PRAISE FOR JEREMY ROBINSON'S
PULSE

"Jeremy Robinson's latest novel, *Pulse*, ratchets his writing to the next level. Rocket-boosted action, brilliant speculation, and the re-creation of a horror out of the mythologic past all seamlessly blend into a roller-coaster ride of suspense and adventure."

—James Rollins, *New York Times* bestselling
author of *The Last Oracle*

"*Pulse* contains all of the danger, treachery, and action a reader could wish for. Its band of heroes is gutsy and gritty. Jeremy Robinson has one wild imagination, slicing and stitching his tale together with the deft hand of a surgeon. Robinson's impressive talent is on full display in this one."

—Steve Berry, *New York Times*
bestselling author of
The Charlemagne Pursuit

"*Raiders of the Lost Ark* meets Tom Clancy meets Saturday matinee monster flick with myths, monsters, special ops supermen, and more high tech weapons than a Bond flick. *Pulse* is an over-the-top, bullet-ridden good time."

—Scott Sigler, *New York Times* bestselling author
of *Contagious* and *Infected*

"Greek myth and biotechnology collide in Robinson's first in a new thriller series to feature the Chess Team... Robinson will have readers turning the pages."

—*Publishers Weekly*

MORE...

PULSE

JEREMY ROBINSON

St. Martin's Paperbacks

This is a work of fiction. All of the characters, organizations, and events portrayed in this novel are either products of the author's imagination or are used fictitiously.

PULSE

Copyright © 2009 by Jeremy Robinson.
Excerpt from *Instinct* copyright © 2010 by Jeremy Robinson.

For information address St. Martin's Press, 175 Fifth Avenue, New York, NY 10010.

Library of Congress Catalog Card Number: 2009007583

ISBN: 978-0-312-38153-0

Printed in the United States of America

St. Martin's Press hardcover edition / June 2009
St. Martin's Paperbacks edition / March 2010

St. Martin's Paperbacks are published by St. Martin's Press, 175 Fifth Avenue, New York, NY 10010.

10 9 8 7 6 5 4 3 2 1

For Hilaree, again, my best, still

ACKNOWLEDGMENTS

The writing of *Pulse* created several challenges for me in terms of military and genetics knowledge. I was fortunate enough to be discovered by readers who are not only experts in these various fields, but also willing to consult on a variety of topics that took the book in exciting directions and root my sometimes whacky theories in a bed of hard facts.

Todd Wielgos, senior research scientist with MS Chemistry. Your advice and insight into the world of genetics improved this novel in amazing ways. This book could not have been written without your help.

As for military and weapons advice, I have three patriots to thank. First is Major Ed Humm, U.S.M.C. (Ret.). Your advice on weapons and tactics was invaluable and contributed realism to my depictions of the military. Further weapons insight (and shell samples) were provided by Rick "The Gun-Guy" Kutka. I now know the difference between .45 and .50 caliber bullets. Ouch. And finally, for tips on the mysterious world of Delta, a very special thanks to brigadier general and author of *Sudden Threat*, A. J. Tata.

Of course, there are bound to be portions of this novel

where I stretch the boundaries of science and weaponry. Any such incidents or errors are mine alone.

I must also thank: Stanley Tremblay, my right hand-man who worked with me every step of the way, from research to marketing. Walter Elly, your masterful web knowledge and passion for my books continue to make the daunting process of marketing more fun and exciting. Peter Wolverton, my editor at Thomas Dunne, for making my first experience with big publishing a fun and exciting experience. Elizabeth Byrne, also at Thomas Dunne, for always being a cheerful and speedy aid. And finally Scott Miller, my agent at Trident Media, for discovering me so many years ago and sticking with me while I honed my skills. I hope to work with you all on many more projects to come. Thus begins the quest for world domination!

Lastly, my wonderful family: Hilaree, my courageous wife and biggest supporter. Aquila, my creative and energetic daughter. Solomon, my loving and brave son. And little Norah—who in my last acknowledgments had yet to be born or named—you are beautiful and peaceful. I love you all.

If a man is offered a fact which goes against his instincts, he will scrutinize it closely, and unless the evidence is overwhelming, he will refuse to believe it. If, on the other hand, he is offered something which affords a reason for acting in accordance to his instincts, he will accept it even on the slightest evidence. The origin of myths explained in this way.　　　　—Bertrand Russell

Where does the violet tint end and the orange tint begin? Distinctly we see the difference of the colors, but where exactly does the one first blending enter into the other? So with sanity and insanity.　　　　—Herman Melville

If all else fails, immortality can always be assured by spectacular error.　　　　—John Kenneth Galbraith

PROLOGUE

Nazca, Peru, 454 B.C.

Hundreds of feet pounded the dry soil, filling the air with the ominous sound of soldiers on the march. But these were not soldiers. They were followers, worshippers of the man whose strange ship had landed on the lush Peruvian shore only a week before, the man who now led them on a trek away from their fertile homeland and across the arid, lifeless Nazca plains.

He marched without cease, without pause for food, water, or rest. With each merciless day their numbers dwindled. The women and children turned back first as hunger and responsibility to their kin overruled their desire to worship the visiting deity. The men who continued following the silent stranger fought against their parched throats and scorched feet, determined to see where the giant would lead. One by one, the weakest men fell to the hard-packed, roiling hot sand and died slowly under the blistering gaze of the sun.

When the man finally stopped in the shade of a tall hill he turned and cast a cool gaze at the remaining twenty-three men—all that remained of the one hundred thirty-seven who'd begun the journey alongside him. They were the strongest and bravest of the tribe, surely worthy of whatever honors the man-god would bestow.

Without a word the giant man removed the lion skin that covered his head and back, pulling the intact beast's head up and away from his own. His sweat-dampened, curly black hair clung to his forehead, but the man paid it no heed. Nor did he wipe away the beads of sweat rolling into his dark brown eyes and into the heavily scabbed gashes running across his chest, back, and legs.

When the giant first arrived on the sandy shore of their village, his resistance to the deep wounds coupled with his tall, six-foot-five height—towering more than a foot above the tallest man in the tribe—had convinced the native Nazcans of his god-hood. The mysterious lion skin that covered his head and back told them he had journeyed from the land of the gods. The club he carried, stained dark with old blood, showed him to be a warrior worthy of respect and awe. But the blood-soaked, woven sack he carried, which wriggled and twisted in his hands and filled the air with a strong copper flavor, revealed he guarded the remains of some ancient evil. At first glance, the size of the object held within the sack made many think he had killed a large boar, but the copious amount of blood constantly dripping from the still-moving body within convinced them otherwise. Nothing mortal could survive so much blood loss.

The giant man knelt and plunged a finger into the hard earth. The small stones and sand that made up the surface of the plains slid away as he outlined a pattern with his finger. After finishing, the man stood again, met the eyes of the men still standing, and waved his hands out over the flat plain at the base of the hill. He then pointed to the central aspect of his drawing, then to a large stone, fifty feet away. The side facing away from the hill looked flat and stood more than ten feet tall and just as wide, but the back side curved out like a boulder. It stood on its edge where the flat side met the rounded, and balanced precariously. To the men it looked like a gnarled, giant melon that had been halved and discarded aeons ago by some ancient god.

The men understood. The strange stone would be the central head of the unearthly creature the man-god had drawn. As the sun set, the men worked in the cooling air. As night came, they labored under torch and moonlight and fought against the frigid, desert air, desperate for food and water, but craving to please the man-god. By morning the oversized reproduction of the giant's drawing was complete. From top to bottom it measured five hundred feet; from side to side, three hundred feet. The light brown lines of the drawing stood in stark contrast to the dark pebbly skin of the plains, making the massive illustration truly magnificent.

The men staggered under the fresh blazing sun as it sapped the rest of their strength and sucked the remaining moisture from their bodies. With each drop of blood from their raw hands, their lives ebbed farther away. Each man knew his life would end in the desert, but they fought the urge to flee, believing that the man-god would reward them for their faithful service. They staggered as a group, dazed and bewildered, toward the head of their drawing, where the giant waited.

He stood next to a deep pit he had dug in front of the large stone, where the two lines from either side of the drawing converged. The men stopped on the opposite side of the pit and waited. The giant raised the sack over the pit, allowing the still oozing blood to drip down into the sand below, where it dried instantly and turned to ash. The men murmured about the strange magic that turned blood to ash, but all remained rooted in place, as much from exhaustion as from a desire to see what might happen next. As the man freed the sack from his grasp, it fell into the pit, landing atop the ashen drop of blood.

Upon striking the hot, dry earth, the sack began to writhe, violently at first, but then more slowly. As the wet blood on the outside of the sack turned white and dry, it stopped moving altogether.

The men waited breathlessly for what might happen next. When the man-god raised his hand and pointed, fear and horror gripped their exhausted bodies. Had they known their fate, not a single one of them would have followed the giant or helped carve his design. Their eyes filled with fear and desperation, but as the giant's grip tightened on his club, they knew flight would serve no purpose. Not one of them would make it outside the borders of their drawing without meeting a blunt end.

The man pointed again, stabbing his finger into the pit. This time the men obeyed, crawling down into the pit. With quivering legs and shaking hands, the men waited to see what would happen next.

The man drank from a wineskin that hung at his hip. The last few drops of the black liquid within dribbled onto his tongue. He swallowed and turned to them again, his body appearing stronger than ever, but his face revealing something more—remorse. The look of regret lasted only an instant as resolve returned to the man-god's eyes.

For the first time since arriving, the giant spoke. His voice shook the sand at the edge of the pit. They didn't understand a word of the man's speech, but found the tone of his voice, the strength of his frame, and the energy of his gesticulations to be inspiring. Confidence returned to the men and several even smiled, as the man-god raised his club to the sky and shouted. They cheered with him, raising their bloodied fists and shouting at the sun.

But their shouts of victory turned to screams as a large object suddenly blotted out the sun above them. Before their tired minds could make sense of the massive object, it descended and crashed with a thunderous boom, after which only the sound of a single pair of sandaled feet could be heard, crunching across the plains, headed west, toward the coast.

GAMMA

ONE

Peru, 2006

Todd Maddox stepped out of the Eurocopter EC 155 and ducked instinctively as the rotor blades continued chopping the air above him. The flight from LAX in Los Angeles to Captain Rolden International Airport in Peru had been uneventful, and the copter ride from the airport to this unknown destination blessedly smooth. But discomfort struck him hard as he exited the copter's air-conditioned interior and entered the humid jungle air of eastern Peru's Amazon rain forest.

His sunflower yellow shirt became like sticky, wet papier-mâché, gluing itself to his body. His styled hair, held in place by a thick film of pricey Elnett hairspray, dissolved into a heavy goo that oozed over his forehead. Out of his dry, Los Angeles element, Maddox grunted and cursed under his breath as he held tight to his briefcase and jogged toward the glass double doors that seemed so out of place in the thick green jungle.

Doubt filled his mind as he neared the doors. Was this worth it? Could he stand all this heat and humidity? The pay would no doubt be amazing and the company, Manifold, was renowned in the world of genetics. But the job description, well, there hadn't been one. Simply a five-year contract and ten thousand dollars for an interview, take it or leave it. He hoped to learn more during this one and only interview, but if the work they wanted him for was anything less than groundbreaking, he'd be on the next flight back to sunny, dry Los Angeles. His job there with CreGen paid well and made headlines occasionally, but the chance to work for Manifold was too good to not, at least, consider. Of course, when he agreed to an interview he had no idea it would take place in the Peruvian rain forest.

The double doors swung open and Maddox ran through like he was escaping a torrential downpour; given the amount of moisture clinging to his dress shirt, beige slacks, and now slick hair, it wasn't much of a stretch.

Inside the hallway, cool, dry air blasted from air-conditioning vents along the ceiling. Maddox's forehead stiffened as the hairspray dried again, several inches lower than when it had first been applied.

"Humidity does a job on each and every one of you metrosexuals the boss brings down here," said a deep voice.

He looked at the man who had opened the door. He hadn't been spoken to with such disrespect since high school. He glared at the man through his Oakley black-rimmed eyeglasses. The man was tall, and given the bulges beneath his form-fitting black shirt, not a scientist. He filled his voice with as much disgust as he could muster and said, "Excuse me?"

"I'm just screwing with you, man." The stranger slapped him on the shoulder—which hurt—and laughed. He extended his hand. "Oliver Reinhart. Head of Gen-Y security here at Manifold Gamma."

"*You're* in charge of this facility?" he asked, wondering if he'd have to put up with this goon long term if he took the job.

Reinhart rubbed a hand over the back of his buzz-cut skull, letting the short hairs tickle his hand. "I oversee security at all the facilities, Alpha through Epsilon. I go where the boss goes."

"Ridley?"

"That's the guy."

Maddox blinked. Richard Ridley reached legendary status when he formed Manifold ten years previous using a three-billion-dollar inheritance. At first no one took his company seriously, but then he began acquiring the best minds in the field, some straight out of MIT, Harvard, and Berkeley. The company soon flourished, making rapid advancements in the fields of genetics and biopharmaceuticals. "Richard Ridley is here?"

"You're a quick one," he said with a smirk. "I can see why he hired you."

"He hasn't hired me."

Reinhart stepped past him and started down the stark white hallway. "He has. You just don't know it yet. C'mon, follow me."

Maddox looked at the burly man's face. A scar ran down his cheek, but other than that, the cleanly shaven face looked, more than anything, young. No more than thirty. Figuring the young Reinhart got his kicks by pretending to be head of security and jerking recruits around by dangling Ridley in front of them, he said, "You look a little young to be head of security. What are you, thirty?"

Reinhart answered the questions quickly. "Twenty-five. We're called Gen-Y for a reason. You won't find anyone over twenty-eight in my crew."

"Doesn't the lack of experience—"

Reinhart paused. He fixed his eyes on Maddox's. "Killers are born, not made."

As though on cue, two more security guards rounded the corner and walked past them, eyeing him and nodding their heads at Reinhart, like friends in a club. Both looked barely old enough to shave, though their bulk and cold eyes confirmed Reinhart's statement. He'd entered a den of vipers.

Still, it seemed irresponsible to hire such young people for security. Then again, eighteen-year-olds were common on any battlefield. Given Reinhart's buzz cut and military posture, he'd probably seen some time in Iraq or Afghanistan before landing the job here. There weren't many military people his age who hadn't. He decided to drop the subject and fell in step behind Reinhart, following him through a maze of hallways.

Reinhart stopped next to a door and opened it. He motioned to the door and grinned. "After you."

Maddox sighed and walked through. The room on the other side stopped him in his tracks. The white marble floor reflected the numerous shades of blue and green from the jungle canopy and sky, which glowed bright above the fifty-foot-long, arched all-glass ceiling. Incan statues lined the ruby red walls and a long oriental rug ran down the center of the room. The rug led to an enormous reception desk that looked more appropriate for a high-profile Hollywood literary agency than a genetics company. The serious-looking redhead behind the desk looked over her glasses at him and smiled briefly.

"Tell her who you are and she'll take it from there," Reinhart said.

Unable to take his eyes off the expansive reception hall, Maddox heard the door whisper shut. Reinhart had left. Though young, the man's presence concerned him. What would happen if he turned Ridley down? He pushed the question from his mind and focused on Reinhart's explanation of his job. If he really was Ridley's personal guard, he wouldn't be here all the time . . . or would he? No one really knew where Ridley spent his time. Reinhart said "Manifold Alpha through Epsilon," which meant there were at least five Manifold locations. Maybe more.

His approach to the reception desk was watched by the bloodred eyes of the twelve Incan statues that lined either side of the room. Their twisted and angry expressions did little to calm his nerves. He paused in front of the desk as the redhead held an open palm up to him. She held a phone against her ear, listening. "You can go in," she said, after putting the phone down. She reached under the desktop and pushed a button. A door to the right of the reception desk slid open silently. He tightened his grip on the briefcase and headed for the door, unsure of what to expect on the other side.

The office was sparsely decorated with more Incan art. Masks hung on walls and statues stood in the corners. Large, green plants made the whole scene look like some ceremonial cave. He realized some of the plants must be mint, as the room smelled strongly of fresh peppermint, the kind his mother had grown in their greenhouse.

At the center of the room sat two black sofas, facing each other. Between them, a short, hand-carved coffee table held two glass teacups, a steaming clay teapot, and a manila folder. Richard Ridley himself sat on the sofa facing the door, his bald head gleaming under the room's stylish track lighting.

He had seen photos of Ridley in articles and promotional materials from conferences, but he looked taller and more confident in person.

Without standing or offering a hand, Ridley motioned for him to sit on the other couch. Maddox sat down and placed his briefcase on the floor next to him. Ridley poured two glasses of tea, drizzled honey into both cups, then handed one to him. A waft of peppermint filled his nose, opening his eyes and causing him to sit up straighter. He took a sip and swallowed. The liquid seemed to invigorate his mind as the peppermint was absorbed into his bloodstream.

"Fresh-cut peppermint tea," Ridley said, taking a sip and then placing his glass on the coffee table. His gravelly voice was impossible to ignore or mistake. Maddox had heard it before and, expecting it, was able to keep his mind from wondering how a man with such a sinister-sounding voice could be so successful. "Amazing what a simple brew can do for the body. It doesn't hold a candle to what you've been involved in, though it probably tastes better."

Maddox smiled, trying not to look nervous.

"I've been following your work quite closely. Your breakthroughs with the Wnt pathway and limb regeneration in embryonic chickens."

Maddox's eyes widened.

Ridley grinned. "Why don't you explain it to me."

Maddox grew excited. He never expected to be in a position to explain something to *the* Richard Ridley. "As you know . . . may know . . . the Wnt pathway is a network of proteins that, in essence, tells a growing fetus where, how, and when to grow limbs. But it becomes dormant after birth. Mother Nature's kill switch so to speak, preventing uncontrolled additions, like a sixth finger growing on the hand when you get a cut. What we tried to do was reactivate the pathway in adults so that when a finger is cut off, the active Wnt proteins tell the cells to grow new ligaments, bones, and muscles, not just a layer of new skin."

Ridley cleared his throat. "But—and correct me if I'm wrong—the Wnt pathway, while a brilliant attempt, is a rather embarrassing dead end."

Maddox hunched as his ego deflated. Ridley knew more than he was letting on.

"But"—Ridley waggled a finger at him—"you're already pursuing a different path, aren't you?"

A *lot* more than he was letting on.

Maddox remained silent, knowing that any verification of his current work would be a breach of his contract with CreGen and would lead to his firing and probably legal action against him. Just being here, instead of vacationing in the Caribbean where he was supposed to be, would be enough to get him fired.

"You don't need to say anything. I know it puts you in a . . . situation. So I'll say it for you. You've managed to regenerate limbs on rats—tails, legs, even ears."

Maddox's eyes widened. "How do you know that? We haven't published—"

Ridley held up his hand, silencing him. "Please. Let me

finish. You've also partially regenerated limbs on pigs and sheep, though with less success. But the crème de la crème is what *you,* and you alone, have managed to do with . . . humans."

"Now wait a minute," he said, sitting up straight. "The work on sheep and pigs is highly classified. There is no way you could—"

Ridley raised his hands. "And yet, I do. Corporate espionage is a wonderful thing. Don't think your bosses at CreGen haven't sent spies in our direction. If not for Mr. Reinhart and Gen-Y, you'd probably be privy to Manifold's secrets as well." He leaned forward. "I notice you didn't mention the human experimentation."

"That's because there isn't any," Maddox said, looking at the floor.

Ridley smiled, put his glass down and picked up the folder on the tabletop. He opened it and began reading. "Boy. Fifteen years old. Admitted to Mass General Hospital because he sliced off the tip of his left index finger while . . . trying to dissect a frog in his basement. The year was 1986." He looked up. "Sound familiar?"

"How did you get access to my medical history?"

"If I can bypass security at CreGen, do you really think HIPAA stands a chance?" He closed the file and returned it to the tabletop; then, like a striking snake, he grabbed hold of Maddox's left hand. He held it up, inspecting the perfect left index finger. "You regenerated your fingertip. Not on the clock, mind you. On your own."

Maddox yanked his hand away and sat back, crossing his arms.

"No need to get upset. I admire your tenacity, even if it is inspired by vanity." He removed a folded piece of paper from his trousers pocket and slowly unfolded it. "Tell me how and I'll show you what's on this piece of paper."

"What could be on that piece of paper that would make me tell you something like that?"

"Your future," he said. "Aren't you interested?"

Maddox held out for five seconds and then said, "Pig bladder extract. It . . . helps construct the microscopic scaffolding for incoming human cells and emits chemical signals that stimulate the regrowth process."

"That's . . . unusual," Ridley said, then smiled.

"Pig extracts are used in diabetes treatments, producing islet cells that help reverse the disease in humans when transplanted."

"So you figured they could also help regrow limbs."

Maddox shrugged. "At the time. Beyond that it's another dead end. The process doesn't work."

Ridley nodded. "Then your research has stagnated?"

He didn't answer the question. He couldn't answer the question. It was too embarrassing to admit failure on something he'd spent his life on. Besides, he could see that Ridley knew the answer.

"As a young man, before all this," he said, waving his arms at the room around them, "I was obsessed with maps. I would chart land routes from one point to another, say Beijing to Paris, over and over until it appeared I had exhausted all the possibilities. But then I tried something different, like your pig bladder, I turned the map upside down and new possibilities emerged. But this technique ultimately ended in frustration as I once again ran out of possibilities. Using my father's resources I turned to a final resource that is both hard to come by and often quite expensive—the ancient past. I purchased ancient maps from dealers around the world, legal and black market. Trade routes were revealed. Secret passages. Tunnels dug and forgotten. Each map revealed more. In this way I came to learn that the ancient past is one of the best ways to uncover secrets in the modern world. It is a belief I hold to this day and a lesson you will soon learn . . . if you're interested."

"I . . . don't know if I can."

Ridley laughed like it was the stupidest thing he'd ever

heard. "You regenerated your fingertip. You have ambition beyond the scope of CreGen, who, may I remind you, takes credit for your discoveries. But you're stuck, just like we are. You can regenerate a fingertip. So what? Kids under the age of eleven sometimes regenerate severed fingertips. You merely extended the age limit on fingertip regeneration."

"By twenty-two years!"

Ridley smiled. "Impressive, I know. But it's not the golden goose, is it? Full limb regeneration. Organ regeneration. Spine, brain, memory regeneration. Those are the real prizes."

Excitement overtook Maddox's concerns. He could see that Ridley just might give him the keys to the kingdom, but he had a few requirements. "I want credit."

"Done," he replied, handing Maddox the slip of paper he'd just finished unfolding. "My offer. Accept it and I will reveal the past that will take us to the future."

As Maddox read over the few lines of text, his eyes widened with each word. He was being offered more than the key to the kingdom; this was the key to the universe! Unlimited research funding, a salary that would make him a multimillionaire, and some of the best names in the business would be at his disposal.

"Do you accept?"

Maddox nodded slowly. This was not the kind of proposal to chew on.

"Very good." Ridley took a sip of tea and got comfortable, his big body stressing the limits of the sofa on which he sat. "The problem with the Wnt pathway is that no one has been able to break what I call the 'natural barrier.' Humans can sometimes regenerate fingertips, as you've shown, but no one has been able to figure out what molecular pathway triggers this kind of natural regrowth. Pathways for triggering regrowth in other parts of the human body simply don't exist."

"You believe I can overcome this?"

"Not at all," he said with a chuckle. "I would prefer to follow a different path. Something less conventional."

"How about nAG proteins?" Maddox said. Motivated by the compulsion to impress the man, he continued before Ridley could respond. "When a salamander loses a limb, blastema cells clump around the wound. Blastema cells can form bones, organs, brains—anything. Humans have them as embryos, but stop generating them after birth. The cells grow and divide, eventually becoming the amputated structure. The nAG protein directs the blastema cells, telling them what to become: muscle, veins, skin, etcetera. If we can find the human version of adult blastema cells and trigger the nAG proteins to communicate certain signals, the potential human regeneration is fantastic. But salamanders take more than a month to regrow a limb less than an inch long. The duration would be much longer for humans. Maybe a lifetime. But I'm sure that's a hurdle we can jump when we get to it. With these resources I imagine I should be able to unlock just about any secret."

Ridley just cocked an eyebrow. "Not bad. Perhaps worth pursuing while we hunt down my pet project."

Maddox did his best to suppress a sigh. Inwardly he shouted for Ridley to get to the point, but all he managed was a timid, "And that is?"

The big man smiled without a hint of malice for the first time. "The fountain of youth isn't some waterfall out here in the jungle, Maddox," he said, then pointed at his chest. "I want to live forever, and the key to that treasure is locked away inside our DNA. In our genetics. And in our past."

"You want to live forever?"

"Who doesn't?" he said. "But I really just want to live long enough to take this company as far as it can go. I'm an entrepreneur at heart, and my vision for this company has always been beyond its means, even now. You unlock the secret to regeneration and I might just live long enough to see my dreams come to fruition. We'll make a boatload of money, too."

Maddox almost laughed, but then realized the man was completely serious. He'd never considered that regeneration in the extreme could vastly extend lives, never mind immortality.

"How well do you know Greek mythology?"

Maddox folded his hands and leaned back. "Better than most I suppose. It fascinated me as a child after watching *Clash of the Titans*. But my knowledge is based on personal research, not actual academics."

Ridley nodded. "There was a . . . creature. Perhaps one of a kind. Perhaps the last of its kind. Who knows. What's important is that this creature had the ability to regenerate limbs, including its neck and head, very quickly."

"And you think this creature still lives today or its offspring still live today?"

"No. If it were still alive, we'd know. The myth states that it was killed . . . by Hercules."

"I see," Maddox said, wondering if Richard Ridley was losing his mind.

Ridley saw the doubt in his eyes and became very serious. "Do not mistake me for a crackpot, Maddox. I have uncovered manuscripts beyond the legend of Hercules. Documents that have nothing to do with the legend. Records of ravaged herds. Destroyed villages. Missing hunting parties. For centuries no one knew what caused all the death and destruction. Not until Hercules, that is."

He stood, walked to a wall safe, punched in a key code, and opened the solid metal door. He removed a thick glass case that held a single, aged document. "I bought this document on the black market for one hundred thousand dollars before knowing it was authentic. Knowing what I know now, I would have done anything to obtain it . . . and on two occasions, a rival group, whose identity I have yet to discover, tried to take it from me. It is truly priceless. As some have proven, it's worth dying for." He sat again and held the case out for Maddox to inspect.

"What language is this?"

"Greek. It's been dated to 460 B.C., mere years after Hercules's fabled encounter with the creature. Far too soon for legend to have set in."

Maddox stared at the document. Its age and plainness somehow lent credence to Ridley's claim.

"It makes no mention of Hercules, though it clearly insinuates someone killed the beast. It offers only a description of the creature, so that it might be identified and dealt with properly should one be encountered again."

"An ancient field guide," Maddox said, beginning to feel the first pangs of excitement.

"Precisely. And do you know what I found?"

Maddox waited in silence. He clearly had no idea.

"The description of the creature in this purely historical text is nearly identical to the mythological description. Perhaps the feats of Hercules have been exaggerated through time and legend, but the details of the beast were so fantastic to begin with that no one in the past twenty-five hundred years felt the need to exaggerate its appearance or abilities. Because of this I am compelled to believe that many of the other aspects of the story are also real. Based on the details of the myth, finding the creature's burial place may be possible. If the creature has been well preserved, recovering its DNA would change everything we know about physical regeneration. Mr. Maddox, we must find the Beast of Lerna's final resting place and extract its DNA. The prize is eternal life."

"Lerna . . ." Maddox leaned forward, his eyes wide with realization. "My God. You're talking about the Hydra."

Ridley smiled wide and toothy.

"That's . . . crazy."

Ridley chuckled. "And that's exactly what I'd expect a scientist to say." He locked his eyes on Maddox's.

"The great scientists of human history all had something in common. Einstein. Galileo. Da Vinci. Hawking. . . . Imagination. They are all brilliant scientists, but they also had the guts to tap what was previously considered fantasy, science fiction, heresy. If the human race didn't pursue the impossible we'd still be staring up at the moon having never set foot on it."

Maddox knew he was right. He'd gone down that path when he regenerated his own finger. But even if the Hydra had existed, they would still have to locate its grave and extract viable DNA. It just didn't seem possible.

"Let me put it to you this way: Would you rather take a risk on something, that if successful will propel your name to the top of the list of great scientists, or would you rather it play it safe and return to a company that takes credit for your work? Remembered or forgotten?"

"You really believe in this?"

"I'm staking my eternal life on it."

Maddox smiled. He would have said yes because of the pay alone, but if Ridley turned out to be right, he might not only get his name into the history books, but also live long enough to see it. "I'm in."

TWO

Nazca, Peru, 2009

On the previous Monday, George Pierce had begun his workweek as usual. At eight a.m. he lectured to his ancient history undergrad class at the University of Athens. The subject had been the rise of Athenian influence. Lecturing never thrilled him and the subject was bland; the real interesting work usually happened postlunch, when he oversaw the archaeological efforts on a recently discovered shipwreck off the island of Antikythera, where a fortress had also been discovered. They had found evidence of repeated attacks on the citadel, with perpetrators and defenders being identified as Rhodians, Spartans, Macedonians, and Romans going back to the time period Pierce most loved, 2000 B.C. and earlier—the time of myth and legend—which is why the shipwreck fascinated and excited him.

He had yet to voice his theory on the ship's identity, as it would be extremely controversial. He had evidence that supported his ideas, but nothing concrete. For that he would need the ship's nameplate or, even more unlikely, a log book. But three months of recovering artifacts and cataloging them at the university had yielded little. His single most compelling piece of evidence, an iron medallion, was being kept safe and secret by his colleague

Agustina Gallo, one of the few people he trusted in all of Greece.

As was now usual, his Monday came and went with no further discovery of any great importance. Pierce returned home to his university campus apartment, sat down, and opened his e-mail. After reading the single e-mail in his in-box, he canceled the ancient history class three weeks from the semester's end and put Agustina in charge of the Antikythera excavations.

Less than a week and more than eight thousand miles later, he arrived in Nazca, Peru, where he stared at crude Greek letters carved into a stone, stunned and silent. Slowly, he reached out and felt the symbol scratched into the stone above the inscriptions. He'd seen it before, but would keep its meaning to himself, for now. He moved on to the letters, tracing them with his fingertips, convincing himself that what he saw really existed. He'd been searching for signs of the great ancient civilizations completing the journey to the Americas long before Columbus—the Vikings and Romans in the northeast United States were nearly common knowledge among his peers—but the Greeks in South America . . . in *Peru,* now that would rewrite history.

The e-mail he received disclosed a report about a new nine-headed geoglyph, a massive drawing in the earth created thousands of years ago, from a friend in the U.N. who oversaw worldwide heritage sites. The 175-square-mile region in which the famous Nazca lines were found had been declared a world heritage site in 1994. The very first Nazca drawings, discovered in 1929, didn't reach true worldwide fame until planes began flying over the desolate region and people began spotting more geoglyphs—a lot more. From the air, massive line drawings in the desert floor emerged that could not be discerned from the ground. Some, reaching lengths of a thousand feet, could not be seen in their entirety below an altitude of fifteen hundred feet. The geoglyphs came in all shapes and sizes, from spiders to monkeys to men and deities. The discovery of any new geoglyph in the region was immediately reported to the U.N., not because important information might have been gleaned, but because even though the region was officially "protected," looters still pillaged most finds long before researchers set foot in the country.

As a precaution, all archaeological finds had to be cataloged, researched, and removed to secure locations before news of a new find reached the looters, who would descend like vultures. The geoglyphs rarely held anything more interesting than potsherds and crude digging tools, but surveying and photographing the ancient drawing before the image was marred by the looters' tire tracks was equally important.

During the initial aerial photography session, a large stone that looked like half an egg rising from the desert at the end of the odd creature's central neck leaped out at the photographer. A geoglyph with a three dimensional feature had never been found before. The following day, a team hurried to the site, inspecting the stone and the area around it. All were amazed when they found an inscription on the stone, but no one could read it, though one young college intern recognized the language—Greek.

The discovery had been made one day before Pierce received the e-mail. Given his previous work with the U.N. World-Heritage Commission and his expertise on ancient civilizations, Pierce had been called to the scene. After three plane flights and a long, bumpy, and dusty jeep ride, he arrived on site, where a small base camp had been set up on the hill that overlooked the glyph. He'd exited the jeep only ten minutes ago and, upon seeing the nine-headed glyph, had run down the hill to where he now stood. He stared at the Greek inscription on a stone that couldn't possibly have come from Greece, which meant that someone from Greece had been to Peru, to this very spot, more than two thousand years ago.

He turned to Molly McCabe, the U.N. heritage commission archaeologist who'd first documented the site from the sky. The Irish woman had been researching the glyphs since the late eighties and had spent more time in the desert than anywhere else. Generally, the Nazcan geoglyphs were her area of expertise, but she couldn't even recognize Greek, let alone read it.

"You're sure the site was untouched? This has to be a hoax," he said.

"No tire tracks for miles around," she said. "You can't hide those here. No wind. No rain. No erosion. Once something scratches the surface it stays scratched. That's why the geoglyphs have lasted for thousands of years. If someone had been out here in the past two thousand years with a vehicle or so much as a donkey, the evidence would still be plain to see. I suppose someone could have walked here, but only a fool would do that."

"Why's that?" he asked, as he gently brushed the inscription clean.

"It'd be a death sentence. You couldn't carry enough water to get you here and back to the world without dehydrating. You'd be a dried-out husk within a month." McCabe huffed and ran a hand through her long, gray ponytailed hair. "So?"

"So . . ." he said. "What?"

"What the hell does it say?" she said, throwing her hands up.

"Right. Sorry." Pierce usually took his time with new discoveries. If he had things his way the whole glyph would be fenced off then segmented into a grid of strings so the location of any discovery could be marked and later scrutinized. He preferred to work slowly and methodically, but he also understood that time was an issue. With each passing day they risked word reaching looters, who had perfected the art of the nighttime raid, focusing on expensive research equipment as much as ancient relics.

He looked at the inscription again, marveling at the text.

Εδω ειναι θαμμενος το θηριο πιο ασχημη. Φλογα και το ξιφος του Βορρα εκανε αθανατο κεφαλι, παντα κατω απο την αμμο και πετρα. Να προειδοποιησει ολους που διαβαζουν αυτα τα λογια. Λαβουν σοβαρα νποψη τους φρουρους 'ανοικτα ακρα και να κρατησει στεγνη τη γη φοβουνται σας μετα το τερας και τη γευση τους μεγαλειωδαις εκδικηση

The carving was crude, but the stone, like the surrounding desert, hadn't been weathered in two thousand years. The inscription was still as legible as it had been when it was first inscribed.

He translated the lines of text, writing down letters in his small notepad without reading the results in full. McCabe bounced a nervous leg next to his face as he crouched to translate the lowest line. He glanced at her leg and noticed it was quite fit for a woman in her fifties.

"Twenty years ago, George, you might have had a chance," she said with a grin. "Now I prefer men my own age."

Pierce smiled and made a final note. "You can't make an exception for me, Molly?"

"George," she said, leaning close to his face.

"Yeah?"

"Read the damn inscription."

Pierce chuckled and read through the inscription that he'd translated. His face fell flat. "It's a hoax."

"George, I guarantee you, this is not a hoax. What does it say?" Her voice was a barely contained shout.

Pierce read from the small notepad. "Here is buried the beast most foul . . . Fire and sword did sever the head immortal, forever entombed beneath sand and stone. Be warned all who read these words. Heed the screaming guards within and keep dry the earth lest you wake the monster and taste its mighty . . . vengeance."

McCabe's brow furrowed. "It's a grave?"

Pierce rubbed his eyebrow while he thought. Then, like a horse at the races, he bolted back up the incline. McCabe chased after him. Gasping at the hot, dry air, they stopped at the top of the hill where the U.N. World-Heritage base camp had been set up—a small village of tents and trucks. He turned around and looked at the geoglyph with new eyes, which quickly widened. "It's the Hydra."

She squinted. "Hydra?"

Pierce looked at her, his orange-tinged brown eyes blazing. "The Lernaian Serpent. The nine-headed swamp-dragon. Child of Typhon and Echidna."

She shook her head. It was all gobbledy-gook to her.

He took her by the shoulders and spoke quickly. "Herakles—"

"Who?"

Pierce sighed. No one knew the man's real name anymore. "Hercules. He was the bastard son of Zeus and Alcmene, a human woman. Because of this, he suffered the wrath of Hera, Zeus's jealous wife, who eventually made him go insane. He killed his wife and children. To overcome the madness he stayed at the court of King Eurystheus, seeking purification. He remained there for twelve years and during that time faced twelve trials, or labors. His second trial pitted him against a nine-headed creature called the Hydra. . . . He killed it by—" He froze like an ice cube defying the intense heat of the Nazca plains.

"What is it?" she asked.

"He killed it by severing its central head—its immortal head—and cauterizing it before it could grow a new body." The possibilities spun through Pierce's mind as he continued speaking in a monotone, trancelike voice. "Most legends say that he buried the head under a large stone. . . . How old is this site?"

"Carbon dating came back at four hundred to five hundred B.C., why?"

"Some scholars, including me, believe Hercules was a real person who lived around four hundred fifty B.C." His eyes widened. "The time fits. Boating in Greece became very important during that time period. Their victory at the battle of Salamis against the Persians was primarily because of their naval might. It might actually be possible that an expedition lead by Hercules reached the shores of Peru."

"The ancient Greeks had sailboats?" she asked.

"Yes," Pierce said, rubbing his eyebrow. "Cargo ships. They weighed up to one hundred fifty tons and made the Greek empire very rich from trade. But it may not have been a cargo ship. There was one ship at the time, renowned for its crew and vast explorations. You may have heard of it. The *Argo*."

She stifled a chuckle. "As in Jason and the Argonauts? I saw the movie, George. Ray Harryhausen may have been a genius with clay, but it's just a story."

Pierce looked at her, grinning. "You should do some research on scientists the U.N. sends to help you, Molly."

McCabe's smile vanished. "What . . . ?"

"A year ago I discovered an ancient Greek crew manifest for a ship named the *Argo* in a tomb dated to four hundred B.C. Looters had taken the major artifacts, but the manifest, along with other rotting documents, remained hidden in a crevice. Forty men were listed on the manifest. One of them was Hercules."

"Why didn't I read about this?" she asked. "Didn't you publish?"

"The manifest was stolen."

"By who?"

He shrugged casually, not wanting to retell the story about the two cloaked men who broke into his lab, knocked him unconscious, and stole the manifest, or explain who he thought they were. Nor did he want to tell her about the Antikythera excavation and the sunken ship they'd found, despite its bearing on this conversation. His trust took time to earn. "Who knows? But I promise you, it was real. Hercules existed. He wasn't the son of Zeus, but he lived and breathed . . . and maybe, just maybe, visited Peru. The proof could be down there." Pierce pointed to the stone.

McCabe grabbed his shoulder. "George." He met her eyes, which were squinting as she smiled. "We need to get under that rock."

He nodded slowly, still stunned.

"And George," she said. "We're going to need security. If word of this gets out there will be no stopping the looters. They'll come in numbers a U.N. badge can't repel."

Pierce snapped out of his haze. "If you have a satellite phone, I know just the man."

THREE

Ostrov Nosok, Siberia

Four invisible specters slid across the frozen sea. Concealed from head to toe in white, military-issue thermal armor, the Delta team moved toward their target—a terrorist training camp. The Aden-Abyan Islamic Army had opted for the deserted wasteland of Russia's Siberian north rather than the boiling deserts of their native Yemen. It was unknown how long the camp had existed or if Russia knew of its presence, but one thing was clear . . .

"It's time to blow this place sky fucking high," said Stan Tremblay, call sign "Rook," into his throat mike, which allowed the others to hear him despite the whipping arctic winds. "Talk about maximum shrinkage—it's so cold out here I might have to change my name to Susan."

The four prone figures shook slightly with laughter. From a distance they would be indiscernible from the surrounding snow and ice, of which there was an abundance surrounding the U-shaped island. Up close they'd look like nothing more than clumps of snow, disturbed by the wind. The only fault in their camouflage was the two one-inch slits in their antiglare snow goggles, but an enemy would have to be within five feet to see the aberration. By then it would be too late.

A dull roar from behind caused the group to become motionless once again. Shin Dae-jung, call sign "Knight," focused on the noise. A vehicle was approaching quickly across the ice, coming from behind and closing on their target. "Motion on our six," he said. "Heads down. Don't move."

The four Delta operators planted their faces in the snow, judging distance and speed from the whine of the engine and the vibrations in the ice beneath their bodies. It was going to pass by them—and close.

"Deep Blue, this is Knight. Do you see incoming target?"

After a faint hiss and click, the cool voice of a man they had never met, yet who watched out for them from above via satellite, came loud and clear through the team's specially modified AN/PRC-158 personal role radio. The radio, which could be used for both voice communication and data transmissions, contained GPS chips that allowed the team to be tracked around the world. The only catch was that there was a one-second delay. "Copy that, Knight. Zooming in on him now. Still one hundred yards out. Looks like two on a snowmobile. They're heading straight for you."

"Are they a problem?"

"Armed, but not looking for a fight. . . . Wait. Queen, you're about to become roadkill. Might want to roll to your right."

"Copy that," said a crisp, feminine voice. Zelda Baker, the lone female member of the team, call sign "Queen," waited motionless as the snowmobile and its two occupants barreled toward her.

"Two rolls to the right," Deep Blue said. "On my mark. Three . . ."

She tensed, waiting for the signal and hoping that Deep Blue took the one-second delay into account. The vibrations in the ice shook her jaw and the sound of the engine roared in her ears.

"Two . . ."

For a moment she wondered if she'd hear Deep Blue's signal over the racket, but then a voice came through, loud and clear, "Go!"

Queen rolled twice to the right, keeping her limbs tight and movement quick, she buried her face in the snow just as the snowmobile passed on her left, its track rolling over the edge of her sleeve. A moment later, the whine of the engine slowed and then idled.

"No one move," came the whispered voice of Deep Blue, as though the men on the snowmobile might hear him through the team's earpieces.

Twenty feet from the team, the two men turned around on their seat. They scrutinized the snow with squinted eyes. Their bodies were concealed behind thick layers of thermal garb and furs. Each had an AK-47 strapped to his back. As the engine idled one of the men stood and held his AK at the ready. He stepped toward the team, scanning the snow.

The voice of Deep Blue returned. "When I say your name, it means they're not looking at you and I want you to take the shot."

The heartbeats of the four Delta operators remained steady and strong, each waiting to be given the signal that would trigger the taking of two lives. Not that either man's death would weigh heavily on any of their consciences. These men were murderers and terrorists and the team's whole purpose for being here was to kill every last one of them. But the plan had been to catch them all inside the facility while they hid from the elements, and blow them to bits, not to engage them in an unnecessary firefight. Under normal circumstances a Tomahawk cruise missile strike would do the trick, but being on Russian soil, a missile attack would be interpreted as an act of war. Better to hit them from the ground and keep things off the radar . . . literally. By the time the Russians discovered the site, it would be nothing more than frozen ashes.

"Hold on," Deep Blue said. "You're clear."

None of the four heard the engine rev up or leave, but if Deep Blue said they were clear, they were clear. All four looked up just in time to see the closest man slump to the ground, a gurgle escaping his slit throat, which loosed gouts of blood onto the snow. Behind him stood a white wraith, staring at them through two thin slits.

"Miss me?"

"King, how in the hell did you get here?" Rook said as he stood.

Jack Sigler, call sign "King," cleaned his faithful seven-inch KA-BAR knife in the snow. Behind him, the second man was leaning on the snowmobile, a slow trickle of blood still draining from his neck. "Been here for five minutes. Wanted to see if you guys talked about me behind my back."

"Bullshit," Rook said, dusting the snow from his white, second-generation FN SCAR-L assault rifle with attached 40mm grenade launcher. Out of the five, he was most in love with his weapons, which also included two .50 caliber Magnum Desert Eagle handguns, one strapped to each hip beneath his snow gear. They were as children to him—very deadly children.

"Motion at the target site," Deep Blue said. "Looks like you've been made."

King lifted the head of the man who had died upon the snowmobile; his blood had already frozen in a pool around the vehicle. He opened the man's jacket revealing his slit throat and a throat mike. "Damnit. I'm getting really tired of these third-world jerks getting their hands on this kind of technology."

"It's the damn private sector," Rook said. "Highest bidder gets the tech. They don't give a rip who gets killed as a result. If they don't pull the trigger, innocent blood isn't on their hands."

King reached into his pocket and pulled out a small

device with a touchpad and small screen. "Won't be any innocent blood spilled today." He began punching buttons as he spoke. "How many outside the complex?"

"None yet," Deep Blue said, "but you've got a Sno-Cat with five, maybe six unfriendlies on their way out."

"Copy that," King said as he finished pushing buttons. Behind him, the island transformed into a volcano as a plume of fire and smoke mushroomed into the air, accentuated by a resounding boom. A shock wave kicked up a wash of snow that momentarily obscured their vision. When the snow cleared, a smoldering island lay in the wake of the blast, with several secondary explosions from fuel supplies still erupting across the land. But at the center of it all, charging straight for them, was a white, tank-treaded Sno-Cat. One man leaned from the window, taking aim with an AK-47, while two men on top brought their own AKs to bear. All three began firing.

The team dove to the snow, knowing they would disappear from view. "I've got this," Knight said, as he crawled up behind the snowmobile, using the vehicle and its lone, dead occupant as cover. He unslung his PSG-1 semiautomatic sniper rifle and took aim at the Sno-Cat. He knew the vehicle wasn't meant for a firefight, so it most likely didn't have bulletproof glass. Looking through the sight he found the driver's head. He could see the man shouting at the others.

Knight slowly squeezed the trigger and a single round burst from the weapon, its retort echoing across the open expanse and drowning out the popping AK-47s. He watched through the scope as the windshield held its own, denting inward slightly where the round struck. Bulletproof glass. Damn.

Knight took aim again, preparing to unleash a semiautomatic barrage of sniper rounds. The Sno-Cat was moving and jostling on the ice, which made the shot even more difficult, but few people on the planet were his equal with a sniper rifle. He held his breath and squeezed off fifteen rounds in rapid succession. The windshield became awash with white pockmarks, but the one in the middle grew wide as eight of the fifteen rounds found their mark, striking the same place as the first round and punching a hole in the bulletproof glass. Three rounds in all made it through the window, but only the first made contact. There wasn't a head left for the second two to strike.

Even without the driver, the Sno-Cat continued toward them. More than that, without the driver, the Sno-Cat wouldn't stop once it reached them. AK-47 fire continued to pepper the snow around the group, but as is so often the case with terror groups, they had atrocious aim and little self-control.

Rook looked down the sight of his assault rifle. "I have to do everything I s'pose. Bend over, ladies, here it comes." A dull pop signified the launching of a grenade. The two men on top saw it coming and leaped from the roof of the Cat. The others took the grenade's full force as it ripped through the Cat and turned their bodies into little more than Campbell's Chunky Soup.

The two survivors clambered to their feet, clutching their AK-47s, and beat a hasty retreat back toward the island's rocky shoreline in search of cover.

"My turn," Queen said.

As the two men made a beeline for the smoldering complex, they fired aimlessly over their shoulders, peppering the ice behind them and posing no real threat to the team.

Queen heaved the dead man off the snowmobile. A sheet of frozen blood lifted away with his body and shattered when he fell to the ice. She took his seat and said, "You'd think with a big secret training facility, these guys would be better shots."

"Blowing yourself up doesn't take much aim," King said.

She revved the snowmobile's engine. "Right." The snow-mobile burst forward. She brought it around in a wide turn, building speed, and then was off like a bullet, streaking toward the fleeing men.

"Hey, King," Knight said, holding up a white Heckler & Koch UMP submachine gun.

King sighed. It was Queen's weapon. And he knew she hadn't forgotten it. The woman was the smallest member of the team, but like the savage wolverine—a terrier-sized weasel capable of taking down a moose—what she lacked in size she made up for in ferocity and brute strength. It wasn't always easy to see past her feminine face, but the woman was built like a powerhouse, so much so that no one on the team dared arm-wrestle her. It wasn't certain she'd win, but if she did, the loser would be cursed by a lifetime of taunting from the others.

Queen closed in on her targets. The men, now out of ammo, simply ran for their lives. If the men had conserved their ammo, she would be dead, but the men had as little sense as they did time to live. Queen was upon them.

The man closest to her—the one she intended to kill first—tripped and fell into a heap on the ice. He ruined her plan, but then she was always open to improvisation. She opened the throttle and plowed over the man just as he picked up his head. The front of the snowmobile struck the man's head with a sickening crunch. It was sloppier than she liked things to be, but she couldn't argue with its effectiveness. She returned her focus to the other man, whose frantic run carried him quickly across the ice.

Queen stood on the seat of the snowmobile as she prepared to attack. The man looked over his shoulder, his eyes wide with fear and confusion. It was obvious he'd expected to be gunned down. Upon seeing her charging toward him, no gun in sight, he stopped and stood his ground.

At least he's brave, she thought. And then, as she closed to within twenty feet she reached up and pulled back her white hood and goggles, letting her wavy blond hair flail in the wind like the tentacles of an enraged squid. She wanted him to know she was a woman.

When a smile crept onto the man's face, she knew her free hair had had the desired effect. He was underestimating her.

Queen leaped into the air and flew toward the man, arms outstretched and wearing a smile of her own. The man reached out to catch her, no doubt intending to squeeze the life out of her, but he'd never get the chance. As she collided with the man, she wrapped one of her thick arms around his neck, squeezed, and then used the impact of their bodies striking the ice to suddenly increase the pressure.

The result was a loud crack as the man's spine snapped. His brief encounter with Queen was akin to being hit by a bus. She stood, waltzed back to the snowmobile, and headed back toward the others. She glanced down at the man she'd run over as she past. His neck was bent back at an extreme angle.

"Piece of cake," Queen said as she rejoined the team after a quick drive past the burning Sno-Cat wreckage.

Knight held out her weapon. "Show-off."

She took it with a smile that, combined with her bright blue eyes and blond hair, could disarm most men—and terrorists—with a glance. She looked past Knight to the silent member of the team. He'd said nothing and moved little since the combat had begun. "Hey, Bishop, not in the mood today?"

Erik Somers, call sign "Bishop," shrugged. "Didn't see the need." He hoisted his belt-fed M240E6 machine gun onto his shoulder, while holding a chain of white bullets. The rapid-fire stopping force of his weapon alone would have been enough to stop the Sno-Cat and take out the men who'd fled, but he was a man of few words and reserved action.

Queen shook her head. She loved to see Bishop in action, and was always disappointed when he held back. He was a one-man wrecking crew. Still, she did enjoy taunting him when a mission finished without him firing a shot. "For such a big man you must have a pair of raisins between your legs, Bish," she said as she turned back toward the others, unaware that a speeding projectile was headed straight for her head.

When the snowball hit, Queen dove, rolled, and made ready with her submachine gun. But there was no enemy, just Bishop, whose chest shook with laughter.

Queen stifled a smile, dropped her weapon, and pounded toward the unmoving Bishop. "You lily shit bird . . ."

"Save it for later," Deep Blue's voice said over the headset. "That blast lit up the infrareds like the Fourth of July. If anyone had a bird over the area, they'll come looking. Hump it back to LZ Alpha double-time and come home."

Queen pointed a finger at Bishop. "You're lucky." She did her best to sound pissed, but the smirk on her lips revealed otherwise. Bishop remained still and silent.

Deep Blue spoke again. "And Queen, put your damn hood back up."

"You heard the man," King said. "Let's go home."

"King, I just got word that your two-week jaunt has been approved," Deep Blue said. "That means you're all getting some R and R. Enjoy it while it lasts."

"Where you off to?" Queen asked.

"Peru," King said. "An old friend needs my help."

"You going to see action?" Rook asked. "Should we come with?"

The four of them looked at King at once. He couldn't see their eyes through the small slits in their goggles, but he could tell they all wanted in . . . *if* there was action to be had.

"Thanks, but no," King said. "Should be a walk in the park."

"Bogies twenty miles out and closing," Deep Blue said. "ETA, five minutes."

"But now it's time to run," King said.

The group broke into a sprint toward the forested coastline where a still-classified UH-100S stealth Blackhawk transport helicopter, piloted by some boys from the

160th Special Operations Aviation Regiment, also known as the "Nightstalkers," stood ready to speed them away.

King took one last look over his shoulder. He'd counted seventy-five men and women in the camp. The explosives he'd planted had killed the majority of them. Two more had fallen to his knife. And yet the number of dead on his hands this day was a drop in the bloody bucket he'd filled during his ten years with Delta. For the briefest of moments he grew weary of the death and violence.

Then he remembered who these people were, what they had done, and what they would do if they weren't stopped. He had witnessed the horrors of war, the blood and havoc. Fellow soldiers had died in his arms on several occasions, some riddled with shrapnel, others missing limbs or simply sprayed down by bullets. War and its tragedy were familiar to him. But they paled in comparison to the horrors wreaked by terrorists. To kill a soldier in battle was something he could justify, something he could live with, but to slaughter innocents, to willfully infect the world's population with fear, was madness that served the needs of a few radicals.

In his line of work, civilian casualties were sometimes unavoidable, but he abhorred the news of innocents caught in the crossfire. It stood against everything he fought for. That the organizations he fought against served to inflict as many civilian casualties as possible, that they cheered and celebrated the deaths of innocents, infuriated him. He'd seen the remains of men, women, and children blown to pieces by suicide bombers who targeted cafés, markets, and schools. He could identify the glazed look in the eyes of a man willing to take his own life in order to spread fear and spark wars. He recognized the heart of his enemy as evil.

So he waged his war against terrorism as a member of Delta, never hesitating to pull the trigger if it meant saving innocents. It was gruesome work, but necessary. Noble even. As King forged across the ice he looked back one last time at the ruined island. Another terror network brought to its knees. With seventy-four potential suicide bombers inside the complex and the average number of deaths caused by each suicide attack placed at ninety-five, he'd just saved roughly seven thousand innocent lives.

"Checkmate," he whispered.

FOUR

Nazca, Peru

Sitting in the office in which he'd interviewed three years previous, Todd Maddox reviewed the latest batch of test results. He scoured through the nearly fifty pages, searching for a clue as to what was going wrong with his test subjects. With the Hydra's burial place eluding Manifold's best efforts, Maddox had focused on his nAG protein theory. He'd made remarkable progress in the field of regeneration, no one denied that, but with each regeneration his subjects, animal or human volunteer, went stark raving mad. What good was a regenerated limb when all the subject used it for was mayhem?

Despite his early enthusiasm, Ridley was beginning to doubt. He didn't come right out and say it, but with every failure, he increased the pressure. The man had made most of his dreams come true, but he was a controlling task master with little tolerance for delays or setbacks. Even in the wake of his amazing strides forward, this last step back from the goal of perfected human regeneration had brought the man's wrath down like a digital maelstrom. E-mails, phone messages, and faxes from Ridley bombarded his office. The message was simple every time—"work harder," "think faster," "I'm not getting younger"—and the increased pressure had kept him awake for days. Even more stressful was that he had to apply that same pressure on the people working under him. He'd been well liked at his previous jobs. Here he lived and worked constantly feeling that a mutiny could break out at any moment. Ridley had never once mentioned firing him. Not even a hint. But the thought was always in the back of his head, urging him to make progress. He didn't want to risk losing all he'd worked for.

His bloodshot eyes burned, his sinuses stung, and a tickle at the back of his throat warned of an ensuing cold, but he ignored the symptoms. It would be well worth suffering through the illness if it meant securing the prize they'd sought for so long.

But the test results revealed nothing new. The subjects reacted to every possible combination of genetic tinkering in the same way. Rapid healing of the body caused swift degeneration of the brain, resulting in insanity and lack of intelligent thought. From rats to humans, each became frothing mad, brutally violent, and ravenously hungry. Some, who were allowed access to food, ate themselves to death, their regenerative abilities not able to keep up with their appetites. Others tore off their own limbs to escape their bonds only to have the limb grow back and send them deeper into madness. In the end, the failures were incinerated alive. Killing them had become a challenge since biological and chemical agents had no permanent effect. Bullets in vast quantities did the trick, but no one wanted to clean up the mess afterward. Maddox couldn't help but feel sorry for the volunteers. He never spoke to any of them—they arrived sedated—but seeing what they turned into . . . They were supposed to be helping people, not turning them into monsters.

His laptop chimed, signaling the arrival of an e-mail. He moved his hand to the mouse and clicked the "delete" button. He didn't feel up to reading more of Ridley's taunts. As he did so, he noticed the subject line was different from

Ridley's usual. It read simply: Fwd: Item found—details inside—pls pay.

He quickly opened the e-mail software's trash bin and read the e-mail.

The first line, added by Ridley, read: Expect a delivery soon.—R.R.

He looked at the forward information below the note.

From: Matthew Bronleewe [mailto: matt.bronleewe@ un.org]
Sent: Tuesday, June 21, 2009 8:33 AM
To: r.ridley@manifoldgenetics.com
Subject: Item found—details inside—pls pay

It was from one of Ridley's many contacts scouring the globe for any sign of the Hydra's burial site. That this e-mail came from a source within the U.N. made his stomach twist. This wasn't some black-market hooligan trying to make a quick buck. Bronleewe could lose his job, or worse, if he was found out. With so much at risk, the information had to be pertinent. When the first photo came through, his suspicions were confirmed. This was real.

When a second and third photo came through, he laughed. The first photo showed an inscription carved into a rock. He couldn't make out a word of it and scrolled down to the next image. Upon seeing it he stood from his leather chair, covered his mouth, and stared at the aerial photograph of a large drawing etched into the earth that depicted a nine-headed creature. He moved back to the laptop and scrolled down, bringing the third and final photo onto the screen. Staring back at him was the dark-haired, browneyed face of a man he didn't recognize.

Following the photos were a few lines of text:

George Pierce—U.N. Heritage Commission's Archae-ologist. On Site.

Inscription claims resting place of Hydra head.
Excavations have begun.
Site dated to 500 B.C.—roughly.
Private security en route. ETA, 72 hours.
Nazca, Peru—14"42'42.23S—75"12'05.84W
923029345

Maddox pieced together the information. The man in the photo was George Pierce, the U.N. Heritage Commission's man on the scene. Possibly an expert on the subject of Hydra. They had seventy-two hours, less by now, to get someone on site before some kind of security showed up. Private security. Not U.N. Interesting. Coordinates for the site came next, followed by a bank account number. The source would get $10,000 for the tip and an extra $100,000 if it panned out. Manifold had already spent $220,000 on previous tips that had them scouring several sites in Greece and others around Europe, but none had gleaned even the smallest hint of the treasure they sought. Other than the documents Ridley had already secured, it was almost as though someone had destroyed all historical record of the creature's genuine existence. It survived only in myth.

But it wasn't a myth. Ridley had shown him that much. The Hydra was real. Hercules as well. He had no doubt about it—not anymore. Maddox looked at the photo of the inscribed stone. This was *very* real. That it was in Peru struck him as odd, but again, who really knew where myths originated?

He also found it strange that this drawing in the sand, made twenty-five hundred years ago, depicted the Hydra in its legendary, nine-headed form. *Perhaps the historical Hercules perpetuated the first legendary aspects of the creature,* Maddox thought. He would have bolstered his reputation while frightening people enough to keep them from investigating his claims. A theory worth pursuing . . . at another time.

As hope crept back into his thoughts, he picked up a

small vial of lemon and eucalyptus oil and breathed deep through his nose, allowing the aromatic scent to fill his sinuses and fend off his growing infection. His appreciation of natural remedies had grown since meeting Ridley, and he used everything from oregano oil to echinacea to strengthen his strained immune system, but it had also inspired his work. Nature held many secrets. Uncovering them was the trick. Maddox breathed deep again, feeling a slight sting deep in his nose. He'd need to be healthy and rested if the prize he'd sought for so long finally arrived at his doorstep.

His instant message software chimed as a message appeared on-screen.

Get back to work in case this doesn't pan out, but be ready.

"Bastard," Maddox said before closing the laptop. But he believed Ridley would come through. The man had delivered on every promise to date. He'd probably steal the discovery, which didn't thrill Maddox, but he'd learned the occasional theft or subterfuge went a long way in his field. The greater good would be served. And he had yet to truly deliver on his promises to Ridley. A vastly extended life span as a madman wasn't very marketable, though he often wondered if Ridley would choose eternal madness over death. He seemed downright terrified of dying. He pushed the thought from his mind. If he could recover the Hydra's DNA and unlock the secrets of its genetic code, death might be an issue that Ridley would never have to face.

It wasn't a question of solving the puzzle of regeneration. That, to an extent, had been accomplished. It was the effects of regeneration on the mind. For Hydra to have survived into adulthood, a sound mind would have been required. True, it was probably an unintelligent creature, but the negative effects of regeneration that he had witnessed so far caused severe reactions even in the dumbest of creatures. Hydra must have had certain genes that blocked or negated this effect. The idea normally sent his mind spinning, but right now all he could think of was sleep.

Maddox sat on his office couch, which more often than not served as his bed, covered up with a lab coat and closed his eyes. A few more tests out of the thousands already run would garner little useful information. But a rested mind combined with the prize soon to be plucked from the U.N.'s grasp might just unlock the secrets to immortality.

Then again, maybe not.

He opened his eyes and sighed. Sleep would not come. He climbed off the couch and shuffled toward the office exit, pausing at the desk to pilfer some caffeine pills from a drawer. He popped two in his mouth and resumed his slow journey back to the lab. There was always time for a few more tests.

FIVE

Nazca, Peru, two days later

King smiled as the dry desert air whipping past pulled the moisture away from his body as quick as he could sweat it out. The intensely flat plains made driving an open-air jeep at ninety-five miles an hour irresistible, and he found himself enjoying what he thought would be a very boring trip. The same could not be said for his skittish passenger, his driver, Atahualpa—the man who was supposed to be behind the wheel of the old brown jeep.

Atahualpa now wished he hadn't accepted King's twenty dollars, but work for people of Incan descent was in short supply these days. He typically ferried tourists out into the desert on sightseeing tours, but they didn't pay well because fierce competition drove the prices down. The occasional science expedition paid better, and still other, less savory clients, paid even more handsomely. But work during the summer months slowed to a trickle drier than the sands, and twenty dollars extra, just to sit in the passenger seat, had been impossible to pass up. The only other benefit he saw to King driving is that they would arrive at their destination in half the time, though he knew arriving too early sometimes created complications as well, and his fare was already a full day ahead of schedule. He'd been assured the accelerated timing wouldn't be a problem, but King struck him as a dangerous man to cross, and that made him more nervous than the jeep's speed.

Glancing down at the GPS guide attached to the dashboard—the only hint of modern technology in the jeep—King could see they were approaching the heritage site base camp. He eased up on the gas and laughed when Atahualpa's body relaxed. The old Incan had probably never driven so fast. *Try a HALO jump,* he thought, *then you'll really understand speed.*

They'd been able to see the lone hill from miles away, but as it grew taller, King could make out a line of white, U.N.-emblazoned tents atop the mesalike hilltop. How anyone could be so brazen as to try looting such an obviously large operation was beyond him. Of course, they were an hour's drive from the nearest village and help would be a long time coming. But really, how valuable could Nazcan artifacts be?

If not for King's trust in Pierce's judgment, he'd never have agreed to spend his leave-time in the middle of nowhere. His ideal break included a cross-country motorcycle trek, the occasional hangover, and at least the potential for a romantic fling. Protecting a bunch of history geeks in a dry, windless desert had never been high on his list of things to do. Still, he'd left a day early, eager to see his old friend. If not for the accident that took his sister's life, this visit would have been a family occasion, not just two old friends reuniting.

The jeep slowed considerably as King drove it up the hill's steep incline, making sure to stay within the tire tracks of the vehicles that had preceded them. Pierce had briefed him on all the protocols for protecting the delicate environment surrounding the new World-Heritage site. At the top of the list: minimal human impact. That included keeping tire tracks to a minimum. The origins of most lines crisscrossing the plains could be traced back to modern vehicles, which often cut through the original ancient geoglyphs, sometimes before the glyphs had been discovered, sometimes long afterward.

He drove between a pair of tents and parked in the center of camp, far away from the other parked vehicles. Not a single person came to greet them or find out why they were there. *They really have* no *security,* he thought. He shut the jeep off and listened.

Nothing.

No people. No wind. No life.

The place was as still and quiet as the moon's surface.

King jumped out of the jeep, unzipped his backpack, and pulled out his .45 caliber Sig Sauer p220 handgun. He snuck the gun into Peru by taking an army flight headed to one of the three radar stations the U.S. manned. He'd had to rush to make the flight, but it'd been worth it. If he was walking into a fight with armed looters, his raised palms wouldn't intimidate them much. The handgun clip held only seven bullets, but the .45 caliber rounds had massive stopping power. If the target still stood with seven rounds in him, a wooden stake and holy water might be the next best weapons of choice. He slapped in a clip and chambered the first round.

He held an open hand at Atahualpa, who nodded vigorously, never taking his eyes off the ominous handgun. The empty base camp combined with his suddenly raised hackles frightened the man. He'd seen enough people shot in the desert to know that help never arrived soon enough.

Moving methodically, letting his weapon lead the way, King worked his way through the small camp, peeking into tents, checking out cars, and looking for signs of a struggle. He found nothing.

An organic murmur tickled his ears. He spun, searching for the source, but found nothing more than Atahualpa's frightened eyes. He pointed to his ear and made a quizzical expression.

Atahualpa cocked his head to the side, listening. He began shaking his head, no, but then stopped as the odd noise rose in volume. He nodded and ducked lower in the seat.

The noise sounded human, but more like a group of people buried beneath the sand. Atahualpa sat up suddenly and pointed over the far side of the hill, opposite from where they had come. The man had good ears.

King headed for the side of the hill, using a pickup truck for cover. He still couldn't see anyone, but the sound came much clearer now. Definitely a lot of people, but were they in pain? Several voices were high-pitched, almost frantic. He rounded the pickup and spun over the edge of the hill, still leading with his weapon, which came to a stop right between the eyes of a chubby local woman. *"¡Oh Dios! No disparen!"*

King lowered the weapon quickly. Twenty-odd people were gathered on the hillside, all looking down. Several looked back because of the woman's shouting, but he had tucked the gun into his pants at the small of his back. *"Lo siento,"* he apologized in Spanish. Delta operators were required to speak several languages. As Spanish was the fourth most spoken language in the world, learning it made sense. He could also speak Arabic and Mandarin. *"Pensé que estaba en peligro. Saqueadores. Soy amigo del Doctor Pierce. Por favor, ¿dónde está él?"*

The shaken woman didn't reply. He took her gently by the shoulders and smiled at her. "Please," he said, switching back to English. "Where is Dr. Pierce? I am Jack Sigler. His friend. He was expecting me."

"Jack Sigler." The woman nodded, recognition filling her eyes and pointed down the hill, past the sitting workers, and said, *"La cabeza del dragón."*

The dragon's head?

King began to wonder if the woman had heatstroke, but then he followed her shaky extended finger, looked past the sitting workers and saw the dragon. Even upside down, the massive drawing in the sand looked intimidating. Far in the distance he could make out its sharp, pointed toes and thick body. Rising out of the body were nine necks, each jutting out at a slightly varied angle, four on each side and one up the middle, like a neatly arranged vase of flowers. At staggering heights, the necks bent ninety degrees and ended with serpentine heads. The central neck shot straight toward the hill, ending at a large domed stone. This was the object that held the group's attention.

The earth around the base of the large stone was covered in small piles of sand. A large tunnel had been dug beneath the stone. Though the hole was cast in darkness, a shifting light moved within. Pierce was *under* the dragon's head, looking for the artifact he thought might cause looters to descend on the site.

"*Gracias,*" he said to the woman.

She just turned and walked quickly away, mumbling to herself.

Moving like he belonged among the waiting workers, King strode down the hill, doing his best not to frighten anyone else. But he saw the sideways glances cast in his direction and heard the nervous chatter after he passed. Seeing the dusty, outdoorsy garb the workers wore, both locals and imported, he realized just how out of place he looked. His scruffy black hair that stuck up like Hugh Jackman's portrayal of Wolverine on a bad hair day coupled with his black cargo pants and tight, black Elvis T-shirt was apparently not hip fashion for archaeology sites.

As a cumulative murmur of concern rose up behind him, he shouted for Pierce in his best playful voice. "Hey, George, you in there?"

King stopped at the tunnel entrance, noticing the odd-looking inscription carved into the stone above the hole. He put his face over the hole and shouted, "Hello. Anybody ho—"

Pierce shot out of the hole, his face only inches from King's. King jumped back, earnestly startled.

"Thought you military types didn't scare so easily,"

Pierce said with a smile, but the smile struck King as odd, almost forced. Something had shaken Pierce up.

"I've looked into a lot of dark holes and seen a lot of awful things, but your ugly mug has them all beat," King said, trying to keep the mood light. But when Pierce's rigid smile disappeared he could see the mood in the excavated space would be as heavy as the stone atop it looked.

Pierce waved him down. "I guarantee you; you've never seen anything as gruesome as this." He slid back into the tunnel. "We just entered a few minutes ago."

With a last glance at the group of onlookers, King felt a twinge of apprehension. Whatever had been buried beneath the stone was long since dead. Dead things didn't bother him. It was the people outside he didn't trust. He looked over the crowd and saw only kind and interested eyes. Atop the hill he saw Atahualpa watching. He gave him a wave. Atahualpa gave a halfhearted wave back, then turned and walked away.

Probably still shaken up from my driving, King thought with a grin. After a four-foot crawl he entered a small chamber lit by a single battery-powered lantern.

As King's eyes adjusted to the dim light, the scene resolved around him like a Polaroid picture. His mouth opened along with his dilating pupils.

"What . . . happened to them?"

SIX

Nazca, Peru

Twisted limbs and gnarled faces leaped out of the dark, more shocking and horrible than any hack-and-slash horror movie King had ever seen. The bodies were not only more gruesome than the imaginings of even the sickest Hollywood mind, but they were also very real. The eye sockets were sunken, but not empty. Each contained an off-white, dry orb that was surrounded by dark tan skin stretched tight like overworked leather. In some places, the ancient skin had ripped, revealing jawbone, ribs, or pelvis. Dried clothing lay in tatters on the dirt floor around the bodies, the natural fibers having rotted and fallen long ago.

King peeled his gaze away from the twenty-odd corpses lying about in the seven-foot-deep, ten-foot-wide hollow. Pierce stood at the center of the space next to an older woman he recognized from photos Pierce e-mailed him; Molly McCabe. "George, this is . . ."

"Disturbing," McCabe finished. She held her hand out to him. "Molly McCabe."

"Exactly," King said, then shook her offered hand. "Jack Sigler."

"As to your question, what happened here is what we're trying to figure out."

King returned his attention to the corpses surrounding them. Something awful had transpired here long ago.

"Near as we can tell," George said. "They were buried alive."

King knelt down and inspected two of the petrified cadavers, making sure not to touch anything. "And dehydrated."

"Mummified by the extreme dry heat," George said. "They've been perfectly preserved, in situ, from the day they died."

King leaned forward, staring at a mummified head that had been crushed flat on top. "How do you know they were alive?"

George pointed to the dimly lit ceiling where several dark lines crisscrossed the surface.

"Blood," King said, recognizing the dark hue. "They tried to claw their way out."

"There are finger gouges all around the edges, too," McCabe said. "But they probably suffocated fairly quickly after the entrance was sealed."

"Some of them were dead before then," King said.

McCabe looked surprised, "How do you know?"

King smiled and pointed to three of the bodies. "Crushed skulls. All three of them. Either they had their heads bashed in before they were buried . . ."

"Or?" George asked as he ran a finger along the jagged edge of one of the crushed skulls.

King stood and took the lantern from George. He held it up to the stone ceiling above one of the flat-headed men, revealing a splotch of color matching the scratch marks. "Or," he said, "this rock was dropped on top of them. Those with slow reaction times died quickly. From the looks of it, they got off easy."

McCabe crossed her arms. "I know you're here for security, but what exactly is your experience that you're so sure about what happened here?"

"Just spent a lot of time around dead people," he said, deflating McCabe's curiosity. "Figuring out how someone died is second nature now."

"There's no way," Pierce said, ignoring King's comment. "This rock must weigh . . . unless . . ." He rubbed his eyebrow and turned away, deep in thought.

"Well," McCabe said to King, forcing confidence back into her voice. "Given your . . . experience with gruesome crime scenes, perhaps you'll be more useful than a hired gun?"

King lowered the lantern and held it out so he could see Pierce again. "Speaking of that . . . why would you need security for a bunch of dead bodies? They can't be worth much to looters. What did you think was down here?"

Pierce snapped out of his thoughts and met King's eyes. "Not what do I *think*. What do I *know*." He stepped aside revealing what looked like a gray stone on the floor of the hollow. It's what they had been looking at when King entered through the small tunnel.

King looked down at the object, hardly impressed. "Looks like a rock."

"Look closer," Pierce said.

He knelt down and examined the object's surface. It looked like concrete, but more flaky. He could see a slight crisscross pattern, like some kind of fabric. Then he noted the shape—large on one end tapering down to the other, like some kind of animal's head. As his imagination set to work, the details came to life. On the small end, a pair of rises looked like a snout. Halfway to the top, another set of bumps looked like eye sockets. He stepped back and looked at it as a whole. "Looks like some kind of head. Like a giant snake head."

"A two-foot-long snake head?" McCabe asked.

He looked at Pierce and shrugged. "A prehistoric snake?"

"Something much more ominous," Pierce said.

King began to reply, but paused as a rise of voices filtered through the tunnel entrance, indiscernible, but clearly growing in volume.

"The natives are restless," McCabe said, then turned to Pierce. "You can tell him all about your theory after we get that thing out of here. I'll go settle down the crew."

Pierce looked through the tunnel but only saw blue sky above. "They probably just want to know what we found."

McCabe stopped in front of the tunnel. Ignoring the circle of bodies, McCabe forced a halfhearted smile. "Think you two strapping young men can handle that?"

"We'll take care of it," George said.

King nodded as he moved toward the petrified head. He'd seen scenes like this fresh with smoldering blood, flesh, and bullets. It disturbed him to think that atrocities like this happened so long ago; he'd always hoped that at some point in man's past there was peace, but here was evidence again that mankind could be as horrible as any monster conjured by the imagination. He wouldn't lose any sleep over this scene, but he took no joy in being desensitized to death.

Pierce took a large empty satchel from over his shoulder and opened it up in front of the artifact. "Lift up this end and I'll slide the bag over it."

King lifted the head. It was a lot heavier than it looked. King grunted from exertion.

Pierce slid the bag over the head, covering two thirds of the object. King placed it back on the floor of the cave, suddenly craving a drink from his few seconds of work. How anyone could have spent the time and energy to create the line drawing above was beyond him. Even here in the shade, the air was still plenty hot and dry enough to wither a man until he looked like a raisin.

Pierce took the satchel strap and dragged the object toward the tunnel. "Let's get out of this sweat lodge and catch up over a beer. I'll tell you all about our little friend here, too. I'll pull, you push."

George ducked into the tunnel, pulling the satchel behind him. King followed on his hands and knees, pushing the artifact with his hands, leaving the lantern behind. He would return for it after getting the heavy son-of-a-bitch artifact out of the hole. He squinted as Pierce climbed out, letting the sun blaze down. With a final heave he pushed the object out and followed close behind. But when he emerged from the hole and looked at Pierce, his face was twisted with an awkward discomfort King had seen on so many faces before—right before—he shot them.

King spun, following Pierce's gaze and came face-to-face with the muzzle of a triple-barreled handgun he'd only seen in demonstrations, the Metal Storm O'Dwyer VLe. Its electronic firing system used no moving parts and didn't require a clip or magazine. Bullets were stacked inside the barrel, separated by propellant. Some Metal Storm weapons using more than three barrels launched projectiles at speeds of up to one million rounds per second. They were the future of battlefield weaponry, but King had never heard of them being utilized in actual combat. Last he heard the technology was still in the R&D phase in Australia, but that did little to comfort him. The handgun lined up with his skull could fire three rounds in under a second without recoil until after the third bullet left the muzzle. His head would be obliterated. Of course, the first round would do the job on its own. The second two just added insult to injury.

SEVEN

Peru

Seth Lloyd had never been fond of James Bond, *Mission Impossible,* or even Nancy Drew, but as he snuck through the dimly lit, electronic-smelling Manifold Gamma computer lab, he wished he'd paid attention and taken notes on how to be a super sleuth. In the confines of a computer system, he could enter and exit at will, hacking networks, opening backdoors, and dismantling firewalls with ease. But the real walls, doors, and security cameras, not to mention the guards watching them, twisted his stomach and had him running to the bathroom before attempting this final act as a Manifold employee.

Seth sat down at his assigned computer, a twenty-four-inch iMac with all the trimmings running Linux, trying to look as normal as possible. He carried a coffee, now cold after his trips to the bathroom, a clipboard full of notes, and wore his funniest T-shirt, that read: *There are ten different kinds of people in the world: those who know binary and those who don't.* He doubted any guard watching would be smart enough to figure out the joke, but he hoped they'd spend enough time on it so as not to notice his computer screen or see the thumb drive he'd inserted into the USB port behind his cup of coffee.

He set to work on the keyboard and found his fingers too shaky to type at the speed he required. Needing to calm down, he turned on his iPod, scrolled down through the list of downloaded tunes, selected "My Hero" by the Foo Fighters, and placed the small earphones in his ears. He returned to the keyboard bolstered by the song's lyrics and heavy beat.

After opening the diagnostic tools he typically used in the lab to make sure the network was up and functioning glitch free, he opened his own personal software from the thumb drive. The small program ran behind the diagnostic window, allowing him to work without worrying about his program being seen on-screen, but it also meant that he had to work blind. He'd memorized the keystrokes, commands, and timing over the past week, since he'd broken into Manifold's database for fun. He'd done it like this, working secretly behind his diagnostic program, which did most of the work for him.

His fun had been short-lived when he uncovered a list of Manifold clients behind an ultra-secure firewall. The list included numerous terror organizations and violent regimes. Several were on the waiting list for something called Project Lerna, so he dug deeper while his subconscious told him to run. As a computer tech and network wizard, he never knew what the geneticists he worked alongside were doing. He knew it was high tech, like everything Manifold did, but he would never have guessed it involved rapid human regeneration. He'd been fairly anarchist throughout most of his twenty-three years of life, even as a child, but this flew in the face of decency. The technology would clearly be used to suppress people worldwide, and that spoke to his inner rebellious core and started his act of corporate treachery in motion.

He first attempted to hack into the system from the outside, which would have negated the need for his own personal Mission Impossible, but the firewall held its ground against every trick in the book. The only way past it was to connect, physically, behind the firewall. And the only place to do that was here, in the computer lab, which had been created for the sole purpose of maintaining the internal network protected by the firewall.

Without seeing it, Seth set the first data transfer in motion, downloading nearly two gigabytes of information to his thumb drive. He began counting down the two minutes it would take for the data to transfer.

When a hand touched his shoulder, he jumped and nearly fell back in his chair. Standing above him was David Lawson, second in command of Gen-Y security and head of the Manifold Gamma security force when Reinhart wasn't present. He'd always been nice enough, but he had seen Lawson during training sessions and knew what the twenty-one-year-old was capable of. He pulled the iPod earphones out and put on his best smile.

"Damn, man, you scared the hell out of me."

"Sorry," Lawson said with a grin. "You're not scheduled to run a diagnostic until next week. Had to come see what was up. You know how it is."

"Yeah, right. I was downloading some files last night and noticed the transfer rate lagging a bit. Wanted to make sure we didn't have a problem."

"What'd you get?" Lawson asked, growing excited. Seth provided most of the young security guards with a supply of video games. They had training and high-tech gadgets, but had very little to actually do. Most were starved for action and the games he provided were as good as it got most of the time.

"Call of Duty Six Beta," he said, hoping Lawson wasn't up on his video games enough to see through the lie.

"Beta? Sweet. Can I get it from you when you're done in here?"

Seth's ass twitched as his nerves began to chew at his insides. "Never finished downloading," he said quickly. "Too slow. Once I find the problem I'll start it back up and should have it for you tomorrow."

"Awesome," Lawson said. "I'll let you get back to work then." He turned and headed for the door, then stopped and said, "Just sign the check-in sheet when you leave so there's a record of you being here. I don't want to get canned because you forgot to sign in."

Seth gave a thumbs-up and looked back at the screen. The two minutes were long since up, so he clicked the "Safely Remove Hardware" button and pulled out the thumb drive, quickly replacing it with a second. His father, a carpenter, had always said, "Measure twice, cut once." He'd seen the logic behind the saying and had incorporated it into most of his life. If something could be doubled quickly, he did it, just in case something happened to the first. He worked over the keys and set the transfer in motion.

Two more minutes and he'd be home free.

After walking through three hundred feet of intersecting hallways Lawson entered the red-lit security suite and sat in one of the two leather chairs, giving him a view of the nearly one hundred security monitors.

"What's going on?" asked Simon Norfolk, a slender young man with a crew cut. He sat back in the chair with his feet on the countertop.

"Move your damn feet," Lawson said, swatting at his partner's legs.

"There isn't a security camera in here," Norfolk said. "Calm down."

"You're getting crap all over the counter. You want to be responsible when this stuff stops working because some idiot got dirt in the system?"

Norfolk took his feet off the counter and wiped away the dirt that had fallen from his deep-treaded black boots. "Happy now?" When Lawson didn't reply, Norfolk smacked his arm. "So what the hell is king geek doing in the computer lab?"

"Noticed the download speed was slow last night so

he's running a diagnostic on the network." Lawson looked at the image of Seth sitting in the computer lab. He squinted and watched as Seth's fingers flew over the keyboard. He was typing in commands, but the diagnostic software wasn't responding. "That's weird."

Lawson moved the image from the small monitor in front of him to the forty-inch screen at the center of the massive display. "Is it just me or is the diagnostic software finished?"

"Looks that way," Norfolk said.

"Then why is he still typing?"

"Better yet, what the hell is that?" Norfolk pointed to the side of the coffee cup where a small portion of the thumb drive could be seen, plugged into the USB port.

"Son of a bitch," Lawson yelled as he leaped from his chair and pounded out of the security suite with Norfolk hot on his heels. They covered the distance to the computer lab in twenty seconds, but when they barreled through the door, Seth was nowhere to be seen. His still-spinning chair revealed he had just left, and fast.

"Sound a general alarm," Lawson said, sending Norfolk on his way. Then he charged through the computer lab, drew his nonlethal stun gun, and headed through the far exit. He shouted angrily, "Seth!"

Seth heard his name roll down the hall like a tsunami. He rounded the corner, panicked and confused. He had never planned to escape on foot. He had never planned to get caught. But now it was one or the other. Looking back over his shoulder, he failed to notice the woman in front of him and crashed into her, sending them both to the floor.

Seth picked himself up quickly, nearly vomited with fear when he saw the Gen-Y security uniform, and then sighed with relief when he saw the woman wearing it— Anna Beck. Despite her girl-next-door good looks, which normally put him on guard, she was one of the few people at Manifold he considered a true friend, and regardless of her employment by Gen-Y, decided to trust her.

"Seth," Beck said, "what's going on?"

He thrust one of the thumb drives into her soft hand. "Look at it," he said. "But don't tell them about it."

"Tell who?" she asked.

"Seth!" Lawson's voice carried up the hallway.

Seth's eyes went wide. "Them. Please, just do it."

She looked at the thumb drive, nodded and said, "Okay. Just tell me what's going on. Maybe I can—oof."

He punched her as hard as he could, sending her to the floor, gasping for air. "Sorry," he said, then ran toward the stairwell that would take him to the exit and the jungle beyond.

A moment later, Lawson rounded the corner. "Where is he?"

After sucking in a breath and standing without help from her compatriot, she told the truth. "Outside. We'll never find him." She leaned against the wall and slid the thumb drive into her pocket. As she watched Lawson run to the stairwell she wondered what could be important enough to cause an average guy like Seth to risk his life. It wasn't Lawson that would kill him—only nonlethals were allowed to be used on Manifold employees. It was the jungle that would do him in. Seth hadn't spent more than a few minutes in the jungle and had avoided every training session Gen-Y had offered Manifold employees. He'd be lucky to survive the next few hours.

EIGHT

Nazca, Peru

King stared at his reflection in the chrome goggles of the masked man pointing one of the world's most lethal handguns at his head. He was happy to see his face didn't reflect any of the surprise he felt at finding himself caught completely off guard.

He quickly counted five men, all dressed, head to toe, in black, liquid-cooled suits—nicer than anything the U.S. military provided. Their eyes hid behind reflective goggles that blocked sun and dust; the remainder of their faces were covered by metal masks that supplied clean air and water to each man. He recognized the suit technology. It was similar to a prototype he had tested, that had yet to receive final approval—funding—for field use.

"Jack Sigler, call sign, 'King,'" said the man holding a pistol to King's head. His voice sounded electronically distorted, like a more metallic Darth Vader. "You're a day early."

King really had to work hard at hiding his surprise now. His call sign as a Delta operative was classified information. Not even Pierce knew he was Delta. Only his team and a handful of government officials had access to his information.

"I would have baked cookies if I knew we were having company," he said. He scanned the area quickly, ignoring the gun hovering in front of his face. Three of the dark-clad men were putting the kneeling excavation crew into zip-tie handcuffs. He fought the urge to curse when he saw the driver, Atahualpa, helping them. *No wonder he was so nervous when I drew my gun,* he thought, *he thought I was on to him.*

A fourth man held a Metal Storm handgun on Pierce and McCabe. Two pulls of the trigger would tear them apart. The artifact-laden satchel lay on the ground between them.

King's mind sprinted through his options. The gun still tucked into his belt buckle held enough rounds to kill all five men if his shots were accurate—and he had no doubt they would be—but by the time he'd killed the man next to him, three bullets would no doubt be fired into Pierce or McCabe. With taking action on the back burner, he decided to pursue the next best strategy: information gathering. "What do you want?"

The man's trigger finger twitched ever so slightly.

"They're after the artifact," McCabe shouted, kicking sand at the man guarding her and Pierce. She'd stood up to enough brooding men in her life to not back down because of a threat.

"Settle down, lady," the guard said, taking aim at her head.

"Go to hell," she said. Pierce took her arms and held her still as she tried to rush the man.

King admired her fight in the face of overwhelming odds, but knew it would get her killed. The situation had to be resolved quickly, even if it meant letting these guys get away. "Just take what you came for and go."

The man standing over him knelt down and, with a low growl, said, "I intend to." He stood and stiffened his aim at King's head. "Take Dr. Pierce. Leave the others to roast. And shoot the bitch."

"No!" King shouted. For a fraction of a second he moved forward, out of the tunnel, but his instincts told him to duck back inside. Had he ignored his instincts the three bullets fired from above would have struck his head instead of the tunnel wall.

Drawing his Sig Sauer, he moved back to the entrance. He'd start dropping bodies as soon as one crossed his path. But the only thing he saw through the tunnel exit was a grenade. It bounced to a stop two feet inside the four-foot tunnel, pin pulled and about to explode. He dove away from the tunnel, covered his ears, opened his mouth, and pressed himself against the cave wall and two mummified corpses.

Three rapid-fire gunshots echoed through the tunnel just a moment before the grenade exploded, sending a plume of dust and a wave of pressure into the small chamber. The force smashed King's head against the hard-packed earth, knocking him unconscious.

NINE

Nazca, Peru

Pierce stared down at the limp body of Molly McCabe. Blood pooled around her, spreading out onto the hard-packed sand and pebbles like a mudslide through a suburban neighborhood. In the day's heat, the blood would be dried within the hour, a permanent stain on the desert marking the passing of a woman he had come to respect and enjoy. He fell to his knees next to her body and checked her pulse. He knew there wouldn't be one, but it was all he could think to do.

"Dr. Pierce," said one of the masked men as he picked up the satchel containing the artifact. "You're going to have to come with us."

He looked at the man through his tears. He longed for McCabe's spirit and strength, but the sight of the strange-looking pistol still in the guard's hand combined with the three holes in McCabe's chest deflated any thoughts of heroism. He wasn't King . . . and King was. . . . He stood up.

King represented what little family he had left. His parents were dead, his brother a drug addict, and King, the man who had nearly been his brother-in-law, had always been there for him.

The man in charge took aim at Pierce, recognizing the look of a man about to do something foolish. "Hold on, Pierce," he said, and then turned to the man who shot McCabe. "Fix her up."

The man knelt down next to McCabe and tore open the top of her shirt. He wiped the area over her heart, where the three bullets had torn through skin and bone, with a white cloth that smelled strongly of alcohol. The man discarded the now bloody rag, took a small pack from his pocket and removed a red liquid–filled syringe. As the man took aim over her heart, Pierce moved to stop him, but he was knocked to his knees and put in a submission hold by one of the other guards who'd finished zip-tying the crew.

"Watch," the guard said, holding Pierce's head just feet from McCabe's dead body.

After five seconds, the holes in McCabe's chest shrunk and closed. Pierce stopped struggling and watched in silence, waiting to see what would happen next. A small undulation beneath the skin of her neck caught his eye. She had a pulse. Then he noticed her chest rising and falling. McCabe was alive.

"You brought her back to life?" he asked as he looked at the man in charge. "How is that possible?"

"Regeneration," the man said. "You know all about that, don't you, Doc?"

He looked at the artifact hanging from the man's shoulder.

Hydra.

"She'll be fine," the man said, lowering his gun. "Now please, come with us."

Pierce nodded slowly. He knew in the end he had no choice, and they did save McCabe. He looked at the now damaged stone, its inscription ruined by the explosion. Regret tore at his insides. King had been his oldest friend, as close to family as you could get without sharing a blood relative. It made him sick to think it, but he hoped the grenade had killed King. Being stuck alive under that rock . . . he'd seen the faces of those men, roasted alive. No one deserved that fate. "Sorry, Jack," he said as he allowed the men to bind him in zip-tie handcuffs.

When he first saw them, Pierce thought these might have been part of the same group who stole the *Argo* crew manifest, but while these men held just as keen an interest in a Hercules-related artifact, their high-tech weapons and military precision set them apart from his previous attackers, who were much more . . . primitive. Those men had been passionate about protecting the secrets of the past, even if it meant destroying it. But these men, if they truly were interested in Hydra for its regeneration abilities, which seemed entirely likely given the miracle he'd just witnessed, were more interested in unlocking ancient secrets.

The men holstered their weapons and led Pierce up the incline, back toward the U.N. base camp. As they walked, the leader shouted back to Atahualpa, "Keep them tied up for two hours, then let them go."

"What about my money?" Atahualpa asked. A wad of cash was tossed his way. He caught it and smiled. "Two hours. Right!"

As they reached the top of the hill, Pierce looked back and saw Atahualpa sit down in the sand. "Oww!" he shouted as something bit his neck. His first thought was that a scorpion or spider had stung him, but he caught a glance of a syringe before a wave of nausea struck. His vision blinked out next.

Though he could no longer see, Pierce could still hear, though his consciousness quickly faded. He raged, unable to move, as one of the dark-clad men said, "That's mean, boss."

"Why's that?"

"Would have been nicer to just shoot them all in the head than leave them with her. She'll tear them to bits when she wakes up."

"Too bad I'm not nice."

Pierce groaned as the men's laughter roared in his head, bent and distorted by his delirium. He lost consciousness as his body flopped down onto a hard surface and an engine roared to life.

TEN

Nazca, Peru

King woke to a hard object poking his ribs. He grabbed at it and pulled it away, tossing it to the side. It clattered across the floor of the pitch-black, resealed burial pit. He realized he'd thrown a bone, probably one of the mummified men's arms.

Colors danced in his vision as he opened his eyes wide, searching for any sign of sunlight that might signify an escape route, but saw only phantom colors. He knew he hadn't been unconscious long because the colors he saw were created by his eyes adjusting to the pitch dark of the tomb. He experienced the phenomenon every time he went on a night mission. That first plunge into darkness always filled his vision with reds, purples, and greens.

Two other indicators told him he hadn't been out long. First, he was still breathing. There couldn't be much air inside the chamber and the lack of light also meant a lack of air passage. That was good news and bad news; good because he wasn't dead yet, bad because he soon would be. The second indicator was that he was only beginning to feel thirsty. Dehydration would set in soon enough as the sun-baked sand cooked him like a roast pig in a

Hawaiian imu pit, but for now he was functioning fine, except for the ringing in his ears.

Damn grenade.

King stood and smacked his head on the ceiling. "Damnit!" he shouted, bending down. The center of the pit stood seven feet high, but the edge, where he'd been thrown, shrunk to just under five feet. He shuffled to the center of the pit, hunching until his foot struck something, filling the chamber with a metallic clang. He bent down and searched with his hands until he found the source of the noise—the lantern.

He felt the electric lantern's body, searching for the power button. As he did, he wondered if he really wanted to light the chamber. What good would it do him? Any sunlight peeking through wouldn't be able to compete with the lantern light. He'd never see it. And he'd have to look at the ugly mugs of the mummified men surrounding him, reminding him of his fate. Buried alive. Mummified by the scorching sun and moisture-sucking air. But when he found the button, he decided he'd rather die being able to see. He said a quick prayer and pushed the button.

Light filled the small chamber, revealing a circle of horrified expressions, eyes pale, mouths agape, fingers torn to shreds, heads bashed in. Most of the men had survived the blast, being dead already, but several had been tossed and shattered after being blown across the chamber and striking the far wall.

The light blinked out as King pushed the button again. Perhaps it was best to keep it extinguished. *Bullshit,* King thought, then switched the light back on. Doing his best to ignore the never-fading shocked expressions of the corpses, he circled the chamber, hammering away with the butt of his handgun where the earth wall met the stone above. The sand and stone, packed in tight, couldn't be budged, even where the entrance used to be. Without a shovel, there would be no getting through. Still, he had to try.

For ten minutes he hammered at the wall where the

entrance once was. After loosing a small chunk he began clawing at it with his fingers. Progress came slow and he noticed each dust-filled breath doing less and less to satiate his body's craving for oxygen. His physical exertion used more oxygen than his body at rest . . . or unconscious. He stopped digging and rested his hand against the wall. After a few breaths, which he attempted to slow, a dull ache in his fingertips caught his attention. He looked at his hand and found it covered in blood. He pulled his hand away from the wall and saw bloody finger marks matching the ancient, dry stains left by the men first buried here.

He had become one of them.

King looked at his fingertips, rubbed raw and bleeding. He couldn't escape. And though someone would come looking for him long before the moisture-wicking air transformed him into a mummy, he'd still be just as dead.

Accepting his fate as each breath he took sucked more oxygen out of the stale air and replaced it with more carbon dioxide, King sat down between two of the mummified men. He looked at each and grinned, finding humor in the fact that he was dying slowly at an archaeological dig rather than being blown to bits or riddled with bullets during combat. "This is gonna suck, right?"

The heat of the chamber pounded on his body, clinging to his black Elvis T-shirt and pulling the water in his body to the surface and away. He longed to remove his clothing, but found himself unable to move. His eyes lulled as his mind and body began shutting down. The only consolation he felt about dying was that he wouldn't be awake to experience it.

As his head slowly tilted toward his shoulder, his thoughts turned to Pierce. He'd failed his friend. He'd never failed so grossly at a mission, but even that would have been forgivable—war was hell and even the good guys sometimes lost. But Pierce was his friend. This never should have happened and he'd never forgive himself for it, not that he had long left to self-deprecate.

In his waning moments, King resolved that if he returned as a ghost, he'd haunt the bastards that did this for the rest of their lives. And if he somehow survived, he'd make them wish he were a ghost. His vision failed and his head thumped heavily against the skull of his neighbor. He'd become one more sacrifice for the sands to absorb.

ELEVEN

Nazca, Peru

The darkness consumed.

Reality twisted, then fled, and the surreal invaded.

King floated past lines of bodies, brutally disassembled and strewn across the desert. A battle had taken place. No. He'd seen battles. This was a slaughter. The stars above glistened like beads of water, thick and wet, stuck to the black blanket of the sky. The view spun away as his ethereal form drifted higher, sliding away from the grisly scene and up toward the heavens.

King had never pictured death. In his line of work a fear of death often quickened its arrival. Fear of pain did wonders, but fear of death could immobilize even the most well trained soldier. But this—floating out from his tomb, drifting over the dead, and rising up—defied even stereotypical near-death experience. Where was the white tunnel? The relative to guide him on? Shouldn't his sister be here? Where was Julie?

"Julie," he said. "Show me the way, Jules."

There was no reply, only the sensation of rising through a thick ooze. His thoughts turned to Hell. The bodies. Clearly tortured. The cold. He felt cold. Was Hell cold?

Maybe Hell really did freeze over. Ha. He wanted to laugh, but could not feel his body. He no longer had a body.

He tried to will his spirit, or whatever this was, in a new direction, but he continued up and away, steadily forward to an unknown destination. The stars beckoned to him, then faded from view. He slipped back into the abyss thinking of his sister again.

"Sir," a voice said. "Drink."

Liquid filled King's mouth. He took a breath. Gagged. Sat up quick and felt a blow to his head like a spike being driven through. The pain pulsed there like a flashing street-light.

"Stay still," the voice said, barely a whisper. "She will hear you."

"Julie?"

"No. The old one."

"Who are you?"

"Atahualpa."

King's eyes shot open as his mind fell back into his body. The vision. He wasn't floating. He'd been carried. But that meant— King squeezed his eyes, erasing the nightmare. With fresh eyes he took in his surroundings.

Atahualpa knelt next to him. The man looked pale. Perhaps from the moonlight. Perhaps something more. The stars above, no longer bulbous, twinkled in the crisp, clear night sky. They sat in the dirt between two parked trucks. Atahualpa handed him a bottled water. "Drink."

King took it and downed all twelve ounces. The liquid, cooled by the desert night air, chilled his stomach and quenched the fire in his mouth and throat. He felt life returning. He took a second bottle offered by Atahualpa and pulled from it more slowly, allowing the liquid time to be absorbed by his body and offered as a feast to his dehydrated cells. He met the doe-eyed driver turned traitor's eyes.

"You saved me. Dug me out."

The man nodded.

"Why?"

"They said no one would be hurt."

King didn't like the sound of that. His mind replayed the field of dead from his vision. He prayed it was a vision. "Who was hurt?"

"I could hear them screaming. I hid in a truck. For hours I hid. Then the screaming stopped. I looked from the window and saw her."

"Who?"

"The old one. The gray-haired woman."

"Molly?" King sat up straight, fighting the throbbing pain in his head. "She's alive?"

"She is the devil's."

King sighed. Information steeped in religious paranoia would do him no good. "Skip what you learned in church and give me the facts."

Atahualpa squinted. "I have never been to church. But I know a devil when I see one. Blood covered her body. Red. Pieces"—he sniffed, fighting back tears—"there were pieces of bodies . . . their insides . . . clung to her body. To her lips. Her belly . . ." He arched his hands out and around his own belly. "Like a pregnant woman. Filled with their bodies."

King tensed. "Whose bodies?"

With a shaking finger, Atahualpa pointed the way. "The workers."

King realized he was pointing toward the dig site, toward Pierce's dragon. He launched to his feet and stumbled, catching himself on the side of the red pickup's flatbed.

"You must be quiet," Atahualpa said. "She fled into the desert, but who is to say she will not return."

"I'll take my chances," King said, draining the remainder of his second water bottle, then staggering toward the dig site. A hand on his shoulder stopped him.

"Take this."

King turned and found his handgun offered. It was a peace offering. He could have let him dry out in his tomb. Judas wanted to team up. His pleading eyes begged. Forgive and forget.

King took the gun, checked the magazine, and slammed it back home. He turned to Atahualpa. The man had been duped and used. King had done the same to men just like him. Desperate for money or food. Willing to trade trust for survival. King nodded at the man. Forgiveness granted.

They fell in together, walking low, slow, and quiet. If there was danger lurking in the dark desert the only warning they'd get was the sound of feet crunching stone. King fought against waves of dizziness, and kept his gun aimed at the dark, willing his eyes to dilate just a little bit more, suck in the moonlight. They reached the hill's crest and looked down.

Melding with the dark, bodies lay in the sand, still resting where they had the previous afternoon. But no heads turned at their approach. Several lacked heads altogether. King felt himself descending back into the hell he drifted by as Atahualpa carried him from his desert tomb. It wasn't a nightmare. It was real. How many bodies lay scattered across the hillside was impossible to tell. Body parts and organs splayed across the scene held in place like sick sculptures by congealed and sun-dried blood. The sand was thick with the stuff. It crunched beneath his feet, chipping away like maroon crackers.

King held his shirt over his mouth and nose as the slightest breeze brought the rising stench down around them. He'd smelled death before, but this—bodies and organs exposed to the blistering heat of the day, cooked and bleached—he was reminded again; this had been no battle. These people were slaughtered.

He found the woman he'd startled and knelt down beside her body. What was left of it. A leg was missing. Following a trail of blood he saw it had been used to bludgeon a man's head. Her arm, still attached, was missing large chunks from shoulder to elbow, as though an ogre had mistaken it for a corn cob. He lifted the dry arm, stiff and heavy and inspected the missing flesh. The bite marks were unmistakable.

Human.

King tried to imagine a tribe of cannibals descending on the group of workers. It was the only thing that made sense. But it lacked any kind of logic. There were no cannibals in Peru, and they certainly couldn't run around the desert eating people without drying up and withering. Plus, he had an eyewitness.

"How did this happen?"

"The woman. Molly."

King shook his head. "Not possible."

Atahualpa made a stabbing motion over his chest. "They shot her. Dead. Injected her with something. She came back. They were gone when she woke up. I offered her water. Like you. She said she was hungry. Tried to bite me. I ran through . . ." He motioned through the dead bodies. "She stopped at the first man." Shaking his head, rubbing out the images, he pointed to what little remained of the first man. Bones and bits of flesh. A large stain. And next to it what looked like a pile of vomit.

King found several piles throughout the scene. If his story was true, she was eating her victims, vomiting them up, and moving on to the next. One after another, the zip-tied crew had no chance of escape. "You could have cut them free."

Atahualpa looked down. "I am not a brave man."

King finished searching the bodies for familiar faces and found none. McCabe was missing, which corroborated his story. But Pierce was missing, too.

"They took my friend?"

"Yes."

"Alive?"

He nodded.

"How did they leave?"

"Truck," he said, pointing north. "That way."

King rushed away from the blood-soaked hillside and entered the camp. Atahualpa stayed behind him, urging quiet, but King ignored him, rummaging through tents and personal belongings of the deceased. He found a flashlight and turned it on. His search sped more quickly and he found what he'd been looking for—a satellite phone. He turned it on and basked in the green glow of its digits. Help was a phone call away. Then he noticed a photo on the floor of the tent. It sucked the breath from his lungs. He placed the phone down and trained the light on the photo. Julie and George. Smiling. Happy. Streamers in the background revealed a party. The sparkle on her finger reflected the promise of what was to come. A life never lived. He picked up the photo, put it in his pocket, and dialed the phone.

After a few clicks, the connection was made and the phone on the other end began to ring. A digital female voice answered. "Hello, I'm sorry, but we cannot come to the phone right now. If you leave your name, number, and the time of your call, we'll get back to you as soon as possible." With the recording finished, the line beeped.

"King," he said.

"Voice print confirmed."

The line beeped three times, then clicked. "That you, King?"

King felt his body relax. Deep Blue. "I need some help down here."

"You need company?" Deep Blue's voice became serious. King didn't ask for help unless people were dead and someone had to pay for it.

TWELVE

New Hampshire

The thick foliage covering the forest floor crunched beneath the feet of the approaching men. Each held their weapon nervously in front of them, twitching back and forth, looking for a target. Looking for him. Rook.

He took a slow deep breath, inhaling the scent of wet earth and decaying leaves. The smell of home. Growing up in the woods of New Hampshire, Rook felt more at home here than anywhere else. A twig snapped just feet from his face and brought him back to his current situation.

Fifteen combatants had been whittled down to three. These two and one more in hiding. Their plan wasn't half bad. These two were bait. The third would take him out with a barrage from the overgrown rhododendron. Of course, if they'd known they were standing two feet in front of Rook, buried beneath the thick foliage, they might have rethought the plan.

"What do you see?" came a whispered voice from the rhododendron. *Amateurs.*

"Nothing, man. Shut up," the closest of the three replied.

"I don't get it," the third said. "This guy is old. Should have been a cakewalk."

Rook did his best not to laugh. These pipsqueaks just guaranteed themselves a no-holds-barred ass kicking. No pain, no gain, girls. He took aim and squeezed his weapon's trigger twice, unleashing two consecutive three-round bursts. Both men dropped to the forest floor, writhing in the wet earthy leaves, holding their red-stained crotches. They hollered in pain.

The kid in the bush began shouting. "Where is he? Where is he!"

"We're dead, man. And I sure as hell didn't see him."

A shrill ring cut through the air. *Damn,* Rook thought as he rose from his concealed position to answer his emergency line. The thing was a social nightmare. He couldn't turn it off in theaters, at a game, or while kicking some University of New Hampshire kids' asses at paintball. He had to be available at all times and that meant the damn phone had to be on at all times . . . except during a mission . . . and this little outing was not being funded by the U.S. government.

The two kids on the ground shuffled away from him, fear in their eyes as he rose looking like an evil Sigmund the Sea Monster. He pulled off his head gear, revealing his dirty blond hair, long goatee, and blazing blue eyes. He lowered his DYE DM8 paintball gun to the ground and held a palm up toward the third kid now rushing out with his rifle aimed. Looking like some Norse god ready for battle, Rook's hard gaze and outstretched hand stopped the kid in his tracks.

"Time out. Need to answer the phone," Rook said.

"Dude, shoot him!" one of the dead kids yelled.

Rook opened the phone and placed it against his ear. "I'm here." He kept his eye on the kid with the itchy trigger finger and listened. "On my way." He closed the phone, pocketed it, and turned his full attention to the lone survivor.

"There's no freakin time-outs in paintball!" one of the grounded kids shouted.

"And dead people don't talk," Rook said, then looked at the last man standing. "Time in."

The kid cocked his head. "Huh?"

Rook pulled his side arm and fired from the hip. A red blotch exploded on the kid's facemask, blocking his view and effectively killing him. He picked up his gear and started his trek out of the four-acre paintball course known locally as GLOP.

One kid started whining. "Cheap bastard!"

Rook raised his paintball gun and pulled the trigger, peppering the kid from head to toe with paintball pellets, each stinging like a bee. The kid danced and shouted in pain, looking for cover, but found none.

When the paintball canister emptied, Rook lowered the gun and grinned at the paint-coated kid. "*Now* I'm a bastard."

He headed into the trees and quickly faded from view. The rest and relaxation shooting college students provided would have to wait. King called for backup and that meant that somewhere, shit was hitting a fan.

Ocracoke Island, North Carolina

In between tides, small waves settled gently onto the shore, sifting through the sand with a soothing hiss. A slight breeze bent the sea grass growing tall and green on the dunes that separated the sand from the island's tree line and small town beyond. The beach was pleasantly devoid of the tourists that packed the more popular mainland beaches, which was just the way Queen liked it. Being able to tan her curves free from gawking male eyes and an endless barrage of one-liners so corny even Rook wouldn't use them was how she believed a vacation should be spent.

A whistle in the distance caught her ear and caused a wave of discomfort to pass through her bikini-clad body. *Ignore it,* she thought. The whistle sounded innocent, like a dog call, but in her experience, any sign of men on a beach was the end of her relaxation. The whistle came again, closer this time. Crinkles formed around her eyes as she willed the passerby to keep on passing by.

"Tito! Come back, boy!"

No such luck.

A dog.

Queen opened her eyes to the smiling face of a half-soaked golden retriever. It carried a drool-laden tennis ball in its mouth and wore a blue bandanna. Had it just been the dog, she would have happily played fetch with it until the sun dipped below the horizon, but her luck had run out. The dog's owner, probably a local or part-timer on the island, swaggered up wearing rolled up blue jeans and a loose-fitting white dress shirt. Silk by the looks of it. His curly near-mullet and scruffy face completed the image of a 1980s stud starring opposite Julia Roberts. He smiled as he took the dog's collar.

"Enjoying the beach?"

"I was," she replied, doing nothing to hide her annoyance at his presence.

After a brief frown he found his self-confidence again and forced a smile. "I can tell you're pretty stressed. Why don't you let me—"

Queen held up her fist and extended her middle finger. She held it there as the man shifted from surprise to deflation and finally to anger.

"Hey, you—"

Her cell phone rang loudly. She popped it open and put it to her ear. She listened, then hung up after saying, "You got it." She stood, looked at the man, and said, "Who names their dog Tito?" She then quickly wrapped herself in a towel and retreated from the beach, leaving her chair, cooler, and novel as mementos for the emotionally castrated man.

Land O'Lakes, Florida

Thirty feet below the surface, Knight poked his head out of the ship's flooded hold to see if the coast was clear. It wasn't. The cloud of rapidly moving silver bodies pursued by scores of frenzied hammerhead sharks still blocked out most of the shimmering blue surface above. Normally, hammerheads didn't attack people. With only twelve reported unprovoked attacks on humans they were one of the safest sharks to swim with. But in the midst of a feeding frenzy, everything within reach of their snapping jaws was fair game.

Knight had come to Florida to visit his aging grandmother, his last surviving relative, but he could only take so many bingo games and retreated to the coast. He rented a boat, scuba equipment, and headed to the coordinates of one of his favorite shipwrecks. The *Anne Marie* was a cargo ship, sunk by a U-boat during World War Two. While much of its cargo had long since been raised to the surface, the inside of the solid-steel ship still held scattered remnants of a time and war that would soon see its last survivors die out.

Knight checked his oxygen levels. Fifteen minutes. On such a shallow dive he didn't need to stop to decompress, so reaching the surface could be done quickly. He had time to wait, but if the human garbage disposer twisting above the wreck didn't ebb or move away, he'd have to choose between asphyxiating on an empty tank or being torn to shreds. With the frenzy well into the thirty-minute mark, he felt sure it would slow down soon enough.

A vibration on his side caused him to flinch back into the ship. He thought for sure he'd come face-to-face with a hammerhead, but found only open water. The nudge came again and this time he recognized it as his phone vibrating. He opened a pouch on his side and removed the phone, sealed in a Ziploc bag. Its blue glow filled the dark ship's hallway. He answered it, pressed the phone hard against his ear, and heard Deep Blue's muffled voice. He pushed "1" on the phone twice, letting Deep Blue know that he had received the message but was unable to reply audibly.

He tucked the phone back into the pouch and peered out of the portal once more. His fifteen minutes disappeared with a phone call. The giant ball of fish and shark above continued to twist and coil in on itself. Chunks of fish floated down toward him where smaller sharks and predatory fish took advantage. Even they might take a bite at him. But he had to risk it.

He kicked out and away from the wreck's protection and stopped on the sandy bottom. He took one long drag from the oxygen, then purged his tank. Bubbles exploded toward the surface in a cloud of energy. The sharks ignored it at first, but when their prey fled from it, the sharks followed. As though flying up through the eye of a tornado, Knight kicked hard, heading toward the surface, rising with the cloud of bubbles. As the bubbles reached the surface ahead of him, the water suddenly cleared and the wall of silvery fish began to close in around him. Massive bodies pounded through with jaws wide open. With only feet remaining on either side, Knight hit the surface and launched himself up and over the side of the small motorboat. As his legs cleared the water he felt something blunt strike him. He rolled onto his back, looking down expecting to see flesh torn away, but discovered himself fully intact, though a rising bruise revealed where a shark had blindly rammed him. He started the engine and hammered the throttles, gunning for the shore.

Fort Bragg, North Carolina

The right hook came like a blur, connecting with Bishop's cheek. He stumbled back a step and kept his guard up, waiting for the next attack. It came in a three-punch combo. He blocked the first two. The third snuck by but only glanced off his shoulder. He bounced around the ring, eyeing his opponent—a beefy freshly crew cut recruit who thought he could take on the world with a pistol and win. And after spending ten minutes pummeling the older Delta operator he believed it more than ever.

He came in straight and sloppy, wide open. Bishop allowed the kid to throw his punches. Five of them this time. Three blocked. Two connected. The last was a good shot that connected with Bishop's forehead and knocked his head back.

"That's more like it," he murmured.

"You say something, old man?" the kid said as he walked around Bishop sporting a cocky grin.

What the recruit didn't know is that the only people on base who would fight Bishop in the ring were recruits. Everyone else knew better. They knew he liked the pain. Absorbed it like a sponge and released it in a burst. Right now he was nearly full up. When the fight ended Bishop would retreat to his small ranch just off base, put on Vivaldi's Spring mvt 2: Largo and meditate, controlling the rage that had built up since childhood.

An unplanned and unwanted birth, his Iranian parents had abandoned him on the side of a road. Found parched in the desert, he became a black-market baby. Bought by a British organization posing as parental buyers, he was eventually adopted by an American family at the age of two. Raised in the U.S., he became Erik Somers. His life reflected the American Dream, but at his core, those two years, the ones lived while his soul took root in his body, left him raging inside. Before joining the military he'd been something of a bar room brawler, but first as a Marine, then a Ranger, and now an elite Delta operator, he had found the discipline—and outlet—he needed to control his rage.

A flash of red caught Bishop in the gut, followed by a second to the temple. The bystanders cringed with loud "oohs!" but not because of the pain Bishop was being dealt, but because they knew it would be returned on the recruit, and then some.

Sufficiently motivated, Bishop changed his stance. That alone caused the kid to back off. Bishop hadn't changed a thing since the fight began. He merely hopped around the ring, accepting punches. But a new presence in the gym caught Bishop's attention. Brigadier General Michael Keasling, commander of the Joint Special Operations Command (JSOC), a task force commissioned with making sure U.S. special ops weaponry and tactics were the best in the world. The man didn't make social calls and he never made an appearance at the gym. The grim look on his mustached face confirmed Bishop's fear. Something was wrong.

Keasling didn't make a motion. Just met Bishop's eye. Bishop nodded. The fight was over.

But not for everyone. The recruit saw the moment of distraction and took it. He came in low and swung up with a massive uppercut. But Bishop was no longer playing the part of punching bag. As the punch came up, Bishop tilted his head back. The gloved fist caught nothing but air, throwing the large man off balance. Bishop followed up the dodge with a quick blow to the recruit's midsection, doubling him over. He chased it quickly with a crushing right hook that put the kid on one knee. Had the recruit been less cocksure he would have let it end there, but this one would get himself killed in combat if his ego wasn't broken. The third punch spun the kid's head around and put him on the mat.

As the men watching cheered him on, Bishop shed his blue gloves, dropped them to the mat, and slipped between the ropes. He toweled the sweat from his body as he approached Keasling. "Is it King?"

Keasling nodded. "The others are on their way back. You ship out in three hours."

"Where to?"

"Best guess at this point? Peru. But the exact location has yet to be determined."

"What happened?"

"Mercs killed a bunch of civies on King's watch. Kidnapped his friend, too. He's out for blood," Keasling said. He started to leave, then paused. "Leave the dog tags. This one's off the books."

Bishop nodded. The general left without another word.

Bishop entered the showers and stood beneath an ice-cold, high-pressure spray of water. He leaned his hands against the wall, closed his eyes, and controlled his breathing. Vivaldi would have to wait.

THIRTEEN

Ayacucho, Ica, Peru

King sat in the jeep, foot eager to hit the gas. As the engine clicked and cooled he forced his hands to release the steering wheel. A painful tingle filled his hands as blood rushed to fill crushed digits. He and Atahualpa had followed the mercenaries' tracks through the Nazcan desert and into the mountainous region that divided the desert from the jungle. The wet dirt roads created an easy trail to follow at first, but as they neared larger cities the tracks became muddled in with others and disappeared. They'd resorted to questioning locals. Luckily, the large silver SUV driven by the mercenaries stood out to those who had seen it speed past.

Atahualpa dashed out of a small house on the outskirts of town built from corrugated metal and tree limbs. His help had been indispensable so far. King could get by in the modern, Spanish-speaking portions of Peru, but here, where Quechuan was the language of choice, he was lost. Atahualpa spoke English, Spanish, Quechuan, and several other Peruvian dialects, some close to extinction. Hopping into the jeep, he was all smiles.

"Good news?" King asked.

He nodded. "I know where they're going."

King raised a skeptical eyebrow.

"They headed northwest," Atahualpa pointed toward a muddy dirt road leading northwest. "That way. There is only one village. Jauja. My cousin lives there."

King took the steering wheel again and hit the gas, having never taken the vehicle out of drive. "What else is in Jauja?"

"Farming village. Cows. Goats. Not much else." He looked at King. "It is dead end. No roads out."

"Nothing?"

"Just the river. Rio Urubamba."

"Where does the river lead?"

"Why would they use the river?"

King shot him an annoyed glace and slammed into a water-filled pothole as a result. Water splashed onto the windshield and slid away.

"The river goes nowhere," Atahualpa said. "Just jungle. Rain forest. But we cannot go there. If we get lost no one will find us."

King tapped the GPS unit attached to the jeep's dashboard. "I won't get lost, and you're not coming." King dodged a second pothole and slammed the gas to the floor. Mud shot into the air behind the jeep as it reached eighty miles per hour. He was closing in on them. If they took the river instead of a plane, that meant they were close. He'd find them in the jungle.

An hour later they reached Jauja. Atahualpa jumped from the jeep, clearly thankful to be alive after King's sprint to the village. Speeding in the open, flat desert was scary enough; the mountainous jungle, with its tall cliff dropoffs, twisting turns, and overgrown roadsides had terrified the man. King would get no argument from Atahualpa over leaving him behind. The man had paid his penance by helping get King this far. Now it was time to pay back the money he'd earned selling them out.

"I need a boat," he said to the nervous guide.

Atahualpa nodded and led the way through the small village. Homes of reed and corrugated metal stood on stilts that kept them safe from seasonal flooding. Clothes hung on lines stretched between huts. A brown capuchin monkey tied to a rope sat on an old wooden fence staring at King intently as a group of girls doing one another's hair didn't spare a second glance as they passed. They seemed invisible to the rest of the village, who either didn't care about strangers in their midst or, more likely, had a recent run-in with less friendly strangers. King kept his eyes open for a silver SUV. It had to be there.

Then he saw it, by the wide, lazy river. A burned-out husk. Any evidence of the men who'd been inside had been erased. An old man dressed in what had once been a suit coat, now tattered and dirty, approached from a hut by the river, his toothless mouth spread wide with a smile.

"My uncle," Atahualpa said. The two embraced and began speaking quickly in Quechuan. Atahualpa turned to King after a few minutes of rapid-fire discussion. The old man was nodding. "He says the men we are looking for went upriver. He has a boat and will sell it to you for five hundred."

"Does he have a gun?"

Atahualpa asked. "Yes, but it is old. A rifle."

It wasn't ideal, but there were no alternatives. "Tell him I'll take both for five hundred."

Atahualpa relayed the message, then smiled. "He agrees."

"Good," King said. "Now pay the man."

Atahualpa blanched. But he did not question King. They both knew where the wad of money in his pocket came from. He paid his uncle, who then led them to the river. The long wooden boat held an outboard motor that looked ancient but well maintained. While the old man fetched the rifle and a gas can, King retrieved his gear and the GPS unit from the jeep. After loading his bag into the boat, King took stock of the river and jungle. The dark water flowed slowly and would make for easy travel as long as it stayed that way, but trees and overgrowth filled the river side opposite the village. With the sun already lowering on the horizon, he'd probably have to spend the night in the boat. He looked at Atahualpa. "Are there crocodiles?"

"Caimans, yes," the man answered. "But they will not attack you in the boat. The jaguar is what you should watch for."

"Right."

The uncle returned and placed a ten-gallon gas tank at the rear of the boat. He handed King a World War Two M1 Garand rifle loaded with eight .30 caliber rounds. It was old but reliable. The eight rounds combined with the eight in his handgun gave him sixteen shots. Not a lot when going up against a team of high-tech mercs, but all he needed was to take down one of them, then he'd pay the pain and misery forward with their Metal Storm weapons.

"Make sure the bodies are found and buried," King said. Atahualpa nodded. "Including McCabe."

Fear filled his eyes as he recalled the horrifying events of the previous day, but he nodded again and said, "I will. All of them."

King still had trouble believing McCabe could have killed all those people so viciously, but he had no other explanation, and no other recourse but to rescue Pierce. McCabe was missing, probably dead. And only Atahualpa had survived the attack. His goal was singular and he was locked on target like a stinger missile—King gave the engine's starter cord a yank and opened up the throttle, puttering into the middle of the river—a very slow moving missile.

FOURTEEN

Ucayali Region, Peru

The Rio Urubamba slid silently through the dense jungle like a boa constrictor hunting for prey. It meandered side to side in vast curves, sometimes nearly looping around on itself. If not for King keeping the old boat at full speed he wouldn't have made it much more than a mile from Jauja. As it was, he doubted he'd traveled more than a few linear miles from the village. But this was the way his adversaries had come and he had yet to see a gap in the jungle where a boat could land.

With the sun lingering just below the horizon, night would soon descend. He knew he should stop for the night, tie off to a tree and sleep, but he couldn't shake his guilt over losing Pierce, not to mention the lives of McCabe and the dig crew. But all of their deaths combined didn't outweigh the pain of allowing Pierce to be kidnapped. As strange as it was, his old friend was all he had left of his sister. With her death, he and Pierce had drifted apart some, like parents of a killed child—each reminded the other of Julie. They kept in touch over the years, but could never close the distance. When King received the invitation to Nazca he saw it as a chance to heal old wounds and regain a friend. Instead, he'd lost him, perhaps for good.

With the stars beginning to emerge in the slit of sky visible through the overhanging jungle canopy, King could no longer ignore the growing darkness. Capsizing in the Amazon at night would be a quick and most likely painful way to die. He tried not to picture the creatures lurking beneath the brown water—caiman crocs, piranha, anaconda—but every now and then something beneath the surface would nudge the boat enough to rock it from side to side. In the dark, with his balance off, even a small nudge might be enough to send him overboard.

As King began searching for a tree to tie the boat to, a small sandy beach opened up in the jungle. He made a beeline toward the shore and landed the boat. After shutting off the motor, he climbed over his bag and made his way toward the front of the long boat. If this had been the point where the others had landed, it would be written on the beach. He inspected the sand and found a series of clear tracks—all animal. The small beach led back into the jungle, no doubt merging with a game trail. Pierce was further downstream, perhaps already off the water, perhaps dead.

King forced the thoughts of Pierce's fate from his mind and began setting up camp. He broke out his small tent, built a quick fire, and began boiling river water to hydrate one of the MRE meals he'd brought. A sports bar probably would have been more nutritious and tasty, but the MREs were easy to get and King was used to them. Besides, a hot meal couldn't be beat. King read the label. Tonight was buffalo chicken and corn bread. Not bad. He shook the contents out and saw a small pack of Charms candy. The brightly colored sweets found in only the occasional MRE were considered bad luck by most in uniform, more so if actually eaten. King picked up the packet, tore it open, unwrapped the first lime-flavored sugar square and popped it into his mouth. He never relied on luck.

And the candy was good.

As the dark blue sky turned black, King's line of sight

was reduced to what the fire lit—the beach, a 330-degree enclosure of jungle, and a small stretch of the lazy river. Above the river, between the trees, he could make out a slice of night sky that contained more stars than he could see from Fort Bragg. With no major city for hundreds of miles, this was one of the few places left on earth where the unadulterated night sky could be seen in all its glory. Just the small sliver of sky above was impressive.

After downing his buffalo chicken and butter-slathered corn bread, he doused himself in bug repellent and laid back on the sand, staring at the slice of night sky. His mind craved to plot and plan his actions for the morning, but beyond waking with the dawn and following the river there was nothing to plan. He had to be fluid and roll with the punches as they came. The type to plan out details in advance, King wasn't thrilled about the prospect of winging it, but he still had no doubt what the final outcome would be—lots of dead bad guys. He just hoped Pierce wouldn't be among the dead.

King raised his arm over his face and pushed a button on his watch. It glowed green in his face. Nine o'clock. Seven back home. Time to check in. King removed the satellite phone he'd taken from the Nazca dig site and breathed a little easier. At least he could coordinate this part of the mission. He dialed the number and waited for the call to go through. After the familiar digital recording played King spoke his call sign into the phone and was connected.

"Any leads?" Deep Blue asked without a greeting.

King felt confident that the man had been moving fast to make things happen on his end, and so Deep Blue's curt voice didn't faze him. King had never met the man. No one on the team had. But he was able to pull strings in Washington and the military like no one else, and King, for one, didn't need to know the man's identity. In this business, anonymity meant freedom to act, and Deep Blue seemed to have that in spades. "If a lazy day on the river counts, plenty," King said. "Otherwise, nothing."

"The team is in the air and on their way south. Go ahead and activate your GPS unit now."

King placed the phone down and removed the GPS unit pilfered from Atahualpa's jeep and switched it on. "It's on," he said into the phone.

"Give me the serial number."

King read the number and waited as he listened to Deep Blue's fingers fly over a keyboard half a world away.

"Got you," Deep Blue said. "Keep the unit on you at all times. We'll drop the others right on top of you ASAP."

"If I'm still on the river when they get here they'll need transportation."

"Copy that. I'll figure out the details. You just stay alive."

"That's the plan."

"Don't worry about your buddy, King. We'll get him back."

King felt bolstered by Deep Blue's confidence. He hadn't realized how deep his doubts about retrieving Pierce had become. "I'll call back when I've got Pierce."

"You do that."

King hung up and switched off the phone, conserving the battery. The night settled around him again with the sound of birds chirping, monkeys calling, and an assortment of foragers scrambling through the underbrush. He was surrounded by life, but all he could see was the dancing fire, which began to die down. King gathered several branches from a fallen tree and tossed them on the fire. The damp branches sizzled but caught, popping as the gases inside heated, then burst. Sparks flew. The music and dance of the fire distracted him as the dry heat sucked away the dense jungle moisture and relaxed his body. Laying back on the sand, King's thoughts drifted.

But before his imagination took root a shriek in the distance snapped him up into a sitting position. He waited, breath held, for the sound to repeat. The shriek came again, like a B-movie actress letting loose. King drew his pistol. He thought the sound had grown closer, but the acoustics in the jungle were impossible to gauge. The air was thick with humidity. The canopy reflected sound at odd angles. And the density of trees, foliage, and other physical barriers was so random that sound became fluid. Full of life. Unpredictable. The sound could have come from fifty feet away or a mile. He would never know. What he did know was that the rest of the jungle had fallen silent.

King stoked the campfire into a raging inferno that would last the night and crawled into his tent, taking the Sig Sauer handgun and M1 Garand rifle with him.

Predators were hunting.

Despite the danger lurking in the rain forest, sleep came surprisingly easy that night. But his dreams were filled with the dead—past, present, and soon to be. His subconscious concocted several horrible ways for Pierce to meet his fate. In each dream, King would run to help but found his body slow to respond, as though weighted down by some invisible force. At one point he reached for his weapon and found only a TV antenna. The surreal dreams left him feeling groggy in the morning, even after a full night's sleep, but they conveyed a crystal clear message—deep down, King didn't think he could save his friend.

At the first hint of light, King unzipped his tent, doused the fire's remaining embers with sand, and repacked his bag. He looked at his watch. Five-thirty. He doubted the men he was after would wake so early. This was his chance to gain some ground. King took the GPS unit from his backpack and checked the battery. Its small screen glowed strong. The battery indicator showed it still held a three-quarter charge. More than enough. He repacked it and placed the bag in the boat.

King lifted his leg to climb into the boat, but froze midstep. Smoke. Just a hint carried on the breeze. His campfire had obscured the smell before, but this was no campfire. He knew the difference between burning wood and the chemical smell of a modern structure in flames. King looked at the dark blue sky, just now shedding its stars. A brown haze drifted lazily in the breeze, rising from perhaps a mile away.

He was close.

He climbed into the boat, took an oar, and began pushing out into deeper water where he could start the engine. Before the front of the long boat pulled free of the damp sand beach, the boat rocked from a sudden impact. Off balance from pushing with the oar, King spilled over the side and into the water. Pushing off the muddy bottom, he launched to the surface expecting a giant fish or snake to try swallowing him whole. He fumbled for his sheathed KA-BAR knife as he kicked for shore.

But no attack came.

He climbed on shore, caught his breath, and searched for what had struck the boat. He began thinking it must have been a free-floating log, but a splotch of yellow next to the side of the boat told him otherwise. King stepped back into the boat, moving toward the object lodged against it. From the yellow and white fur covered in black spots, King could see the animal was a jaguar. Clearly dead. But what had killed it?

After pushing the body away from the boat with the oar, King inspected the body. The big cat would have been a prime specimen when alive, but now . . . The lower half of its body had been torn away. Water-logged entrails floated free in the water's currents, but no blood stained the water. The cat had been dead for hours, perhaps all night. His first thought was that a caiman had caught the cat off guard in the water, but a series of straight, two-inch-long puncture wounds didn't look like croc bites. Something else had killed the jaguar—the Amazon's top predator.

As the body drifted downstream, carried by the river, King followed it with his eyes. He nearly fell out of the boat again. Carcasses littered the river, some intact, some in pieces. Monkeys, birds, cats, crocs, and rodents. Nothing had been spared. A slaughter had taken place while he'd slept. It was probably only his raging fire that kept him safe. King yanked the engine cord and launched the boat as fast as it could go. He kept his .45 in one hand and steered with the other, ever vigilant.

There was something much worse than the average predator lurking in the jungle. Something that made a meal out of jaguars and crocodiles . . . and it wasn't human.

FIFTEEN

30,000 Feet

A sudden brilliant light turned the insides of Pierce's closed eyelids bright red. He woke with a start, launched into a standing position, and then just as quickly fell down. He felt a hand take his arm and help guide his fall so that he landed on the same padded bench he'd been sitting on.

"Easy now," came a deep voice. "The drugs are still wearing off."

"Where am I?" Pierce asked, rubbing his eyes.

"With friends," said a second voice. "Take these."

Pierce felt two pills placed in his hand. "What are they?" His world was spinning and his mind was only half with it, but he wasn't going to take a drug without knowing what it would do to him.

"Caffeine pills. They'll help counteract the sedative you were given . . . which should never have been given to you in the first place."

Pierce sensed that the man speaking really was irritated about his being sedated and decided to trust him. "Water?"

A bottle was placed in his other hand. He opened his eyes a crack and looked at his hands. Two small blue pills in one. A bottle of Poland Spring water in the other. He popped the pills in his mouth and swigged the water. It was cool and refreshing. The pills dissolved quickly and took effect within seconds. A tingle ran up his spine and when it reached his skull it was as though a switch had been thrown and his mind came rushing back to him.

Pierce looked up and saw two men looking down at him. One was tall and bald, wearing an expensive-looking suit jacket. The other wore dress slacks, a perfectly pressed shirt, and a red tie that complimented his groomed face, hair, and hands. Both wore kind smiles and had intelligent eyes. Assuming they were some kind of authority, he asked, "Did you catch the men who kidnapped me?"

The tall, bald man's crow's-feet crinkled around his blue eyes as he held out his hand to be shook. Pierce took it with apprehension. As they shook hands, the man said, "Richard Ridley. Happy to make your acquaintance, Dr. Pierce. *I* am the man who kidnapped you." Ridley smiled wide.

Pierce looked at the other man, who now wore a frown. He pushed away from the men and found he had nowhere to go. Glancing around quickly he noticed the small white room was actually a cell.

"Well, not me," Ridley said. "But men who work for me."

"What do you want?"

"The Hydra."

Pierce felt like he'd been punched. The man's statement was so self-assured, so plain and blunt. Was he serious? Pierce decided he was, and realized that lying would do no good. "Why?"

"I believe you were given an example of what we can do?"

Pierce remembered the three bullet wounds in McCabe's chest. How quickly they healed. How her life returned. "Regeneration." Pierce glared at the man. "You could have just asked."

The man crossed his arms and gave Pierce a skeptical

look. "You and I both know that as soon as the Hydra head's authenticity was proven, no one would be allowed near it until whatever government agency claimed it was finished with it. In other words, never. You and McCabe would have no doubt disappeared along with the relic."

Pierce didn't argue. He'd had the same fears as well. But he couldn't forget the savagery of the attack on the camp. "My friend, Jack Sigler. What happened to him?"

"Your 'security,' yes." Ridley flashed a smile and chuckled. "He came a day early. An unfortunate turn of events. I'm sorry for what happened. Truly. It's not how I envisioned things turning out. But you should know that both of your friends are alive and well. The crew was freed, as promised, two hours after you departed. They dug Jack out from under the stone. No one was seriously hurt."

Pierce couldn't shake the feeling that there was more. He remembered a wave of apprehension before passing out. Something the kidnappers had said. But it escaped him. "Why did you take me?"

"It never hurts to have an expert on the subject in question," Ridley said.

"And we like to give credit where credit is due," the other man said. "When we announce our findings, you will receive credit for your part in the discovery."

"And you are?"

"Todd Maddox," he said. "I'm the lead geneticist here. I developed the regeneration serum that . . . saved your friend. It should never have happened in the first place."

Pierce detected guilt in the man's voice. He seemed earnestly displeased with the situation. "Am I a prisoner?"

"Not at all," Ridley said. "In fact, I was hoping you'd join the team."

Pierce squinted at the man, making no effort to hide his skepticism.

"You'll be given full access to the artifact and may study it any way you want," Maddox said. "All we require in return is that you help us unlock its secrets."

This all seemed too convenient, too well packaged to be real. But what choice did he have? He doubted these men would let him walk free. Even if King, McCabe, and the rest of the crew had been unscathed, they were still criminals. High-tech looters. He also had no doubt that King would come for him. That meant keeping the status quo for as long as he could. "Take me to it."

Ridley laughed and looked at Maddox. "He's as ambitious as you." He turned back to Pierce. "I'm afraid that's not possible right now."

"Why not?"

Ridley pointed to the side wall. "You have a window. Look for yourself."

Pierce stood and balanced himself against the wall. The floor had shifted beneath him. He looked through the small oval window and held his breath. The ocean sparkled far below. They were in an airplane.

Ridley clapped him hard on the shoulder like they were old chums. "We have more than a thousand miles and thirty thousand vertical feet between us and Manifold Beta. Care for some tea in the meantime?"

"What is Manifold Beta?"

Ridley grinned wide. "Wonderland."

SIXTEEN

Ucayali Region, Peru

Not more than twenty minutes later, after dodging and plowing right over hundreds of small corpses, King came to a dock. He'd been so close. The single boat tied to the dock had been burned to a char, just like the SUV. They were covering their tracks. But burning a single boat could not produce the amount of smoke he'd seen. King stopped the boat's engine and coasted to the dock. He tied off, slipped on his backpack, and slid into the jungle, his M1 Garand leading the way.

Following a well-groomed path, King found the jungle floor clear of all but the tallest and thickest trees. King looked up at the thick canopy. *Clearing the jungle to build, but keeping the natural camouflage,* King thought. *Smart.*

The terrain dropped and a valley opened up. Inside the valley lay a smoldering ruin of what was once a very large, modern facility. King took little comfort from the lack of movement. Something awful had taken place here. It wasn't the smoke still sifting free from the ashes or the coppery taste of blood in the air. It was a gut feeling. The hair on his arms raised. His spine tingled.

A wailing shriek, the same as the previous night, ripped through the jungle. It was louder, closer than he'd heard before. He knelt, raised the M1 to his shoulder, and waited for some sign of movement. Something was out there. Something that had somehow survived the slaughter of the previous night. King's breath caught in his throat when he realized the only thing that could have survived the mass killing was the killer.

King moved slowly down the hill, taking aim at any hint of movement or ideal hiding spot. The sound did not repeat and he detected no signs of life. He had yet to be discovered. His need for clues outweighed his primal instinct to run as he stood inside the ruins, picking out details. A few squares of linoleum flooring survived the blaze. The partial remains of a three-pronged, type-B outlet—American.

After a half hour of slow, methodical searching he found little else. He'd heard a few more shrieks, but they sounded more distant. Still, he kept his guard up. He ended his search at the remains of a helipad. Had Pierce been taken out of here by air? Had he just missed him again? Or was his body among the ashes? King forced the thoughts from his mind and looked down at the charred complex. It was vast, taking up several acres, and given the amount of ash and rubble, had stood more than a couple stories tall. *Probably reached right up to the canopy,* he thought.

A loud slap on the helipad pavement spun him around, rifle at the ready. A body lay writhing at his feet. A thirteen-foot boa constrictor perfectly camouflaged for jungle living twisted on itself as blood oozed from several two-inch-long punctures. King looked up and was surprised to see trees over the helipad. Looking to the right he saw the trees clear at an angle, reaching out to the sky. His eyebrows rose. The helicopters would have come in at an angle through the trees, allowing the helipad to remain covered by the canopy. Gutsy and a bit extreme. Whoever ran this place did not want to be found. He realized they'd probably detected his approach on the river the day before and bugged out.

The snake twitched madly, then died.

King knelt by its body and inspected the wounds. Just like the jaguar. Where chunks of flesh hadn't been bitten away, dozens of pairs of deep, straight wounds covered the body. A wet shriek from above, followed by a second fleshy whack made King jump. A large lump of short reddish-brown fur smacked the helipad next to the snake. King couldn't see what kind of animal it was, but the thing was clearly dead. Upon impact its body had burst, spilling guts and gore out over the cement.

He aimed the Garand up, looking for some kind of predator lurking in the trees. Whatever it was, it had returned and no doubt knew of his presence. Worse, he stood near two of its kills . . . its food. It would want them back. He felt sure.

As King stepped back, his boot squished through the spilled gore. He looked at it and realized the guts didn't look right. There were no intestines or other internal organs, just chunks of flesh. As he stepped closer King realized that only the creature's stomach had burst. The mass of flesh spilled from its barrel-shaped body, some scaled, some hairy, some unrecognizable, came from whatever it had eaten. A sickening feeling took hold of his stomach. Using the rifle as a prod, King nudged the dog-sized creature, rolling it over. He recognized it. A capybara. The largest rodent on earth, it sported two sets of massive incisors, above and below. The source of the odd wounds and the overnight slaughter. *This* was the predator!

Before he could think about how a vegetarian rodent could accomplish such a thing, the capybara twitched. After falling nearly seventy-five feet onto concrete and bursting open, the thing was still alive. Wondering if it was his imagination, King leaned in with the Garand and poked its head. The reaction was instantaneous. With a shriek, the capybara snapped its jaws and bit the barrel of the rifle, severely chipping one of its teeth. The scream, the same that had been unnerving him since the previous night, coupled with the sudden savagery caused him to stumble back. The rodent yanked its head to the side and tore the rifle from his hands.

As the capybara began lifting its body from the ground, King did the only thing he could think of. He ran. To his amazement and horror, the capybara shrieked and charged after him, guts and the partially eaten remains of its victims dragging from its still open belly.

Working his way through the burned-out complex, King hoped to lose the creature, but it seemed to never tire and was surprisingly fast, even with its stomach open. He never looked back at it though. He could hear it fine. Its claws clicked on the hard, burned hallway floors. Its teeth snapped loudly, like a manic chatter. And its shriek pierced the air like a siren.

Atahualpa's words returned to him. His description of McCabe. What she'd done to those people. The teeth marks on the animals here might be different, but the results were the same. He pictured McCabe, feral and savage like the capybara and grimaced as he realized Atahualpa had been telling the truth. As his lungs began to burn from sucking in deep breaths of the acrid air, King realized he needed to end the chase or he'd end up another gnawed corpse.

He drew his .45, stopped, and spun around. He dropped to one knee, took aim, and froze at the sight. Froth sprayed from the rodent's mouth with every breath. Its eyes were peeled wide, unblinking, and zeroed in on him. Its teeth chattered endlessly. Rapid-fire Morse code. The hair on its back stood on end like an angry dog's. And its entrails, now covered in ash, whipped between its legs as it ran. The thing had become 150 pounds of savagery.

As the capybara closed the distance between them, King wondered what kind of person could create something like this. It was obviously the result of some genetics experiment gone awry. But to what end? And why let them loose? As King looked down the .45's sight, meeting eyes with the killing machine, it became clear.

To kill me, he thought.

Not today.

King pulled the trigger sending a .45-caliber bullet into the capybara's side. Flesh exploded on contact. The giant rodent fell and rolled through the ash. King stood and stepped closer. He took aim again. The wound was healing. As the wound sealed the capybara shook and frothed in a psychotic rage, even more savage than before. Before the creature could rise again, King took aim and pulled the trigger twice more, effectively reducing the beast's head to pulp. The body fell still.

King covered his mouth with a bandanna as he breathed heavily. He leaned over the dead creature and shook his head. Three .45-caliber rounds. Three. One was enough to kill most creatures on four legs, let along a giant tailless rat. But it had taken three . . . two to the head. A distant shriek tore him from his thoughts.

Another one.

A reply came from behind, closer.

Then a third.

Damn. King ran for the helipad where the Garand rifle still lay next to the dead constrictor. He'd need it if he was going to survive the hour.

A shriek tore through the clearing.

Hell, he'd be lucky to survive another ten minutes.

SEVENTEEN

Ucayali Region, Peru

Puffs of ash exploded with each footfall as King sprinted through the labyrinth of what were once hallways. But this was no tall walled maze. He could see the end goal in plain sight: the helipad and his M1 Garand rifle. Veering from the hallway, he opted for a more direct route. He bounded over the remnants of walls as he cheated his way through the maze, arriving at the helipad just as the first new capybara entered the clearing.

King dove to his stomach hoping his black shirt and pants would conceal his position in the ash. He doubted the thing could smell him with all the soot in the air. The capybara was smaller than the first, but quicker on its toes. It bounced around the ruins, sniffing here and there, all the while frothing and chattering its teeth like an oversized guinea pig gone berserk. Shrieks in the distance told him more were coming. There was no way he could face them all at once, and lying here, just waiting to be found was not how he played the game. King slowly took aim with the rifle. Eight shots. He couldn't miss.

The rifle's report echoed through the jungle. The capybara hit the leaf-ridden jungle floor and spasmed as though having a rapid-fire seizure. Then it snapped back onto its feet, spinning in circles. It stopped suddenly, eyes on King.

The thing shrieked as it dashed for King.

"Son of a bitch . . ." King fired twice more. Both misses.

The capybara hopped the outer wall of the ruins with ease and charged toward King. He fired twice more. The giant rodent fell, twitched, and continued its charge. The smaller round shot right through the creature without mushrooming like the .45 rounds. As a result, the damage was minimal.

As the beast closed to within thirty feet, King squeezed the trigger several times until a loud ping sounded from the rifle. The locking bolt sprang free and ejected the spent clip, allowing for the next clip to be slammed home. But King had no more clips.

And even less time.

The capybara launched into the air, its jaws open and two-inch incisors ready to bury into King's skull. King drew his KA-BAR blade and slammed it down just as the capybara was about to make contact. The blade pierced through the creature's back, slammed it to the helipad where the blade slid into a crack, pinning it in place.

King fell back, leaning on his hands, breathing heavily.

A shriek sounded to his right. He saw a flash of teeth.

A single shot boomed from his .45.

A splash of blood covered his body just before the now headless, hundred-pound rodent landed in his lap. King kicked it off and stood, looking for more attackers. Three more capybaras entered the far side of the clearing, already running toward him. King checked the magazine. Three bullets.

A shriek at his feet made him jump.

The capybara pinned to the helipad vibrated and spewed fluids as it pulled its body through the knife, slicing itself in half yet healing just as quickly. King placed the barrel of the .45 against the rodent's head and pulled the trigger. Its head disappeared and its body stopped moving.

King knew retreat was his only option. He searched his memory for what little he knew about capybara. They were semiaquatic. A glance at the dead rodents by his feet confirmed it. The river was out. As far as he knew, they couldn't climb trees. But the first he'd encountered had fallen from a tree. In their enraged state they might be able to climb trees, and navigate quick enough to catch a slow moving boa, but it did fall. The canopy might be his only chance.

As King looked for a suitable tree to climb he frowned. The trees had been trimmed clear of any low-lying branches, no doubt to afford room for the complex hidden here. The three capybara entered the complex, making a mess of each other as they snapped and vied for the front position, but they never slowed. They'd be on him in seconds. King holstered the handgun, tightened his grip on the KA-BAR knife, and leaped from the helipad. He struck a tall, smooth tree and nearly fell to the jungle floor, but he stabbed his knife into the tree's flesh and held on. After wrapping his left arm around the tree and tightening his grip, he pulled the knife out and stabbed again. Higher. Then pulled himself up. He repeated the movements three more times. Grip. Stab. Pull. Then stopped to take stock of the situation.

Before he could turn, the tree shook from an impact. A capybara landed on the jungle floor, kicking its legs madly in the air. A second launched itself at King and struck the tree, just below his feet. It, too, fell to the ground. As the third prepared to jump, King quickly withdrew the knife and stabbed higher, pulling himself up.

The third rodent jumped, struck the tree, and clung to it. Its dull claws, powered by unceasing mania, held tight. King's eyes widened as the creature began moving up. He let go of the tree, holding only to the knife. He risked a fall, but couldn't pass up such an easy target. He drew the .45 and fired down. Half of the capybara's face splattered against the tree, then began regenerating. He pulled the trigger again, finishing the job, and spending his last round.

After dropping the gun, King returned to climbing. The two remaining capybara followed, clawing their way up the tree. In the same way King used his knife, they used their upper teeth. Stab. Pull. Stab. Pull.

The chop and scratch of the pursuing capybara kept time with King's movements. But he didn't look down. He didn't want to see if they were gaining. He just focused on the task at hand, moving toward the glowing green canopy above. When he reached the first branch, nearly one hundred feet above the jungle floor, he took hold and pulled himself up. After sheathing the knife he looked down. The capybara had five feet to go.

As King looked around to find the best path through the canopy branches, a shadow fell over the area, like a cloud blotting out the sun, but this shadow grew darker, and larger. King ducked, knowing something was falling from the sky. It crashed through the canopy, snapping branches and, for a moment, stopping the startled capybaras. The sudden cacophony was followed by a loud voice, "I'm down, but in the trees, Queen, over."

King looked up and saw Rook fighting to free himself from his parachute, now tangled in the branches. He'd been speaking to Queen through his throat mike. "Rook!"

Rook jumped back and nearly fell from the tree. "Gah!" The two men's eyes met. "King, what's the sit—" Rook saw the frothing capybara snapping at King's feet. "Oh, hell . . ."

"I need a weapon!" King shouted, stretching out his hands to the man he knew would be carrying an arsenal.

Rook quickly slipped his assault rifle from his back and tossed it to him. After a quick flick of the safety, King aimed down at the capybara closest to him and pulled the trigger. Plumes of red liquid rained down from the tree, coating the jungle floor. The capybara fought the barrage as its wounds healed, but King adjusted his aim and took off the creature's legs. It fell to the forest floor followed by the second, also missing its legs.

The two capybara writhed on the jungle floor while their legs began growing back. King took aim and pulled a second trigger with his middle finger. The weapon coughed and sent a 40mm grenade flying through the air. The capybara disappeared in giant ball of fire. The explosion shook the canopy of the entire clearing and sent the tree King and Rook clung to swaying. They hung on tight until the danger was over.

Armed and reinforced, King felt his confidence return. Though he couldn't see them, he knew the rest of the team clung to trees somewhere nearby. "Everyone stays in the trees," he told Rook. "Shoot anything that looks like an overgrown guinea pig."

Rook relayed the message and then peeled himself away from the tree. Still not free of his parachute, he turned around to give it a yank and came face-to-face with the blank-eyed stare of a corpse. He jumped back, but quickly caught himself, swallowing a gasp. "This a friend of yours, King?"

King climbed the branches to Rook. "What'd you find?"

Rook leaned back revealing the dead body of a young man. His T-shirt had been ripped open and his stomach eviscerated. The rest of his body was covered in two-inch puncture wounds.

King pushed past Rook and quickly searched the body. He found an ID card in his pocket. He handed it to Rook. "Ever hear of Manifold Genetics?"

Rook looked at the card, shaking his head. "Seth Lloyd. Tech support. So how does a guy who deals with the blue screen of death end up a treetop munchie for a psychotic rat?"

King noticed a lump under what little remained of the young man's T-shirt. He reached under, took hold, and yanked it free. A thumb drive. "Maybe we'll find some answers on this?"

"Or a lot of porn."

A boom rolled through the canopy. King recognized the report as a sniper rifle. Rook listened to a voice in his headset. "Knight bagged one of your guinea pigs."

"Tell him to take off its head."

After Rook relayed the message a second boom shook the leaves. After a few minutes, the sounds of jungle life returned to the area. The last of the super-predators had been killed. Within a year the burned-out complex below would be reclaimed by the jungle. No trace of its existence or the slaughter wrought by the capybara would remain. The only remnant of the facility and what had taken place here sat in King's hand. A small, eight-gigabyte thumb drive taken from a dead tech-support kid.

"Where to, boss?" Rook asked.

King handed him the thumb drive, not wanting to put it in his wet pants pocket. "Civilization."

BETA

EIGHTEEN

Pope Air Force Base, Limbo

After making their way out of the jungle via an air-dropped riverboat and catching a flight back to the States, King, Queen, Rook, Knight, and Bishop returned to Fort Bragg two days after touching down in the Peruvian rain forest. After showering and changing into fresh clothes, they returned to Pope Air Force Base, known simply as "the Pope," and met in a room attached to Delta's personal hangar. The few Delta teams elite enough to perform covert missions referred to the room as Decon, short for decontamination. But Rook had given the room his own name: Limbo—the place between Heaven and Hell. It was where they met at the beginning of every mission, to be briefed, and the end of every mission, to debrief. The name stuck.

At first glance, Limbo looked like a corporate office meeting room. A long oval table hemmed in by eight leather executive chairs filled the center of the blessedly air-conditioned space. A perspiring pitcher of ice water sat on the table with some glasses. A silk bamboo palm tree sat in the back corner, its vibrant green providing contrast to the blank beige walls. The room's technology was concealed—video projectors, computers built into the tabletop, satellite uplinks, and a series of flat-screen monitors hidden inside the walls. When not in use, the technology hid so those in the room could fully concentrate on whatever life-and-death matter was at hand. Today, it was Pierce, and King was noticeably tense as he sat at the back of the table.

King's leg bounced as he rested his elbows on the table. Pierce had been kidnapped and there was nothing they could do about it. They didn't know who they were up against or where to start looking.

They'd given the thumb drive to Lewis Aleman, Delta's personal R2-D2. But he was no short, stocky robot. His lean body stood at six-two, and when he ran at the track, the man's legs appeared as fast as his fingers on the keyboard. Though no longer a field operative, he could still outrun anyone on the team. He seemed part machine as he interfaced with computer systems, hacking networks and retaining information with more reliability than a hard drive. He liked to say that he could do the work of two NSA supercomputers, and no one doubted it. Whatever was on the thumb drive, King knew Aleman would make short work of any encryption, but he'd barely had time to take a shower and shave before being called back to Limbo.

Now they were all here, waiting silently. Queen had her nose in a book. Bishop sat back in his chair, eyes closed, his breathing slow and controlled. Knight typed out an e-mail on his PDA—probably to one of his many women friends. Rook leaned far back in his chair, twisting back and forth. For the most part, all of them were relaxed, which didn't seem fair given the circumstances, but it wasn't their friend who had been kidnapped.

The door leading to the main hangar opened and General Keasling entered with Aleman in tow.

"Hey, Mike," Rook said with a sarcastic smile.

Keasling stopped in his tracks and shot Rook a look that could make a fainting goat fall over dead. "You Delta pipsqueaks might not use rank, but I'll be damned before I let a little turd like you call me anything but 'General.' You got that?"

Rook stood at attention and worked hard to suppress a smile. Though his position on this most elite team couldn't be revoked short of a presidential order, Keasling could make his life very uncomfortable. He had a long history of getting under the general's skin for no other reason than to see the man's face turn beet red and his nostrils flare like a dragon preparing to burn down a village. "Yes, sir. Sorry, sir."

"You address me as anything other than General Keasling and I shit you not, I will have you bunking with the green recruits and on latrine duty for the rest of your damn life. Now sit your ass down."

The give and take between the two usually helped lighten the team's mood and often signified the start of a briefing, but today, King failed to see the humor. He rolled his neck with a sigh. "What did you find?" he said, leveling his gaze at Aleman.

"One moment." Aleman sat at the head of the table while Keasling stood to the side, hands behind his back. He pushed down on the table in front of him. A seventeen-inch square of tabletop depressed and then popped up revealing a computer screen and keyboard. He took the same thumb drive King recovered in the jungle from his pocket and inserted it in the tabletop PC's USB port. After tapping a few commands into the computer, a massive digital TV screen appeared, like an apparition, in the wall behind him, its beige surface fading as a minute electric charge shifted the color crystals in the screen, which could mimic any color or pattern including the most complex plaid. The screen blinked to life, matching the display of the small screen built into the table. A larger folder opened, revealing two more. They were named REGEN and CLIENTS.

Aleman double clicked the REGEN file and then opened several documents within. As images, videos, and text documents appeared on the screen, he organized them so all could be seen. "I've uploaded all this to your units if you want to browse on your own or double-check something."

"Just break it down for me, Ale," King said. "Short and sweet."

"Short and sweet." Aleman rubbed his stubble-covered chin. He stopped, sat forward, and said, "We're dealing with some real bastards. You've already experienced their advanced technology—weapons, field equipment, and genetics. Previous to your encounter I wouldn't have believed a single corporation could achieve as much."

"You sound envious," King said.

"You're not?"

King's only response was a slight purse of his lips. He was envious. They all were. As Delta operators they were accustomed to outgunning and out-teching their enemies. Being on the other side of the coin made them all uncomfortable.

Aleman continued. "The company behind all your trouble is Manifold." A logo appeared on the screen—a stylized DNA strand surrounded by a circle of five red blocks, all connected at the corners. "They're a genetics company with, we believe, five main locations. Best guess, the facility you found burned down in Peru was one of them. Given the way you described what burned—just the facility and not the surrounding jungle—tells us this was a controlled burn purposely set to erase all traces of the facility's owners, while at the same time keeping the ruins hidden beneath the canopy.

"This," he said, bringing up a black-and-white photo, "is Richard Ridley. He started the company after receiving a large inheritance from his father, who killed himself on Ridley's twenty-first birthday. Shotgun. Real messy. Police report says that Ridley found him. Most of what they do is off the grid, probably illegal in most first-world countries, but given their burgeoning bank accounts, they're no worse for wear."

Here was the man responsible for Pierce's kidnapping. King made a mental note of Ridley's face. He wouldn't forget it. "Can we skip the rest of the who, for now, and move on to the why?"

"Will do," Aleman said, then shifted the open files on-screen. "This is where things get strange. Manifold is working on human regeneration. They're taking what nature has given to species like salamanders and transferring the ability to humans, with staggering yet limited success. Picture a soldier stepping on a mine and losing his legs. Typically he . . ." Aleman looked at Queen, who'd been watching silently with her arms crossed, "or she, would die or be bound to a wheelchair. But these guys. What they're doing is, well, the legs wouldn't just grow back over time, they would start growing back before the soldier's body hit the ground."

"We've seen it," Knight said. "I put a softball-sized hole in the side of a capybara and the thing started healing on the spot."

"But they went nutty," Rook said. "Their minds were gone."

"And that's where Manifold is stuck. With each injury and healing, their subjects go progressively more mad. Look at this." Aleman hit a button and a video on the screen began playing. The date showed June 17, 2009, only two weeks previous. A woman lay strapped to a table by her ankles and wrists. She wore only a paper gown over her dark skin. A male voice spoke, "Subject has been injected with serum D-twenty-four. All preexisting health conditions including a tumor and diabetes have been tested for. She's now clean. Heart rate and blood pressure are normal, well, normal for a super human." The camera shook as the man chuckled.

"I am now going to make an incision across her throat, severing the jugular." The man's hand reached out, a scalpel at the ready. He paused as the blade hovered over the woman's throat. "At the first sign of duress, clear the room," he said to someone unseen.

"I know the drill," the man off-camera replied.

The blade slid across the woman's throat, cutting deep. As blood spat from the fresh wound, it stopped just as quickly. The man withdrew the blood-soaked blade, but the wound had disappeared. "C'mon, lady," he said, looking at the vitals displayed on several beeping and blinking monitors. The heartbeat pulsed hard. Then again. And again.

"She's going . . ."

"Better clear out, Doc."

The camera shook as it spun, catching a blurry view of the other man in the room. They exited, closed and locked a thick metal door. When the camera came into focus again, it was shooting through a thick glass window. The woman's back arched high and then slammed back down on the table. Her eyes opened wide and she screamed, pulling at her bonds. Unable to free her hands and feet, she flew into a frenzy, pulling and yanking her wrists. Blood splattered against the window. A slick, blood-covered hand shot free from the tight leather manacle, but the second was stuck firmly in place. The woman looked at her bound hand and launched at it, biting with every pound of pressure her adrenaline-powered jaw could deliver. Bones snapped. Flesh flew. The woman roared as the hand tore free and blood pulsed from her wrist. But even as she held the bloody stump up, the hand began to grow back.

The shot turned away from the woman and filmed a split second of a long hallway before cutting off. The glimpse was short, but they all saw the hallway lined with thick windows, some covered in blood, others containing unconscious people on gurneys and still others receiving blow after mad blow from the crazed people inside.

"Kind of makes me glad they burned the place down," Rook said.

Aleman closed the video. "We've identified the woman

as Salwa Batori, a native Peruvian woman. Her husband reported her missing three weeks ago. She had three children. We've also identified one of the men in the video."

"I didn't see any faces," King said.

A photo appeared on the screen. The man looked young, but strong, and had a military-style crew cut. "We were able to compress the motion blur details into a static image. It's not perfect, but with his face already in the system, he was an easy match."

"Who is he?" King asked.

"Ex-Navy SEAL," Keasling said. "Oliver Reinhart. Dishonorably discharged after his first mission. Went on to form a private security force called Gen-Y. They hire straight out of the military, mostly other dischargees who have less scruples, but some are good soldiers drawn by the high pay and higher tech they get to use. And these guys are seriously high tech." He looked at King. "Metal Storm weapons are only the tip of the technological iceberg with these guys. Hell, they knew who you were. That kind of intel is, well, let's just say some security heads are rolling. In some ways their hardware technology is beyond ours because they're willing to use weapons and equipment we won't touch until they've been tested for years. The one big advantage we have over them is experience."

"They've seen enough action to know what they're doing," King said. "They had me dead to rights. I just got lucky."

Keasling nodded. "And they're connected. That's the real reason for the rush." He looked at Aleman. "Open the second file."

The videos and images disappeared, replaced by an open folder with a single text document labeled "Clients." The text document opened and a list of names, addresses, and phone numbers appeared on the screen. King didn't recognize the first three names, but after that it was a veritable who's who of terrorism and third-world dictators.

Keasling scratched his head, then leaned his hands on

the tabletop. "If even one of these organizations got their hands on this technology, even in its unperfected stage, it could drastically shift the balance of power in the world. And if what they took from the U.N. dig site helps them finish the job, we may be running out of time."

"This is official, then?" Queen asked.

With a nod, he added, "Deep Blue is putting together the logistics and coordinating with the necessary forces. So put your tags back on if you haven't already."

"And George?" King asked.

Keasling sighed. "As much as all of us want you to get your friend back, he's got to take a backseat for now."

King ground his teeth. He knew the call was the right one, but that didn't make it an easier pill to swallow. King's only consolation was that they had taken Pierce in the first place. That meant he had something to offer them. He pictured the crazed and bloodied woman from the video, fearing that they'd simply taken Pierce as a test subject. He forced the thought from his mind. They'd taken him specifically, for a reason. But they'd kill him eventually. Of that, King had no doubt.

"Don't worry, King," a familiar voice said, coming from the room's speakers. They knew he'd been listening, as he always did for briefings. But the mysterious Deep Blue tended to stay silent until he had information to divulge or something important to say. "We'll get your friend back."

The screen filled with a silhouetted figure. It was all any Delta operator had ever seen of the man. His general shape showed him to be physically fit and his neatly outlined head revealed him to be either bald or on his way there. His keen sense of strategy and amazing connections hinted at a history in the military, possibly highly decorated. Other than that, they knew nothing about the man except that he was their lifeline, their eye in the sky, and could seemingly mobilize every branch of the military at a whim. King knew the faces of every general who fit the bill and not one of them matched the silhouette on-screen. Of course, King knew, it could easily be a body double.

"You sound confident," King said.

An image appeared on-screen, covering Deep Blue's form. The satellite image showed three small islands surrounded by nothing but blue. "The three islands are Nightingale Island, Inaccessible Island, and the one we're interested in, Tristan da Cunha." The image zoomed in directly over Tristan da Cunha, revealing it as a fairly round island sporting a massive volcanic cone at its center. "The island was formed by volcanic activity. It last erupted in 1961. The island was evacuated, but little damage was done to the settlement. The residents returned in 1963 and the volcano has been quiet since. The only military history we have with the island occurred in 1958. We detonated an atomic bomb not far from the island as part of Operation Argus, which became public knowledge in 2006. We've been fairly unwelcome on the island since, as we never told them about the test or offered to help monitor any potential side effects. For that reason, and that the island is a British territory, we need to keep our presence on the island under wraps. Our friends in the U.K. might not take too kindly to an invasion of their soil, even if it is five thousand miles away from the Queen."

The view zoomed in again, showing a small port town on the northwest side of the island. "Tristan has one settlement. Edinburgh of the Seven Seas. Total population, two hundred seventy-one. Eighty families total. The settlement has grown slowly over the past hundred years, but two years ago a small airport appeared along with this . . ."

A quick slide to the right showed a large, modern complex. Next to it, a long airstrip stretched off-screen. "The facility belongs to a company named Beta Incorporated, which we believe is a dummy corporation for Manifold."

"Assuming this is where you're sending us," King said, "what makes you think this is where they went?"

The image focused over the empty airstrip. "This picture

was taken early this morning." The image updated. A large 747 sat on the airstrip. "This was taken an hour ago. To fly a 747 to an island that is two thousand miles from the nearest continent would take an in-flight refueling. There aren't many companies in the world that can arrange that. Manifold most certainly could."

"So," Rook said, stroking his long blond goatee, "if this island is in the middle of nowhere and we need to get there ASAP without getting shot to hell by landing on their airstrip, what's the plan? I mean, I'm assuming you're going to be tossing us out of another plane, but I'd like to avoid any more close encounters with tree limbs if at all possible."

"You'll be rendezvousing with the USS *Grant*. The *Grant* is a new CVNX class aircraft carrier. She's state of the art, really impressive, but we haven't worked out all the kinks yet. She's accompanied by a full battle group, though, so short of a world war, you shouldn't have any problems. We're just lucky they were out there running tests on the girl or we'd be stuck. Bishop, Rook, and Knight. You will be taking a small boat and landing on the back side of the island. You will keep watch on the settlement from above and provide backup for King and Queen who will pose as a couple circling the globe on their yacht. Disguises and identities will be provided upon arrival."

"So you're tossing us out of a plane then, right?"

"If you miss the aircraft carrier the Atlantic will soften your landing."

"Don't think I can't see you smiling, Blue Boy."

"Wheels up in one hour," Deep Blue said. "Better take your Benadryl now, Rook. I'll be in touch." The screen went blank.

"When I find out who that guy is," Rook said with a smirk. "Right to the moon."

"You heard the man," Keasling said. "Go take a crap or whatever you have to do to get ready. I want you back here in thirty minutes."

King watched as the team exited the room. They joked

and prodded each other, reinforcing the sense of family that would keep them frosty and thinking of their teammates' safety while on mission. But he couldn't bring himself to take part. As strong as his connection was to the members of his team, his connection to Pierce was even stronger. With revenge on his mind, King found it hard to focus on much else, and that, he knew, could be dangerous for all of them.

Bishop paused at the door and looked back at King. He'd been silent, as usual, throughout the entire briefing. He held King's gaze, making sure he had his full attention. "We'll find him. We'll bring him back." Then he left with the others.

Somehow, coming from Bishop, the words rang true. They would find Pierce, of that King had no doubt. But whether or not they'd be bringing him home in a body bag, well, that was another issue.

NINETEEN

Tristan da Cunha

Pierce stood in front of a five-foot-square window, staring out at an endless expanse of ocean. He knew they were on an island, but where in the world, he had no idea. His third-story room provided him with a view of the airstrip they'd landed on, a patch of grass beyond, and then one hundred eighty degrees of ocean. He had yet to see any indigenous animals or birds that might hint at a location, and the only flora he'd seen was the grass, which helped about as much as a toothpick in a knife fight.

The room was an improvement over his cell on the plane. Not only was the window larger and view less unnerving, but the accommodations were comfortable—probably meant for actual employees, not prisoners. A firm twin bed sat in the corner across from a desk holding copies of the *Odyssey, Dante's Inferno,* and several Edgar Rice Burroughs novels, including Pierce's favorite, *The Lost World.* As a child it was the kind of swashbuckling adventure he pictured him and King having as archaeologists. Thanks to *Indiana Jones,* most men his age had the same views of the science. The truth was far more boring, though no less interesting. Of course, he had been kidnapped by armed looters. That had to count for something. He just wasn't whipping his way to freedom.

As the first thoughts of dramatic escape filled Pierce's imagination a sharp knock rattled the door. The guard, Reinhart, who he'd learned was head of Manifold's security force, opened the door without waiting for an answer and tossed a lab coat to him.

"There's a problem with your artifact," he said.

Your artifact. "What's wrong with it?"

"Do I look like a pencil-pushing scientist to you?" Reinhart crossed his arms, letting his muscles bulge.

Pierce slipped the lab coat on, noting a Manifold I.D. card with his name and photo on it had been clipped to the breast pocket. Pierce smirked. "Am I hired?"

"Consider this your ninety-day trial period," Reinhart said.

Pierce fell silent as he moved toward the door. He knew what happened at the end of ninety-day trial periods. You were either kept on board with a hearty handshake . . . or terminated. As he noticed the strange three-barreled handgun holstered on Reinhart's hip he realized that he was probably one of the men who kidnapped him, and after ninety days, if he even made it that long, would be his executioner. He fell in step, walking in Reinhart's massive shadow as they worked their way through a maze of unlabeled hallways.

After nearly two minutes spent in silence, Reinhart pushed through a set of double doors and revealed a futuristic, stark white chamber. Men and women wearing lab coats worked at stations around the five-thousand-square-foot laboratory. Ridley and Maddox turned at their entrance. Maddox approached with a smile. "Welcome to Wonderland, Dr. Pierce."

"This is, ah, something," Pierce said.

"It's more than something," Maddox said, leading Pierce through the room, pointing out machines and equipment as he walked. "We have fifty Zeiss and Olympus microscopes, one at each station, along with fifty automated karyotyping and FISH—fluorescence in-situ hybridization—stations. Each has the capability for multicolored FISH and other molecular cytogenetic procedures. There are ten low-temperature freezers—the long white boxes by the back wall. The giant pills up there," he said, pointing to a line of cylindrical bath tub–sized containers bolted to the wall above several workstations, "those are twenty-one liquid nitrogen storage tanks."

"Isn't that dangerous? Keeping liquid nitrogen above the workstations."

"The only way to breach them is with high-caliber bullets or explosives, and if either are used to burst one of those high-pressure containers it won't matter if they're on the ceiling or the floor."

As they approached the long work table Ridley stood by, Maddox continued his tour. "There are five Barocyclers—really high tech—six automated Vysis VP2000 slide processors, three Axon Scanners, four Thermotrons, and—"

"You do realize I'm an archaeologist," Pierce said. "You're speaking Chinese to me."

Maddox paused, frowned, and then covered the remaining distance to the table in silence. Pierce watched the man, wondering how someone with obvious accomplishments could so easily be offended. His impeccably shiny shoes, hair, and teeth all pointed toward some innate desire to impress those around him.

"You've gone and hurt his feelings," Reinhart whispered.

When they stopped at the table, Pierce saw the Hydra artifact resting at its center, still wrapped in the petrified fabric that fused to the head long ago. Pierce stared at it. Part of him thought he'd never see it again. He'd even started thinking that he'd imagined the serpentine details, that his imagination had got the better of him. But seeing it again now, in the bright white glow of the lab, his doubts vanished. This was the real deal. An aberration at the top of the artifact caught his attention. A hole. "You drilled a hole in it?"

"For a core sample," Maddox said. His voice raised an octave in annoyance. "But it's the same cementlike substance all the way through. We dissolved it in an alcohol solution, but it just turned to paste. How are we supposed to get a DNA sample from paste?"

"I never claimed that you could."

"You claimed it was the authentic head of Hy—"

"If you're trying to pin incompetence on someone else, find another scapegoat."

Maddox's face beamed red. Ridley put a hand on his arm, calming the man.

"Dr. Pierce, please," Ridley said. "He's under a great deal of pressure to succeed. Now, we can banter about this, call names and so forth, or we can cut right to the swift. What say you?"

"By all means," Pierce said.

"Being the closest thing to an expert on the Hydra, you will tell us how we can take a DNA sample from what I've been told, based on your initial assessment, is the authentic head of the mythical Hydra . . . or, Mr. Reinhart can take you to the cliff side, put three bullets in the back of your head, and toss you into the Atlantic." He smiled. "Is that clear enough?"

Pierce tensed from head to toe. He knew a braver man might tell Ridley to shove it, but he really just wanted to survive. He looked up at Maddox and was surprised to see a look of horror on his face. Apparently the man had no idea his employer could be so ruthless. Pierce glanced around the room. The other scientists remained hard at work, having not overheard the conversation. Pierce wondered how many of them knew what was really going on here.

"Well?" Ridley said.

Pierce looked at a long line of tools laid out next to the

Hydra head. With a shaky hand he picked up a scalpel. Pushing hard, he cut into the petrified fabric. With a pair of tweezers he pulled the piece away and placed it on the counter. The four-inch square showed what looked like scales, though they were powdery and gray. He watched it for any change.

Nothing.

"You keep the air in here dry," he said. He had felt the sting of dry air on his throat upon entering the lab and heard the hum of the air conditioners. Most labs kept the air cold and dry to preserve artifacts or other elements, but in the case of Hydra, it kept another reaction from occurring. At least that's what he hoped. The petrified fabric probably kept natural moisture in the air from reaching the Hydra head en route to this facility, but the air in the lab was like the desert at night. Moisture had yet to reach the sample.

He placed a chisel against the exposed area, he held a hammer high and took a deep breath. He let out a long sigh, thinking, *I can't believe I'm doing this.* Then his thoughts turned to what being shot in the back of the head would feel like and he brought the hammer down hard.

A chunk the size of a walnut shot off and fell to the table. He caught it and held it up. It looked no different from a dry piece of dog crap—insignificant in every way. He looked up and found Ridley, Maddox, and Reinhart watching in rapt silence. In fact, the whole lab had gone silent at the sound of hammer and chisel. All eyes were on Pierce.

He stood, picking up a plastic sample dish, and filled it with water from a nearby sink. He returned with the inch-deep water dish and placed it on the counter. He held the Hydra sample in his hand. "Hydra lived in a swamp. The word 'hydra' *means* water. Hercules buried the head in the driest environment on earth." He looked at Maddox, "Alcohol is a diuretic. It does the same thing to cells as it does to the human body—dehydrates."

Ridley smiled.

Pierce dropped the sample into the water. It bubbled like an antacid as air trapped in the miniscule depressions was forced out by the water seeping in. As the water cleared, the sample went from light gray to dark, like water on cement. For a moment, Pierce thought he was mistaken and his life was over, but a twitch of movement caught his eye. The sample bounced like a Mexican jumping bean, twice clearing the water. All at once it seemed to ooze and expand, the top side turning vibrant green, the underside red, fleshy sinews. The water inside the container seeped into every pore of the sample until not a drop remained. The fist-sized chunk looked like a green-scaled filet mignon.

"I'll be damned," Reinhart said.

Ridley pounded the table victoriously. "Well done."

Reaching out slowly, Pierce traced his fingers along the scaly flesh. The scales felt hard, almost sharp. Touching it brought it all home and erased his concerns for his own well-being. He smiled wide, picked up the sample container, and handed it to Maddox, whose hands were shaking, too. "Dr. Maddox, your DNA sample."

TWENTY

Pope Air Force Base

As King looked at the laptop screen, sifting through the information taken from Manifold's turncoat techie, he tuned out the repeating metal on metal clink and stream of curses following them. With a half hour to kill and their gear safely stowed on board the *Crescent*—Delta's very own stealth transport—the team gathered at their usual premission spot next to the Delta hangar bay. Two metal poles, each protruding from a square sand pit, forty feet apart, marked the official Delta horseshoe court.

King sat in one of three lawn chairs, in the shade provided by the massive hangar.

The metallic clink of a horseshoe striking a pole sounded out.

"Damn you," Rook shouted. "Another ringer."

"That's game, right?" Knight asked as he walked the forty feet between the two sand pits. Despite being the shortest and lightest of the Chess Team men, he was also one of the most skilled and deadly of the group, especially from a distance. He liked to say he was only good at three things: being a sniper, horseshoes, and women, but he was one of those people who seemed to be good at everything he tried. So when he walked with his short-legged confident stride and flashed his charming, squinty-eyed smile, no one complained . . . much. Rook sometimes took issue with the pint-sized, dapper-dressed Romeo, as the two were polar opposites, but their tiffs usually ended with laughter.

Bishop, terrible at horseshoes, was almost always paired with Knight, to keep the team game fair. But Rook and Queen weren't much better and the outcome was almost always predictable. If the game wasn't intended merely as a way to unwind before a mission, Rook's blood pressure would skyrocket. Being the front-runner in the race for the world's worst sore loser benefited the team on the battle-field. He never surrendered. But there was no such thing as a friendly game of Monopoly with Rook.

"I'm out for now," Queen said, as she plopped into the chair next to King while Bishop stood watch and Rook and Knight started a fresh one-on-one match. She quickly tied her hair back, looping the blond waves into a tightly wound bun. The early summer North Carolina heat, combined with the black fatigues the team wore, had her sweating, even in the shade. After splashing water from her drinking bottle onto her face, she peeked at King's laptop. "Find anything interesting?"

He just stared at the screen, chewing his lower lip.

She placed her hand on his. "Hey."

King looked up. He hadn't seen her approach or heard her talk. "Sorry. What?"

"What are you looking for?"

"Answers."

"You're wondering why they took your friend. Why they took his artifact."

"It just doesn't make sense," King said. "Why would Manifold be interested enough in an artifact to kill doz-ens of people and then destroy a multimillion-dollar re-search facility to cover their tracks? What could George have to do with all this?"

"How well do you know him?"

King shot a Queen a look.

"Don't give me that look. The path to truth isn't always comfortable." She gave him a shove. "You know that better than anyone."

"The man is terminally trustworthy, honest, and forgiving . . . and I was going to let him marry my sister." He looked her in the eyes. "You already know how that turned out."

Queen nodded. They all knew about Julie's death. An air force training flight. She never saw combat, but served with distinction. As King's early inspiration for joining the military, they all knew her story. He kept a photo of her on him at all times. "He's family. A brother."

"Then he's our brother," she said.

King smiled and nodded. "But I still don't know why they wanted him."

"What was he working on?"

"It was a U.N. dig. Not even his project. He was brought on as a specialist." King brought up photos of the Nazca dig site and the nine-headed geoglyph. "He said this image represented the Hydra."

"Like the mythical Hydra? Hercules and all that?"

"That's the one. You know it?"

"When I learned Greek for Delta I took Greek history and mythology, too."

"Then you're going to love this. Beneath the central head, here"—King pointed to the large stone head at the center of the geoglyph—"George found something, a head. Reptilian. But it was just an old statue. Felt like cement. Nothing worth killing for." He looked Queen in the eyes. "So why would a multibillion-dollar genetics company go to all that trouble for a stone?"

"If it wasn't a stone."

King squinted at her.

"The Hydra myth says that Hercules buried the cauterized Hydra head beneath a stone. It doesn't take much of a leap to assume he'd pick a really dry place as the Hydra lived in—thrived in—water. It made its home in a swamp. It's really not all that unreasonable. Salamanders regenerate limbs like the Hydra was supposed to. Some salamanders grow up to six feet in length. That's today. Twenty-five hundred years ago, animals grew a lot bigger. They hadn't been hunted to extinction and their habitats were still intact. So maybe it was simply an oversized salamander with the disposition of a komodo dragon. Who knows? The real point is: Did George think it was important?"

He thought for a moment. "Yeah."

"Then forget the salamander and *assume* it was the real deal. Manifold obviously is, too. The ancients certainly did. The ancient Greek scholar Apollodorus wrote a text titled *Library*. In it he recorded all of Greek history, from the fall of Troy to roughly one hundred nine B.C. The golden fleece, the Argonauts, the *Iliad,* Ulysses, they're all in there. Here, I'll show you."

She took King's laptop, placed it on her lap, and opened the Firefox Web browser, which connected to the Internet through the airfield's wireless network. Within thirty seconds she had what she was looking for. She handed the laptop back to King. "This is a translation of the original Greek version of the *Library*. I highlighted the portion on Hydra."

King read through the text.

[2.5.2] As a second labour he ordered him to kill the Lernaean hydra.[105] That creature, bred in the swamp of Lerna, used to go forth into the plain and ravage both the cattle and the country. Now the hydra had a huge body, with nine heads, eight mortal, but the middle one immortal. So mounting a chariot driven by Iolaus, he came to Lerna, and having halted his horses, he discovered the hydra on a hill beside the springs of the Amymone, where was its den.

By pelting it with fiery shafts he forced it to come out, and in the act of doing so he seized and held it fast. But the hydra wound itself about one of his feet and clung to him. Nor could he effect anything by smashing its heads with his club, for as fast as one head was smashed there grew up two. A huge crab also came to the help of the hydra by biting his foot.[106] So he killed it, and in his turn called for help on Iolaus who, by setting fire to a piece of the neighboring wood and burning the roots of the heads with the brands, prevented them from sprouting. Having thus got the better of the sprouting heads, he chopped off the immortal head, and buried it . . .

King couldn't conceive of such a thing actually living, but it was clear that Manifold saw the Hydra as the genetic version of the Rosetta stone. If Pierce really had found the immortal head of the Hydra, then in a very crazy way, all this made sense. He couldn't think of any government on earth that wouldn't kill for it. But they wouldn't have to. Manifold would simply sell the formula and make a fortune.

A loud metal ping sounded. The first of the nearly silent horseshoe match. "That's right, sucka," Rook shouted from forty feet away. "All tied up." He lined up a shot, grinning like a kid hopped up on Pixie Stix.

King's wristwatch beeped. He stood as Rook loosed his final shot of the match. The horseshoe sailed through the air, flipping over itself. As it began its descent King reached out and plucked the hard metal horseshoe from the air. "Time to go."

"What's that make it?" Knight said with a grin. "Forty-three games to nothing?"

Bishop chuckled.

Rook's mouth dropped open. "You could've let it hit the ground."

After dropping the horseshoe just shy of the metal

pole, King smiled and headed for the side entrance to the long hangar.

As the team gathered their shed clothing and followed him to the hangar, Rook added, "I swear, we better find King's buddy soon or there is going to be hell to pay."

TWENTY-ONE

Over the South Atlantic

Six hours after leaving the Pope, traveling at mach 2—1,522 miles per hour—the *Crescent* closed to within twenty miles of the USS *Grant*. The *Crescent,* named for its half-moon shape, was the world's first stealth transport plane, and while it had the potential to hold several tons of equipment, it had been converted to be used for special ops covert insertions. Small quarters with bunks could hold sixty troops, but right now, the only passengers were the five members of the Chess Team, the *Crescent*'s most frequent fliers.

The trip had been made in silence as the team slept in their personal quarters. Missions often lasted for several days and sleep was always in short order. The six-hour flight from North Carolina to Tristan da Cunha, while aggravating for King, was a blessing as the team got, in military terms, a full night's sleep. All slept fully clothed, with their gear stowed next to the bunks, ready to go at a moment's notice.

The pilot's voice over the intercom provided the team's wake-up call. "Rise and shine, Delta. We are approaching the LZ and are descending for your jump."

High altitude low opening, or HALO, jumps were the

norm for the team's aerial insertions, but they were landing on friendly territory while the sun still hung on the
horizon. More than that, if they failed to land on the deck
of the USS *Grant,* a cold dip in the ocean would greet
them. While they typically relied on stealth to stay out of
trouble, this time it was all about aim.

With their parachutes checked and double checked
already, they strapped the packs to their backs as they
exited their bunk rooms and moved to the *Crescent*'s rear
loading bay. Rook rubbed his eyes as he stepped in line
behind Queen.

"Aww, the little guy still sleepy?" Queen said with a
grin.

Knight chuckled as he got in line behind Rook.

"Hard to sleep with you grinding up against me," Rook
said, slowly gyrating his hips.

Queen laughed and tightened the straps across her
chest, accentuating the point by showing off the feminine
curves hidden beneath the black jumpsuits they all wore.
"Boy, if you had me, you'd still be dead to the world
tired."

Before Rook could reply, the red light above the red
hatch turned green. He lowered his goggles into place and
took hold of the railing that led to the rear hatch. A moment later, the hatch opened. A torrent of air whipped
through the cabin and pulled at their bodies. The team held
tight as the door opened fully. The view through the back
became solid blue as the endless ocean below reflected the
darkening blue sky above. The USS *Grant* could not be
seen, but it waited for them directly below.

King raised his hand, snapping the team to attention.
His next hand signal would have them all jumping out five
thousand feet over the ocean. He moved toward the rear of
the plane, holding the railing as he leaned out, looking into
the blue abyss. The first of the ships in the USS *Grant*'s
battle group came into view. They were to jump just after
passing the carrier itself, angling toward the ship's massive

deck. The carrier came into view, surrounded by what looked like a fleet of skyscrapers laid on their sides. Five destroyers, two Aegis guided-missile cruisers, three guided-missile destroyers, and two supply ships hemmed in the USS *Grant*, which dwarfed the other ships. Unseen, two Los Angeles–class attack submarines patrolled the frigid waters below the battle group. King had been aboard several different carriers over the years, but had never looked down on one from above. The sheer size of the ships combined with enough firepower to level most of the world's nations humbled him as he gazed down.

What amazed him most was that Deep Blue had managed to retask several hundred billion dollars worth of navy assets in the time it took most people to send an e-mail. And all of it was here for *them*. King shook his head. Deep Blue either had a massive amount of dirt on people in power or knew how to play the military-political game better than anyone else. King decided it was the latter. Named for the chess-playing computer capable of beating the world's masters, Deep Blue had proven himself deserving of the name.

The massive carrier sat still in the ocean, displacing a hundred thousand tons of water and waiting to receive them. After just passing the carrier's bow, King closed his fist and jumped. One by one, the team followed, throwing themselves from the back of the *Crescent* without a second thought.

Knight, the last one to jump, met the open air with a smile. He loved the sense of freedom jumping gave him. In the distance he could make out the speck of Inaccessible Island, which hid them from any eyes on Tristan da Cunha and would obscure their approach. With arms outstretched, Knight followed the diagonal trail of the Chess Team led by King. Like a group of small planes they steered their bodies through the whipping winds toward the deck of the USS *Grant*.

The *Grant*'s 1,092-foot-long flight deck made an easy

target, but sixteen F/A-18 Hornets locked in place provided enough obstacles to make a precision landing, dead center, important. Slamming into the side of a forty-one-million-dollar war machine was never a good idea. Not only could you do millions of dollars in damage, but colliding with a wing after a 5,000-foot drop could take a head clean off. Adjusting his fall, Knight twisted and lined up directly behind Rook's feet. Straight ahead and below he could see the rest of the team. As they closed in on the deck, Knight took hold of his ripcord and watched King's hands.

Six hundred feet from the deck of the *Grant,* seconds from impact and moving at terminal velocity, King made three quick jerking motions with his hand. At once, the team deployed their chutes. With a snap, the descent slowed only four hundred feet from their target. They coasted in a straight line, past the back of the ship, then swung around the bridge and headed for the main deck. The team landed as though choreographed, one at a time, pulling in their chutes quickly before a stiff breeze pulled them from the deck.

Crew with brightly colored jumpsuits—green, purple, blue, and brown, each color designating their specific jobs on the flight deck—ran out and helped collect the chutes of the most unusual deck landing any had seen. They were used to catching roaring jets, not a five-man special ops team.

A tall man with eyes as blue as the surrounding ocean and wearing a bright white officer's uniform approached King with a grin. King took note of the eagle insignia on the man's collar and the four yellow bars and single gold star on his shoulder. He offered a salute, that as a Delta operative he rarely had to do, but when in Rome . . . or on a Navy carrier . . . it was always nice to show the respect expected. "Captain Savile."

The captain returned the salute and smiled. "That was the damndest thing I've ever seen. What the hell was that bird you jumped from?"

"You might have a higher pay grade, Captain, but I'm afraid I get to keep a few secrets."

Savile laughed. "Well, considering the ship you're standing on doesn't officially exist, I won't tell anyone I saw your stealth transport if you don't tell anyone about my next generation supercarrier."

"Deal."

After the team finished freeing themselves from their parachute harnesses, Savile motioned for them to follow him. "We've got cabins squared away for you if you need some—"

"No need," King said. "We need to hit the island before nightfall."

Savile looked at the sun, just about to dip below the arc of blue ocean. "Better double-time it, then. The shorelines around these islands are deadly to approach during daylight and suicidal at night."

"Suicidal missions are what we do," Queen said as Savile opened a hatch.

Savile turned around and looked each of them in the eye. At that moment he realized his five guests had probably seen more action and taken more lives than the ships in the battlegroup and thousands of souls manning them combined—real soldiers—the kind he enjoyed working with.

TWENTY-TWO

USS *Grant,* South Atlantic

"You look like a seventies porn star," Rook said as he gave King a once-over.

King smiled as he looked in the bathroom mirror. The thick black mustache pasted on his top lip, combined with his messy hair; loose, white button-down shirt; and pleated khaki pants was enough to make him laugh, despite the grim situation. He looked ridiculous, though entirely convincing for his role. "I am but a French sailor," he said with a thick French accent. "I am traveling the world with *ma petite cochonne*."

The gray steel door clunked open and Queen entered the cold utilitarian bathroom without a knock. Dressing and undressing in front of each other was part of the job. "Your little pig, huh?"

King grinned as he saw Queen's outfit, equally humorous, though much more flattering.

"Wow," Rook whispered when he saw her short shorts, sandaled feet, and poofy, white half-shirt that did little to conceal the fact that she wasn't wearing a bra. Her long legs, stomach, and arms still held the tan she got during her time on Ocracoke Island and accentuated her toned muscles.

Looking in the mirror next to King, she pouted her red lips and batted her eyelashes. She looked at Rook and with an equally thick French accent said, "Oh *ma puce*, you will burn holes in my blouse if you continue to stare at me with those devilish eyes. Then . . . I will have to rip them out." She waggled a finger at him. "Tsk, tsk, tsk."

The door opened. Knight stuck his head in, smiled at their outfits, and said, "Your yacht is incoming. Time to go."

Queen followed him out the door.

"What the hell is '*ma puce*'?" Rook asked.

"My flea," King said with a grin. "It's a term of endearment."

"Term of endearment, my ass," Rook said as King left the bathroom. He hastily applied a layer of black face paint. "*Ma puce*, huh?" He smiled. "I could live with that."

It was only twenty minutes after their arrival, and the sun was nearly below the horizon. Daylight would only last for another hour as the last of the sun's rays reflected off the atmosphere. The team waited on deck, King and Queen dressed for a private cruise and Knight, Rook, and Bishop clad, head to toe, in black wet suits. Supplies and weapons for King and Queen would be stowed away on their yacht once it arrived, but the other three carried their armaments and supplies on their backs, chests, and over their shoulders. They looked ready to wage war.

Savile stood with them, waiting for the arrival of the vessels the team would take to shore. Seeing King and Queen dressed in their disguises made him grin. He'd heard that Delta often wore disguises, but never pictured them like this.

A chopping in the distance drew their attention.

"You got to be shitting me," Rook said with a shake of his head and a grin.

A slate gray, heavy-lifting CH-53 Sea Stallion helicopter pounded into the air above the *Grant*. But it wasn't the chopper's grasshopperlike cockpit or massive whipping blades that surprised the group, it was the unusual cargo that hung on steel cables beneath the bird: a forty-five-foot dual-hulled catamaran. The pristine yacht gleamed white and bore the name *Mercury*. The Sea Stallion lowered the yacht to the water below the deck of the unmoving USS *Grant,* in the process bringing the cockpit of the helicopter level with the deck. When the cables went slack, the pilot grinned, saluted, then cut the yacht loose. The freed yacht bounced in the high swells but had no trouble staying perfectly upright, thanks to its extremely stable double-hull design.

After the copter peeled away the group approached the deck edge and peered down at the yacht bobbing in the water. "Where did you find a yacht out here?" Knight asked.

"As far as I know," Savile said, "someone on your end tracked the thing using its GPS unit. Had a couple of helos intercept and . . . requisition the ship. I was told the owners were paid twice its value, but they were none too pleased to have their cruise interrupted."

King shook his head, amazed at the resources being pulled together at the last minute. "Deep Blue." He said it lightly, but Savile overheard.

He snapped his head toward King. Deep Blue's call sign had become near legendary in the past few years as he worked behind the scenes and shifted military units across the globe like they were his own personal chess pieces on a world-sized board. "Deep Blue, huh?"

King nodded.

"Suez canal. Two years ago."

King met his eyes. "You were on the *Halsey*?"

"Hell, was that you five?"

Five grins answered the question. "I'll be damned. You guys saved more than five thousand souls that day. Like lightning from the sky." He shook King's hand.

Savile remembered the day well. As captain of the newly commissioned destroyer, the USS *Halsey,* he had been ordered to the gulf, along with the rest of his battlegroup, by way of the Suez Canal. As the canal passes through Egypt, whose relations with the U.S. and her allies is at times strained, the passage of any U.S. military must be completed without incident. Any military action taken in the canal could easily be seen as an act of war. The problem created is that any ship passing through the canal is essentially a sitting duck. Savile found out later that the CIA had picked up chatter about an attack at the canal, something similar to the attack on the USS *Cole* off the coast of Yemen. But the powers that be decided to keep quiet about the threat. Issuing a warning might make sailors jumpy enough to take potshots at the wrong people and set off an international incident.

So when five motorboats powered through the canal, making for the port hull of the *Halsey,* Savile could do nothing but keep watch and hope they were just trying to get a good look at one of the world's most powerful ships. When the five boats passed through the invisible border that marked the point where they could normally open fire, he became worried. Even more so when, despite his warnings via a loudspeaker, the boats continued in a straight line. They nearly sank the USS *Cole* with one boat. This was five. Savile shook his head, realizing what was about to happen, but then someone shouted "Look in the sky!" like some scene right out of a Superman movie.

Savile stepped out of the bridge and saw five black specks flying in at a sharp angle, one behind each of the approaching motorboats. Looking through a pair of binoculars he saw that the five figures were dressed, head to toe, in black and bore no insignias or flags. They swept in, with fabric stretched tight between their outstretched arms and legs, gliding more than falling. At first he feared they were part of a two-pronged attack, but quickly realized that even the most well-funded terrorist organization could never pull off a stunt like that. His suspicions were confirmed when, just ahead of the five approaching boats, the five-man team popped their chutes and immediately opened fire with silenced weapons. In under thirty seconds the five motorboats were disabled and taking on water. The attack had been averted in near silence, leaving only a few pissed-off terrorists trying to tread water as evidence. The five-man team hit the water, disappeared from view with their chutes, and never resurfaced.

"Hate to break up the reunion," Rook said, "but where is *our* boat?"

Savile pointed to a small black zodiac tied to the *Grant*. Rook glanced at the small boat, which looked beyond insignificant next to the *Grant* and *Mercury*, then back at the yacht, then at King and Queen. "Bastids."

Twenty minutes later, Rook clung to the side of the zodiac as a stream of muttered curses flew from his mouth with every lurch up and over a wave. From the deck of the USS *Grant,* the ocean had looked calm, but upon launching they had discovered six-foot swells and a stiff breeze brought on by the cooling night air. Bishop piloted the eight-foot inflatable boat while Rook provided a counterbalance to Bishop at the bow. Knight, whose smaller stature made him the most likely to be catapulted from the inflatable, sat low at the center, gripping a plastic handhold.

Darkness had consumed the ocean as they rounded Inaccessible Island and made a straight shot for the back side of Tristan da Cunha. This helped conceal their approach, but also made each wave a nasty surprise.

The zodiac bounced, catching air as Bishop kept the throttle opened up, and careened into the next wave head on. Frigid water cascaded over the front of the boat, soaking Rook and spraying the other two.

Though the circumstances were uncomfortable and the ride perilous, all three maintained calm. As they approached the island, even Rook's muttering ceased. The mission had commenced and each man knew the life and death of the others depended on their professionalism.

The zodiac sprung up again, but not from a wave. The contact was solid and dead center. Knight bounced into the air as though he'd just landed on a trampoline. He landed next to the now immobile boat. If not for the ocean floor being five feet beneath he would have had to shed his gear or drown. Without a word he began slogging toward shore as waves pounded his back and threatened to smash his body against the rocky coastline.

Rook and Bishop slid out of the ruined boat into the cold water.

"On three," Rook said.

Bishop nodded as Rook began counting. On three they hefted the zodiac off the rock and let it sink beneath the waves, erasing all trace of their incursion to Tristan da Cunha.

"All clear," Knight said from shore. They met on a rocky crag.

Bishop motioned to Knight. "Took a heavy hit. Any damage?"

Knight shook his head. "It'll bruise. I'll be fine."

After shedding their wet suits and changing into dry, jet black fatigues, they donned night vision goggles and, though exhausted and beaten from their oversea insertion, began the long rocky trek toward the small forest that lined the base of Tristan da Cunha's volcano. After setting up camp, their mission would begin in earnest.

TWENTY-THREE

Cow Bay, Tristan da Cunha

The ride aboard the *Mercury* felt closer to a pleasure cruise, which was the intention of the double-hulled catamaran's designers. It cut through the surface, completely stable. Moving at a steady, casual pace propelled by the ship's two outboard engines, King steered toward the small harbor of Cow Bay, the only official and safe way to land at the island. With the surrounding waters lit by four halogen bulbs, he easily avoided the rocky shoreline and made a swooping arc around and between two jetties that protected the harbor from the constant assault of ocean waves.

"Looks harmless enough," Queen said as she stood next to King. Without the pounding surf soaking them to the bone, she remained in her skimpy outfit, absorbing the cooling yet still eighty-degree air.

The settlement of Edinburgh emerged from the darkness, lit by a combination of moonlight and a few streetlights. Most of the buildings, both home and official, were stark white, while their roofs were brightly colored with reds, yellows, greens, and blues. King's attention drifted to the hill just beyond town where a strong glow illuminated the misty air and side of the volcano. He thought it strange that the Manifold facility would be so wide out in the open and glowing like a beacon for all to see. But with two thousand miles in every direction separating them from the outside world, who would be looking?

They cruised past several docked sailboats and fishing vessels. All seemed in good repair but not one looked like it had been built within the past twenty years. Steering toward an open spot on the dock, King saw an old man with a scraggly beard hobbling toward them. "Here comes the welcome wagon."

The old man gave a feeble wave as the *Mercury* slid up to the dock. He seemed slow and ungainly, but deftly caught the tie line as Queen threw it to him. He tied them off quickly, then repeated the process at the catamaran's stern.

"What brings ya to Edinburgh?" the man asked.

King recognized the accent as coming from Massachusetts. By the looks of him, the man had spent a lifetime at sea. Probably a fisherman or lobsterman. He laid on his phony French accent and said, "We are traveling the world. Seeing the . . . ehh, sights. And my sweetheart . . . she wanted to see the world's most remote locale."

"Well, you've found it," the man said, scratching his long, thick beard. "And you'd be wise to leave it."

King raised an eyebrow. "And why is that, monsieur?"

He nodded toward Queen, "This one's going to cause a ruckus."

"Oh?"

"There are two hundred and seventy-one people on this island. Almost two hundred of them are men. And the women here are either married or too young, though that doesn't stop most from marrying at sixteen. You're the first visitors we've had in six months. And there ain't anyone here who's going anywhere fast. You catching my drift?"

"Then add one more married woman to the list," King said.

"Listen, boy, it ain't gonna matter if she's married or

not." He looked at Queen's breasts silhouetted inside her sheer white half shirt and emerging from the low-cut collar. "I haven't seen a rack like that in twenty years and I'm feeling some life in places I'd long since given up for dead."

King smiled. He liked the old man, but not what he was insinuating. He knew Queen could take care of herself, but if the locals turned on them it would compromise the mission. "I see what you are saying. Honey, make yourself decent." He shooed her away with his hands, which garnered a quick glare. She disappeared belowdeck a moment later.

King hopped onto the dock and found the thick old man stood as tall as he did and a good portion thicker. Aged, but with a body earned through hard labor. He shook his leathery hand and said, "Étienne Brodeur, a pleasure."

"Captain Jon Karn," he returned, pronouncing his last name Kahn.

"How did you come to live on Tristan da Cunha?"

Karn eyed him. "Why you want to know?"

"I am a, ahh, connoisseur of life. I am interested in people. You see?"

Karn smiled and shook his head. "You better watch your back, too, buddy. You're about as feminine as the gals here."

King guffawed. "You are from Massachusetts, no? I recognize the accent. We've summered on the Cape Cod."

This got a smile from Karn. "I'll bet you have . . . I'm a Gloucesterman. Third-generation fisherman. But the waters dried up. Fish disappeared. Made living hard. At the time the waters here were thick with fish, so I left home and tried my hand out here in the middle of nowhere. Worked out great for a while. But two years ago the fishing factory burned down. Most folks lost their income. Course, that all changed about a month later when *they* showed up."

Karn motioned toward the distant glow of the Manifold facility. "Most everyone gave up on the fish and went to work for them. Now the lights stay on day and night. We get cable television. High-speed Internet. The works. Me, I liked it here before they came. You don't come to the settlement if you like being connected to the world. And that's just the start of—"

"Is this better, monsieur?" Queen exited the cabin dressed in hiking boots, loose-fitting blue jeans, and a baggy sweater. A sports bra combined with the sweater hid her curves nicely. Her hair was tied in a bun that protruded from the back of a Yankees baseball cap. She'd washed off the makeup she'd applied for her role, but her natural beauty would be impossible to hide without a thick coat of mud.

"Lose the fucking Yankees cap and I won't throw you to the fishes." Karn gave a nearly toothless smile.

"All Americans are Yankees to the French," she said, smiling fiendishly.

"Watch your language, lady," he replied, though he couldn't hide a grin of his own.

Queen removed the cap and tossed it into the water.

Karn nodded. "You should be fine." He caught King's eye. "Just don't leave her alone."

King pulled Queen up and into his arms. "I would never let anyone harm my darling Dominique."

Queen feigned a giggle as she jabbed her thumb into a pressure point on King's back. He winced and covered it with a laugh of his own. "Please, Monsieur Karn. Is there an eatery on the island?"

"An eatery?"

"A restaurant. Someplace we might socialize . . . pick up the local flavor?"

"The local flavor is shit, boy. But if you're in the mood for shit, Jake's Tavern is three streets up on the right. There ain't no sign, but it'll be the only place with lights in the front."

"Merci," King said with a wave. He placed his arm around Queen and they strutted off toward town.

Karn shook his head. "French people." He thought the two were nice enough. He just hoped they could stay out of trouble. Strange things had been going on in Edinburgh since Beta Incorporated had arrived. And more than a few volunteers had yet to return. Including his brother, who had made the trip to Tristan da Cunha with him. He'd volunteered to undergo an experimental treatment for a tumor on his leg. That was a month ago. He hadn't heard a peep from his brother since and was beginning to think he never would again.

TWENTY-FOUR

Tristan da Cunha

Pierce entered a large computer lab with Reinhart right behind him. He'd been summoned from his room once again, this time from a dead sleep. The bright white light of the lab caused him to squint, which in turn caused him to stumble into a chair. The chair shot across the room as Pierce fell back. He managed to stay on his feet, but the corner of the desk caught his funny bone, sending a wave of pain from elbow to fingertip. The clatter announced their entry into the lab rather noisily, but neither Ridley nor Maddox, who stood in front of a large, six-monitor computer display, turned or bid them welcome. Behind the display screens sat rows of slate gray computer towers, whirring and humming as their cooling fans filled the room with heat from the hardworking processors. Judging by the mass of cabling attaching each computer to the next, he could see they were all networked, functioning as one supercomputer. He couldn't guess at how much computing power the system contained, but it was clearly built for something monumental, far beyond the capabilities of a human mind. That seemed to be Manifold's M.O. at least.

Reinhart shoved him forward. "Try not to trip on your shoelaces."

Pierce glanced down at his shoes, just in case. Tied tight. He headed for Maddox knowing that he, at least, had some small amount of decency in him. His reaction to Ridley's death threat earlier was proof of that. But it did little to comfort him as he looked around the vast lab and found it empty. There would be no witnesses for what was about to occur. And though Maddox might have a conscience, Pierce doubted the man would risk his life to take a stand. He clearly prized his research over all else. Probably his life, too.

Rubbing his arm, he made his way past workstations and lab equipment. He stopped at the computer display, acutely aware that Reinhart remained behind him, rather than circling around. Ridley looked up from the sheet of paper he and Maddox had been looking at. Both men wore smiles.

Success.

"Dr. Pierce," Ridley said. "Just in time to share in our little celebration."

Pierce forced a smile and did his best to sound nonplussed. "No balloons or champagne?"

Ridley stood tall, his bald head gleaming in the room's bright light like a polished statue. He looked as monolithic as his deep voice sounded. "Time for that later. A few tests are in order before the true celebration can begin."

"Then you haven't finished?"

"Not completely." Maddox's smile would have been contagious under different circumstances. The man was truly excited. "But we're days away from a final product. Thanks to you, of course."

"The Hydra DNA worked then?" Pierce couldn't hide his interest. The idea that a mythological creature was not only real, but impacting modern-day science was intriguing despite being a prisoner.

Maddox nodded quickly. He handed Pierce the sheet of paper he and Ridley had been examining. Several charts containing series of numbers filled the page. "What am I looking at?"

The page was ripped from his fingers. Maddox held it like a treasured prize. "When I first began analyzing the Hydra sample I thought my equipment was flawed. We recalibrated everything. Used new equipment. The results came back the same every time."

Maddox ran a hand through his messy hair. Disheveled and excited, he looked like some of Pierce's friends. He chuckled as he continued, "At first, things went disastrously. Extracting DNA, while not exactly trivial, has become somewhat routine. Not so with the Hydra sample. We had to break new ground. You see, DNA extraction is performed . . . in water."

"Ahh," Pierce said, understanding.

"The sample continued to replicate and grow, but I'm assuming, without a head or other controlling force in the flesh, it took no shape. We ended up with a three-pound sample. The solution was discovered quite accidentally as we tested the large sample. It turns out that once absorbed, water inside the Hydra flesh became D20—heavy water— its natural and nonreactive state. Using heavy water, we were able to extract the DNA and analyze it. That's when we discovered how truly unique the Hydra is."

Maddox rubbed his stubble-covered chin, eyes looking off into the distance as he relived the discovery. "All life on the planet is composed of the same stuff. We share the large majority of our genomes. That's why you hear things about humans being ninety-eight percent similar to apes, or bananas, or such things. But the Hydra is totally different. DNA bonds in pairs. Adenine pairs with thymine. Quanine with cytosine. They're the building blocks of DNA structure. This is true with Hydra as well, but it's what *binds* those base pairs together that is different. For most of us, it's hydrogen . . . water. For Hydra, it's heavy water. It's this unique bond that allows for the existence of genes not found in other living creatures. We can't simply switch on dormant regenerative genes, we need to introduce them."

"That is odd."

"Odd is an understatement. The word that best describes it is *alien*. Not that I think that's what we're dealing with, but it's as close as you can get without leaving the planet. There is no record of anything else like it, anywhere. Have you ever heard of something being able to grow a second head?" Maddox typed on the keyboard. Images displayed on the six screens: DNA strands represented by double helixes, a series of chemical structures that looked like patterned hexagons bearing labels such as: adenine, thymine, guanine, cytosine, hydrogen, deuterium, and tritium, along with more streams of numbers, and photos of the oversized Hydra sample. Again, Pierce could make little sense of the images, but the man seemed determined to use visual aids. "And that's just the tip of the iceberg. The Hydra is so mind-bogglingly different that just understanding it is slowing us down. We're interested in a single trait, regeneration. But Hydra's extra genes are full of traits that are, for now, undesirable.

"Poisonous breath and a penchant for human flesh," Pierce said.

Maddox caught his breath and looked at him.

"Hydra traits," Ridley said.

"Ahh. Yes. Exactly," Maddox said. "Finding out which genes trigger which traits is our last stumbling block."

"How do you do that?"

"Experimentation."

Pierce began to sweat despite the room's air-conditioning.

Maddox saw his apprehension growing. "Volunteers, of course."

Feeling Reinhart behind him, and the towering Ridley beside him, Maddox's assurance did little to quell his growing fears. Perhaps from the adrenaline filling his veins, Pierce noticed five needles, the syringes filled with red liquid, standing on the counter next to the keyboard. "And those?"

"The first batch. By using a virus, in this case porcine circovirus, a single-stranded DNA virus, as a carrier. The virus crosses the cell membrane and infects the cell with the DNA alterations. The infected cells divide, the virus spreads, the host becomes . . . something new. When we're done, we'll have the world's first cure-all vaccine.

"We've already weeded out the most obvious undesirables. By comparing the Hydra genes to those of humans and virtually every other creature on earth, we were able to remove ninety-nine percent of the DNA. The D20 bond may be different, but the code combinations still match. These first samples contain one fifth of one percent of the remaining genes." Maddox picked up a needle, but left the rubber stopper on the tip. He had no intention of using it. He simply admired it. "If the subject in question is able to regenerate, we'll be able to narrow down our search to the few hundred genes contained in this serum. In the same way, we'll whittle down the potential genes until we're left with one. *The* one. The future of human civilization could be inside this syringe." He stared at the red liquid. After a few silent seconds, he snapped out of his trance. "We'll be able to re-create the human race . . . making us stronger, healthier, and, for all intents and purposes, immortal, soon enough." He put the needle back with the others.

This bit of information was enough to distract Pierce. It seemed unthinkable . . . inhuman . . . godlike . . . to achieve such a thing in such a short period of time. "I've only been here for two days . . ."

Maddox began to explain, but Ridley interrupted him. "All things are possible with enough money."

Pierce understood. "The computers."

Gesturing to the networked computer systems, Ridley added, "The NSA has their one Cray Triton supercomputer. It can handle sixty-four billion instructions per second. Used for breaking encryptions and the like. The system you see here, Yahweh, is the equivalent of five NSA systems, capable of handling three hundred twenty billion instructions per second."

Pierce shook his head. What kind of person names a supercomputer after God?

"With access to the most complete DNA database on the planet assembled over the last three years, Yahweh can dissect any living thing down to its basic genes. It searches for and identifies flaws. It can combine gene sequences of different creatures, creating superior chimeras. And it made short work of identifying the one percent of Hydra's genes that make it unique."

In short, the machine was capable of breaking life down to its smallest components and rebuilding something new. Hence the name. Yahweh. God.

"What I don't understand, is why you explained any of this to me."

"You were part of the discovery," Maddox said. He gave Pierce a genuine pat on the shoulder. "You deserved to know."

"Thanks," Pierce said, amazed by his naïveté. He turned to Ridley, tired of the game. "What's the real reason?"

Ridley shrugged. "A courtesy."

Pierce took a step back and bumped into Reinhart, who didn't budge—a wall of muscle. Maddox looked confused.

"I thought you might like to know what you were volunteering for."

With the same elbow he'd been holding since injuring it on the desk, Pierce swung around, attempting to smash Reinhart in the nose. If he could knock the man down, escaping and hiding in another part of the vast complex might be possible. He knew he'd never make it through all the defenses, he just didn't want to become a guinea pig. Unfortunately, Reinhart either had catlike reflexes or he'd anticipated the move. Probably both.

With intense pressure, Reinhart caught Pierce's elbow, pulled the arm back, took hold of his hand, and twisted. Pierce's wrist cracked audibly. He screamed in pain as Reinhart pulled him up, holding him by the broken wrist and a handful of hair. Just as quickly as he'd been pulled up, Pierce was thrust down, his jaw breaking upon impact with a desktop. In five seconds, the fight had been taken out of him. And it would be a lifetime before he could forget the pain.

"Your first volunteer," Ridley said. But Maddox put his hands up and backed away. He wanted no part in the action, but also didn't voice an objection. He simply watched as Ridley picked up a needle, flicked off the stopper, and buried the needle in Pierce's neck. Pierce fought, but Reinhart had no trouble holding him down. He felt the warm liquid enter his body. It stung. Then burned. But before he could scream at the pain coursing through his veins, he was struck in the back of the head. As he slumped to the floor, he saw Reinhart standing over him, holding his handgun like a club.

Ridley, too, stood above him, saying, " 'We mortals with immortal minds are only born for sufferings and joys, and one could almost say that the most excellent receive joy through sufferings.' Beethoven said that." Ridley knelt down over Pierce, pulling open one of his closed eyes. "You'll let me know if he was right, won't you?"

Pierce slipped, willingly, into the abyss.

TWENTY-FIVE

Tristan da Cunha

Edinburgh looked insignificant from the top of the island's volcano. After hastily setting up camp within the short-treed forest of Tristan da Cunha, Knight and Rook had climbed the steep grade to a point a few hundred feet below the volcano's crater, leaving Bishop behind to man the camp. They worked their way around the craggy slope to a point that afforded them clear views of both the small town and the much larger Beta Incorporated facility.

Rook peered through a pair of 140x night vision zoom binoculars, taking in the quiet town while Knight checked out the well-lit Beta compound through the lens of his new pride and joy. The XM109 semiautomatic sniper rifle had been waiting for him on the *Crescent* when they boarded. Though the weapon was officially still in development by the Barrett Firearms Company, Deep Blue had managed to get him the most up-to-date version. It seemed only fair that the Chess Team start using weapons as advanced as their enemies. The XM109 fired 25mm-caliber rounds capable of piercing armor and disabling light vehicles with a single shot. If fired against a flesh-and-blood target, little would remain. Head shots were a thing of the past with this weapon. Few vehicles short of an M1 Abrams tank could stand up to it. Not even a regenerative capybara.

"See anything interesting?" Rook asked.

"Minimal guards patrolling the outside. I've counted seven, armed with some kind of rifle I've never seen before."

Rook shifted his view to the facility and found a guard walking along the outer wall's catwalk. "Looks like more of the Metal Storms King described. Three barrels." He lowered the binoculars. "You notice the way that place is built?"

Knight nodded. "Like a prison."

"Yeah. I first thought the walls were to keep people out, but I'm starting to think they're for keeping people in. Now why would that be?"

Rook resumed watching the town. He'd watched a few people entering and exiting homes, walking the few streets, and hanging laundry in their backyards, but little else. The only place of constant action was a small well-lit building he'd seen King and Queen enter twenty minutes ago.

"How's Grandma Knight, these days?" he asked.

Without taking his eye away from the sniper scope, Knight said, "She doesn't know who I am anymore. Thinks I'm her uncle when I visit."

"That bad, huh? Sorry, man."

He shrugged. "That's life. Old age. You know? There isn't much I can do besides accept it."

"Still . . . she's all you got left."

"I've got the ladies lining up, man. There will be little Knights running around before you know it."

"You horny rabbit. I didn't know you wanted kids."

"Who doesn't? You don't?"

"S'pose it would have to be with the right lady."

"Got a lady in mind?"

Rook paused, holding his breath. "I've got Queen . . . and King. Exiting the building."

Knight shifted his view and found them walking toward the dock. Their casual walk told him they hadn't found trouble. That was good news. But their pace also told him they hadn't discovered anything to make them walk fast. That was bad news.

They watched King and Queen return to the catamaran. Moments later, King's voice filled their ears. "Knight, do you copy?"

"I'm here, boss," he replied.

"The townies are a bust on intel. Most work at the facility doing menial labor. Janitors, food services, things like that. I doubt a single one of them has any inkling as to what's going on in there. Queen will be going in for a look. What can we expect?"

"Seven guards outside with Metal Storm rifles. The outer wall is taller than it looked in the satellite imagery, but she shouldn't have a problem getting in."

"Why's that?"

"The guards aren't watching the perimeter. They're watching the building. King, there is something nasty in there they don't want getting out."

"Copy that," King said. "Just watch her back."

"You've got incoming," Rook said suddenly. He watched as a lone man snuck his way between buildings and ran across streets with his head ducked down. "Queen better move out."

"Copy that."

Rook watched as Queen, now dressed in black leaped from the catamaran and disappeared into the dark, invisible to all but Rook's night vision binoculars. "She's clear. You've got a single man headed your way. On the dock now. Looks old, maybe. Long beard."

"An old friend," King said. "No worries. Out."

A click signified that King had switched off his radio. Rook watched as the man approached. King climbed onto the dock and reached out his hand for a friendly handshake, but stopped short. "Oh, hell," Rook said.

Knight took aim with his sniper scope and found King, hands in the air, gun in his face. As Knight turned off his rifle's safety and took aim on the back of the man's head, Rook kept both men in view. King glanced up toward the volcano, almost looking directly at them and shook his head slightly. The message was clear.

"King is shaking his head. Hold your fire," Rook whispered, knowing how close his partner was to reducing the man to a puddle of chum. "Let's see how this plays out."

TWENTY-SIX

Tristan da Cunha

Though the salty sea breeze tickling his nose and rustling the leaves overhead calmed his nerves, Bishop found relaxing impossible. Sitting against a tree at the center of their small makeshift base camp, Bishop's thoughts were with his teammates. He'd heard the communication between King and the others. He knew the level of danger was ratcheting up. But he also knew that if medical care was required, or a place to hide, the base camp would be it. And for that reason he had to maintain his post, no matter what might occur on the other side of the volcano.

Frustration built as time passed without update. Something about this mission, about the strangeness of the psychotic capybara and intent of Manifold Genetics to sell physical regeneration to their enemies had his instincts shouting for caution. But here they were, charging headlong into the unknown. Well, everyone but him.

A pain lanced up his arms as he squeezed his hands into tight fists, nearly breaking the skin of his palm with his nails. *Get a grip,* he told himself. With a deep breath, Bishop forced his muscles to relax. He crossed his thick yet limber legs and breathed deep again, focusing on the distant sound of the ocean and the rustling leaves above.

The scent of earth filled his nose and the exposed skin of his arms prickled with goose bumps at the cool breeze rolling in from the ocean. Clearing his mind of worry, he focused on his current mission—preparation and defense of the base camp.

The camouflage tents assembled within a stand of bushes would only be seen if someone stumbled upon them. Being nearly invisible and far from any trails, they probably could have left the hidden medical gear, weapons, and communications equipment without fear of discovery, but they had no idea what they would find within the protected walls of Manifold's dummy corporation. So Bishop would wait until called upon to act, whether it be attack or medical assistance.

His chest sagged as his thoughts cleared and body loosened. The rage dissipated. Breathing deep once more, he sensed a change in the air. It warmed as the breeze shifted direction, rolling down from the volcano. The trees creaked and swayed.

He stood, looking at the sky through the treetops, looking for signs of a storm. But the sky was clear and full of stars. Another deep breath caused him to gag. Something foul clung to the air.

Again, the hair on his arm rose, but not from the cold this time. He snatched up his silenced 9mm Heckler & Koch USP, determined to defend the camp without exposing his position. Pulling his night vision goggles over his eyes, the forest came into view as the goggles amplified what little light from the moon and stars filtered through the trees. Crouching low, he worked his way toward the volcano's base. With the air pouring down over the volcano, the rancid odor's origin had to be somewhere at the base of the incline. Given the strength of the smell, he knew it was close by.

Leaves crunched beneath his feet as he moved, pausing every few steps to listen. After another five minutes of cautious advance, a loud snap stopped him in his tracks. The sound had come from beneath his foot, but was markedly louder than the crunch of a leaf or break of a branch. He lifted his foot and looked down. Something white extended out of the dark leaf litter that had concealed it from view as he approached. He swept the leaves away. A human femur.

Bishop stood, raised the 9mm, and continued. The smell quickly became nauseating. He raised an arm over his mouth and nose as he passed through a bush and entered a clearing surrounded by large trees that covered the area with sweeping branches and leaves that concealed the site, and its contents, from above. But standing at ground level, he could see the bodies.

Some, the ones providing the stench, were perhaps days old. Bloated and deformed, their bodies hardly looked human anymore, and the lack of heads revealed how they had been slain—decapitation. But the sheer number of bodies filling the shallow pit, both human and animal, caused Bishop to step back. Manifold was infinitely more dangerous than they had surmised.

He looked down at the mass grave before him. It could have been the handy work of Hitler or Stalin or any number of sick-minded dictators. Fresh corpses lay atop and twisted limbs with the further decayed, who shared space with skeletons. Even in a time of war, acts like this were considered criminal, but this site belonged to a genetics company working on the secret of human regeneration. He wondered, with growing revulsion, what would have become of the world if Hitler's S.S. had been impervious to harm. The beaches of Normandy could never have been stormed. The Third Reich could have taken the world. And it seemed the same ruthlessness would be the birthplace of the world's next military horror. Whoever possessed the technology would rule the battlefield.

Blood fueled by adrenaline surged through Bishop's veins as a rage unlike any he'd felt before took root in his soul. Manifold had to be stopped. The others had to be warned. But as he turned to head back to camp, the sound of approaching voices mixed with the frenzy of a madman filled the air. Bishop dove behind a tree just as the men entered the clearing. As three men shouted to one another over the mindless screams of a fourth Bishop stole a peek around the base of the tree. What he saw through the green vision provided by his night vision erased his rage and replaced it with something he felt very rarely.

Fear.

TWENTY-SEVEN

Tristan da Cunha

"Now just who in the hell are you?" Karn asked, keeping his pistol aimed between King's eyes. "And drop the phony French accent."

"How did you know?" King asked, speaking normally, as commanded.

"I didn't know. Not until I pointed the gun at your head and you didn't even blink."

King smiled and looked at the pistol. It was a M1911A1, .45-caliber automatic pistol that took more than its fair share of lives during the Vietnam War. "You're a veteran. Vietnam."

Karn squinted at him, then gave the pistol an angry stare. He felt King's eyes on his face, inspecting the scars just barely visible beneath the man's thick beard.

"Prisoner of war," King said, doing nothing to hide his new admiration for the man. "How long?"

Karn shook the gun, his eyes wide. "I've got the gun. I'm asking the questions. Now step into the boat and take a seat before someone sees us. And keep your hands where I can see them."

King did as he was told, sitting at the back of the boat, hands in plain sight. Karn stepped into the boat and sat across from him, well out of sight of anyone who might be looking on from town, or, King noticed, from a perch on the volcano. Smart man.

"Is your lady friend on board?"

King shook his head, no.

The man looked skeptical. "I wouldn't want to be surprised and squeeze off a round by accident."

"She's *not* here."

Karn settled down into his seat, relaxing his body, but keeping the gun aimed at King's chest. "Now, tell me who the hell you're working for and what you're doing here?"

"I can't tell you who I work for, but I will tell you why I'm here."

He shrugged. "Figured as much. So spill the beans."

"We're investigating Beta Incorporated."

"Why?"

King mulled over how much to tell the man. "They may have links to terrorist organizations. Beta Incorporated is a dummy corporation for a genetics company named Manifold."

"Never heard of 'em."

"Few people outside the genetics world have."

"So why are you here?"

"I just told you."

The man leaned forward with a grin. "You told me why some U.S. brass sent you here. Don't feed me a 'national security' line, either. I'm a good judge of character, boy, and I can see that weight on your shoulders as clearly as I can see my own dick."

King noticed that Karn had lowered the weapon, probably unknowingly. He could have easily lunged across the deck and killed the man, but decided against it. The rest of this town was tight-lipped, but Karn, aside from being abrasive, might prove to be more than a simple informant. He'd made the same observation about Karn that Karn had about him. They both carried a weight on their shoulder, and both had something to do with the facility glowing bright on the other side of town. For that reason, King decided to be honest with the man.

"They took a friend of mine. Kidnapped him right from under my nose. Killed a bunch of civies in the process. All of them were under my watch. I'm here to find my friend . . . my brother . . . and make them pay for what they did."

"Your brother?"

"My sister's fiancé . . . before she died. He's family."

Karn nodded and placed his gun beside him on the bench. The message was clear: they were no longer enemies. "They have my brother, too."

"They've been kidnapping people from town? Why hasn't anyone complained?"

"They're slicker than that," he said. "The population here . . . it's small. Ain't many choices for who you marry. Inbreeding has been a problem. Not for me, mind you. I'm from the mainland. But for the natives, they're, well, they're all family if you know what I mean. It's made for some medical issues over the years. Deformities. Disease. Immune system mumbo jumbo I can't make sense of. Well, these guys came in and got approval to build that monstrosity of a compound after they offered free medical care to folks who volunteered for their programs. Most in town agreed and signed nondisclosure agreements. I did, too. Seemed like a good thing at the time. A few months back, my brother found a tumor a few inches above his dipstick. Scared the crap out of him. So rather than head to the mainland he signed up as a volunteer. I've heard bubkes from him since. They've ignored all my calls, and when I showed up at their doorstep, those pipsqueak security kids roughed me up. Tasered me and dumped me back in town."

"When was that?"

"Last week."

"They've been locked down tight since that plane flew in a few days ago. Then you showed up. I don't believe in coincidences."

King stood and headed for the cabin. He paused at the door. "How well do you know the facility?"

"With the fish factory burned down, we all needed work. I helped build the damn thing. If you're looking for a way in, there's only one I can think of."

King opened the door to the cabin and motioned with his head for Karn to follow. "You know, I don't believe in coincidence, either."

Karn smiled as he stood and stepped toward the cabin. The weight on both men's shoulders lifted slightly as they recognized the other for an ally with the same goal: rescuing family. When Karn entered the cabin his eyes went wide. He looked at King and with a laugh, said, "I may not believe in coincidence, but I sure as hell believe in God, now." He rubbed his hand over the cool metal of a M224 60mm lightweight mortar. "Thank you, Jesus."

TWENTY-EIGHT

Tristan da Cunha

When Queen set out from the *Mercury* she had three plans of attack to gain entrance to the Beta compound. Her first and the most simple plan was to find an unguarded portion of wall and, using a grappling hook, climb and heave herself over. But fifty yards from the wall, her plan was foiled. A puff of gas revealed a crisscrossing maze of laser tripwires that not even a tightly clad Catherine Zeta-Jones could work her way through. If that wasn't enough, she spotted an array of heat-detecting sensors peering out from the twenty-foot wall like cycloptic guardians. She could have beat the heat sensors using the heat shield folded into a four-inch square inside her cargo pants pocket, but using the shield while working a laser maze would have been impossible without wings. Gen-Y knew what they were doing.

Moving through the darkness, she worked her way around the outer wall, careful to keep a good distance between her and the laser grid. She stopped one hundred yards from the facility's main entrance. A dirt road led up to the fifteen-foot-tall, barbed-wire-topped gates. Guard towers rose up on either side of the gate and spotlights illuminated the area. She was sure an array of motion detectors and heat sensors would detect her approach anyway. Of course, she could always go the old-fashioned route by paying no heed to the sensors, killing the guards, and blowing the gate with C4, but King wanted the subtle approach for now. And she trusted his judgment. So she continued along the facility's outer wall, heading toward the base of the volcano, in search of a chink in the security barrier's armor.

She had hoped the volcano side of the facility wouldn't be walled—who would be foolish enough to enter or exit over such a steep grade—but then she realized that these walls were probably created just as much for keeping mindless monsters *in* as infiltrators out. The twenty-foot wall continued right up and across the incline. For a moment, short of a Trojan horse, she couldn't picture a way inside the technological fortress.

Then she saw it.

A sheer cliff rising fifty feet above the wall that ended at a ledge just large enough for her to stand on. From the ledge, she could descend into the compound without tripping any ground sensors and still be low enough not to appear as a blip on their radar.

After shedding and hiding thirty pounds of equipment that would have come in handy in a variety of other scenarios, but now served no purpose, she stretched and took inventory of her remaining equipment. A Heckler & Koch MK23 handgun with twelve hollow-point .45 ACP rounds, a LAM (laser aiming module), and a sound suppressor were strapped to her hip. She had two spare magazines for the weapon. Over her shoulder she held an UMP submachine gun, a light close-combat weapon that held the same hollow-point rounds as her handgun. But without a sound suppressor, the weapon would be reserved for when the gloves came off. Before then she'd use her most deadly weapons: her hands. She slung the heaviest piece of equipment, a T-PLS pneumatic grappling gun, over her other shoulder and started up the volcano's incline.

She climbed three hundred feet, making sure to avoid any sensors hidden within the crags of the volcanic stone, then cut across the mountainside perpendicular to the wall. She reached the cliff base a few minutes later. She stood two hundred feet away from the wall, but only five vertical feet taller. She looked up at the cliff, searching for handholds and found very few in the moonlight.

As a child, Queen would never have pictured herself looking at a wall like this with the intention of climbing it and throwing herself into an enemy compound. Before her mother died and her father hit the bottle, and her, she'd been a bookworm, and despite her good looks had been teased for her mind. As a result, she'd become timid and fearful, even more so when the beatings began. Over time, one fear after another began to manifest. At first it was obvious things like spiders and mice. But then a fear of heights took root. Elevators, enclosed spaces, lightning, and an array of wild animals joined the list. By the time she lost her son, with her fears exaggerated by LSD, she was more timid than a snowshoe hare. Her boot camp psychologist diagnosed her with an anxiety disorder brought on by mass phobias and past trauma. The psychologist suggested she tackle her fears head on, and quickly, or she'd be sent home. The idea was to hold a spider until she no longer feared spiders. But she discovered, after some experimentation, that she no longer feared spiders after she reached out and crushed one.

In this way she didn't simply conquer her fears, she destroyed them. After completing boot camp successfully, she took up hunting, base jumping, and freehand cliff climbing whenever she had enough leave time. It turned out that the wide range of experience garnered from her extracurricular activities and the outright aggression toward fear-inducing situations helped her excel beyond the standards of her male counterparts. She joined the Army Rangers three years after enlisting. Delta recruited her, the first woman in special ops, one year later when her reputation grew to legendary status among the Rangers. She held her own with the men and used her feminine wiles to disarm them and her fists to pound them into submission. The first man to resist the urge of underestimating her because of her blond locks and perky breasts sparred with her for ten brutal, bloody rounds until Keasling called a stop to the fight. King, still bleeding from his right eye and nose, invited her to join his new team on the spot. Having earned her respect, she agreed.

That had been three years ago, the official banishment of the last vestments of her fears. She was Delta now. Fearless. After chalking her hands she launched onto the wall. She felt for handholds, some barely big enough for her to claw onto with her fingernails, and hauled herself up. Halfway up, she discovered a vertical crack, which she jammed her fingers into with each upward lurch. She covered the fifty vertical feet to the small ledge in fifteen silent minutes without even a grunt of exertion to give away her position.

She squatted on the ledge, looking into the compound from above. A long, four-story building stood at the back of the facility, its roof ten feet below her current elevation. On both sides of the main building were what looked like four water tanks. Beyond lay an open courtyard, an air-control tower, and the outer wall and guard towers. It was all very plain, but one thing did catch her eye that had been obscured by shadow in the satellite photos. A tunnel ran from the back of the main building, through the outer wall, and into the side of the volcano.

Though interesting, the tunnel didn't concern her. It was the facility she was absolutely positive existed beneath the surface of the compound that she needed access to. She unslung the grappling gun and replaced the metal hook with a titanium arrowhead. She took aim at the rooftop of the main building, looking for a suitable target and found it in the tar rooftop itself. She pulled the trigger. The grappling gun coughed as 400psi of compressed

air launched the arrowhead towing a black 7mm Kevlar
line behind it. The arrow struck the tar roof, burying deep
with nothing more than a dull thud. The butt of the gun
held a spring-loaded cam, which she jammed into the crack
she'd climbed and triggered the locking mechanism. Two
serrated "axes" sprang out and bit stone. Designed to stop
a free fall, the cam could hold her weight, plus the rest of
the team's if need be. She wound in the line until it was
tight, clipped on a small, high-velocity trolley, grabbed
on tight, and flung herself out over the cliff without a moment's hesitation.

She glided silently over the wall and sailed toward the
main building's roof. She let go as she cleared the roof,
absorbing the impact first with her ankles, then knees, and
ended in the roll. She made no more noise than a squirrel
might. She lay on her stomach, searching for signs of
alarm, but her approach had gone unnoticed. She crawled
to the vent and began unscrewing the four screws that held
it in place.

A scuff of shoe on tar caught her attention, but she
didn't pause. Whoever it was hadn't sounded an alarm
yet, and time was of the essence. She wasn't concerned.
Whoever the unlucky person was, they were about to
discover that God sometimes does throw lightning bolts
from Heaven.

As the fourth screw came up, she heard the wet pop and
felt the sprinkle of liquid on her back she'd been expecting.
Not God. Knight. And the lightning bolt was actually a
25×59mm armor-piercing round that turned the man's
head into mist.

She spun around and caught the now headless Gen-Y
security guard's body before it could hit the roof with its
full force. It wouldn't be loud, but if there was someone in
the room below, they'd surely hear it. Blood oozed from
the body as Queen returned her attention to the vent. She
pulled the covering off and peered inside.

The smooth corrugated metal of the vent's interior

looked solid enough for her to move through with a good degree of silence, but the barely two-foot-square space would make for a tight fit. Still, there was no other choice. Queen gave a thumbs-up toward the volcano, knowing Knight and Rook would see, and slid into the bowels of Manifold Beta.

TWENTY-NINE

Tristan da Cunha

"You son of a bitch! Don't . . . don't!" The scream that followed was the loudest scream Pierce had let loose since Halloween of 1985 when King scared him by jumping out from behind a tree dressed as Frankenstein's Monster. But this one lasted longer and carried the distinct tone of being pain induced, rather than fear. Though fear was certainly part of it. He could feel the scalpel parting the flesh on his side. He saw the bloody blade as Reinhart brought it away from his body. The pain burned at first, then came in throbbing pulses as his blood seeped from his body. After that, it itched, then ceased. And that terrified him.

"What . . . what did you do to me?" He'd asked the question several times already. They'd been at it for nearly an hour—cutting his body, breaking his bones, pulling out his fingernails. They tortured him, again and again, but there would be no information that could stop the torture, because the results of the cutting and breaking was what they hoped to understand.

"We perfected you," Ridley said from his stool across the room. He sat in his tailored suit, well out of range of the spraying blood, watching like Caesar at the coliseum, entertained by the bloodletting, but separated from the visceral experience. He even wore a surgical mask that kept him from smelling the coppery blood.

Then came the questions from Maddox, who, true to his nature, observed and took notes, but wore a mask of horror and refused to actually take part in the "operations." His previous patients remained unconscious during the regenerative testing. But Pierce was different. They wanted him awake and answering psychological questions after each injury. And since this operation required only the skill to inflict injuries, Reinhart was perfectly suited to the job.

"Do you know what day it is?"

No answer.

"What was the subject of your doctoral dissertation?"

Pierce's jaw muscles bulged as he clenched his mouth shut.

"How do you feel?"

Pierce nearly exploded. "How the hell do you think I'm feeling, asshole!"

Maddox jotted down some notes.

"Am I losing my mind!?" Pierce shouted. "Am I going nuts!?"

"Actually, given the circumstances, you're reacting quite normally."

Pierce fought against his bonds, but couldn't move. They'd stripped him down to his boxers and strapped him to an operating table. His ankles, thighs, waist, wrists, and forehead were all strapped tight. "Then it worked. You can stop."

Maddox opened his mouth to respond, but Reinhart stepped forward. He held a long knife in his hand. "I'm afraid we're not quite finished."

Eyeing the knife, tears filled Pierce's eyes. In the past hour he'd taken more abuse and suffered more pain than he had throughout his entire life. When other people would have mentally checked out, passed out from blood loss, or simply died, his new body kept him awake, alert, and alive. And though he now hoped for death, he couldn't help but beg for mercy. "No . . . You don't need to . . . Please."

"I'm afraid it's quite necessary," Ridley said. "You see, some of our previous subjects did well handling small injuries, much less severe than what you've already endured, mind you. Paper cuts, pinpricks, and the like. But when the injuries became more severe—broken fingers, lacerations, puncture wounds—they descended further into a savage mania with each subsequent injury. You have excelled in the first two categories, but I'm afraid we must also run two more. You see, all of our previous subjects, without exception, became raging lunatics after receiving what should have been a fatal injury. Whether it was their first injury or twentieth, the reaction was the same and instantaneous. Normally, Dr. Maddox here would perform the procedure himself, but as you've seen he doesn't have the stomach for operating on subjects while they're awake."

"And against their will," Maddox added, glaring at Ridley.

"He will thank us when we are done," Ridley said, stepping down from the stool. He walked around the operating table, stepping over pools of blood. "He is the first of his kind."

Pierce knew what was coming next. They were going to kill him. But Ridley said there were two tests remaining. "What's the second test? After you kill me?"

Ridley stopped by the door. He propped it open, ready to exit quickly in case things went wrong. "Decapitation." He nodded to Reinhart.

Before Pierce had a chance to look up or scream, the large knife slid between two ribs and skewered his heart. The ruined organ spasmed. Blood filled the chest cavity. But death did not come. Not instantly.

Pierce could see the knife handle sticking out of his chest, though his mind, overwhelmed by the intensity of the injury, had not yet registered the pain. And as the oxygen in his mind dwindled and his vision faded, it seemed the pain would never strike.

But then it did.

A pain deeper than anything he'd ever imagined gripped his body. He could feel his toes throbbing. His guts ached. His fingers burned. Then he realized, this wasn't pain from the knife wound. This was bigger. More profound.

Death.

Though his vision faded, his consciousness remained intact. For a moment he longed to see the comforting white-lit tunnel so many near-death survivors reported. He would be greeted by a loved one—Julie—and escorted to . . . where? But before any of that could happen, a pain, like an electric jolt, shook his body. He opened his eyes and saw Reinhart pulling the knife up and out of his chest.

Now he screamed.

His body, inside and out, itched severely. And though he could not see it, he could feel it healing. Thirty seconds later, he was hale and pain-free. Alive.

"Hallelujah!" Reinhart said in a mock, TV evangelist voice. "He's been born again!"

"It worked?" Ridley asked, stepping back into the room.

Even Maddox had lost his resistance to the procedure. A smile stretched across his face. "How are you feeling?" he asked, skipping the previous questions.

Though he raged at the obscenities done to him, Pierce couldn't help but be thankful he was still alive. Perhaps there was hope? "I feel fi—"

A new pain gripped him. His muscles tensed as an intense itch tore through his body, as though emanating from the bones out. Through gritted teeth, he said, "Something is happening."

He clenched his eyes as the itch entered and filled his head. When it struck deep in his bowels, he opened his eyes again and looked at Maddox. The man jumped back, slamming into a metal cabinet, his face twisted in fear. He looked up at Reinhart. Then Ridley. "Lock the room down!"

Then he was gone. The sound of a metal door slamming shut and locking followed. But it wasn't the locked door, or Maddox's sudden exit that captured his attention. It was the reflection in the metal cabinet Maddox had fallen into. Something . . . inhuman stared back at him. Though distorted by the dent created by Maddox's fall, he could still make out the green-tinged skin and bright yellow eyes. As the face in the reflection mirrored the expression of abject horror on his own face, he realized the awful truth.

He was the monster.

THIRTY

Tristan da Cunha

The shriek sounded like a combination of a hyena's laugh and fingernails on a chalkboard. Clearly not human. But that's what Bishop found most disturbing; the sound *had* come from a man. Watching from his position behind the tree, Bishop saw three men spaced out around the screaming man at their center. Each man held a six-foot metal pole. Attached to the top of each pole was a loop of metal wire. And the loops were tight around the neck of the man. Tight enough to draw blood.

The man struggled but winced in pain as the wire cut his flesh, drawing fresh blood. Despite the man's savagery, the three uniformed Gen-Y security men handled him with practiced ease.

They'd done this before.

The man was led to the side of the grave. Upon seeing the bodies, his eyes went wide. "Don't!" he shouted. "No, no, no, no."

"They must be making progress," one of the guards said. "They couldn't talk before."

"Sorry, buddy," another said. "You're dead."

The man snarled and slashed at the guard, then paused as he saw all three guards tense. "Please, wait! I—"

A slick slurping sound spilled from the man's neck as all three guards pulled back as one. The three wires, pulled in opposite directions, cut quickly and cleanly through the man's neck. Blood sprayed from the severed neck as the body fell, but the guards, already moving back, avoided the crimson geyser.

"Check for regen," the senior guard ordered.

The other two checked the body and head. "Nothing."

"Same here. This dog is down."

Bishop had seen enough. Even though he wanted to barrel from behind the bushes and put rounds in all three men, that was not his mission. He moved slowly back into the darkness without a sound.

A loud beep sounded from the guards on the other side of the pit, followed quickly by a loud voice. "I've got movement."

"Where?"

"Over there. Locked in and sent to your units. Could be a local. Non-lethals." The man ordered a maneuver next, like a basketball coach calling a play. "Op. Tri. Go."

Bishop quickly realized what the conversation meant. The three guards had portable motion sensors. When he moved, it triggered the device and they locked on to him. Now all three were converging on his position, and if he moved, they'd know it. *Damn their technology,* he thought. He scanned the area with his night vision goggles, looking for movement. With his 9mm up and ready, Bishop stood and pounded for the coast. They would be able to track him, but he wasn't about to be a sitting duck.

"I've got him," a voice shouted.

Bishop took aim in the direction of the voice and squeezed off three silenced rounds. The first two struck wood. The third was rewarded with a shout of pain. But the shot was far from lethal. The fallen man shouted, "He's armed!"

A moment later, the trees around him shattered as an amazing number of bullets burst into the air. His ears had registered six separate gun reports, but the explosion of leaves, bark, and branches revealed many more bullets being fired. *Metal Storm,* he thought.

Leaves crunched and twigs snapped behind him. He could hear metal striking metal, too. The guard behind him was reloading the Metal Storm weapon, changing out barrels instead of switching clips. When he was done a second barrage of bullets would tear through the forest, and if the guard's aim improved, Bishop didn't stand a chance. He looked over his shoulder and saw the dark shape of a guard running behind him, taking aim with a three-barreled handgun.

Three shots rang out as Bishop beat the guard to the punch, placing three rounds in the man's chest. He dropped and slid to a stop. Looking forward again, Bishop found what looked like a striking python streaking toward his face. He tried to duck, but was struck by a solid force that threw him back and slammed his body against a tree. A massive weight continued to press against him. He fought against it, making ground, but then the grip solidified. As though caught in Medusa's gaze, his body became rigid. Stonelike.

"Got him!" one of the guards shouted. The man stepped into view and lit the area with a flare.

Bishop recognized the modified weapon in the man's hand as a sticky foam gun, though the foam had been modified to something resembling quick-dry cement.

The other two men emerged from the forest. One had a blood-soaked shoulder. The other had three dents in his chest where Bishop's 9mm rounds struck his body armor. His night vision goggles were ripped from his head as the three men looked at him. "This the guy Reinhart warned us about?"

"Too big. Skin's too dark."

Bishop looked each man in the eyes, making mental notes about their physical appearance. If he didn't get to kill them later he might be able to I.D. them. That is, if they didn't kill him on the spot.

"Let's take him back. Give him to Ridley."

One of the men leaned in with a sick grin. "Looks like you just volunteered for—"

Dust and chunks of dry foam burst into the air as Bishop's hand shot out and took the man by the throat. He squeezed tight and felt, more than heard, a crunch. The man fell limp before the other two had time to react. Bishop shook as he put his whole body into breaking the rock-hard foam. But before he could break free, a pinch in his neck drained his strength. As he became lethargic he realized he'd been drugged.

As consciousness faded he heard one of the men speaking. "Oh God, John's dead, man!"

He stirred in what felt like seconds later, but was actually ten minutes. He felt the ground beneath his heels as he was dragged through the forest by his arms. He willed his eyes to open, but the drugs fought his body, returning him to unconsciousness.

Again, his mind returned for a moment. He lay on his side now. Felt a hot breeze on his face. He managed to force his eyes open. Lights streamed past, buried in stone. Between the lights—blocks of C4. A moment of clarity put the pieces together—they were passing through the volcano. That's how the men had appeared so quickly in the forest. As his thoughts returned to the C4, his body numbed again. As he slipped into darkness once more, a final thought ran through his mind.

They've rigged the volcano to blow.

Ridley, Reinhart, and Maddox stood outside George Pierce's cell, looking through the five-inch-thick glass window as his body changed. The man's skin had turned green and what looked like scales or calcification had begun to cover his body. His eyes had turned yellow and the pupils were beginning to stretch vertically—oblong, serpentine.

"Well, that's a dismal failure," Ridley said.

Maddox shook his head. "Not at all. His body regenerated. We've narrowed the genes down by a great deal. Further refinement is just a matter of weeding out the other bad genes."

"How long?"

"Weeks. A month, tops. Less if we work around the clock."

"Then you're back with the game plan?"

Maddox looked at George, squelched his guilt, and nodded. "This is too important."

Ridley turned to Reinhart. "Round up a new batch of volunteers. Use force if need be."

"We'll have to cut off contact with the mainland before—"

"Do it. We can't—"

"Sir!" The voice was sharp. Loud. And Reinhart recognized it immediately. David Lawson. One of his best. Lawson stopped, looked at Ridley, then Reinhart, unsure of who to address. He chose Reinhart. "Sir, the island has been infiltrated."

"By whom?"

"Same as before. Delta operator."

"King?"

Lawson shook his head. "We hacked into the Fort Bragg database again and found a match. Intel I.D.s him as Erik Somers. Bishop."

"Bishop?" Ridley said. "Ah, chess pieces. Cute."

"King must be here as well." Reinhart pursed his lips, then turned to Ridley. "There is nowhere for them to go. We have superior numbers and know the terrain. I don't foresee a problem."

"Sir," Lawson looked less sure of himself. "We did a satellite sweep . . ."

"And?"

"And . . . there's a full battle group waiting on the other side of Inaccessible Island. We couldn't I.D. the flagship, but it's clearly U.S. Navy."

Reinhart sighed. "Give us one hour to take out King and his crew."

Ridley met his eyes. "No."

"Sir—"

"Our work is too important to risk! Upload then erase the database. Evacuate the personnel to Alpha." Ridley headed for the exit. He paused before leaving, looking back at the three stunned men. "Release the regens. Let them take care of King and his men." He turned to leave, but paused again. "And while you're at it, destroy the island and do something about that battle group."

THIRTY-ONE

Tristan da Cunha

With a grunt, Queen pushed her body through the tight confines of the ventilation duct. With her arms stretched out in front of her body, she could only pull with her fingers and push with her toes. Given the cramped space it was only the smooth surface of the vent shaft that allowed her to move at all.

For the most part, darkness ruled the vent. Only when the occasional beam of light pierced the darkness where a screw was missing did she have a sense of how quickly she moved. And each time the experience was discouraging. Progress was slow. She moved until reaching a junction, then turned right. At the next she turned left, then right again, determined not to move in circles.

As she began to wonder why there were no vents in the shaft, she felt the floor beneath her hand disappear. Taking the edge of the drop-off in her hands, she pulled herself up to the edge and looked down. A pinprick of light greeted her more than one hundred feet below. She reached out across the drop and felt a bare, cold metal wall.

Only one way to go.

A breeze wafted up the vertical shaft. The air smelled of antiseptic. Like a doctor's office. Or a lab. That sealed the deal. She squirmed forward, leading with her arms until she was hanging over the edge by her waist. She looked down. The drop was a killer, but would take her at least three stories below the bottom floor of the main facility. It was her best shot. Her only shot.

Bracing herself, she squirmed forward, then launched downward like a torpedo exiting a submarine. She spread her arms and legs as her body became fully vertical, careful to only make contact with her cloth-covered forearms, legs, and the rubber soles of her boots. If a hand struck the metal, it might stick and be yanked up. If the arm didn't break, her body could twist within the vent and become lodged like an overweight Santa Claus.

Her arms began to burn as the friction between her arms and the vent wall grew. But her fall slowed only marginally. She pushed hard as the feet flew past. She began to slow as the light below grew in size and lit up the shaft with a dull glow. Forty feet from the bottom, still moving fast, Queen saw vent shafts branching off in either direction, both in the path of her bracing arms and legs. To avoid smashing a limb on the tunnel edges, she bought them close again and freefell past.

Having regained momentum, Queen pushed hard against the walls, making more noise than she cared to as the sudden slow jarred her UMP loose from her back. It smacked against the side of the shaft and scraped loudly—metal on metal—as she continued to fall. With five feet left to descend, Queen planted both hands against the walls and put her muscles to the task of stopping. Her arms bent and protested, but slowed her fall to a stop, inches from the vent. Sweat dripped from her nose, trickling between the slats and striking the dimly lit linoleum floor ten feet below.

As she worked on slowing her breathing, she listened to the sounds of the space below. There was the mechanical twitch of working hard drives and whine of computer cooling fans, but no alarms, shouts of concern, or stomping feet. Still, she wouldn't underestimate her enemy.

Bracing her feet against the walls, she removed her hands and placed them on the grate. She shoved. The grate stayed in place, but shook. Its hold on the duct was precarious at best. She shoved again, this time letting her feet go and put her weight into it. With a crack, the hinged grate swung open.

As she fell, Queen snapped her head up, spinning her body beneath her. At the same time she reached behind her back. She landed, ten feet below, in a crouch. A red dot of light from her silenced handgun's LAM shot back and forth across the room as she searched for a target. Finding none, she stayed silent and still, taking in the room. The space was massive and filled with an array of computer stations, laboratory equipment, and several long examination tables. Looking up she saw the vent she'd fallen through twenty feet up, in the ceiling. Across one wall she saw four large containers marked with warning symbols and the words "liquid nitrogen."

Stupid.

She spotted two security cameras at either end of the room. Luckily, neither was pointed in her direction, though both were headed her way. She jumped up, slapped the vent shut, then ducked beneath a desk. She watched as the cameras passed her position and then swung the other way.

She spied a discarded lab coat, slipped out from under the desk and threw it on over her black fatigues. She removed the black covering from her head, twisted her hair into a conservative-looking ponytail, donned a pair of phony glasses and clipped a Manifold I.D. card to her shirt that might fool one of the scientists but would certainly alert security to her scam. With the lab dark and the time passing midnight, Queen had the lab to herself. She sat down at a computer terminal hoping to look like just another scientist working late, and took hold of the mouse. The screen blinked to life, casting her in a sickly blue glow. The cameras would see her now.

A prompt appeared on the screen, asking for a password, which could be a problem if someone was watching the video feed. She tried the most common password used on computer boot screens—none—hitting the Enter key. She smiled as the operating system booted and displayed a variety of folders, icons, and files on the cluttered desktop. But none of that mattered to her. The terminal was just a gateway for the little gem Lewis Aleman had provided the team with before leaving. "Hacker in a bottle" he had called it; a worm that sought out information on predetermined search patterns, slipping past security and erasing all traces of its existence along the way. Queen plugged the small device into the computer's USB port and with a feigned yawn of an overworked scientist began opening random files on the screen, giving the impression that she was hard at work.

An image appeared on the screen and made her pause. Spread out on a table was what looked like a serpentine head. Standing behind it was a man she recognized from photos King had shown her: George Pierce. He looked fine. In fact, he was smiling. Then she recognized the background. The photo had been taken in this very lab. Pierce had been here. Possibly still was. Queen stood and looked over the lab. She saw the lab table from the photo at the center of the room. But the table was as empty as the lab was devoid of life. *Why was that?* she wondered. If they were so close to a staggering discovery, why were they not working around the clock?

As the doors at the far end of the lab burst open with a sound like thunder, she realized why.

THIRTY-TWO

Tristan da Cunha

"Rook to King. Come in King."

Dressed in fatigues, now covered by a black wet suit, King walked across the *Mercury*'s cabin, heading for the radio. He and Karn had taken the *Mercury* around the island and dropped anchor just outside what Karn claimed was a submarine dock. To King it looked like every other slab of rock descending into the ocean, but the old man insisted they'd blasted out a hole big enough for only one thing he could think of: a sub. King picked up the radio. "Go ahead, Rook."

"Things are going to hell fast, King. We've got a mass exodus taking place from the back side of the compound. Looks like scientists and some security. They're skipping town."

Shit, King thought. *How did they know we were here?*

"It gets worse," Rook said. "Bishop is M.I.A. He should have checked in a half hour ago."

"What about Queen?" King asked.

"She's still inside. Haven't seen any sign of— What?"

King heard Knight talking quickly in the background. The signal cut out for a moment, then Rook returned.

"King, we're counting fifteen . . . eighteen people exiting the front of the compound, heading for the main gates and . . . holy . . . King, these people, they're like the capybara. Regens. If they get to town . . ."

King closed his eyes and shook his head. He knew the people had no control of themselves, that they were, in fact, innocents. But letting them live meant the deaths of hundreds more. "Take them out. Protect the town. I'm going in."

King dropped the radio and exited the cabin. He walked to the back of the boat where Karn waited.

"What's got your panties in a bind?" Karn asked.

King held a small, handheld oxygen tank with a regulator attached to his mouth, taking a test breath. The small tank would give him five minutes underwater. "Take the *Mercury* back to the dock. Use anything you find on board to protect the town. I've got some friends that will lend a hand. And see if you can raise the USS *Grant*. Tell them to keep that plane on the ground, but under no circumstances shoot it down."

Karn stared at him, wide-eyed for a moment and then gave a quick salute. He immediately began pulling up the anchor. He turned around to ask a question but King had already entered the water. His swim fins slid beneath the waves as he descended into the depths.

With the anchor up, Karn sat himself in the captain's chair, turned the key, and smiled as the dual engines roared to life. He slammed the throttles forward, launching the yacht forward as though it were a speed boat. "Cavalry's coming!"

He picked up the boat's CB as the *Mercury* pounded over the waves. "USS *Grant*. This is the yacht *Mercury*. Please respond. Over."

No response. "Damnit, *Grant*. I know you're out there! Pick up the line or so help me, I'll sink you myself."

A cold voice came back from the CB, "This is the USS *Grant*. Who the hell am I talking to? Over."

"Gunnery Sergeant Jon Karn, U.S. Marine Corps," he said, then added, under his breath, "Retired. Over."

"Say again. Did you say retired? Over."

A large wave nearly threw him from the chair. He gripped the steering wheel hard with one hand and raised the CB to his lips with the other. "There isn't time for bullshit! I'm working with a fella. Goes by the name King. He needs some help."

Karn waited for a response as he turned the *Mercury* toward the lights of Edinburgh. This time the silence lasted fifteen seconds. He was about to speak again when a new voice came on the line. "This is Captain Steve Savile of the USS *Grant*. What do you need?"

He laughed as the *Mercury* pounded through another large wave, casting a spray of seawater over the deck, plastering Karn's gangly hair and beard against his head and chest. *I'll be damned,* he thought. For a moment it felt good to be back in the thick of things. Then he saw muzzle flashes from the mountainside, like distant fireworks and the rising of panicked voices from Edinburgh.

He opened his mouth to respond, but a sudden series of rapid-fire explosions pounded the air. Rising toward the sky were thousands upon thousands of large tracer rounds. He knew the rounds, designed to be seen, showed the path of even more rounds hidden by the night sky. In all his time in the service he'd never seen such a condensed and massive amount of shells being fired. It seemed impossible. He took note of their southwestern trajectory. The only thing there was Inaccessible Island . . . unless something was behind it.

He crushed down the button on the CB. "Savile! Move your ass! You have incoming!"

He listened for a response, but only heard the distant sound of explosions.

THIRTY-THREE

Tristan da Cunha

Frothing mad, seven regens, both men and women, burst into the large laboratory. Queen ducked behind a workstation and watched as the mindless group snapped at each other like a pack of wild dogs. One caught the arm of another and bit a chunk free. The flesh healed immediately, but the injured regen reacted violently, tackling the other in a bloody frenzy.

Queen crawled toward the workstation that held her thumb drive and Aleman's virus. She had no idea if it had time to do its work, but time was up. If she wanted to leave alive it had to be now.

The battling regens rolled across the linoleum floor, leaving streaks of liquid red as they tore one another apart, healing time after time, descending deeper into madness. The pair fell into a computer terminal, shaking the hibernating machine. The screen blinked to life and played a start-up chime. The sudden light and sound startled the regens and without pause, the group flung themselves at the computer, treating its actions as a sign of life and, therefore, food.

Monitors flew through the air after proving too tough to bite through. Wires snapped and fell to the floor like disemboweled entrails. All the while, the regens worked their way across the lab, headed straight for Queen. She reached up over the desktop and felt for the thumb drive. She found the front of the computer tower and the thumb drive attached below. She grabbed on tight and yanked.

The device removal chime sounded like a gunshot.

Queen held her breath as the regens stopped and listened. In that moment, she knew she wouldn't leave the room without a fight. Never one to take the first blow, Queen unslung her weapon and stood up. As the closest regen's eyes widened, its head ceased to exist. Queen placed three hollow-tip rounds between the eyes of a second. But her luck ran out when she aimed at the third.

The five remaining regens sprang into action, tossing tables and equipment at Queen as they made their way toward her. She realized with horror, that the regens weren't completely mindless. They understood the danger of bullets and were doing their best to avoid them. Queen backed up a small staircase that led to an exit. But with the combination of not knowing where the exit led and knowing the regens would give chase she decided to make her stand here.

She let loose with several volleys of bullets, catching a shoulder here, a leg there, slowing them down, but far from stopping them. With fifty feet between them, she took note of the four large cylinders attached to the wall. They might understand the danger of bullets, but she doubted they could comprehend the danger of the liquid nitrogen stored above them.

She let five more rounds fly after ducking a flat-screen computer monitor flung at her head like an Olympic discus. She struck the regen that threw it in both legs, sending it to the ground. Then she yanked out her weapon's magazine and slammed in a new one. Adjusting her aim, she unloaded the full magazine on the four containers of liquid nitrogen.

As rounds struck the first container it rang with a hollow gong.

Empty.

One of the regens lunged forward, no longer fearing being shot.

Queen drew her handgun with her left hand while she shifted the submachine gun's aim to the next three containers, sweeping back and forth across all three. She squeezed the handgun's trigger as the regen, a balding man with a scruffy beard, reached out for her. The hollow-point bullets made short work of the man's head.

The bullets striking the liquid nitrogen tanks sounded as dull thuds. As the report of her weapon ended with an empty magazine, a violent hiss filled the air as the compressed liquid nitrogen sprayed through the quarter-sized holes.

Writhing in agony, the four remaining regens became drenched in liquid nitrogen, their bodies instantly freezing where struck.

Queen turned to flee before a jet of the quick freeze liquid struck her. Unlike the regens, she could not heal from such a wound. She slung her weapon over her back and stepped toward the door, but found her legs suddenly pulled out from under her. She struck the hard floor with a grunt, losing her sidearm in the process. She rolled over quick and found a legless regen, a woman this time, pretty once, now snarling and covered in blood, pulling itself up her pants legs and eyeing her stomach where a feast of entrails awaited.

On her back, Queen couldn't reach her weapon, which held an empty magazine anyway, and her sidearm was well out of reach. She could feel the regen's nails digging into her leg as it pulled itself up. The regen let out a roar, opened its mouth wide, and, despite Queen's kicking, made a lunge at her stomach.

The regen's teeth stopped an inch above Queen's stomach where she had no doubt it would have made short work of her clothing and flesh. Even the Kevlar vest would do little to stop the regen after it realized the bulletproof garment could be lifted away. With shaking arms, she pulled the regen's head away from her stomach, pulling it by the thick shocks of hair she'd caught in both hands. But it fought her the whole way using strength born of madness and adrenaline.

The mad woman lashed out, striking Queen's arms, slicing gashes into the flesh. Queen screamed in anger, not pain, then gave a yank on the woman's hair that pulled her up and away for only a moment. But it was all Queen needed to slip her legs out from beneath the regen's body and kick hard.

The woman toppled, legless, down the stairs and splashed into a pool of steaming liquid nitrogen. With the majority of her body frozen, she snarled and bit at the air, still trying to get at Queen.

Queen stood, walked to her handgun, and took aim at the woman. "I'm sorry," she said. "You probably didn't deserve this." She fired once, shattering the woman's skull and sending brain matter into the liquid nitrogen where it turned solid and floated like ice cubes in a drink. She fired three more times, dispatching the other three frozen human experiments. Then, as liquid nitrogen began to lap at the top stair, she exited the lab and headed into the unknown depths of Manifold Beta.

Screams rang out in the distance. Gunshots, too. But there was no way to know where she was. Ahead, a light pouring from two windows set into double doors glowed bright in the darkened hallway. With no other direction to go, she headed for the doors hoping not to find more regens or walk into a Gen-Y trap. She prepped her weapon, switching out the magazine with her last, kicked in the doors and gasped.

Strapped to a table at the center of a small lab was the last person she expected to find inside the Beta facility. He opened his eyes and looked at her. "Queen," he said. "Get the hell out of here."

"Not without you, Bish," she said, then pulled out a knife and began cutting through the restraints.

"You don't understand," he said, then his head turned toward the door and his eyes went wide. "Queen! Look out!"

She spun and squeezed her weapon's trigger. A spray of bullets cut across the chest of a regen man. The impact sent him to the floor, but he began scrambling to his feet as though he'd merely tripped. Queen took aim and fired three rounds, destroying his skull, and brain. He fell to the floor, dead for good.

"You don't have time, Queen," Bishop said again, his teeth clenched.

She ignored him and cut his other arm free. But before she could cut his legs free an impact from behind sent her sailing across the room. She rolled with the impact on the floor and managed to get back to her feet just before the regen, a woman this time, leaped at her. Queen fired the weapon, striking the woman's leg, but the regen's forward momentum wasn't stopped.

Queen let go of her weapon and reached up with both hands, catching the forearms of the regen woman before she could slash out. The woman pushed forward, allowing her arms to be bent back. She snapped at Queen's face with her teeth. Over and over, aiming for Queen's nose.

Feeling the woman's muscles tear as she bent her arms back, farther then physically possible, Queen realized the woman would eventually reach her. But she couldn't let go of her arms to stop the woman's face . . . and while a head butt to the face would normally end this match, it would only send the regen into a deeper mania. With the woman's blood-tinged breath filling her nose and mouth, Queen screamed in frustration.

Then she felt the woman torn away. The regen sailed across the room and crashed into a wall.

Bishop stood between them, clutching the knife. He'd set himself free.

Queen quickly grabbed the UMP and took aim, but Bishop stood in the way. "Bishop, move!"

The regen stood.

Then charged.

As did Bishop.

They met in the middle of the room. Bishop ducked beneath the woman's slashing hand and struck up with the knife. The blade entered the woman's chin and entered the brain, pinning the woman's snapping jaws shut. Bishop continued the motion, picking the woman up off the ground, holding only the knife hilt, then smashed her back onto the floor. He was on top of her in an instant, launching punches with his fists like a jackhammer. He stopped when the woman's legs finished kicking.

Queen stood, dazed. She'd never seen Bishop kill someone in hand-to-hand combat. It was brutal on a level she never pictured him capable of. She walked to him as he breathed heavily and placed a hand on his shoulder. He spun around with rage in his eyes.

She fought the urge to move away from him. "You did good, Bish."

He calmed. Looked back at the woman and shook his head. "How can this be good?"

Queen saw him look down at his hands, which she could not see. He shook his head again. When she leaned over to see what had captured his attention she saw his fists covered in blood, but not a scratch on him. The blood belonged to the regen. She wasn't sure what bothered him about it. They all had blood on their hands, usually figuratively, but they'd all killed, Bishop as much as the rest.

He stood and headed for the exit. Queen took one last look at the regen's smashed head and then followed him into the hallway where screams echoed from every corner of the complex.

THIRTY-FOUR

Tristan da Cunha

The only thing King could see through the pitch dark water within the man-made cave was a faint light in the distance. So, like a moth to a flame, he followed it blindly and without slowing or caution. There wasn't time for either. But when the light blinked out, he paused, hovering in the water.

The light extinguishing wasn't what bothered him. It was the way it had disappeared, as though something large had risen from below, blocking the light with its girth. Fighting visions of sharks and giant squid, King started in the direction the light once was. Then paused again. This time for only an instant as he felt a pressure wave moving through the water. He kicked up hard, not knowing where the cave ceiling was, but preferring a collision at his top speed over one with something big enough to create a pressure wave.

The massive object silently passed just beneath him, grazing his swim fins and sending him into a spin. As he careened in the water, King lost all sense of direction. Then he struck a wall, or was it the ceiling? His shoulder ached from the collision. As the object passed, its wake pulled him out, away from the wall, and spun him in the water again. He realized whatever it was had been huge. He frowned as he drew a breath from the handheld regulator. He could normally count on his skills to keep him alive, but this time it had been dumb luck that kept him from becoming underwater roadkill.

With the light in view once more, King kicked toward it with renewed determination—not to complete the mission but to get out of the water before that thing decided to come back or another took its place.

He was soon rewarded as he approached the underwater light mounted to the cave wall next to a ladder that rose out of the water. He shed his fins and small oxygen tank, clasped the ladder, and poked his head out of the water. Upon looking at the cave, he realized how lucky he had been. Old Karn was right. This was a submarine hangar. He'd come within feet of being a stain on the front hull of a submarine.

King climbed the ladder and looked over the cement chamber. Whoever had been here left with the sub. Manifold was clearing out. His gut told him they should do likewise. He'd seen what remained of Manifold Gamma in Peru and doubted that Ridley would allow the secret of this facility to fall into their hands as well. But until he knew Pierce had been taken with them, he wouldn't leave, even if that meant searching every room in the compound, fire or no fire. He had to know.

After removing his wet suit, King opened a solid metal door and ran through a long cement hallway that he guessed ran beneath the airstrip and into the compound. The walls shook as several rapid-fire rumbles sounded from above. He'd never heard anything like it, but his gut told him it was some kind of weapon being fired. Then a different sound filled the tunnel, a deep roar followed by the painful shriek of a 747's engines whining. The plane was taking off. He sprinted toward a second metal door at the end of the hallway, enraged that Ridley, Gen-Y, and Manifold were slipping through his fingers yet again.

With a quick yank, he unlatched the door and, leading with his SOPMOD M4 carbine decked out with a sound suppressor, laser sight, and M203 grenade launcher, stepped out into the brightly lit outer courtyard of the Beta facility. He ducked down as five regens charged out of the front doors of the main building and pounded toward town, shrieking all the way.

He stepped into the open, heading for the doors when two loud reports, like a chain saw being gunned, blasted the air. Falling back, King watched as thousands of shells flew into the air in a three-second burst. This was the source of the rumbling he'd heard in the tunnel. The rounds flew from four massive Metal Storm launchers that could be used to defend against air and sea attacks, including missiles. He grimaced as he realized they'd been hiding inside what they'd thought was four water tanks. Gen-Y had outsmarted and outgunned them. As the glowing tracer rounds flew into the distance and began arcing down, King tensed.

The Grant . . .

Pierce would have to wait after all. With nearly five thousand souls on the *Grant* alone, not to mention the rest of the battle group, the needs of the many severely outweighed the needs of the few. King took aim, and pulled the second trigger of his weapon. The grenade struck the Metal Storm weapon, obliterating it in a blaze of fire and kinetic force. He quickly launched three more after reloading each round, the last striking as a new barrage flew from the final weapon. The tower tipped as the weapon fired and its thousands of rounds punched into the side of the facility, shredding the top three floors of the main building. King prayed Pierce wasn't being held there and ran toward the main doors, ignoring the possibility that the building might collapse from the damage the Metal Storm weapon caused.

Two regens shrieked at him from the darkened doorway, but he didn't slow. He put a bead of red between each of their eyes and with perfect accuracy, let loose with two three-round bursts. The two mindless, now headless, men dropped to the floor.

King entered the facility and found himself facing five hallways, two elevators, and a wide set of stairs. Under other circumstances, he might have hesitated to decide which way to go, but the long, streaked trail of blood leading to and down the stairs was like a giant blinking road sign saying: *this way.* He took the stairs two at a time, descending the flights of stairs, passing several exits but sticking with the bloody trail, sure it would lead to the labs . . . and, hopefully, Pierce.

The blood trail led to the bottom floor, six flights below the surface of Tristan da Cunha; hidden from the world. He pushed the door open and was immediately greeted by screams of anger, both men and woman mixed with shrieks, roars, and the sound of equipment being thrashed.

Moving slowly now, he made his way toward the noise, stopping at a pair of solid metal doors streaked with blood. Using his sleeve he wiped a swatch of the drying plasma away from the door's small square window and peeked through. He recognized the space on the other side. A containment facility like the one in the video, probably identical to the one in the destroyed Gamma facility. This is where they kept the regens . . . and every door on the two levels, fifty in all, lay wide open.

But the room itself held little interest to him. It was the action on the left side, just outside one of the cells. Three regens were hacking, slashing, and gnawing at something hidden from sight. At first he though it was a human victim, but one of the regens was flung across the room. Whoever . . . or whatever . . . stood behind them was fighting back. How that was possible, King had no idea, but when a second regen flew across the room and crashed against the door, its slashed face plastered against the glass window, King knew it wasn't human. Not anymore at least.

King watched as the tossed regens pressed the attack again. What looked like a green hand flew out and caught one in the neck, lopping its head clean off. The second was grabbed and tossed. And the third fell to the floor under a crushing blow to the head.

"Oh God . . ." King said when he saw the creature standing there. It had clearly once been human as it stood on two legs, had two arms, fingers, and a head of hair, but its yellow serpentine eyes, green scaly skin, sharp teeth, and long claws was more monster than human. It wasn't a regen. It was something else.

Something new.

The green creature stomped its foot on the fallen regen's head several times, crushing it to the consistency of chunky peanut butter. Then it turned to the last one, which was just regaining its feet. King noticed that the creature didn't move with the frenzy of a regen. It wasn't killing out of uncontrollable savagery. It was killing with intent. It was intelligent. With a sudden strike, the creature slashed the regen's throat, took hold of the hair on the crazed man's head, and pulled back. Sinews snapped and blood sprayed as the spinal column came apart. The head came free from the body as it fell to the ground, lifeless like the others.

Then the creature wavered. It fell to one knee as several red slashes and bite marks on its skin healed up.

As it fell to one knee, holding its head, King saw his chance to put it down before it could kill anyone. Clearly, it was far more dangerous than a regen. He walked silently into the room, approaching the creature from behind. He realized as he approached that he didn't know if a head shot would do the trick on this creature.

As it fell to the floor, apparently in pain, it began tracing its finger on the floor. It drew a circle in blood, through which it drew two straight lines.

The creature stopped drawing as King took aim. It sensed him somehow. But he didn't pull the trigger. He could see it wouldn't be moving anywhere fast. Was it dying? As it turned over to face him, he could see the pain in its serpentine eyes. It posed no threat. As it looked up at King, its eyes watered and looked pitifully sad. With the last of its energy sapped, the creature closed its eyes, but managed to speak.

"Agustina Gallo," it said, then fell limp.

King didn't recognize the name, but the voice hit him like a .45-caliber round to the heart. "Oh God, George!"

THIRTY-FIVE

Tristan da Cunha

The settlement of Edinburgh leaped out of the darkness as Knight looked through the night vision site of his sniper rifle. From his perch high above the town, he shifted his view from target to target, but through the green-tinged sight it was nearly impossible to tell human from regen. A few he pegged as regens because of the way they loped through town, but the others, mixed in with fleeing, panicked townspeople, couldn't be discerned until they pounced on a victim. And by then, it was usually too late.

He willed Rook to hurry. He could only defend so many people at a distance. Rook would be able to help people up close and personal.

Knight shifted his view as movement caught his eye. A man stood on the roof of a home, swaying back and forth. But was he hiding or stalking? With the facial expressions of mania and abject fear being so similar through the lens, he couldn't tell.

A woman burst from the door and made for the dirt road.

The man leaped.

Regen.

Knight mentally anticipated the man's arch through

the air and fired. The 25mm armor-piercing round struck the regen's neck and severed his head. The body struck the ground behind the woman, startling her. She turned and jumped back as the head rolled by her feet. Then she stopped, put her hands to her mouth, and screamed. Then she fell to her knees and hugged the headless body.

She knew the man.

For a moment Knight wished to be somewhere else, but a second regen emerged from the darkness and kept his mind from escaping the horrors below. He fired twice. The first shot took off the regen's arm. The second, its head. The body fell to the side revealing the woman, torn apart. Dead.

Knight grimaced. He knew a losing battle when he saw one.

"Rook, what's your status?" he said into his throat mike.

"Almost . . . in town," Rook's out-of-breath voice came back. He'd run straight down the mountainside to duke it out in the thick of it, where he preferred to be. But Knight could see even that would do no good. They had to leave the island, and fast.

"I'm on my way down," Knight said. "We need to evac. Will cover as possible on the way."

"Copy that, little man."

Knight took aim, fired a head shot, and then picked himself off the ground. Holding his rifle in both hands, he ran for town, hoping to find the *Mercury* prepped for a quick exit.

Rook leaped a small white picket fence, a remnant of the visions of grandeur the settlers here had for the island, and entered a stretch of road that ran parallel to the ocean. He could hear screams farther in town, but the growing volume of voices told him the action was heading in his direction . . . which was the plan. He intended on becoming a one-man wall, keeping the regens at bay while the locals took to the ocean at the dock.

Rook continued running down the side street, heading for the main drag that lead up from the dock, through town, and all the way to the Manifold facility. As he entered the main street two women nearly bowled him over. Nearly as mindless as the once-men-now-monsters chasing them, they ran past squealing like injured hyenas. Rook shook his head. It always amazed him how, when faced with a violent death, people reverted back to an almost animal-like state. He wondered if that's what drove the regens mad, being pushed to that near-death state over and over until the mind could no longer function outside of it.

He had little time to ponder the idea as the screams rolled downhill. With the main drag lit by a row of bright, Manifold-installed streetlights, he had no need for his night vision goggles, which was just as well because he could more easily pick out the bad guys—they were the ones covered in blood, but still running.

Kneeling to one knee, Rook raised his assault rifle to his shoulder, peered through the scope, and began firing quick, three-round bursts. The locals ducked their heads, as he knew they would, but continued forward, toward the gunfire, somehow intuiting that the bullets were not intended for them. Either that or a death by bullet was preferable to being eaten alive.

"Shake a leg, people," Rook shouted between shots. With his aim so obscured by civilians, Rook could only slow the advancing regens. He was lucky to get a good body shot, never mind a head shot. Despite his efforts, civilians continued to fall. As the main group of locals passed by, thirty people out of the original two hundred seventy-one, he lost sight of the regens.

The group spread around him and passed in seconds. The road ahead lay empty save for a few injured stragglers, which the regens quickly turned on as they healed from the bullet wounds inflicted by Rook. He quickly counted their numbers.

Twenty-seven.

Damn.

Twenty-seven charging normal people would be hard enough to defend against, even unarmed. But these things . . . they could heal like the *X-Men*'s Wolverine on speed.

Rook unleashed with a blaze of gunfire until the magazine was exhausted. Several of the regens lay on the ground, injured, but healing. Remembering the capybara, he took aim at three of the injured regens and pulled the second trigger on this weapon, launching a 40mm grenade. The blast shredded the three injured regens and pocked two more with shrapnel. Rook fired three more grenades as quick as possible, only stopping to reload each round, turning the street one hundred feet away into a crater-filled inferno.

As the road smoldered and smoke rose into the night air, Rook could see movement within, but was unable to tell how many had been dispatched. He replaced the assault rifle's magazine and squeezed the trigger. Bullets flew into the haze, but there was no way of knowing if he was making a difference. As the bullets blazed, a splash of sticky wet liquid struck his face. Blood.

He flinched back, turned, and fired, riddling a headless body with bullets. The body fell back under the force of the bullets. Rook wiped the man's blood from his face. "I owe you one, Knight."

"Almost in town," Knight responded.

A shuffle of stones brought Rook's attention back to the smoldering road. Nineteen regens emerged from the smoke. Open wounds stretched together, linked, and sealed. Within seconds, each and every one of them was hale again. They ran for Rook.

"Better hurry!"

He unloaded the last few rounds from the assault rifle, dropping one of the regens, but there was no time to reload. He dropped the rifle on the ground and drew his two specially made, brushed chrome .50 Action Express Desert Eagles from holsters under each arm. If not for the wrist guards he wore, which locked the guns and his wrists into place, he would never have been able to fire the weapons, which packed enough recoil to snap a wrist. They could punch a basketball-sized hole in anything made of flesh and blood, but each weapon only carried seven rounds. Fourteen rounds total . . . eighteen regens. And he doubted he'd get a chance to reload.

The group charged as the fleeing townspeople reached the dock and began launching boats. They headed straight for Rook.

Aiming carefully, Rook began firing. Three regens dropped, two headless, one missing the better part of its chest. More fell, but not from lethal wounds . . . not for regens anyway.

Another lost its head from the side as Knight came up beside him.

"I never liked the Alamo story," Knight said, squeezing off another perfectly aimed shot.

"Me neither." Click, click. "I'm out." He holstered both weapons, not willing to part with either, and drew his long KA-BAR blade. Thirteen regens continued forward, frothing, growling, savage. Some were still healing from gaping wounds opened by Rook's Desert Eagle. They closed within fifty feet, picking up speed.

Then a grenade clunked to the ground at the center of the group. They paused to look at it.

"The stupid bastards are dumb as shit!" a voice shouted from behind. They turned and saw Jon Karn, loaded with guns and ammo. "Haul your asses back to the yacht. I'll cover you."

Rook opened his mouth to argue, then saw the weapon in the man's hands and thought better of it. Karn held a M134 Minigun mounted on a heavy-duty tripod. The weapon was impossible to wield as a handheld weapon, despite its popular use in movies, but Karn seemed to know that. He kicked open the tripod, knelt down, and fired three bolts into the town's only paved road, locking the tripod down. He stood, pulled the trigger, and as the barrel of the gun began spinning, shouted, "I said move! This is my town. I'll defend it!"

The minigun spat bullets at a rate of four thousand rounds per minute. The first regen struck was split in two from crotch to head.

Listening to the man, Rook and Knight bolted for the *Mercury,* intent on rearming and returning to the fight. As they approached the dock they could clearly see the surviving townspeople powering out to sea on an array of small ships. The *Mercury* and a fishing boat named *Susie-Q* were the only ships remaining. The wood of the dock echoed under their boots, both men stopped short of the *Mercury.* The minigun had stopped firing.

They turned to find Karn falling beneath the weight of two regens who had tackled him from the side. Knight took aim as Karn's screams came to an abrupt stop and a pool of blood slid out over pavement. Knight dropped both regens with a single well-placed round. He lowered the rifle and shook his head.

Rook nudged his shoulder and nodded toward the top of the hill. A horde of regens plunged toward town like an army. "Let's move."

Knight hopped into the boat, while Rook tossed the tie lines in. The dual engines roared to life as Rook climbed in. He reloaded his twin Desert Eagles and began looking for more weapons on the heavily armed yacht. They couldn't stay in town, but they wouldn't be leaving. Not with three members of the team M.I.A.

Better we all die together, Rook thought.

THIRTY-SIX

Tristan da Cunha

Ignoring the potential threat from rampaging regens, King heaved the green, scaly George Pierce over his shoulder and made for the stairs, leading with his handgun. He couldn't believe the state of his friend. And though he tried not to think about what Pierce had become, he couldn't shake the feeling that it was his fault. But at his core he knew it wasn't. It was Richard Ridley and Manifold that ultimately had to answer for what had happened to his friend. Without their actions none of this would be happening, and Pierce would still be . . . human.

King kicked the staircase door open. Shadows shifted on the flight above. He could hear flesh rending from bones and more than one voice moaning in pleasure from the feast. He backed out of the stairway, not wanting to tempt fate by engaging undying enemies with Pierce on his shoulder. His aim, balance, and speed would be off.

A sign at the end of the hallway pointed to the elevators. If they still worked, they might be the only way back up. After a quick run, he rounded the corner to the elevators and slid to a stop, the barrel of an UMP pressed against his forehead.

"Shit, King, I nearly took your head off," Queen said, lowering her aim.

King immediately noticed Bishop standing next to Queen, leaning against the wall. "Bishop?"

"Captured. End of story." Bishop said, then pointed to Pierce. "Who's this?"

King turned to the side, revealing Pierce's scaled face. "George. They did . . . something to him."

Bishop frowned and shook his head in disbelief.

An explosion shook the floors above. King pushed the elevator's call button.

"Elevator crapped out," Queen said. "We need to take the stairs."

"They're occupied."

"Not for long," she said, moving around the corner, weapon raised.

"Let me take him," Bishop said. "I'm stronger."

King noticed Bishop's forehead covered in perspiration. He couldn't remember ever seeing Bishop sweat, even in hot and humid weather. The man's body seemed built to handle high temperatures, but now . . . "You don't look so well."

"Damnit, King." Bishop pulled Pierce from his shoulder and hoisted him up and over his own, handling Pierce's weight as though he were nothing more than a small child. "I'm fine."

A staccato of gunfire ripped down the hallway, followed by Queen's voice. "Clear!"

King didn't like that Bishop had so brazenly taken Pierce, not because he was wrong to do so—he was stronger . . . a lot stronger—but first, the forceful approach was out of character, and second, Pierce was his burden to bear. But he couldn't argue with the fact that Bishop carrying Pierce made sense. "Let's go."

The group ran up the stairwell, avoiding slippery pools of blood along the way. As King took in deep breaths he couldn't tell which was better, breathing through his nose and smelling the thick coppery odor of blood, or breathing through his mouth and tasting it. As they reached the top floor, a series of explosions shook from below.

The place was coming apart.

"Go, go, go!" King shouted as he ran for the open exit. He hopped over the two headless regens he'd shot when he entered and stepped into the courtyard. A series of booms grew louder. Closer.

"Get down!" Bishop shouted, realizing the main building was next in line to be blown apart. He opened his arms and scooped King and Queen into a great bear hug, falling to the ground on top of them and Pierce.

A massive explosion shook the ground and burst the windows on the remaining floors of the main building. Then, with its foundation liquefied, it imploded, shooting out glass and metal shrapnel. Bishop grunted as the debris struck his back.

Muffled explosions continued to sound out in the distance, but the courtyard grew still. Bishop pushed himself up off the others, jaw clenched in pain. He fell to the side, unable to walk.

Queen rolled up and knelt beside him. "You dumb son of a bitch. Why'd you do that?"

"I'll live." He pushed himself up, tore off his shredded shirt and then his flak jacket. Glass and debris clung to it, some pierced all the way through. Bishop inspected it. So did Queen.

She looked at Bishop's back. "You been saying your prayers, Bish? You didn't get a scratch."

Bishop had his eyes clenched shut tight. His eyelids twitched like he was reliving a bad dream. Then he stopped, opened his eyes, took a deep breath, and said, "If God is looking out for me it's not because of anything I've done."

A boom that put the destruction of the main building to shame rocked the entire island. It was followed by a bright orange glow from above. King looked toward the noise and found an unreal sight. Gouts of bright orange lava spewed from the cone of Tristan da Cunha's volcano. A plume of ash rose up and mushroomed in the sky above the island. Rivers of magma poured from fresh blast holes on the side of the volcano, flowing hot and fast. Pyriphlegethon, the mythological river of lava, had been unleashed on earth.

That is their exit strategy, King thought. *The total destruction of the island.*

King could tell by the speed and direction of the flowing lava that the Manifold facility and the whole of Edinburgh would soon be wiped out. Erased from existence. And long before they had time to run through town to the docks. He turned to Queen and Bishop, who had already thrown Pierce back over his shoulder, and said, "Stay close."

After leading them across the courtyard, ever wary of lurking regens, King opened the metal door leading to the submarine bay. He motioned them through, shouting, "Haul ass to the end. We'll figure out the next step when we get there."

Queen led the way, followed by Bishop.

King looked back and found a wall of lava eating through the back side of the facility's wall. It would slow the advance, but not for long. He slammed the metal door closed and locked it tight, praying it would take some time for the lava to melt through. He sprinted down the long cement hallway, its lights flickering as the facility's power died. He caught up with the others as they reached the end of the hallway and the second metal door. Bishop kicked the door open as the ground began to shake more violently. The volcano was hemorrhaging lava. With everyone through the door, King turned to close and seal it. He paused, looking down the hallway where the other end glowed bright orange.

He slammed the door shut and locked it. He turned, facing the others and the submarine docking cave. A cement L-shaped platform held several lockers, tool chests, and storage bins, but there was no clear mode of egress from the interior of the cave. "It's too far to swim out. Look for oxygen tanks, rebreathers, anything."

The lights blinked.

King dove for the nearest lockers, tearing them open and pouring through the contents. Queen joined him. After the first three, the lights went out. With no source of illumination, the bay plunged into total darkness.

Then the darkness ebbed, pushed away by a subtle glow as the metal door began heating from the other side. In the dim orange light, Queen found a flashlight and turned it on, handing a second to King.

"Time is running out," Bishop said, pointing to the metal door. A trickle of molten liquid leaked through a hole at the door's base. Then another.

King flung open a long metal chest. "Here!" He pulled out a sleek, black X-Scooter CSI diver propulsion vehicle and handed it to Bishop. The small handheld machine could pull the two men through the water faster than either could swim. They would make it out alive . . . in fact, he wasn't sure Pierce could even drown and knew Bishop could hold his breath for minutes. "Get him out of here."

Bishop nodded and headed for the black pool of seawater. He jumped into the water, sank beneath the surface, and disappeared with Pierce.

King moved to the next chest and flung it open. Empty.

"Strip and swim, boss," Queen said as she shed her fatigues, weapons, and cartridge belt.

Lava burst through the door, moving like warm honey across the cement floor. A wave of heat filled the space. King tore his clothes from his body as Queen popped the thumb drive into her mouth and dove into the water dressed in her jet black boyshorts and sports bra. As King discarded his pants and stood in his boxer briefs, he saw a pair of swim fins in an open locker. The far end of the locker was already melting into the lava. He acted without thinking, racing against the flow of lava, he grabbed the fins, raced back to the edge, and dove high just as the lava ate the cement at his feet and spilled into the pool. King struck the water and slid away fast and deep. As his momentum slowed, he put on the swim fins and kicked hard into the water, keenly aware that the cave glowed bright around him where it had been pitch-black before. He was even more aware of the water's rising temperature. If he didn't drown, he'd soon be boiled like a lobster.

King gained on Queen thanks to the swim fins. They were fifty feet from the exit, which stood out as a dim, moonlit circle. King pointed to his feet and reached a hand out to Queen. She saw the fins, nodded, and took his hand. They kicked together, increasing their speed. Twenty feet from the tunnel exit, King saw a thick drip of something sinking through the water. A flurry of bubbles flew away from the object as it descended. Then a second, larger blob sunk past. The lava had reached the island's edge ahead of them.

King kicked harder, his legs and lungs burning, as a small stream of lava oozed into the water to their right, filling the ocean with steaming bubbles. King watched the bubbles burst and expand as a second stream of lava struck. They'd be trapped in seconds.

A shadow shot out of the depths like a hunting shark, moving fast and fluid. King fought the urge to stop swimming and face the object, whether it be shark or torpedo, but with gouts of lava about to rain down from above, he kept on kicking . . . and waiting for death to come from above, or below.

THIRTY-SEVEN

Tristan da Cunha

The shadow emerged from the depths, reached out, and took King's arm in a vice grip. He and Queen were yanked up and away as Bishop, still holding the high-powered scooter pulled them away from the mouth of the cave. An explosion of bubbles and wave of heat pursued them as lava spilled into the ocean. With the scooter pulling and King still kicking with his fins, they cleared the area just in time not to be boiled alive, but as King's vision began to fade, a new threat emerged.

He needed to breathe.

Sensing this, Bishop turned the scooter toward the surface and pulled them up. After breaking through the waves, King and Queen gasped for air, taxed beyond their limits, but unwilling to give the grim reaper his due. As they fought against the waves, hands reached down from above and plucked them from the ocean and onto the plush, comfortable deck of the *Mercury*. Bishop started up after them.

Rook reached down to help him up.

"I got it," Bishop said.

He took Bishop by the wrist. "C'mon, big guy. Let me help you—"

"I said I got it!" Bishop twisted his wrist out of Rook's

hand, took hold of Rook's shirt, and pulled him overboard. Rook sank under the water and came back up a moment later. "Bishop, what the hell!"

Standing on the deck of the *Mercury,* Bishop looked back at him. "Just stay away from me, Rook." He stalked away, ignoring the stunned looks of King, Queen, and Knight, and entered the cabin.

King helped Rook back onto the deck. Water poured from his waterlogged clothes. "What was that about?"

"Probably upset about being captured," Queen said, wrapping a towel around her scantily clad body. "He'll cool off soon enough."

"Well, I'm doing like the man said and steering clear of his grumpy ass," Rook said. He didn't like being humiliated, or manhandled, by a teammate. Broken trust could lead to all kinds of trouble on the battlefield. As Rook stripped out of his drenched clothing he frowned and added, "To top things off, the island is a total loss."

King looked up as Knight hammered the throttle, launching the yacht away from the island. The whole of Tristan da Cunha was consumed in lava, smoke, and fire. Edinburgh burned. Manifold Beta sat beneath a pool of molten lava that would cool and harden. The site would take years, perhaps more, to excavate. Even then any evidence left behind would have been burned or melted within the cauldron.

The mission had been a disaster.

Well, not a complete disaster. King looked to his side and found Pierce, if it even was him, lying next to him. His eyes remained closed and breathing shallow. He'd rescued his friend, but at what price? He might have been better off if they'd shot him and been done with it. Now he had to, what . . . live life as an immortal monster? A modern mythological creature?

"Near as I can tell," Rook said, "your buddy is in a coma."

Queen checked Pierce's pulse, holding his wrist.

Checked his eyes. Squeezed his hand hard, looking for a reaction to pain. Nothing. "The regens reacted to regeneration by losing their grasp on reality. They became animals . . . worse than animals. But this is something new. Still not perfected. His mind might be reacting by shutting down."

King listened. It made sense and he was glad Pierce wasn't awake to see himself like this. Still, on the off chance that people in comas really could hear the people around them, he leaned in close and said, "George. It's Jack. Listen. I'm going to take care of things. I'm going to figure out a way to help you. That's a promise."

"We've got trouble," Knight shouted back from the captain's chair. He pointed out toward the ocean. Debris clung to the waves. Body parts, too.

"They didn't make it," Rook said.

"Who?"

"The locals. A bunch launched out to sea."

King ground his teeth together. The submarine. Had to be. He punched the side of the boat and looked back at Tristan da Cunha. The island glowed bright orange like the devil had ascended from the thirteenth level of Hell and settled on the island. A great billow of smoke filled the sky above, blotting out the stars. Ash fell from the sky, the gentle flakes kissing their skin like warm snowflakes.

"Head inside," King said. "We don't need to be breathing this crap."

Rook took Pierce in his arms and carried him into the cabin and lay him down on a comfortable couch. Queen followed. King stepped up to Knight at the controls. "Set a course due north, then come inside. We'll take shifts out here. For now, let's see if we can raise the *Grant* on the radio inside."

Knight turned the wheel, looking at the compass, when he caught a flash of green in his periphery. The luxury yacht came complete with sonar. Something was rising next to them. Something big. "King . . ."

He saw it, ducked into the cabin and came back out with an RPG, ready to launch. Bishop, Rook, and Queen followed him out, similarly armed with a variety of explosive projectiles. He looked at the sonar screen, took aim at the ocean, and waited to fire. The submarine broke the surface one hundred yards away, rising like a breeching whale and crashing back into the water. A massive wave rolled out and away from the sub, pushing the *Mercury* up at an odd angle, throwing off their aim.

The sub was easily recognizable as a Los Angeles–class attack submarine, but King had no way of knowing what kind of sub Manifold had got its hands on. He took aim again, as the *Mercury* settled in the water. The others followed his lead. The sub approached slowly and stopped ten feet away. Too close to launch torpedoes and not sustain damage. The message was clear: *We come in peace.* But King maintained his vigil. The sub could easily ram them, letting its conning tower tear the *Mercury* in two.

Only when the top hatch opened and two men in U.S. Navy uniforms stepped out, hands in the air, did King relax. The two sailors were followed by Captain Savile looking like a drowned cat.

He lowered the RPG staring at the captain, his mouth open in shock. He realized immediately what the captain's presence and physical appearance meant. Something awful had happened to the USS *Grant*.

"Get your people on board," Savile said to King.

"How many were lost?"

The side of Savile's mouth twitched for a moment. "Five hundred thirteen dead or lost so far. Maybe more. The *Grant* is wounded, listing, but not sunk. She'll make it."

"Those sons-a-bitches," Rook muttered.

"Get what you need," King said to the others, "and take George. I'll sink the *Mercury*."

"Hey, King," Savile said.

"Yes, sir."

Savile looked at the glowing remnants of Tristan da Cunha. "Did you get them?"

King felt his stomach lurch as he heard the eager tone in the captain's voice. He wanted to know the bastards that sunk his boat and killed his men had paid for their crimes. But they hadn't. They'd escaped right out from under their noses. King let them go again. King's silence and cold eyes said what words couldn't.

Savile shook his head. "When you find the man who sank my ship, make him hurt."

King nodded. It went without saying. Manifold and Gen-Y had not only drawn first blood, but second blood, too. The only acceptable solution was to draw third blood . . . and much more of it.

ALPHA

THIRTY-EIGHT

Pope Air Force Base, Limbo

A day after their failed mission, the team found themselves once again sitting in Limbo. They had been plucked from the ocean by helicopter, rendezvoused with a second aircraft carrier, and flown in the navigator's seats of five F/A-18 Super Hornets. The thumb drive data had been sent ahead to Aleman via satellite but only contained useless fragments of information.

Aside from retrieving Pierce, the mission had been a total failure and then some. A town had been destroyed. Two hundred seventy-one foreign civilians had perished, and while the proper authorities had been notified by a "passing vessel" of Tristan da Cunha's destruction, the world would never know it wasn't a volcano that killed all those people. After counting and recounting it turned out that six hundred seventy-two sailors had died in the attack. And the government's first CVNX-class, eleven-billion-dollar aircraft carrier and billions in aircraft had nearly been sunk to the bottom of the ocean. The military term FUBAR (fucked up beyond all recognition) didn't do the mission justice. If the whole mess hadn't been swept under the rug and buried deeper than the Mariana Trench, it would have gone down in history as the military's single most expensive mission, outside of a war, and would be recorded in history books for centuries to come.

On a personal level, the feud started by Bishop tossing Rook into the ocean had continued as neither man spoke to the other. A rift was growing on the team and that usually meant bad things. If someone didn't get injured as a result, someone would end up quitting. If they weren't reconciled by the mission's end, King would be forced to send one of them packing. The alternative was to risk all their lives. For now, the two would be separated. King spoke to Deep Blue in private, arranging the break.

On top of all that, Pierce showed no signs of coming out of the coma and still looked more like the Creature from the Black Lagoon than a human being. If that wasn't bad enough, the brightest minds in the U.S. government, from the CDC to folks who didn't officially exist at Area 51, couldn't make heads or tails of the skin and organ samples taken from Pierce. It seemed he was no longer fully human. He wasn't only not human, he wasn't like anything in recorded history. But King knew there was something similar. The artifact stolen from the Nazca dig site. It was real. Had to be. The Hydra. They'd somehow extracted and transferred its DNA to Pierce.

As King sat, waiting for Keasling to arrive, his anger at the situation built. He wanted to be reprimanded. Shouted at. Something. But it was business as usual. They'd underestimated their enemy. King. Keasling. Deep Blue. All of them. With such a big noose, it seemed no one would be hung. So long as the right people were caught in the end. Then the noose would belong to them.

Keasling entered and looked the team over as they sat around the table, sullen-faced and quiet. Even Rook remained silent. Aleman entered a moment later and took a seat at the table. He was straight-faced, but couldn't hide the tiny smirk at the sides of his mouth.

He'd found something.

Keasling frowned. "The time for licking your wounded

egos is over. You look like a bunch of first graders after a recess fight. Snap out of it."

They did. Faces hardened. Postures straightened. Each turned their guilt into anger. They'd been trained to do it when it needed to be done. They'd deal with the guilt later, when there was no one left to kill. Hell, killing the right people could actually relieve the guilt. Knowing how many people would die if Manifold succeeded and sold its formula to terrorists or dictators made the lives and billions lost seem like chump change . . . chump lives.

The screen glowed to life. Deep Blue sat in shadow. "How's everyone holding up?"

"We're ready to kick some ass," Rook said.

Deep Blue nodded. "Good. And that will come soon enough. But first there are two mysteries that need solving. The first is Manifold's new location. We know they had at least five large facilities, all secret. Two of them are now destroyed thanks to their cut-and-run, slash-and-burn tactics."

"Bunch of pansies," Rook said.

"Effective pansies," Deep Blue added. "After Aleman confirmed the thumb drive contained no useful information I set the CIA to the task of finding any evidence of large facilities being built in the United States."

"You think they're here?" King asked. "Right under our noses?"

"Almost. They're in New Hampshire."

Rook looked surprised. "Where at?"

"Your backyard. Pinckney."

"Little town, north of Plymouth?"

"That's the one. A few boaters off Rye reported seeing a submarine beneath their boats. The Portsmouth Naval Shipyard was put on high alert. Nothing turned up, but it put our attention on New Hampshire and Maine. It took a lot of digging, but we found evidence that something large had been built in Pinckney. Tolls and weigh stations reported large amounts of material entering the area, but never appearing on the grid again. A lot of building material went in and never came out. But that's not all. As you know, we've been testing Pierce with the hopes of understanding and reversing his condition. What we've found is that his healing ability is greatly increased in the presence of radiation."

King sat up straight, his voice tinged with anger. "You're exposing him to radiation?"

Deep Blue held up a hand. "Nothing more significant than the background radiation found naturally in certain environments."

"The Granite State," Rook said, understanding. "The whole state is riddled with the stuff."

"Which contains ten to twenty parts per million of uranium," Aleman added.

Rook nodded. "The uranium decays and escapes as radon gas. My grandmother had to move because her foundation leaked the stuff like a sieve."

"The town of Pinckney is situated in a valley that rests between several large mountains of granite. If Manifold discovered the effect of this background radiation on regeneration, then it makes sense that they would retreat to that location. The problem is, finding the facility has proven impossible from above. They're most likely underground, so we need boots on the ground. King. Knight. Bishop. I want you to handle this."

"Why not just flood the area with troops?" Knight asked. "Smoke 'em out George W. style."

"They'd see us coming long before we smoked anything out," Deep Blue said. "We don't want them bugging out this time. If it takes you a little longer to find them, fine. Let them get comfortable. Catch them with their pants down. And don't let them escape again."

Rook began to object. New Hampshire was his home state. His people. But Deep Blue beat him to the punch, "I know all the reasons you want to go, Rook, but there's more. I'll let Aleman explain."

Aleman sat up straight and cleared his throat. "The symbol Pierce drew, the circle with two vertical lines . . . It took some research . . . *a lot* of research. But I found it mentioned in an archive of the Natural History Museum of all places. Turns out, quite appropriately, that it's a symbol for Hercules. To be specific, the pillars of Hercules, also known as—"

"The Strait of Gibraltar," Queen said. She leaned forward, elbows on the table. "Some legends say that Hercules formed the strait by striking through a mountain with his club, but most believe he traveled to the strait to fetch the Cattle of Geryon, a giant with six arms, three heads, and three bodies. His tenth labor."

"Hydra was his second?" King asked.

Queen nodded. "Seems he kept the true distance of his travels to himself, though. Gibraltar was supposed to be the farthest he traveled."

"That's right," Aleman said with a grin, clearly impressed by Queen's knowledge. "Which brings us to Agustina Gallo."

"You found her?" King asked.

"Well, there were two hundred fifty-seven women with the name, worldwide, but only one of them is an expert on Greek mythology."

"Where is she?" Knight asked.

Aleman smiled. "Greece, of course."

"You're sending me to Greece?" Rook asked, doing nothing to hide the annoyance in his voice.

"You and Queen," Deep Blue said. That alone seemed to settle Rook down, but Deep Blue continued, "Queen speaks the language, and as she's shown us, isn't too shabby when it comes to Greek mythology. But Rook . . . you're needed to complete her cover story."

Rook's right eyebrow rose a centimeter. "And that is?"

"Queen will pose as a local. Your guide. You'll be the loud, obnoxious, American tourist."

Rook sighed, bit his lip, and shook his head, clearly

frustrated. But he didn't argue. He knew he was perfect for the job.

"Your plane leaves at seventeen hundred hours. Bags have been packed for you. Posing as tourists you'll have to take a commercial flight in. Get your passports stamped. The whole deal. So no weapons. If you run into trouble, which you shouldn't, head to the U.S. embassy or take a boat to the naval base in Souda Bay on Crete. Dr. Pierce seemed to think Gallo was important. I need you two to find out why. In the past twenty-four hours she hasn't answered her phone or checked her e-mail. We don't know if she's busy, antisocial, or otherwise disposed, so stay alert. Any questions?"

No one offered any. The screen went black.

Keasling stood. "Hit the road gumshoes. Don't come back unless you've got Manifold by the balls, or I'll have your balls in my own personal vice."

Queen grinned.

"What are you smiling about?" Keasling said. "You've got more balls than the four of them combined. Now move your asses."

THIRTY-NINE

Greece

Flying as civilians meant a flight first from Raleigh, North Carolina, to Boston, then to London, and south to Greece, where they landed at Athens International Airport—Eleftherios Venizelos. Rook had done his best not to complain, but on the flight to Greece, after already spending eight hours on a plane, decided to start practicing his American tourist cover by complaining that the seats were too tight for his bulk. To his surprise, he and Queen had been moved to first class mid flight and given a bottle of champagne. Apparently, Greece wanted loud, obnoxious tourists . . . and they wanted them drunk and spending money straight away. While neither Rook nor Queen imbibed the spirits, Rook did save the bottle, stowing it in his very American, Boston Celtics gym bag.

They checked into their hotel posing as a vacationing couple, which drew looks of pity for Queen as she was dressed in a form-fitting navy blue top that accentuated her eyes and a flowing black skirt that matched her stylish sandals and highlighted her taut tan legs. She spoke the language fluently and short of her blond hair, fit in with the locals. Rook on the other hand, dressed in high-top sneakers, tight blue jeans, and a sports jacket, was easily spotted as a stereotypical American tourist. The looks they received from everyone, including the cabbie, the hotel doorman, and the checkout clerk all asked the same question of Queen: *Why are you slumming with this clown?*

After checking in at the Electra Palace Hotel and, like a perfect gentleman, carrying Queen's bags to their room on the tenth floor, Rook dropped the bags on the room's king-sized bed and wiped a bead of sweat from his forehead. "I swear if I hear any Beauty and the Beast jokes in English or Greek I'm going to snap."

Queen opened the shades looking out over the Plaka, the oldest and most prized neighborhood in Athens, the white buildings glowing orange in the light of the setting sun. The streets had long ago been blocked off to cars, though delivery men on speeding mopeds weren't uncommon. Locals and tourists mixed and mingled on the ancient streets lined with cafés, shops, and restaurants. Scents of coffee, ouzo, and flaming sausage wafted up from below. But most impressive was that the small neighborhood's prime real estate was located at the base of Athens's most famous landmark, the Acropolis, upon which stood a symbol of the ancient world's glory, the Parthenon. The site was breathtaking. Another time. Another life. Queen would have enjoyed this little trip . . . but there was work to do.

She turned to Rook, tried not to laugh at his outfit, and asked, "Care for a gelato?"

"That's like ice cream, right?"

"Better."

"I'll believe that when Ben and Jerry start selling gelato at four bucks a pop." Rook opened the door, leaving behind their bags, which held clothing they never intended on wearing but helped to complete their cover story. Getting stopped at customs with an empty bag on vacation could have drawn attention. And Rook would be more than happy to leave the awful clothes behind. He'd questioned the need for such an elaborate cover, but it wasn't known whether or not Pierce had given Manifold the same information. Until they knew otherwise, they had to watch their backs—unarmed—and play the part of an American odd couple.

"So when are you and Bishop going to patch things up?"

"When he stops acting like a prick we'll be golden."

"And if he doesn't?"

Rook stopped and looked at Queen. "The guy won't talk to me or anyone else. He looks on the verge of snapping someone's head off. I'm just going to give him space and hope he comes around. We all should. He'll work it out on his own. Always does. Let's talk about something else. This subject is too distracting."

Rook continued walking.

Queen decided to drop the subject. Rook was right. Preoccupation with personal issues compromised the mission.

On the streets of the Plaka, Rook found it easier to forget the trouble with Bishop . . . and his awful outfit. There were enough loudly dressed tourists talking it up with crisply dressed locals that he and Queen fit in. The hum of vehicles faded as conversations in a variety of languages filtered out of the street-side cafés. As they walked by a restaurant with tables spilling out onto the street, a maître d' took Rook's arm and spoke perfect English, "Sir, you absolutely must try our giant shrimp!"

Rook pulled his arm away. "Maybe later, chief."

"Our dishes are the best in the Plaka. Moussaka. Pastitsio. Souvlaki. You can't go wrong."

Rook's impatience neared its end. The short maître d' was about to get an earful when Queen ribbed Rook with her elbow and said, "*Parakalo agnoiste to filo moy. Einai toso trahys oso einai omorfos. Tha epistrepsoyme gia na epileksoyme ta piata sas argotera apopse.*"

The maître d' chuckled. "*Oraios?*"

Queen gave the man a look that could kill. "*Nai.*"

The man bowed with a smile and let them continue on their way.

"What'd you tell him?"

"That we would be back later. For supper."

"What's *'oraios'* mean?"

Queen took a side street. "This way. We're almost there."

The street led uphill and ended at the tall wall of the Acropolis. The back street narrowed as they climbed the hill, becoming little more than a three-foot-wide path between gleaming white homes staggering up the hill. The old stone homes were decorated with pots of flowers that filled the air with a sweet fragrance that fought for olfactory dominance with Athens's summertime smog.

They entered the Anafiotika, a group of small homes that spent a large portion of every day in the shadow of the Acropolis. With the sun now setting, this portion of the city was already cast in darkness. It was here that the search for Agustina Gallo truly began. The archaeologist had made her home in the world's most celebrated archaeological site, in the oldest part of the city—three thousand years old—surrounded by archaeological sites like the Tower of the Winds, the Mosque of Mehmet, not to mention the Parthenon itself. The city was the birthplace of Plato's Academy and Aristotle's Lyceum and had done more to advance democracy in the ancient world than any nation, including America, could claim to have achieved in the modern. But what brought archaeologists to Athens, even more than the ancient sites, were the modern institutions. Athens University and Archaeological Society along with several prestigious museums—the National Archaeological Museum, the Epigraphic Museum, the Byzantine Museum—and more could be found here. Two archaeology laboratories, seventeen archaeological institutes, and fourteen archaeological libraries completed what Rook called an archaeologist's wet dream. And at its core was the home of a woman who may or may not have something to say about the symbol George Pierce had drawn in blood before falling into a coma.

After walking up a series of steps leading between two homes, Queen found the number she was looking for. She approached the small white home's maroon door and knocked.

Rook stood behind her, trying not to look too foolish while he scoured the path up toward the Necropolis and back toward the Plaka for signs of trouble. Finding none, he turned back toward the door as it opened and nearly fell back as one of the most beautiful women he'd ever laid eyes on in person smiled at them. From her straight black hair and deep brown eyes, he took her as a local, but when she spoke English with a sweet southern drawl as out of place in this ancient city as Rook's clothing, he had to work hard to keep himself from dropping to one knee and proposing.

"Ya'll lost?" she said.

"Agustina Gallo?" Queen asked.

"The one and only."

Queen squinted at her. "How did you know we spoke English?"

Gallo nodded at Rook. "Captain America here was a dead giveaway. Hey, you're not friends of Chris Biggs, now are you? He's always sending folks my way. Like I have time to give personal tours of the Plaka."

"Actually," Queen said. "We're friends of George Pierce."

The woman seemed taken aback, then fearful. "George? Is he okay?"

"I'm afraid not. Can we come in?"

She looked unsure. "You have something to do with all the answering machine hang-ups from an unlisted U.S. number?"

Rook nodded. "Haven't checked your e-mail yet, have you?"

"I just got back from a weeklong stint at an excavation I'm covering for George while he's gone. I've only just arrived home."

"Agustina, we're with the U.N.," Queen said. She felt bad lying to the woman, but just because Pierce seemed to trust her didn't mean she was truly trustworthy. "George has gone missing. We really need to speak to you."

Gallo stepped back inside the house. "C'mon in."

As they stepped inside the house, following Gallo into a quaint sitting room, Queen gave Rook a taste of the old evil eye. "Close your mouth. You're drooling."

They sat in comfortable chairs around a coffee table. The room, built like a roofed atrium, was decorated with a mixture of small Greek statue reproductions and oil paintings of flowers. Queen noticed the paintings were signed in red, by Gallo. Apparently she was a painter as well.

Gallo sat across from them, lines of concern still etched into her forehead. She flattened her skirt over her legs several times, chasing wrinkles that didn't exist. Pierce apparently meant something to this woman. She leaned forward, elbows on knees, hands wringing together. "What's happened to George. He wasn't attacked again, was he?"

Despite Gallo's beauty distracting Rook from the impending interview, a single word caught his attention.

Again.

FORTY

New Hampshire

With a population of 1,532 people, downtown Pinckney, New Hampshire, consisted of a post office/general store, a church, and not much else. Its main tourist attraction were the Ice Age Caverns, a series of cliffside caves that formed as the last of the ice-age glaciers retreated. But the single most populated area in town was the Pinckney Bible Conference Grounds. During the winter months the population on the conference grounds swelled to 160 on weekends when schools, youth groups, and winter sports teams rented the center's Prescott Lodge for snowy getaways. But during the summer months, the number of visitors blossomed to over a thousand people, increasing the town's summertime population to just over 2,500. Not only did the lodge fill up, but also the campground's six cabins, forty-nine privately owned cabins, and more than three dozen RVs.

As King, Knight, and Bishop rounded the final turn on route 27, passing a small pond on the left, then Prescott Lodge, they got their first views of the campground where they'd rented a cabin. With the campground representing the most densely populated area in town, they wanted to be there to protect the people in case things went sour and an army of regens was released. But as they passed the swing set, volleyball court, and swimming pool, it became apparent they would have a hard time fitting in.

Not only were they three single men staying in the same cabin, but they were also large, weathered, and lacked kids. Their clothing also stood out. King in blue jeans and a Doors T-shirt; Knight wearing black designer pants and a loose, white button-down shirt; and Bishop, muscles bulging beneath a tight long-sleeved navy blue shirt and cargo pants. To fit in with the summertime revelers, they would have to change into shorts and T-shirts. King made a mental note to go out to the department store they'd passed and get new clothes before mixing it up with the locals. The only one among them that might help with meeting and discreetly interviewing people for leads was Thor, a one-hundred-pound, thick-headed golden retriever. He was picked for his friendly disposition and love of children, but he was also one of the best tracking dogs in the military.

King steered the massive, cherry red Chevy Tahoe into the main entrance where two kids sat at a makeshift lemonade stand. He gave them a wave and a grin. They waved back, eager to make a sale, but he drove right past. A quick glance in the rearview made him laugh. One of the kids flipped him off. Good Christian kids. Still human.

"It's your third left," Knight said, looking at the directions sent to them by the family that owned the cottage.

They entered the campground proper. To the right was a baseball field, a soccer field, and a green and white building sporting a sign that read "Snack Shack." Some kids sat on a picnic table drinking sodas while others played shuffleboard. A pair of old men wearing pastel-colored slacks and white polo shirts sat in the shade sipping iced tea and watching the kids. Grandparents, King realized. This place had history.

On their left was a small, brown registration building and a churchlike bookstore painted white and green to match the Snack Shack. They turned after the bookstore, onto a dirt road cutting through the forest—Praise Street—and pulled up to a small white cabin that bore a name that insinuated enough to stand out in stark contrast to the ultra-conservative campground: Honeymoon Nook. Reading between the lines, the cabin could have just as easily been named Love Den.

Knight slid down from the passenger seat, landing on a bed of brown pine needles that covered the wooded campground's forest floor. One-hundred-foot-tall pine trees swayed and creaked high overhead, buffering the wind and blocking out the sun and its heat. He looked at the cabin's nameplate. "Rook has got to see this place."

They entered the cabin using a key hidden in the cabin's utility shed. Inside they found a large living/dining room furnished with a collection of old rocking chairs, a dining room table, and a mishmash of dining room chairs. A pellet stove sat to the right, not yet installed, and four doors exited the room. The first to a master bedroom taken up, for the most part, by a king-sized bed. There was a second bedroom with two twin beds, a bathroom, and a small kitchen. The air, though a little musty, was cool and easy to breathe.

Bishop sat in one of the chairs and picked up a 2000 issue of *Time* magazine featuring Bill Clinton on the cover. The chair groaned under Bishop's bulk, but held him. He grunted in approval, the first positive communication he'd had with any of them recently. While he normally didn't talk a lot, something about him had been different since Tristan da Cunha. He'd been more on edge. He did what was asked of him and made curt reports, but stayed distant from his teammates.

King entered with Thor on a leash and cut him loose. The dog ran through the cabin, smelling everything. He returned from the master bedroom with a chew toy, compliments of whatever dog stayed here previously.

As King and Knight did a security check on the cabin, looking for exit routes and scanning for bugs, a knock cut through the silence. Bishop stood and answered the door. Two boys, no older than ten, stood at the door. When they saw Bishop their eyes went wide. "Whoa . . ." the first said.

The other, after swallowing, asked, "Is . . . is Josh or Matt here? We saw the car . . . You're not related to them, are you?"

Bishop shook his head, no.

"You've got huge muscles!" the first said with a grin.

Bishop's patience grew thin. He didn't have time or desire to chat it up with the local kids. He fought a growing urge to slam the door in their faces. Realizing his emotions were suddenly, without reason, spiraling into chaos, he looked away from the kids and took a deep breath. He listened to the wind whispering through the tall evergreens. He breathed deep a second time, filling his barrel chest with pine-scented air. When he looked back down, calm returning, the boys were still staring at his large right arm, which bulged as he gripped the door.

He let go of the door. "What are your names?"

"Mike and Nate."

He dug into his pocket and gave both boys each a dollar. "Mike and Nate, go get a soda."

The kids ran off, talking loudly about the giant they'd seen. When their voices had faded into the distance, Bishop turned around and found Knight and King staring at him like he'd grown horns. He grinned. Something about this place, not necessarily the people or environment, but something, relaxed him. Put his mind at ease. And for that, he was thankful. His old feelings of rage had been more powerful over the past few days. So much so that he thought he would eventually lose the fight. Here, he felt something else.

Hope.

the silence. Bishop stood and answered the door.

FORTY-ONE

Greece

"What do you mean, *again*?" Rook asked.

Gallo sat back, her mouth closed tight. She wasn't entirely sure who her two visitors were or what they wanted. Perhaps they were the source of George's trouble? He had left quickly, and mysteriously.

"Look, Ms. Gallo," he continued, "Pierce is in a good amount of trouble. Life-threatening. If you know something, spill the beans."

Queen cleared her throat. "Please."

"Who are you, really? The U.N. would have left a message. You all hung up nearly fifteen times in a row."

Queen considered the request. The woman wasn't stupid. "We're friends. That's all we can say."

"Friends," Gallo said with a scowl. "No offense, but if George had been friends with you, I'd know about it."

"First," Rook said, his patience waning, "I don't normally dress like this. Second, seeing as how Pierce's life is dependent on you helping us, I'd recommend you throw caution to the wind and—"

"Jack Sigler," Queen said. "Do you know him?"

Gallo squinted at her. "I've never met him. But George has talked about him. Keeps a photo of he and his . . ."

"Sister," Queen filled in. "Julie. He was going to marry her."

"I know."

"Then you know how much Jack means to him."

She nodded.

"We work with Jack. He's like family to us and Pierce is like family to him. You see where I'm going with this?" Queen's voice grew louder. "You ready to help us?"

Gallo paused, looking at both of them.

Queen pulled out a piece of paper and slapped it down on the coffee table.

Gallo looked down at the single image on the page, the symbol Pierce had drawn. She gasped and clutched her blouse, just above her heart. "Where did you see this?"

"Pierce drew it in his own blood," Rook said. "Just before saying your name and slipping into a coma."

Tears filled Gallo's eyes.

"You know what this is?"

"The pillars of Hercules. It represents the Strait of Gibraltar. During Hercules's tenth trial he—"

Queen held up her hand. "We know all this. We were hoping you might be able to tell us something *more*. Something not as well known."

She picked up the piece of paper with a shaky hand and looked at the drawing. "It's a very old symbol, but not yet well known. It represents several things, all connected, but different. Visually it represents the pillars of Gibraltar. Its first true use was as a crest for Hercules."

"Like a logo or brand name or something?" Rook asked.

"Something like that. But it later became the symbol for an organization formed thousands of years ago, the Herculean Society. Their edicts, George believes, is to protect the real legacy of the historical Hercules. To safeguard his secrets. His discoveries."

"They believe Hercules was real?" Queen asked.

"Hercules *was* real. And he wasn't the bastard son of

Zeus. He was as human as us, but far more brilliant. George has long believed that Hercules gained his godlike strength through alchemies."

"Magic?" Rook asked, doing nothing to show his skepticism.

"Science," Gallo said. "Using plant extracts, known poisons in miniscule quantities—"

"Homeopathy," Queen said.

"Yes." Gallo looked at Queen, taking stock of the woman who was not only sexy and strong, but also smart. "Combining his knowledge of these things and conducting countless experiments, we believe Hercules was able to refine . . . serums I suppose you'd call them. Perhaps he created ancient steroids. Or perhaps some kind of adrenaline booster for times when superhuman strength was called for. There are many stories of Hercules using poison to defeat his enemies, including the blood of Hydra. It's all speculation at this point. George's best evidence—a crew manifest—was stolen by the Herculean Society; at least that's who George thinks they were. That's the first attack I mentioned."

The three sat in silence, each processing the information. Rook sat upright. "Could he have used something against Hydra? Something to keep it from regenerating?"

"The Hydra story mentions Hercules severing the immortal head with a sword, then cauterizing the wound. The only mention of poison is what he took from Hydra's blood."

Rook looked disappointed, but Queen spoke up. "What if the story is wrong? Stories that old inevitably suffer the effect of verbal history. The poison could have been used against Hydra."

"I suppose." She cocked an eyebrow at them. "What's your interest in Hydra?"

"It's . . . complicated. Leave it at that for now," Rook said and then pressed on. "This Herculean Society. You said they've been trying to protect the secrets of Hercules. Removing a poison used against Hydra from the Hydra story would have been a simple thing if they've been around for as long as you say they have. Right?"

"Yes, but— Listen, these people will kill to protect their secrets. They nearly killed George last year to recover the crew manifest that mentioned Hercules by name, and that was simply evidence that the man wasn't just a myth, never mind that he was a fully human alchemist."

Rook sat forward. "We can handle them."

"You're sure?"

Rook smiled. "It's what we do, lady."

"Did Pierce tell you about the manifest before it was stolen?" Queen asked.

"He called the moment he found it."

"And how long after that was it stolen?"

"The following night," Gallo said. "Why? Wait, you don't think I—"

Rook sighed and stood, walking to a small table where a portable phone sat. He cracked open the back of the phone, pulled out the batteries and then squeezed two of his thick fingers inside. He pinched down and pulled out a small device the size of a nickel. He tossed it onto the coffee table where it spun for a moment, then lay still in front of Gallo.

She picked it up, knowing what she was looking at, though she'd never seen a listening device before. "They're listening in on my phone calls?" She placed the bug down on the table and pushed it away.

"Probably Pierce's, too." Rook said. He picked the bug up, gripped it tight and snapped it in half. "Did he call you before going to Nazca? Did he say anything specific about what he was doing there?"

"Nothing over the phone. We met in person, at a café, before he left." Gallo pointed to the broken bug in Rook's hand. "How did you know you'd find that?"

Rook took his seat. "Like I said, it's what we do."

Gallo sat back in her chair, still clutching her chest.

"Now let me preface this by saying I'm not being a pervert." He pointed at Gallo's chest. "Are you going to show us what you're hiding in your shirt?"

Gallo looked down at her hand, which had been holding the object hidden beneath her blouse, the single piece of evidence George had to support his theories. He'd entrusted it to her care. Its heavy weight around her neck now felt like a burden, and with some relief she pulled the chain up and over her head, allowing the iron medallion to twist in the air. The dull gray metal, beaten and worn, spoke of its long history, but the symbol it formed—a circle cut through by two straight lines—the insignia for the Herculean Society, Hercules, and the Strait of Gibraltar meant so much more.

She held it out and Queen took it. "Where did you get this?"

"George found it. On a shipwreck. He was overseeing its excavation when he left. I've been in charge since then. He asked me to keep it safe."

"And he just happened to find this on a shipwreck," Rook said.

"Not just any shipwreck . . ."

Queen held the medallion up, letting a ray of sunlight gleam from the few smooth areas polished by the seafloor. She let out a slight laugh and smiled. "The *Argo*."

"What is the Argo?" Rook asked.

Surprised by Queen's knowledge, Gallo paused before replying, "Designed by Athena, the *Argo* was this ship Jason and Argonauts used to track down the Golden Fleece. Perhaps the first Greek warship in history and manned by a famous crew that included Hercules. His name was on the manifest."

"Pierce actually found the *Argo*?" Queen asked.

"He thinks so, but—"

"We need to see it," Queen said. "There must be something Pierce wanted us to find."

"That's impossible," Gallo said. "The wreck is fifty feet below the surface. Excavations are slow, surrounded by a gaggle of undergrads and security provided by the Greek government. Getting you past security would be hard enough, but searching the wreck for something meaningful. It could take months."

All three sat back, deflated by the dead end.

"Maybe the Greek government will give us access? Blue can pull some strings," Rook said to Queen.

She shook her head. "They'd want to know what we're up to."

"Blue can lie."

"It'd still take too long to find something. We can't just—"

Gallo sat up straight. "George would have known the excavation was off limits. He wouldn't send us there."

"Then where?" Rook asked.

"The university. Everything taken from the excavation is cataloged at the University of Athens. He must have found something before leaving."

"Can you get us in?" Queen asked.

"I don't have security clearance for the vault. I always go with George." Gallo stood. "But I'll try."

"Vault?" Rook said. "They keep the artifacts in a vault."

"Much of what we find is priceless," Gallo said. "Believe me, people would kill for it . . . people would die to protect it."

Rook nodded. "People have."

After a five-minute walk out of the tight neighborhood, the three sat in Gallo's cramped Volkswagen Fox, and rumbled off, over the cobbled streets, toward the University of Athens. If Gallo had thought to check the rearview mirror she might have noticed the two shadowy figures in pursuit, leaping from rooftop to rooftop. She might have noticed that the two figures avoided patches of bright light. And she might have seen them leap onto the roof of her vehicle, which would have been the only evidence that they now bore two additional passengers, because no one heard a thing.

FORTY-TWO

Greece

After driving over a speed bump that felt more like a springboard, Gallo pulled up to the Ilissia Gate that lead to the heart of the university's main campus. A streetlamp lit her face through the car's windshield. Her lip quivered as she held her I.D. up to the armed guard. Despite passing through the gate, sometimes daily, she had never entered the campus for less than academic reasons and her gut reminded her of it every few seconds. The guard waved her through.

After passing through the main gate successfully, she began talking about the history of the buildings as they passed. Like a nervous tour guide on her first day, Gallo gave a verbal dissertation on the Informatics building, the Energy Policy and Development Center, and the School of Theology building before pulling to a stop at the outer edge of the parking lot for the School of Philosophy, which housed the Archaeology Department and its vault. She put the car in park, and looked at Queen sitting next to her, and Rook, sitting hunched over in the rear of the small car. Both grinned at her.

With a huff she said, "It's not like I break into my own university every day, you know."

"It's not every day I cram myself into a sardine can, either," Rook said. "Can we go now?"

They entered through the side door of the six-story, utilitarian building that looked more like a hospital than a place where works of art and history were studied. Gallo waved to students who recognized her and smiled nervously as they shot odd looks at Rook. They entered a stairwell and descended two levels. Gallo stopped in front of a door marked Basement Level 1: Archaeology, Anthropology, V.

"Through this door is a long hallway. Pierce's office is down here, too. The vault is at the end of an adjacent hallway. There will be one guard, Sebastian. He will recognize me, but only full-time staff are allowed unscheduled visits to the vault." She took a deep breath, licked her lips, and added, "But I'll try."

They entered the basement hallway, passing Pierce's dark office on the way. The hallways, though underground, were well lit from above and accented by the occasional sconce hanging on the green walls. The red industrial rug lining the floor masked their approach, but Gallo stopped them well away from the corner that lead to the vault and motioned for them to stay put. After taking one more deep breath of the basement's stale air, she rounded the corner and headed toward the vault. Despite the intimidating title, the vault was little more than a warehouse with one entrance—a thick steel door that required a keycard to enter. A keycard that hung from Sebastian's neck.

Sebastian smiled at Gallo as she walked toward him. He tipped his hat toward her and in his best English said, "How are you, Dr. Gallo?"

She smiled. Sebastian had a reputation as being a ladies' man. Given his smile and use of the English language whenever she spoke to him, she didn't doubt it. The man was charming. But the gun at his waist also meant he could be deadly. "I'm fine, Sebastian, how are you?"

"I was bored, but now . . ." He held his hands out toward her. "You have arrived. How can I help you?"

Doing her best to hide her twisting stomach, she replied, "I was hoping I could look at a few items in the vault. I don't need to remove anything, I just need to confirm—"

Sebastian was shaking his head. It seemed he took his job more seriously than his flirting. "I'm afraid you'll have to make an appointment or return with Dr. Pierce."

"You know he's out of the country."

He shrugged. "I'm sorry, but I could lose my job. Were it in my power, I would take you anywhere you wanted to—"

"There you are!" Queen's voice echoed down the long hallway. Sebastian leaned over and looked around Gallo. Queen strode toward them, smiling wide. "A girl could get lost in this maze."

She stopped next to Gallo and extended a hand to Sebastian. He shook it, smiling wider. "And you are?"

Queen mocked surprise. "What, you can't see it? We're cousins."

Sebastian glanced at Gallo, his expression fiendish. "Cousins. Perhaps I can show you—oof!"

Queen yanked on the man's arm. He fell toward her as her knee came up and met his gut. When he doubled over, Queen brought her entwined fists down on the back of his head. He collapsed to the floor.

Gallo backed against the wall, hand to mouth.

"He'll live," Queen said, then whistled down the hall.

Rook walked quickly toward them as Queen wasted no time removing the keycard from Sebastian's neck. They entered the vault a moment later, where Rook secured the guard with plastic zip-tie handcuffs.

Despite her shock over Queen's violence, Gallo maintained her composure and when Sebastian was secured, said, "Follow me." She led them through rows of shelves containing an assortment of artifacts, labeled drawers, and unopened crates. Despite the age of the room's contents, the tightly controlled atmosphere in the room smelled more of ozone thanks to the four air conditioners that kept the air dry and temperature even. During blackouts, this was one of the few locations on campus that had a dedicated generator.

Gallo paused in front of an aisle. "This is it. Everything on both sides of this aisle represents what we have recovered from the shipwreck. My instinct says to ignore the drawers because they hold the smallest objects, usually potsherds or coins, but since we don't know what we're looking for . . ."

"I'll take the drawers," Rook said.

They set to work, inspecting every artifact, but most were clearly irrelevant—shards of rotted wood, ancient tools, bowls and cups. Nothing stood out as important.

After twenty minutes of searching Rook loudly closed the last of the drawers. "There's nothing worthwhile here. It's like looking through some ancient guy's trash."

"There's got to be something," Gallo said.

Queen shook her head and put down a sword hilt. "Maybe somewhere else?"

Gallo stood up straight. "You're right." She looked at Queen. "When George found the amulet he didn't catalog it. He hid it."

"Before he gave it to you?" Queen asked.

Gallo nodded with wide eyes. "In his office."

They exited the vault, leaving the still unconscious Sebastian behind. Feeling a sense of urgency, they began running. After rounding the corner to the main hall, Queen stopped short, reached out, and stopped the other two.

"What is it? What's wrong?" Gallo asked.

Rook saw immediately. "Pierce's office. The door is open."

"Look at the lights," Queen said.

All of the lights leading to Pierce's office, both ceiling and sconce, had been broken.

They crept to the door, unsure of who or what they'd find inside.

"Maybe it's a janitor?" Rook asked.

Gallo shook her head. "They don't break lights."

Glass shattered from within the room, followed by a heavy crash as something heavy fell over.

"Stay back," Queen told Gallo. She stood to the side of the door and whispered to Rook. "Whoever is in there, shouldn't be. I'll hit the lights, you go in swinging."

Rook nodded. Queen counted down from five on her fingers. With her last finger down, she slid into the room and flicked the light on just as Rook barreled in, fists clenched. But the sight inside the office locked him in place.

Two figures, enormous and cloaked in black, leaped up and let out twin shrieks of agony. As one sprung onto the desk at the center of the room and lashed out and up with a wooden staff, Rook caught a glimpse of what looked like ash gray skin. Then the lights shattered and darkness returned. The shrieking was replaced by the sound of fast movement.

"Oh sh—"

Rook was struck head on and flung from the doorway. He sailed across the hall and into the wall, which dented inward beneath his girth.

Gallo screamed as two shadows moved like liquid, out of the office and down the darkened hallway. But it wasn't just their cloaked appearance that frightened her, or that they moved on all fours, like animals, it was that they were running on the walls. They disappeared into the gloom, but could be heard exiting through the stairwell.

Queen exited the office, ready for action, but found only Gallo hiding behind a potted plant and Rook struggling to stand. She helped Rook up. "You okay?"

"Never better. What the hell were those things?"

Queen shrugged and looked at Gallo. "I-I don't know. They looked like . . . they looked like wraiths."

"Wraiths," Rook said. "That's just spectacular. So why were wraiths in Pierce's office?"

She shrugged, looking wild-eyed.

"Agustina," Queen said, "we're almost done and they've gone. Does Pierce keep a flashlight in his office?"

"You're sure they're gone?"

Rook and Queen just waited. Gallo entered the office slowly. They could hear her inside, shuffling through paper, fumbling. There was a loud crash as something shattered, followed by a whispered expletive. Light filled the room a moment later, glowing from a small desk lamp. A broken jar of candy sat on the floor, but that was just the beginning of the mess. The office had been ransacked. Filing cabinets had not only been opened, they'd been destroyed. The desk drawers had all be torn out and upended. The couches had been slashed and gutted.

"Hold on," Rook said. He moved to the phone, one of the only items in the room that remained untouched. He hit the call button and said "Nice try assholes," before popping open the back, tearing out the batteries and removing a bug, which he promptly smashed. "We're good."

Rook moved behind the desk, where the two dark-clad figures had been hunched. A three-foot-square safe sat on the floor, beaten but secure. "This is what they were working on." After wiping a finger along the edge of the safe where a line of plaster clung, he looked at Gallo. "Where is this safe typically?

Moving slowly, Gallo stepped over a coatrack and took hold of a crooked painting. She lifted it to reveal an empty space in the wall.

"Impossible," Rook said as he tried lifting the safe. "This thing weighs a ton. I doubt four men could move it."

"Do you know the combination?" Queen asked from the door where she was keeping watch.

"Nine, seventeen, nineteen, ninety-five. That was supposed to be their wedding date. George and Julie."

Rook ignored her and dialed in the numbers. He opened

the safe a moment later. Inside lay a single piece of wood, shaped like a bust, but worn and indistinct. He took it out and placed it on the desk. "Great, another chunk of old wood."

"George wouldn't have saved this without reason." Gallo looked at it up close. She could just make out what used to be a face, possibly wearing a helmet, which led to a slender neck, shoulder, and pair of breasts. On the right shoulder sat a figure, whose details had not yet fully faded. An owl. Gallo gasped. "It's . . . she's . . . Athena. This must have been a small part of the *Argo*'s prow."

"But why would George want us to find this?" Rook asked.

"The prow of the *Argo* was made from a tree taken from the sacred forest of Dodona, where the world's first oracle presided. From prehistoric times up through Greek history the site was revered as a place of prophecy. It was believed that the prow of the *Argo* held this power, too, perhaps aiding Jason in his quest."

"A prophetic tree," Rook said. "What's it got to say for us now?"

Gallo leaned in close. "Maybe nothing." She dug her finger into an odd notch where the neck met the head. She could see that it had been worked recently, pried at, probably by Pierce. Something clicked and the head twisted to the side revealing a cylindrical space within the neck. "Maybe everything."

Filling the space was a single cylinder. It slid easily from the bust, where water had not yet reached. It was a tube-shaped piece of pottery that had been sealed with wax, but had already been carefully cut. Gallo traced a finger along the cut. "This is what he wanted us to find."

She opened the tube and found a parchment inside. She pulled it out, laying it on the table. Defying everything she knew about archaeology, Gallo slowly unrolled the parchment, which was in extraordinary condition. Her only consolation was that she knew Pierce had already done the exact same thing. Flakes fell from the sides, here and there, but the document was still intact.

"A map?" Rook said looking down at the image. Several coastlines had been hand drawn on both sides of a large island. Text filled the spaces of the land masses to the left and right. "The text is ancient Greek and faded. It will take time and equipment to enhance and translate."

Queen left her post by the door. "Could George have translated this?"

"Too much of the text is faded. A few words here or there maybe, but not on his own. Besides, I don't think it's the text he wanted you to find."

"What then?"

"I recognize this island," Gallo said. She looked at each of them, stopping at Queen. "It's Gibraltar, twenty-five hundred years ago."

"You're sure this is it?"

Gallo lifted the map and held it in front of the lamp. The backlit map revealed a watermark at the center of the island—a circle with two lines through it. "The Herculean Society."

"What's in Gibraltar?" Rook asked.

Gallo shrugged. "Maybe nothing."

Rook grinned. "Maybe everything. Right, I get it."

"Whatever it is, George believed it might help."

"And it's all we've got." Queen rolled up the map and reinserted it into the bust, which she placed back in the safe and spun the lock. "Did Pierce keep a weapon?"

"In his top desk drawer. He got it after he was attacked."

Rook found the tipped drawer and searched beneath it. He found a 9mm Glock. "Not bad."

"Am I coming with you?"

"Did those things see you?"

Agustina thought on it. "No. They never looked in my direction."

"Then you'll be safer staying here."

"But I'll be arrested."

Queen took her by the shoulder and looked her in the eyes. "Go back to Sebastian. Wake him. Cut him lose. Tell him you were coerced, that we would have killed you both if you didn't cooperate."

"What if he doesn't believe me?"

"He will," Queen said, then delivered a hard slap to Gallo's face, splitting her lip.

Gallo cringed in pain, but understood the reason for it. "Thank you."

Then, as easily and quietly as the two wraiths, Queen and Rook entered the hallway and disappeared into the darkness.

FORTY-THREE

New Hampshire

Three days had passed without incident. Knight had reconnoitered much of the forested mountainsides within the borders of Pinckney without finding any evidence of construction. King had spent the time getting to know the locals, who he skillfully interrogated without ever raising an eyebrow. He'd asked everyone he came across about new construction in the area, convoys of trucks, everything he could think of. No one had seen a thing. Bishop remained holed away in the Honeymoon cabin, researching the area on the Internet, mapping out a search pattern for Knight, and meditating his rage issues away, which was made simpler thanks to the relaxed environment provided by the cottage and surrounding natural world.

But they were all getting anxious. The clock was ticking.

As had become habit, King took Thor for a walk, leading him out across the large grassed quad that led to the Tabernacle, then the trailer park, and the official "dog walk" beyond. The time alone provided King with an opportunity to think and take stock of any changes in the scenery.

But nothing seemed out of the ordinary. Birds chirped from the fringes of the forest. Morning dew clung to the quad's close-cut grass. Gleaming white clouds rolled past in the distance, behind Stinson Mountain. The air smelled clean, despite the yellow clouds of pollen that filtered down from the pine trees with every stiff breeze. And always, the sounds of children, both seen and unseen, called from all corners of the campground.

He paused to take it all in. The place was a haven. *All the more reason to find and stop Ridley,* King thought. He gripped the leash hard in his hand and his frustration at their inability to find Manifold. *Three days. Three damn days.*

As he stared at the ground, thinking about what tactics might work better than the current subtle approach, King failed to notice the car bearing down on his position. It wasn't until the brakes were applied, screeching the car to a stop, that he looked up and saw the front end of an old station wagon stop five feet short of barreling him over. Through the brown dust kicked up by the stopping car, he caught site of a figure moving swiftly from the driver's side door.

He reached under his T-shirt behind his back, gripping the hidden handgun. Just as he was pulling it out, the newcomer emerged from the dust. King shoved the handgun back into his pants and put on a smile.

"Now just what in the name of Pete do you think you're doing?"

Mrs. Scranton. Eighty years old, white-haired, and wearing a loose-fitting light blue, flowered dress. Full of fire, and apparently brimstone as well.

"Mrs. Scranton. How nice to see you again," King said. He'd first made her acquaintance two days ago when she commented on his choice of T-shirt—his Elvis T-shirt no less.

"This mongrel is . . . is relieving himself all over the quad!"

King looked down. Thor stared up at him with his big innocent eyes, still squatting. A fresh mound of rank feces sat behind him. At that moment, King missed Rook. He tried to imagine what Rook would say in such a situation, but failed miserably in his attempt. "Guess he needs to lay off the bran, huh?"

The old woman's sour face reminded King who he was talking to. Bran issues probably hit too close to home.

"I do hope you brought a plastic bag for that mess?"

King's smile said it all. Nope.

"What was your name again?"

King missed the question as he caught site of a woman standing outside the Snack Shack. She was looking right at him. After a few seconds of eye contact, more than could be chalked up to a casual glance or even physical attraction, she ducked inside the building and disappeared into the darkness within. King tensed. The way the woman carried herself—like a soldier—stood in stark contrast to everyone else he'd seen in town.

A shrill scream snapped his attention back to Mrs. Scranton. Thor, feeling frisky after relieving himself was kicking dirt with his back legs, all over Mrs. Scranton. She huffed and made her way back to the car. A series of contorted facial expressions mixed with more than one kind of grunt, gasp, and growl told King she was going to tell the campground's higher-ups and anyone on God's green earth that would listen about this incident. He gave as friendly a wave as he could muster as she started the engine, but it only seemed to enrage her further. Pedal to the metal, she nearly ran them over as she peeled away, rounding the quad, turning toward the campground exit and skidding to a stop in front of the registration building. As she stormed inside, King looked down at Thor. "We're supposed to be undercover. That means not drawing any unnecessary attention you dumb mutt."

But the incident had given him something, though he didn't know what yet. He headed toward the Snack Shack, determined to find out who the mystery woman was.

* * *

Knight followed the dirt road that rounded a corner and up a hill at the backside of the campgrounds. The road didn't exist on the campground map and was too covered with trees to see where it went via satellite. It was one of the few patches of terrain in Pinckney he hadn't checked out, so he decided to have a look. He doubted he'd find anything worthwhile, though. The campground owned hundreds of acres going back into the mountains, and no one would have been able to build up here without the campground's knowledge. But there wasn't much territory left uncovered and he doubted he'd missed anything.

He stayed five feet in from the road, just in case someone drove past. It wouldn't do him much good to be seen dressed in all black, carrying a MSG3 selective-fire rifle over his shoulder. That kind of news would travel fast in a small town. It might not be believed by the locals, but if Manifold caught wind, they would send out the hounds for sure.

At the top of the hill, Knight found an abandoned horse stable and three large, brown buildings. An old kids camp by the looks of it. The largest building, a long, rotting structure full of broken windows, bore a sign that read "Mess Hall." The other buildings, smaller and in equal disrepair, held signs that read "Administration," "Nurse," and "Snack Shack 2." The place had once been a part of the campground below, but had been left to rot long ago. Nothing of interest, though.

Knight continued on, following the dirt road. He passed a rainwater- and tadpole-filled in-ground swimming pool and a rusted swing set. A small utility building full of deflated inner tubes came next. Then, after a sharp turn and short hill, he arrived at what looked like a kid's camp straight out of a B horror movie. There were twenty-odd brown cabins arranged in a U. The dirt road ran up and around the cabins, exiting into the forest on the other side of the campground.

He crouched low, hidden by a pine branch, and swept

the area, keeping track of the sounds and smells of the place. Convinced no one was around, he entered the campground. The wooded center of the camp was full of campground obstacles in disrepair. Tires half buried in the ground. A zip line now tangled in branches. A tire swing with no tire. The place looked like it would have been fun once. Now it was a ghost town.

A distant sound caught his attention. A hum. An engine. Perhaps a semi on route 27 echoing off the mountains. Perhaps something else. Knight made his way to the back of a cabin, climbed a nearby tree and threw himself to the cabin's roof as easily as a chimp, breaking off and taking a pine branch on the way. He lay flat, covering his head with the pine branch, and peering over the top with a pair of reflection-free binoculars. A glint of light caught his eye. A blue pickup truck. Nearly as old as the camp by the looks of it.

He took aim with his rifle. The weapon didn't have the range or power that his assortment of sniper rifles did, but it was amazingly accurate at a distance—more so in his hands—and its automatic fire made it the superior choice for a wooded firefight. The truck drove slowly through the campground, working its way around potholes and fallen branches.

Knight noticed three things right away. For an old car the engine sounded mint, powerful even. When it did strike a pothole, the suspension handled the jolt with ease. But it was the two clean-shaven, serious men in the cab that really caught his attention. Not only did they look too well put together to be vacationers, but their eyes looked harsh—something he had yet to see in the small, friendly town. As the truck passed, Knight saw that its flatbed had been covered by a blue plastic tarp. *They're hiding something in there,* he thought. Could be anything from pot to manure, but he decided it was worth his time to find out what.

Moving quickly, Knight shed his backpack and weapon.

He placed his GPS locator inside the backpack and activated it. The device would alert the others to come looking and let them do so with ease. But GPS wasn't without its limitations. Inside a cave, or underground facility, the GPS would fail and his trail would disappear. Luckily, they'd prepared for such a possibility. He removed a small spray can labeled SprayTrack from his pants pocket and pointed the nozzle at himself. He doused his body in a cloud of clear mist. The odor wasn't strong, not to people, but it would be easy for Thor to track. The dog would be able to follow his scent for days, following the smell well beyond the range of a GPS transmitter. The GPS tracker would get the team here. Thor would take them the rest of the way.

With the truck twenty feet past his position, Knight jumped down from the cabin and ran through the woods to catch up. Without the weight of his backpack and weapon, he covered the distance in near silence. Running low, he bolted from behind a tree and clung to the backside of the pickup, feet on the bumper, hands on the rear hatch. So far, so good. Getting inside without being seen in the rearview— that was the trick.

After thirty seconds, he got his chance. The truck hit a series of pounding bumps where spring floods had washed away the road. As the truck thundered up and down, Knight used the momentum to fling himself over the back and under the tarp. He closed his eyes as his body struck the flatbed with a thud, hoping he wouldn't be found out. When the truck continued on its way, he sighed and opened his eyes and looked to see what secret the truck held.

A pair of dull gray eyes stared back at him.

FORTY-FOUR

Rock of Gibraltar

The chartered flight, courtesy of a U.S. government spending account, touched down at Gibraltar airport shortly after dawn. It was the fastest way to cover the distance, but the small airport's lax security also allowed Rook to sneak along Pierce's Glock. Rook had also used the change of scenery and mission as an excuse to change his clothing. He now wore more functional cargo pants, T-shirt, and hiking boots. Queen had changed into similar clothing. Gibraltar was built on a steep incline that descended from the base of the "rock" to the ocean. The combination of ancient fortresses, caves, tunnels, and sloped city streets translated to a lot of hiking. Rook noted that even in cargo shorts and a tank top, Queen managed to still look more European than he did. Too much "backwoods and flannel in you," she'd explained.

Unsure of where to begin their search, they took a "tour the rock" taxi, which drove them to all the local sites, starting with downtown Gibraltar. The city, being property of the United Kingdom, was a mix of British pubs, shops, and bright red phone booths better suited to a London street corner than a Mediterranean city. But the population density of the city made finding any kind of clue as to the location of the Herculean Society impossible.

They continued the taxi tour, requesting to be taken to the oldest sites on the island. With the Society being so interested in history they hoped they would make their home, as Gallo had, as close to an archaeological wonder as possible. St. Michael's Cave, a stalactite- and stalagmite-filled cavern sometimes used for operas and ballets, proved to be an impressive site, but home to nothing more than tourists and a large, out-of-place auditorium.

Next came the Great Siege Tunnels, which Rook hoped would turn up something. The labyrinth of tunnels were one of the island's first true defense systems. Built and used to defend the island between 1779 and 1783, they were later used during World War Two. The dark, low ceiling tunnels were full of history, violence, and death, but were vastly predated by anything as old as Hercules.

Visibly discouraged, their cabbie and personal tour guide, Reggie, took their mood to be a result of discontentment. He was a kind man, full of smiles, but his British name combined with dark skin and rigid features made his true nationality a mystery. His mixed accent, as well, was impossible to place, at times sounding Indian, other times Spanish, and occasionally British. "I will show you the best Gibraltar has to offer and introduce you to our most famous residents."

It sounded like a lead worth following, so neither argued. They became even more interested as they approached a large fortification high above the city. "The Tower of Homage," Reggie explained. "The oldest structure in the city."

The car stopped in a large parking lot, nearly full. The tower itself stood to their left, tall and impressive. The double-door entrance was closed. "What's in the tower now?" Rook asked.

Reggie answered from his rolled-down window. "Her Majesty's Prison Service."

Rook shook his head. "Well, there goes that theory. Unless her majesty is in league with the Herculean Society."

Queen ignored him, walking to the hillside wall. The view of Gibraltar below and the blue-green sea beyond was impressive. Once again, they found themselves in an ideal vacation spot for history buffs and revelers alike. Rook stood beside her. "I'm not a big fan of needles or haystacks. Put them together and I'm bound to get pissed."

When she didn't reply, he looked at her. She craned her head one way and then the other. To their left was the city. To their right, a line of hotels along the beaches. "What are you looking for?"

"How old is this castle?" Queen asked and then answered before Rook had a chance to process the question. "A.D. 711."

Rook began to ask a question, but she held up a brochure she'd picked up at St. Michael's Cave, answering the question of how she knew the build date. "Okay, what's your point?"

"This is the oldest structure on Gibraltar. But it's not old enough."

"And?"

"And we've only seen half the island."

"That's because the other side is a thirteen-hundred-foot vertical drop into the Mediterranean."

Queen handed the brochure to Rook and pointed to the bottom of the third foldout. He read the text aloud, "Gorham's Cave. Twenty-eight thousand years ago, Neanderthals made their home on Gibraltar. Not only were they the first hominid settlement, it is also suspected they were the last of their kind. Over one hundred three artifacts have been recovered including spear tips, knives, blah, blah blah. Yeah, I see where you're going. So where is it?"

"At the bottom of a thirteen-hundred-foot drop." She smiled. "But we can also take a boat."

A sudden blur of motion caught Rook's attention, but

he reacted too slowly to avoid the approaching creature. It launched from the wall, clung to his back, and assaulted him with its small hands, groping in his pockets and in his waist. "What the hell!"

Rook spun and struck the animal with his arm, knocking it away. As it bounced off the cement sidewalk and bounded back up to the top of the wall he got his first look at the creature—a brown-furred, tailless macaque. One of the island's famous Barbary Apes. But it wasn't just the sudden appearance of the macaque that opened Rook's eyes wide. It was what it held in its hand—a 9mm Glock.

Rook felt the small of his back. Nothing. "Son of a bitch."

Though the macaque held the weapon handle out, Rook didn't want the gun to discharge outside Her Majesty's Prison Service. Explaining why a macaque had a handgun covered in his fingerprints, stolen from a ransacked office at the University of Athens would take some time. More time than they had. Even with Deep Blue's vast political influence.

As Rook reached out for the weapon, the macaque hissed and bared its teeth. Rook dove for the weapon, but the creature was too quick. He looked at Queen, who was watching and smiling. "A little help?"

"I've never seen two monkeys fight before."

Rook grunted, then dove for the macaque again. This time it leaped onto his back and off again. That's when Rook noticed Reggie approaching. "It's okay," Rook said. "You don't need to help."

"I see you have met our most famous residents? Do not worry. This is a simple matter," Reggie said. "You just have to know how to negotiate."

Rook watched as the man took out a chocolate bar. Reggie and the macaque slowly reached out both hands, each taking hold of what the other held. It was like watching a back-alley drug deal. He let go of the chocolate and the macaque disappeared over the side of the wall. "Here you go, sir," he said, handing the weapon to Rook, and then added, "Do not worry, sir. I will not speak of your weapon." He pulled up his shirt, revealing his own handgun. "The streets can be dangerous at night. Especially for tourists. You were wise to bring it."

"We were hoping to visit Gorham's Cave," Queen said, wanting to change the subject.

"A magnificent place. Unfortunately, closed to the public."

"Is there anyone there now?"

"Indeed. Archaeologists have been working on the site for many years."

Queen reached into her pocket and pulled out a wad of cash. "Are you sure there isn't a way to get a private tour?"

Reggie grinned and scoured the area for any bystanders who might overhear before saying, "I might be able to arrange transport to the cave . . . but you must deal with the archaeologists—and consequences—on your own."

FORTY-FIVE

New Hampshire

After tying Thor to one of the deck chairs and ordering him
to stay, King entered the Snack Shack through its bright
green, double screen doors that announced his entrance
with a loud creak. He was about to greet Fred, the man behind the counter, when he noticed the dining room was
empty. The double doors on the other side of the room
swung back and forth. She'd just left.

"What can I get for ya?" Fred asked, but King ignored
him and walked to the swinging doors. He pushed them
open slowly, fearful of a trap. But the woman was walking
quickly toward the woods. She glanced over her shoulder
and met King's eyes again.

She ran.

The trees enveloped her quickly and she disappeared
from view. King burst from the Snack Shack and sprinted
toward the trees. Upon entering the forest, he drew his
weapon. There was no doubt in his mind that this woman
was with Gen-Y and he couldn't let her escape, even if it
meant putting a bullet in her leg.

He could see her ahead, weaving in and out of the trees.
Despite her weaving, she ran in a straight line. King was
impressed by her speed and agility as she cleared fallen

trees and brush with ease. His urge was to take a shot or shout for her to stop, but if there were others around he didn't want to attract their attention. It struck him then that she hadn't called in help yet, either.

Still wary of a trap, King forged ahead, slowly closing the distance. He lost sight of her as she rounded a moss-covered boulder, but something had changed in her gait as she disappeared. She wasn't running full out. She was slowing.

King bounded up the rock instead of around it. At the top, he leaped off, landing behind the woman, who had indeed stopped, and placed his gun against the back of her head.

Her hands came up quick. Empty. "I'm not armed!"

King dug his hand beneath the back of her shirt and removed a Metal Storm handgun. "Funny, you look armed."

"I meant I wasn't going to use it." She turned to face him. Her face was hard, but pretty, framed by shoulder-length brown hair. "Look, I came to find you."

"You knew where to find me?"

"Not you, no— I hoped to find someone. And I found you. But I couldn't risk being seen with you out in the open."

King kept his weapon aimed. "Who are you?"

"Anna Beck," she said, glancing left and right like a nervous animal.

King realized this was not a sanctioned visit. "So, what is a member of Gen-Y security doing at a Bible Campground? Come to ask God for forgiveness?"

King thought she would flinch at the revelation that he knew who she worked for, but the woman just met his stare and then dropped a bombshell of her own.

"Jack Sigler. Call sign 'King.' I have shoot-to-kill orders for you. We all do."

She knew who he was, too, just like the men in the desert. He mentally replayed the event, remembering the body shapes of the black-suited mercenaries. None were women. Beck wasn't there. Lucky for her. "And yet you didn't shoot."

"Not everyone at Manifold knows what's really going on. Most of the scientists know what they're working toward, but they have no idea that the volunteers are actually kidnapped, then murdered. And they certainly don't know that the technology they think will usher in a new age of health, long life, and prosperity will be sold to the highest bidder."

"But Gen-Y does?"

"Some of them, yes. But not all."

"And you're one of the people in the know?"

"I am now. I was given this." Beck pulled out a small USB drive and handed it to King. It matched the one found in the Amazon.

"I have one just like it," he said.

Beck's eyebrows shot up and relief swept across her face. "You found Seth! He risked his life to get that. I didn't understand what was so important when he gave it to me, but— How is he?"

"Seth, I'm afraid, never made it out of the Amazon. He's dead."

She slumped and leaned against the boulder. The news struck her hard. Seth was a good guy.

"If it's any consolation, his life wasn't lost in vain. If we hadn't found him, Manifold would have finished its work unhindered on Tristan da Cunha."

Beck frowned. She'd been there.

"How many people died?" she asked.

"Nearly nine hundred. Including the island's residents and over six hundred U.S. sailors."

"No . . ." she whispered, then found her voice again. "I was in the army. Served a tour in Iraq, then jumped ship."

He looked her in the eye, sizing her up, then guessed. "Too good at your job? At killing."

She nodded. "Some people are born to play basketball or cure cancer. I seem to be really good with a submachine gun. But it's not in my heart. I didn't want to kill people for a cause I wasn't one hundred percent sure about."

"So . . . you took the security job because what? You believe in Manifold's cause?"

"On the surface, yes. The PR garbage touts them as a humanitarian company out to solve the world's problems. Makes them look noble. Like something worth dying for. Or killing for. But they're no better than the people who sent me to Iraq, except that they pay better. But honestly, I didn't think we'd ever see any action. And I never thought I'd be one of the bad guys."

"How many more are there like you?"

"In Gen-Y?"

He nodded.

"If I thought there were others I wouldn't be here alone." The statement reminded her to check for eavesdroppers again. "Some of the others aren't that bad, but do I think they would leave the money and status behind . . . ? What do they have to look forward to? It's not like people are lining up to hire Iraq vets these days. Going to war makes you a 'hero' to everyone but employers. At least for soldiers on the front lines, putting bullets into people. You can't do that and not have demons."

King nodded. She was right of course. It's what you did with the demons that mattered. But he wasn't a shrink and now wasn't the time to talk military philosophy. "Is there anything new on this thumb drive I should know about?"

Beck stood up straight. Back to business. "As far as I know, it's a copy of what you already found."

He pocketed the drive. "I'll take it anyway. Just in case." He looked her in the eyes. "Then the next big question I have is: What's to keep me from taking you in right now?"

"In fifteen minutes I'll be late and they'll know something is up. But if you want me to stage some kind of coup on the inside you can forget it. The Gen-Y's won't go for it and the scientists, well, they're scientists. They wouldn't stand a chance. Besides, I think they're done."

It was King's turn to stand up straight. "They've finished?"

"The labs are empty. I've only seen Maddox and Ridley working. If they're not done, they're close."

"Tell me about Maddox."

"Todd Maddox. A pretty-boy genetics wiz. From what I've heard, he came on a few years back, after Ridley hit a brick wall, and got things back on track. On the fast track, really. A good guy, I guess. But real squirrelly lately. Afraid."

"If he knows what's going on, he should be terrified. We all should be," King added. "But is he one of the bad guys?"

Beck chewed on that, but before she could answer, a shout, full of fear, rose in the distance. King looked back toward the campground, but couldn't make anything out. When he turned to face Beck again, she was in motion. Her foot connected hard with his chest, toppling him over. The impact jarred her weapon from his hand. She picked it up and bolted. King took aim as she fled, but held his fire. She'd dropped something next to him. A sheet of paper.

He looked at the page and found a hand-drawn map of the valley. She'd drawn Stinson Mountain and campground as reference points, then the mountain just behind the campground. There was an X through it and a hastily written, X marks the spot. They weren't only in their backyard, they were actually on the campground's property. Which meant someone here knew where. *It's amazing what good people will do for money,* he thought before thinking of Knight, who was reconnoitering dangerous territory. But warning Knight would have to wait.

King hid his weapon and dashed back to the campground where he could hear more distant screaming. Fred stood outside the Snack Shack, hand on his forehead, looking at the woods on the other side of the quad. A plume of smoke rose from the trees. "What's happening?"

Fred turned to him, his face struck with panic. "Fire."

Through the trees, King could see a cottage just inside the woods. Fire licked at the first-floor windows while smoke billowed from the second floor. "Whose cabin is that?"

"Doug and Linda Crowell. Elderly couple." Fred looked at him. "They had grandkids visiting this week, I think."

"Call nine-one-one," King said. He unclipped Thor's leash and launched across the quad like a heat-seeking missile, heading for the burning cottage. Thor stayed right by his side. He wasn't sure what he could do to help against the fire, but he doubted Pinckney had much in the way of a fire department, and Plymouth was a fifteen-minute drive. What he was sure about was that he'd sworn to protect the people of this country, and if that meant pulling them out of a burning building, so be it.

A small group was already gathered in front of the cabin. He stopped next to them and asked, "Is anyone home?"

An older man responded. "I was able to steal a peek in the first-floor bedroom and living room. Didn't see Doug or Linda. Must be out."

King didn't like taking the man's word for it, but with flames gutting the entire first floor, what choice did he have? Even thirty feet away the heat felt intense.

A scream switched off King's apprehension in an instant.

"The children are still inside!" a woman shouted.

"Stay!" King shouted at Thor, before heading for the front door and kicking it in. But the added oxygen fed the fire. King jumped back as a vortex of flames shot from the front door. A man helped him sit up and urged him to back away. The building was impossibly hot, set to collapse and a death trap for anyone who entered. King looked around for something that could help. A hydrant. Ladder.

A puddle to roll around in before running in. But there was nothing. Then he saw the crowd, now thirty people strong. They were praying.

For what? A solution? The children's souls? "Damnit!" King shouted in anger. One of the woman closest to him opened her eyes and looked at him, in anger at first, then in wonderment. But she wasn't looking at him. She was looking behind him.

King turned just in time to see a fast-moving blur enter the cabin. While the others burst into frantic chatter about the man who'd just entered the building, King took up where they left off, saying a prayer for the man who he'd just seen enter: Bishop.

FORTY-SIX

Rock of Gibraltar

As the small motorboat bounced up and over a large, blue-green Mediterranean wave, the base of the vertical stone face of Gibraltar's famous rock could be seen clearly. A small rock-strewn shoreline rose up perhaps ten feet from the water where it met a cliffside covered in caves. The caves, massive where they met the elements, narrowed into dark tunnels into which eyes adjusted to the bright sun could not see.

They had elected to approach the caves in broad daylight in an effort to remain inconspicuous. After all, they were just a couple of Swiss tourists interested in seeing the famous Gorham's Cave.

The hum of the engine faded as the pilot, a man who refused to give his name or remove his sunglasses, idled toward the shore. Just before the boat struck the stony shoreline, the pilot reversed the engines, stopping the boat a few feet from shore. Without waiting or bidding their driver farewell, Queen and Rook hopped into the knee-deep water and waded to shore.

A tan man with long, black curly locks and a scruffy beard charged out of the cave entrance. He didn't talk, but his body language spoke volumes. He was fairly large, just a little taller than Rook, and had confident eyes and sculpted forearms. In fact, his eyes were so deep, so keen with wisdom that Queen stopped short of the shore. There was something different about this man she couldn't quite peg.

The boat powered away, out to sea. Regaining her composure, Queen motioned to it and spoke with a passable Swiss accent. "Your face says we should not be here, but as you can see, he has left us."

"Why are you here?" the man asked, crossing his arms over his chest.

"Our guide in town," Rook said, also laying on a Swiss accent. "He said the Gorham's Cave was the most magnificent sight on Gibraltar. That the history is so spectacular. That no man, or woman, should miss the opportunity to see the cave. To experience our shared history."

"He was right on all counts, except that you are not allowed in the caves. No one is. Not without an official invitation, and those are only given to archaeologists and anthropologists. Which I'm guessing neither of you are."

Queen pouted. "I am afraid not. You are sure about this? That we may not enter?"

"Quite."

She looked at Rook. He smiled in a friendly way and shrugged a "Why not," still acting the jovial vacationer part.

"I must apologize, sir. We have not been entirely honest with you."

The man stood his ground, but did raise his eyebrows.

"You see, we were sent here by a friend. She told us to visit the caves. That we would find them fascinating. She lives in the shadow of the Acropolis in Athens. The Plaka district. Perhaps you have been there? A beautiful place this time of year."

"Wonderful gelato," Rook added with a smile.

The man stood silent for a moment, and then said, "I do not know her."

Queen reached into her blouse and pulled out the amulet recovered from the *Argo*. The worn Herculean Society symbol glittered in the sun. The man squinted, frowned momentarily, and then put on a warm smile. "Ahh, I see you have a special invitation then."

"We had hoped so," she replied.

The man thought for a moment, then headed for the cave entrance. "Follow me."

He led them through the large mouth of the cave, into the darkness beyond. The tunnel had been largely clear of debris, but the floor was all but invisible in the darkness. If not for the light ahead, allowing them to keep watch on the man's head, he could have easily left them behind. "You can lose the accents," the man said. "I know you're Americans."

Rook didn't bother asking how the man knew, and didn't argue the point. He dropped the accent and asked, "I didn't catch your name."

"Alexander Diotrephes." He hurried on, into the light.

They entered a large chamber, lit by several standing halogen lamps. The floor was covered in a grid of intersecting strings—an all-out archaeological dig was indeed underway. Several workers looked up at them, watching with suspicious eyes, but none said hello. Alexander waved to them and they returned to work. "Please stay on the path. A single step could destroy thousands of years of history."

Rook took note of the two-foot-wide path, lined by strings. It wound its way through the cave. Whoever had laid down the path had meticulously worked their way through the cave, avoiding any and all archaeological finds, which were marked by small, bright orange flags.

"We have cataloged one hundred and twenty artifacts including knives, spear tips, and bone fragments. But our greatest discovery makes the rest of this seem trivial."

"The last holdout of the Neanderthals is trivial?" Queen asked.

Alexander stopped in front of the rear wall of the cave. It appeared as though they'd hit a dead end. He flashed a smile. "You wear the symbol of our founder," he said. "I'm sure you know his name."

"Herakles," Queen said, using the ancient pronunciation.

Alexander nodded, then stepped aside, revealing the Herculean Society symbol etched in the stone wall. He continued to the side and then disappeared into the wall. Queen and Rook followed after the man and found a cleverly disguised entrance that could only be seen up close. He waited for them in a dimly lit staircase. "What we have here is a citadel of sorts. This is where Hercules spent his last days on earth, teaching his ways to his followers, safeguarding his secrets and ensuring his status as a god among men."

"Then he wasn't a god?" Rook asked as he followed Alexander and Queen down a winding staircase, making sure to keep a watchful eye behind them. If things went wrong, the cave system was a strategic nightmare.

"Hardly. An amazing man. The *most* amazing man. Worthy of adoration and praise. But fully human. That is the legacy of the historical Herakles. The pinnacle of humanity. The bar for which we all grasp."

A solid wooden door blocked the way at the bottom of the stairway. Then he surprised them again by flipping open a faux rock and revealing a hand print identifying pad. He placed his hand on the pad, and waited as a blue light passed over his palm and fingers twice. The door unlocked and swung inward, allowing them entrance.

The room on the other side was as modern as it was large. While the stone walls, stalactite-covered ceiling, and ancient carvings revealed the cavern's age, the computer terminals, lab tables, and rows of refrigeration units spoke of a long-term, modern occupancy. If there had ever been evidence of Neanderthal occupation here, they had long since been crushed underfoot . . . or vacuumed off of the splendidly polished stone floor.

Rook felt sure that this is what Pierce must have suspected. And with no one else around, it was time to drop the ruse and get some answers. Rook drew Pierce's 9mm and aimed it at Alexander. "Sorry, buddy. But we're going to ask you some questions and we're going to need some answers. And fast."

Rook expected any number of reactions from the sizable man. He'd seen tougher men urinate, weep, and buckle at the knees when confronted with their own death. But Alexander reacted by grinning and chuckling. He knew something that allowed him to keep his calm, to the point of casually accepting the presence of a gun. He sat down on a stool, clasped his hands on his lap, and asked, "What is it you want to know? Hmm?"

As Queen and Rook looked into the now excited eyes of Alexander Diotrephes, they failed to notice the two figures approaching them . . . on the ceiling.

FORTY-SEVEN

New Hampshire

Word about the man who had entered the blazing inferno spread through the campground faster than the fire could devour the house. The crowd swelled to nearly a hundred people. Women gasped as the story was told. Men explained why they hadn't charged in. Kids watched with wide, nervous eyes. King made a mental note of the teenager taking video of the scene on his cell phone. If Bishop made it out alive, that was one video that couldn't be allowed to make it onto YouTube. If he didn't make it . . .

King tried to ignore the possibility. But it had been nearly a minute since Bishop had entered the cabin.

The whine of fire engines sounded in the distance. Plymouth was responding quickly. If the fire spread, the whole campground could go up in flames. Just as King began to focus on the possibility of having to evacuate the campgrounds, an explosion blasted a hole in the cabin's roof. Smoke billowed from the fresh, four-foot hole. King shook his head in frustration. The place was falling apart. Bishop was—

The smoke split as a figure launched from the hole, clearing the remainder of the roof and plummeting two stories to the ground. A sound like snapping branches shot out as the man struck the ground. His legs had broken from the impact. The man fell to his side and rolled to his back, as if protecting something in his arms.

Despite the thick black coat of soot, King recognized Bishop's bulky form. Thor did, too. The dog whined at Bishop. No one else would recognize him, though. The kid with the video camera would probably make a small fortune from the video. He grit his teeth and clenched his eyes shut as an intense pain racked his body. He rolled onto his knees, holding his torso up with one and still clutching the other, and a thick blanket, to his chest.

King walked closer, wary despite knowing it was Bishop. Something didn't feel right. Part of him wanted to run over and support his friend who was clearly in severe pain. But another part of him, a voice he wanted to squelch, but couldn't, shouted just the opposite. Run.

Bishop should *not* have survived.

Still King moved closer.

Bishop's skin was twisted and bent. Beat red. Melted. The elephant man and Quasimodo combined had nothing on him. His breathing was deep and fast, rough and ragged. Primal. Frantic. He had been altered, inside and out, re-shaped by flame into a monster.

The crowd saw this, too, and stepped back as King took another step forward. Motion on Bishop's face stopped him. Something was changing.

A woman hollered in fear and pushed her way back through the crowd. She'd seen what King was now seeing.

Something impossible.

As Bishop began to bellow—in rage or pain, it was impossible to tell—his charred skin flaked away before their eyes, falling to the dirt road like soft feathers. Some pieces were caught by a breeze and carried off above the crowd. People ducked and shouted as the burned, papery flesh hovered in the air. As the skin fell away, it was replenished by a new layer. Fresh hair grew atop his skull, which had been burned bald in the blaze. The red, gnarled skin on his face smoothed and straightened. Thirty seconds after leaping from a burning building, nearly on fire himself, Bishop's shout sounded human again. He had been healed.

As Bishop's scream faded, King headed off the crowd before they could jump to any conclusions about the man in front of them. Good or evil. Angel or demon. Religious people tended to go one way or the other. Either way, he had to get Bishop away from these people. How he failed to realize Bishop had been injected with the regeneration serum on Tristan da Cunha was beyond him. He should have realized it when Bishop had taken the brunt of the explosion and survived without a scratch. The question was: Would Bishop lose his mind?

As he knelt down next to Bishop, King could see smoke and steam rising from his flesh and burned clothing. The man had endured the horrors of being burned alive and survived. He kept his right hand behind his back, ready to draw his weapon if necessary. It would be an awful thing on so many levels, but if Bishop went regen on this crowd of people, few, if any, would survive.

Placing his left hand on Bishop's shoulder, he said, "Bish . . ."

Their eyes met. When he spoke, his voice was like a growl. "I'm here. It's still me. But if I lose control . . . If I become like the others. Use it." He looked at King's arm, still behind his back, ready to draw his weapon. "Take my head off."

Nothing further needed to be said. Both men knew the score. If Bishop lost control, his head would soon follow. It was the merciful thing to do. Bishop would rather die than hurt an innocent, or a team member for that matter.

"The kids?"

Bishop uncurled his hunched body as he stood. He held a ball of blankets in his arms. As he reached his full, towering height, the blankets fell open revealing two unconscious children, free from burns.

The crowd erupted with cheers. A slew of "Praise

Jesus" and "Thank the Lord" went up. The clamor was drowned out by the blare of two fire engines rounding the corner and entering the woods.

"They . . . need to be treated . . ." Bishop said.

"Take your time," King said, taking the kids one by one and laying them on the ground, far from the blazing home. Thor licked their faces gently, then lay down beside them. Being compassionate wasn't part of the dog's job description. He was just being a golden retriever.

As King checked the kids over, feeling for pulses, listening to their breathing and watching their little chests rise and fall, the crowd kept a safe distance from him and Bishop. He could hear them whispering about Bishop, but ignored their words.

When King finished with the kids, Bishop took his arm. For a moment he looked enraged, but it could have just as easily been the discomfort of his quickly healing wounds. "There is no time." He winced as pain shook his body. He growled lightly, tensed, and then returned to himself. "Knight activated his GPS. I was on my way to get you. He's found something."

"Or some*one* found him."

"He could be in trouble."

Two firemen cut through the crowd and approached. After giving Bishop a wide-eyed once-over, they turned their attention to the kids on the forest floor. "What the hell happened?"

"He saved them," someone shouted.

"They need to be treated for smoke inhalation," King said. "They'll live."

"Was there anyone else inside? I was told the home belongs to an elderly couple," one of the men said, then looked at Bishop again. "And . . . is he . . . okay?"

"The house was empty," Bishop said. "I checked all the rooms."

"You . . . went in there?" the fireman asked, looking up at the burning cabin.

With furrowed brows and anger in his voice, Bishop replied, "No, I always roll around in soot before I—"

Before he could finish, two streams of water blasted the cabin as the fire crews attacked the blaze. But they were too late. The weakened structure collapsed. As the second floor and attic crashed down, smoke, sparks, and hot embers shot out among the crowd, sending folks scattering. The two firemen covered up the children, shielding them with their bodies.

But when the smoke cleared, the two men who had saved the children from the fire, and their dog, were gone. The crowd searched the surrounding woods for the men, but they'd disappeared.

Like angels.

After fifteen minutes of slow, but bumpy, travel, the pickup truck came to a stop. Knight peeked out from the side of the tarp and saw the driver look up and wave. He couldn't see the recipient of the wave, but guessed a camera was watching because what looked like a moss-covered rock wall moved into the mountainside and then slid away, revealing a subterranean tunnel leading inside the mountain. He ducked beneath the tarp as the truck drove forward. Looking through the back of the tarp, Knight saw the secret door close behind them as double sets of ceiling-mounted lights passed by on the ceiling above.

He lowered himself down again and looked at his fellow passengers. After searching their bodies he discovered the gray-haired, liver-spotted couple were Doug and Linda Crowell. Both were over eighty and owned a cabin in the Pinckney Bible Conference Grounds. Both were alive, though severely sedated. What Manifold wanted with them was anyone's guess. Neither were scientists. Doug carried a long-since-expired mill worker I.D. card. And given the amount of flour on the apron Linda wore, the only science she was currently involved in was the chemistry of making snickerdoodles.

As the truck slowed, Knight peeked out. They were about to enter a large loading dock of some kind. He hated leaving the couple. They reminded him of Grandma Daejung, but staying would only get him killed. And their chances of survival dropped with his death. Knight slipped silently from the back of the truck and dove into the shadow of a support beam.

The truck stopped in a brightly lit parking area. The driver and passenger were met by two more men dressed in security uniforms. Gen-Y. The four men joked and laughed as they casually pulled the elderly couple from the back of the truck, took them by arms and ankles and carried them away. After the group left, the loading bay went dark.

Knight entered the space, comfortable in the dark, and checked the door. Locked. A dull green light caught his eye. He approached it slowly, wary of a motion sensor. But as he neared, he made out the shape: a downward pointing triangle positioned eight feet up on the wall. He searched the wall, finding the door's central seam. He worked his way left and found a single button. He pushed it. It glowed bright yellow and the double doors slid open. A large freight elevator. "Going down."

Knight stepped inside and scanned the options. The levels were labeled by letters: G, L, Y, and P. He chose to start at the beginning and work his way through. After pushing the G button, Knight took out his silenced Sig Sauer and smashed the overhead light. Crouched in darkness, he waited for the doors to open again.

Thirty seconds later they did. After his eyes adjusted to the bright light streaming in, he moved slowly into a hallway. A loud repeating pop filled the air. The sound repeated over and over, each time followed by a guttural grunt. His nose caught the ripe smell of human sweat and his imagination filled with images of regens, torture chambers, and human guinea pigs strapped to tables. He knew Manifold was fully capable of producing all three.

He slid against the wall, approaching a four-foot-by-eight-foot window that looked in on the room where the sounds and smells came from. He took a deep breath and prepared to steal a glance. With a practiced quickness, he could look in the room, memorizing every feature to sort out in his own time. But when he turned his head and looked into the room, his head locked in place. What he saw was so outrageous, he couldn't look away.

FORTY-EIGHT

Rock of Gibraltar

Alexander Diotrephes crossed his legs and leaned back on a lab table, cool as can be, and answered the first question Rook posed, "George Pierce is an archaeologist. A fine one at that. But his allegiances are in the wrong place."

"What do you mean by that?" Rook asked.

"He is committed to revealing history to the world."

"You're an archaeologist. You disagree?"

"Did I say I was an archaeologist?"

Rook thought about it. He hadn't.

Queen circled Alexander slowly. "And the problem with learning from history?"

"History is doomed to repeat itself no matter how much we know about it. There were two world wars, virtually back to back, facing the same enemy. No one learned from the first war. No one doubts that there will be a third world war. It's as much a part of our future as the wars of our past. But digging up the past isn't just useless, it's sacrilege. When ancient relics, theories, and . . . intellectual properties are dug up by archaeologists like Pierce, they automatically take a kind of finders-keepers mentality. He believes that he has complete freedom to reveal what may have once been a closely guarded secret to the world.

I simply say it is not the place of archaeologists to make such a decision."

"You expect archaeologists to track down the descendants of the original owners?" Rook asked.

"Or the descendants of the grave they're exhuming, yes. Do you think the pharaohs wanted to be dug up and displayed in museums, or ground into powder and sniffed like drugs, or sold at auction? The modern world talks about religious freedoms and protections, yet we so quickly ignore the beliefs of those who came before simply to satiate our curiosity. It's offensive."

"Cry me a river," Rook said, then looked at Queen. "I'm betting he's a vegan, too."

That got a grimace out of Alexander. "Do you know who I am?"

"Not a clue."

"And yet, you come here, armed, and expect me to answer all your questions?"

"Looks that way."

"Looks can be deceiving."

A shadow fell over Rook. It hammered him in the back. He fell forward, losing the handgun beneath a lab table. A second form fell from the ceiling, but Queen dove out of the way, rolled to her feet, and raised her fists. But there was only Alexander, sitting with his cocky smile. She noticed his eyes flicker, ever so briefly, behind her. She turned and kicked out, catching her attacker by surprise. She was happy to hear a grunt and crack of bones.

But when she turned to face her foe, it had retreated to the shadows. She could just make out the swaying head and shoulders, but could clearly see the yellow, reflective eyes.

Rook crouched and dove for the gun. Just before his fingers reached the weapon, a dark hand reached out and snagged it. There were five fingers, but the cracked, gray skin and impossibly thick fingernails looked inhuman.

Rook stood in a flash. He recognized the skin. These were the same things they found in Pierce's office. He looked for it, but the creature had joined the other in the shadows.

"Do not be afraid," Alexander said, looking as relaxed as ever. "The weapon made them nervous. You'll be fine . . . until I'm finished with you." He spun on the chair, facing Rook. "Now it's my turn to ask the questions. Who are you?"

Both remained silent. Torture would not gain that information. Alexander could see as much. "Very well. We all have our secrets. But I know you've been to the University of Athens. Interrupted our recovery efforts."

"Hope you got my phone message," Rook said.

Alexander grinned. "Indeed. You spin words like a minstrel. But it seems you also found what they"—he glanced into the shadows—"were unable to retrieve. You were lucky to turn on the lights. As you can see, they're quite sensitive. Now, what is your interest in George Pierce?"

"He's a friend," Rook said.

"And?"

Queen sighed. Divulging information had not been the plan. "He's been poisoned."

"Indeed. By whom?"

"A genetics company."

"For what purpose?"

"According to you, that isn't information worth sharing with the world," Rook said.

"Clearly you thought I could help with this poison. Why come here otherwise?"

"We didn't know what we would find," Queen said. "Agustina Gallo. Those were the last words Pierce spoke before he fell into a coma." Queen held up the Herculean Society symbol. "He drew this symbol in his own blood."

Alexander sat up straight. Interested. "That doesn't sound like Dr. Pierce to me."

"He wasn't himself," Rook said.

"Then, *what* was he?"

Again, they stayed silent. In the silence Queen could hear clicking from the shadows. The yellow eyes had disappeared, but she could sense the two . . . things in the dark.

"He found something, didn't he? Something dangerous? Something men . . . would kill for." Alexander rubbed his chin, then looked at Queen. "Please. Tell me where he found it. What country?"

Queen figured that knowing the country would do little good in figuring out what ancient Greek artifact had been found halfway around the world, so she divulged the information hoping it would keep the conversation going and buy more time to turn the tables. "Peru."

The man's eyes widened. "Nazca?"

"How did you know that?" Rook asked. "Another bug?"

"It can't be . . ." He was on his feet now. "A genetics company you said?"

Rook nodded, noting that the aggressive tone in Alexander's voice had been replaced by concern. "You know what he found, don't you?"

He looked them both in the eyes, sizing them up. His countenance softened. "Follow." He led them across the room, away from the shadows, toward a row of glass-faced refrigerators. "Do you know what the Herculean Society does?"

"Protects the 'legacy of the historical Hercules,'" Queen said.

He nodded, then continued toward the refrigerators. "We have led the world to believe that Hercules was a god among men; that his prowess and stature were out of reach to all of humanity. In truth he was a scientist of sorts. The first geneticist if you will."

Steam billowed from the refrigerator as he opened it. He reached in and pulled out a test tube holder that contained six vials, each filled with brown liquid. He took one out and shook it, clouding it to near black. "I never thought I would need these . . ."

He replaced the test tube holder and handed all six vials to Queen. "The elixir will block the genes that allow for regeneration. It was a temporary fix for the Hydra. For Dr. Pierce . . ." He shrugged. "Two for the creature. A small dose for Dr. Pierce should be effective. Use the rest to make more if needed. Eternal life is a burden. A curse. The planet will not be able to survive an eternity of the human race."

She looked at the vial, then back to Alexander. "You're letting us go?"

"As I said before, some secrets are better left buried. The Hydra should have never been exhumed. History will repeat itself yet again." Alexander pushed their shoulders, turning them to the exit. "Go. Now. You will not be harmed. Go!"

"If you know so much, you could come with us," Queen said. "Help us."

He laughed. "You would have me locked up when finished."

"We can make arrangements."

"I'm afraid not. I long ago promised someone I loved that I would refrain from getting directly involved in the world's problems. I'm afraid this is the best I can do. You see, unlike the rest of the human race, I honor the past. Now go!"

Alexander shoved them forward, and neither slowed. They had what they came for and knew how to find him again if need be. They raced up the stairs and entered the main cavern. The people working on the Neanderthal artifacts stood and watched them wind their way through the maze of strings. A few moved toward the back of the cave, but then stopped. Rook looked back. Alexander was there, motioning that everything was fine.

As they approached the bright Mediterranean Sea through the dark cave, Rook took hold of Queen's arm. "Something he said just registered."

"What?"

He pointed to the test tubes. "Two for the creature . . ."

FORTY-NINE

New Hampshire

Bishop paced in the small Honeymoon Cottage living room. It was uncharacteristic for him to show any kind of impatience or exasperation, but given that others in his position had succumbed to madness by this point, he was doing well enough. King sat at the dining room, looking at the screen of a laptop. The silhouetted view of Deep Blue looked back.

"I had the map you sent analyzed and compared to topographical maps of the area surrounding the campgrounds. If the map Beck gave you is accurate . . . and not some kind of trap, you should find Manifold somewhere beneath Fletcher Mountain. I've got a team covering every square inch of the site for possible entry and egress points, but they've covered their tracks fairly well."

"If Knight followed protocol we'll have all the intel we'll need." He pet Thor's head.

"I'll contact your PDA if we find anything," Deep Blue added. "Good hunting. Oh, and King . . . the gloves are off. I don't care what kind of a coverup we need to generate at the end of this. Manifold cannot be allowed to skip town again. Do whatever it takes."

The screen went blank.

Bishop stopped his pacing. "We ready?"

King turned and faced Bishop. "Think you can contain that rage building within you for a little while longer?"

"You know I can."

"Then let's go."

The two men climbed into the Chevy Tahoe with Thor. The engine roared as King pulled out of the pine needle–carpeted clearing that served as a driveway and drove through the campground. As they passed by the quad, King took note of the pickup soccer game, and farther beyond, at the baseball field, two long strings of kids playing red rover. As much as he wanted to wipe Manifold off the map, doing "whatever it takes" could not involve allowing these people to be hurt. He frowned as he realized that was probably why Manifold set up shop at this location—off the beaten path, but human shields abounded.

After passing through the campgrounds, they drove up a tall hill and discovered what looked like an abandoned kids camp. The GPS tracker on King's PDA showed their current position was just under a mile from Knight's signal. Not wanting to get too close and set off security, they pulled into the woods, covered the vehicle with camouflage netting and pine branches, then set off on foot, fully armed and led by Thor.

After ten minutes of hiking, off path, toward Knight's signal, they came upon a clearing full of cabins. They crouched at the side of an incline, searching the area for signs of movement, organic or electronic. Seeing nothing, they stood and moved up behind one of the decrepit brown cabins. King checked the PDA. "We're right on top of the signal."

The trees above swayed in the breeze. Bishop looked up. "Or the signal's on top of us." He placed his machine gun, muzzle up, against the cabin, locked his fingers together and lowered them, palms up. King placed a boot within Bishop's large hands and was quickly launched to the cabin's roof. He laid low on the roof, waiting in silence to see if the movement had garnered any kind of response. Even the snapping of a twig would be enough to tip him off. But other than the twitter of birds and swish of wind through pine needles, the forest was silent.

He turned his head the other way and found Knight's backpack, rifle, GPS transmitter, and an open can of Spray-Track. He shut off the tracking unit and placed it into the pack, which he dropped over the side to Bishop's waiting arms. While Bishop hid the pack inside a rotted fallen tree, King leaped down from the roof with the rifle and Spray-Track. He slung the weapon over his shoulder before kneeling down to Thor. He held the can out to the dog. "Do your stuff, boy. Stay quiet."

The dog whined in response. The "stay quiet" command had been developed to keep dogs from barking when stealth was required.

Thor entered the U-shaped campsite, sniffing the ground. He stopped in the middle of the dirt road and whined again. Scent found. "Follow. Slow."

The dog began following the trail, walking at a casual pace with his nose to the ground. King and Rook kept pace, from twenty feet within the woods. Anyone watching the road would see a loose dog out for a stroll.

Twenty minutes into following the scent trail, King noticed a tree mounted camera sweeping back and forth. It was small and camouflaged, but its movement in a direction opposite the current breeze gave it away. They waited for it to point toward Thor, then bolted past before it swung back around. Best-case scenario, they wouldn't think anything of the dog. Worst case, they had a shoot-to-kill order for the special ops dog, too.

After another five minutes of slow going, mostly to be sure they didn't trip any alarms, they saw Thor stop and sit. The trailed ended at an overgrown vertical wall at the base of the mountain. This was, no doubt, an entry point into Manifold's subterranean facility, but they couldn't get any closer. Queen had noted, in her report on Tristan da Cunha, the amount of visual, infrared, and motion sensors the Manifold facility had had. He doubted this would be any different. They would have to find another way in.

King whistled a command that would sound like any of the local birds, but Thor recognized as a simple command: go home. The dog stood, turned, and just as casually backtracked. He would follow the SprayTrack back to the campground, their own scent trail back to the Tahoe, and the car's scent back to the cabin where he would wait for their return.

Laying low in a patch of tall ferns, King turned on his PDA and waited for a connection. He looked at Bishop, whose eyes were still on the hidden entrance. He looked like he was about to blow the door down and open up with his machine gun until every last living thing inside keeled over. When he saw Bishop's hand on a grenade he realized that might actually be what he had planned. He placed a hand on Bishop's arm. "Soon."

Bishop took a breath, released the grenade, and nodded.

A text message scrolled across the PDA's screen as it was received and decrypted. It read:

Found ventilation on Fletcher. Also, potential helipad. Actual pad obscured. Same as Amazon. Take your pick.—DB

A map of Fletcher Mountain loaded next. Two vents were marked with red circles. The helipad with a blue question mark. "Thoughts?"

"I think I'm too big to fit in a vent shaft."

King smiled. "Good point."

After circling the base of the mountain for a half mile, they began their upward climb. The grade was fairly even, but fallen trees and scads of oddly shaped boulders slowed their climb. After reaching an elevation of one thousand feet, they headed sideways again, stopping twenty minutes later on the opposite end of the mountain, directly above a helipad. Once again, the trees had been cleared diagonally so that a helicopter would have to fly into and under the canopy. The pad was currently empty, but two armed guards stood to either side of the pad, scanning the forest below.

King looked at Bishop, whose facial expression asked a very simple question, "Now?"

King nodded, but then held his index finger to his lips. The message was equally simple. Kill them quietly. The men split up, each moving toward their intended target. The battle for Manifold Alpha was about to begin.

FIFTY

New Hampshire

With widening eyes, Knight peered through the large
glass window, forgetting for a moment to conceal himself as he watched a spectacle beyond comprehension.
The forty-foot-long, twenty-foot-tall, and equally wide
room was brightly lit from above. Red lines stretched
across the highly polished hardwood floor. But it wasn't
the boxy room's size or lack of decoration that held his attention, it was the two people throwing themselves around
the space, grunting, stretching, and occasionally cursing
when the ball was missed. A racquetball court in a science
facility would have been odd enough. But the two players
on this court fought for the ball and victory like combatants
at the coliseum. It would have normally been an impressive
sight, except that the man and woman inside looked older
than Knight's own grandma. Pushing eighty, at least, if not
older.

Their sweat-soaked white hair lay plastered against
their heads. Their muscles looked firm and healthy. Only
their faces defined their age, wrinkled and wizened. The
man dove for the ball, missed, and slammed into the glass
in front of Knight. The man's lip split, but as he stood and

regained his composure, the lip healed. The man noticed him, gave a smile and a wave, then went back to playing as the woman smashed a devastating serve. The two were back at it, playing what had to be one of the most intense games of racquetball Knight had ever seen. They had regained their youth. They were happy to be alive. So happy that they didn't notice Knight's unusual black garb or the silenced weapon in his hand.

As his sense of reality returned, Knight noticed a video camera mounted high in the corner of the court. The couple was being watched. Guinea pigs. But a success story? Knight wasn't sure. For all he knew, one of them might break a hip, go mad, and eat the other. He stepped away from the window, steering clear of the camera, and proceeded down the hall. He passed rooms full of exercise equipment, a basketball court, a boxing ring, and a pool. The facilities were probably created to entice new minds to work for Manifold, but they clearly never got a chance to use them. Not only was there not a soul around, but the equipment looked brand-new. Of course, there was always the likely possibility that the scientists chose not to use the equipment.

He entered a men's locker room at the end of the hallway. He checked for security cameras. He didn't think there would be any, but he wouldn't put it past Manifold. They didn't seem to have any compunction when it came to issues of morality . . . or in their case, immorality. After seeing no visible signs of security, he rifled through the lockers. Most were empty. One held a candy bar wrapper, long since discarded. One of the last he checked held some clothes. He looked them over. Plaid pants and a yellow button-down shirt. They no doubt belonged to the old man playing racquetball, and would do little to help him blend in. On a whim he pushed open the bathroom stalls, one by one. The first three doors clunked open. The fourth made a thud. Knight looked behind the door and smiled. A long, white lab coat hung from a hook on the back of the door. Knight slid it on and headed for the door.

As he rounded the corner out of the locker room he slammed into something moving fast and fell to the floor. Dazed, he sat up and looked at the person above him, expecting to see a security guard. Instead it was the old man, reaching down with a hand and a smile. "You all right, son?"

Knight took the man's hand and stood. He forced a smile. "You're built like an oak tree, sir."

"Thanks to you people." The man slapped Knight's shoulder. It hurt. A lot. "You've gone and found yourself a miracle cure."

"I didn't catch your name on the memo," Knight said.

"Bobby Jackson."

"And how did you find out about the program?"

"I was in Plymouth Hospital. Terminal cancer. Few weeks to live. Your fellas came and picked me up one night. Snuck me right out. Next day I was shooting hoops. Today racquetball. I'm a new man."

"And your partner on the court? How is she?"

"Louise? She's fantastic."

"Your wife?"

"My wife has been dead for forty years, son. And I hope she gave up looking down on me a long time ago, 'cause I'm aiming to get lucky tonight."

Knight laughed. "Well, good luck with that, Bobby."

"Luck won't have nothing to do with it," Jackson said as he entered the locker room. "I'm the only one in her age group that can keep up!"

Knight couldn't help but smile at the old man's innocent enthusiasm. Youth regained had to be an amazing feeling. But the ramifications were disturbing. Manifold was close to success, if they hadn't already achieved it. Knight hurried down the hall trying his best to look like a scientist in a hurry. As he passed the racquetball court, the woman exited and flashed a healthy grin. No dentures, either. Her teeth had grown back in. "Good game, Louise?"

"I'll get him next time," she said, then headed toward the locker rooms. She rounded the corner as Knight entered the elevator. He pushed the button for the next floor down, labeled L.

When the doors opened, he entered the hallway looking as casual as possible. He took a left without hesitation and didn't bother looking for security cameras. To anyone watching it would look like he knew exactly where he was going. Thankfully, he found the beige hallways well labeled and full of scientists wearing similar lab coats. He passed signs for archives, cryogenics, computer lab, and, most disturbingly, a morgue. But none held his interest enough to check out in person. His chosen target was well labeled above all others: Research Wing.

As he rounded a final corner he found the research wing blocked by a security door that required a pass card. He looked at his watch, head down, and plowed into a pair of talking scientists. He apologized three times, never meeting their eyes like a frightened dog, then continued toward the door, a freshly pilfered security card in his hand. He swiped the card and entered the secure wing.

The hallway on the other side was devoid of people, but he could hear voices farther on. He continued down the hallway, once again doing his best to look like he knew where he was going. He turned twice, following the voices, then realized they were fading. Rather than backtrack he took two rights and then a left, getting back on track. As the voices grew louder, he slowed, then, upon reaching a windowed lab, stopped. He knew it would look suspicious to anyone watching, but it might look equally suspicious to anyone inside the room. Especially with the hallways so empty.

He peered into a large lab, full of computer terminals,

large pieces of equipment he didn't recognize, and a dozen people sharing champagne. He took note of the people in the room. He didn't recognize several of them, but he could see Richard Ridley pouring the champagne. The Gen-Y guy, Reinhart, abstaining from the drink. And Todd Maddox, imbibing greedily.

Ridley held up his glass. "To our success!"

Cheers rang out. Knight made mental notes of the others in the room. A few scientist types. Harmless. In addition to Reinhart there were four more Gen-Y security men. Too many to charge in with a lone weapon. He'd take a few with him, maybe even Ridley, but he'd be killed in the end and would tip off Gen-Y to the team's presence. He was about to head back the way he came when Ridley took Maddox by the shoulder and led him away from the others. Knight reached into his pocket, pulled out a personal sound amplifier. He plugged in a set of earbuds and placed a small suction cup against the glass. The device worked like placing a cup against a wall, but with crystal clarity. With its invisible laser pointer directed towards Ridley and Maddox, the digital processor inside the device blocked out any signal outside its scope, essentially silencing the other voices in the room.

Ridley's voice filled his ears, pushing the small earbuds' bases to the limits. "How long before we can be sure?"

"We're testing the second couple now. They're responding well to physical injuries."

"Skip ahead to intense testing. I want to know if it's safe by the end of the day."

Maddox nodded.

"And when you're done, cut off one of their heads. The Hydra was said to replace a single decapitated head with two new ones. I need to know if that is a concern."

"It shouldn't be," Maddox said. "Different genes would direct the number of heads grown and we've isolated the regeneration gene. I don't foresee—"

"If you happen to lose a head during your very long lifetime, do you want to spend the rest of your days with polycephaly? We should also know if the body can regenerate from the severed head . . . or if a new head will grow from the body. Or both. If not, we'll have to do our best to avoid guillotines."

"Mmm." Maddox looked at the floor. "Listen, Richard, I know what we've done is amazing. It will save lives. Countless lives. But I can't help but feel bad for the lives that were lost."

Ridley sniffed and rubbed his nose. "You've heard the expression about broken eggs and omelets, I'm sure. It applies here as well. Except that we've done much more than create an egg and cheese patty. I would have willingly sacrificed a thousand lives. Two thousand. More. With billions to benefit, my conscience is clear. Always will be." He laughed at Maddox's wrinkled forehead. "Relax, Todd. You have accomplished the impossible. By dawn we'll be immortal."

Maddox smiled. Ridley made a good point. His feelings of guilt over the deaths he helped cause had already faded some. In two hundred years they would be a vague memory. He sipped his champagne. In the meantime, work and alcohol would dull his conscience.

Knight had heard enough. He had to risk getting word to the others. Manifold had to be brought down, and now. By the next day they'd be facing an immortal security force. He headed back the way he'd come and found an elevator. He entered the elevator, pushed the button for the top floor and took out his PDA. He turned it on, took a deep breath, and attempted to make a connection. A status bar on the screen glowed blue, then flashed red. A message appeared on the military modified device.

Signal blocked . . .

Digital device detection network found . . .

Shutting down . . .

The screen went black, just as the lights in the elevator flashed red and an alarm sounded. The doors opened as Knight pocketed the PDA. In his peripheral vision he caught movement. Someone drawing a weapon. He drew his handgun and swung it around, aiming the silenced muzzle at the face of a beautiful woman, whose three-barreled Metal Storm handgun was aimed at his forehead.

FIFTY-ONE

New Hampshire

Using the soft layer of pine needles coating the forest floor to quiet his approach, King sidestepped down the mountainside using trees for cover along the way. Bishop descended the incline on the other side of the helipad. The two guards stood chatting, oblivious to their presence. King stopped behind a tree trunk and peeked around the edge. He took in every detail of the guards. Their boots were polished and their black uniforms free of wrinkles. Military discipline. They bobbed from one foot to the other as they talked. Disciplined, but bored. He listened to their voices. One was nasal. The other cracked occasionally. Disciplined, bored, and young. King took note of the Metal Storm weapons strapped to their waists. And deadly.

He was about to signal Bishop, who was hiding on the opposite side of the helipad now, to attack, but noticed a wire rising out of one of the men's collars. It merged with the man's earpiece behind his ear. *Damn,* King thought. The two sentries wore health monitors. Checking in by radio was often time consuming and could give away positions. Using a heart monitor was a newer method of knowing guards were still alive and kicking. They were no doubt being monitored by cameras as well. King looked for cameras and found two. One was scanning back and forth, the other, up and down. Not only would the guards have to be subdued alive, the job would have to be completed in a very short amount of time.

King relayed the information using a series of hand signals. The message was crude, but the team knew how one another thought and Bishop came to the same tactical conclusion that King had. At least King hoped so. He wasn't sure how Bishop would handle himself in combat now, with every injury threatening to make him a raving psychotic. It was only the man's long time practice of rage control that kept him in check.

He watched the cameras move back and forth, up and down, their timing just slightly off like windshield wiper blades matching a musical beat for a few seconds, then fading away. The cameras would only match the required angles for two passes every twenty minutes or so. King watched, as the horizontal camera swung toward Bishop at the same time as the vertical pointed down. As they reversed direction, he signaled Bishop. This was his chance.

The vertical camera reached its highest point just as the horizontal pointed fully in King's direction, making those watching the feed temporarily blind to what was happening on the helipad. Amazingly silent for his size, Bishop launched over the fallen tree he'd taken cover behind, covered the distance to the helipad, and struck out with one of his big fists just as the guard facing him noticed. The man's face had barely registered surprise when Bishop's blow connected with the side of his head. The guard crumpled to the cement helipad. The second reached for his weapon, but Bishop's hulking arm, which had flashed past the second guard's head in order to strike the first, wrapped around his neck. Bishop spun, picking the man off his feet, and smashed his head into the stone wall. The man fell limp in his arms.

Fighting the urge to continue pummeling the men, he took the first by the collar, kept the second in a head lock and dragged them both behind the fallen tree. He ducked down just as the horizontal camera faced his position. The whole attack had taken just under fifteen seconds. To the camera, it would look like the men either vanished or simply stepped within the door frame where the cameras couldn't see. Bishop checked their pulses. Strong and regular.

The waiting began again as the cameras began their dance, but within three minutes, both King and Bishop were standing beneath the cameras, out of view and ready to storm the castle. The metal door looked like it could take a direct hit from an RPG, but its weakness lay in the technology that kept it locked. Gen-Y might be high tech, but when it comes to breaking and entering, the CIA had all the best tools, and thanks to Deep Blue, so did the Chess Team.

To the right of the door was a fingerprint analyzer, card swipe, and numerical keypad. Bishop swiped the card he'd taken from one of the guards. The fingerprint pad glowed blue. Bishop place a fingerprint mold made from the same unconscious guard's finger against the pad. The phony finger was scanned. The light turned green. Just then, King popped the front panel off the wall mounted device, revealing three wires—yellow, red, and black. Power cables. He pushed them aside and found the maintenance port where new key codes could be input. King plugged his PDA in, activated a program created by Lewis Aleman, and let it run. The program snuck past the firewall, inserted a new key code, then displayed the number on the screen. King smiled when he saw the simple number. "One through five," he said to Bishop, who keyed in the code. The door unlocked and slid silently open. King unplugged the device and slipped inside the door behind Bishop. The door closed and relocked behind them.

King led, sound-suppressed assault rifle at the ready. From here on, it was shoot to kill. He doubted Gen-Y monitored the life signs of the interior guards, and the silenced weapons would keep things quiet, to a point, but their luck could only hold out so long.

The short hallway ended in a stairwell. They took it down one flight and entered the first floor they came to. The stairwell exited into a long hallway. Brown metal doors lined both sides of the hallway. King knelt and took aim. Bishop took up position behind him.

"Looks like a college dorm," Bishop said.

As a man exited a room and walked away from them, towel around his waist, King realized that wasn't far from the truth. It was a barracks. Hopefully for the scientists, not Gen-Y. The man walked into a room at the end of the hall, this one had no door. A bathroom. Voices came from the room as two men inside greeted the newcomer. The words couldn't be discerned, but it was clear the two men were exiting. King and Bishop maintained their aim.

Two Gen-Y guards, dressed in uniform, exited the bathroom. They headed in the opposite direction, but one looked back over his shoulder. His reflexes were quick. One hand took hold of his partner while the other began drawing his Metal Storm pistol. He got out a partial word, "Hosti—" Then two large holes burst in his forehead, splattering blood, bone, and brain matter on the hall wall. The other guard didn't have a chance to reach for his pistol. He fell on top of his partner, gagging on his own blood as it drained from a gaping wound in his neck. Five seconds later, he was dead.

"Oh my God!" the man in the bathroom yelled.

King and Bishop ran down the hall and greeted the toweled man in the doorway, pointing their weapons at him. His hands shot up. His towel fell down. He made no motion to pick it up or hide himself. He was terrified. A scientist. "I'm not armed!"

Bishop looked the man over. "We can see that."

"We're not going to hurt you," King said. "What's your name?"

"Christopher Graham. Assistant geneticist." His hands shook. "Who . . . who are you?"

"The good guys."

"Who are the, ah . . . the bad guys?"

King rose a single eyebrow and glanced at the Gen-Y security guards, then back to Graham. The message was clear. *Manifold.*

"Oh . . ." His hands lowered as his face fell flat. "Oh. Oh, dear. I didn't know anything. I swear. I just—"

King held up a silencing hand. "Listen, Chris. I need you to return to your quarters and stay there. Tell anyone you see to do the same. If you tell anyone we're here . . ."

"I won't. I swear! I won't—"

The lights dimmed. The halls filled with bright white strobes and flashing red lights. An obnoxious alarm sounded loudly. Too late. The jig was up. Bishop moved to cover the hallway exit. King looked Graham in the eyes, his gaze intense. "Where can I find Richard Ridley?"

FIFTY-TWO

Rock of Gibraltar

"This is nuts." Rook sat on a bench pretending to read a newspaper, looking relaxed despite his drenched and itchy feet. They had followed, on foot, the sometimes submerged shoreline around the rock of Gibraltar in order to reach the city. Queen sat next to him. Together they eyed the security situation at the civilian Gibraltar airport. The six-thousand-foot-long airstrip stretched from one side of Gibraltar to the other, marking the border between the United Kingdom territory and Spain. The airport had been built and expanded by the U.K. for military use during World War Two, but in 1987 the airport was reduced in status to a civilian-run facility. Which suited Rook just fine. Security, from what he could see, had been reduced to one checkpoint, perhaps with an armed guard, and barbed wire on top of a chain-link fence. Some people even strode back and forth across the landing strip to reach Gibraltar from Spain, which made what they were attempting that much more insane.

Beyond the fence, a family who had just strolled across the landing strip entered the small reception building and stopped briefly at the check-in desk. A guard, armed, stood and checked their passports before letting them through.

He would pose a minimal threat, but neither wanted to injure a man for just doing his job.

"Over the fence, then," Queen said.

"Ayup." Rook checked his watch. Their ride would arrive in ten minutes.

After leaving Alexander Diotrephes and his strange cave of Herculean Society secrets, they'd jogged the half hour back to the city of Gibraltar, retrieved their clothing and equipment from a lock box, and placed a call to Deep Blue. He related what King had learned from Beck and that they were in the process of infiltrating the facility, which Knight had apparently already entered. Rook grumbled about not being part of the raid, but after Queen mentioned the test tubes acquired from Alexander, and what they were meant for—one for Pierce, two for the creature—Deep Blue decided it was best to get them both to the New Hampshire Manifold facility ASAP. The *Crescent* scrambled ten minutes later, en route for Gibraltar. That was nearly two hours ago.

Rook checked his watch again. Almost time. He looked to the west. Bright white clouds hovered in the blue sky. Seagulls danced about. Kites flew high at the distant beaches. But nothing else.

Then he saw a black, straight-flying boomerang cut through the clouds and swoop toward the ocean. "That's our ride."

Queen jumped up and ran across the street. Rook followed close. She quickly scaled the chain-link fence, tossed the thick wool blanket over the barbed wire, and heaved herself over. Rook was up and over, just as quickly. As he hit the pavement on the other side, the guard inside the reception building noticed them and made for the door. But they were already in a dead sprint for the tarmac when he exited and shouted for them to stop.

Screeching tires tore up the pavement behind them. Rook looked back. Two armed jeeps roared from a garage.

The lax security wasn't as lax as they were led to believe. "Run faster!"

They ran at an angle toward the end of the runway, knowing that the *Crescent* would need almost all of the six thousand feet of pavement to fully stop. It was the equivalent of a mile-long sprint. Both Delta operators could achieve the task, but neither could outrun a speeding jeep . . . or bullets.

Shouted voices rang out from behind them. The jeeps were closing in. "Stop or we'll be forced to shoot!"

Rook was about to split away and allow Queen, who was carrying the container of test tubes like a football, to escape, when a massive gust of wind nearly knocked him over. Tires squealed as brakes were applied. The massive black plane appeared silently, like an apparition. When the brakes were applied and engines reversed, the thunderous roar drowned out all else. Rook looked back. It had also stopped the guards in their tracks. The *Crescent* looked more like a UFO than any other kind of aircraft. It was something no civilian had seen before, and something these guards would never see again. On top of that, any airport, tourist, or surveillance camera, along with every other electronic device for a square mile, was now dead thanks to the EMP discharged by the *Crescent* before landing. Distant cameras would record the passage of the giant plane, but the details would be lost in the mash of pixels. No one would know what landed there that day.

The *Crescent* never came to a complete stop, but a staircase did descend. Rook and Queen leaped on it and climbed inside as the plane began spinning around on the tarmac. Both made it to their seats just in time to be plastered to the back of their chairs by massive G-forces. They were aloft and breaking the sound barrier thirty seconds later. New Hampshire, Manifold, and their teammates awaited them at the end of a two-hour flight. Until then, they would prep the serum for use against a mythological creature and hope they wouldn't have to use it.

he lax security wasn't as lax as they were led to believe.

FIFTY-THREE

New Hampshire

"All I need is one shot," Knight said. "And I won't miss. So why don't you put the gun down."

Knight was shocked when the woman actually complied. Then she surprised him.

"You're with King, aren't you?"

Knight just stared at her, wondering if he should knock the woman unconscious and be on his way. But he wanted to find out what she knew about King, and he had issues attacking women he'd rather be asking out. She was his type—a chiseled beauty. He exited the elevator, keeping the gun leveled at her chest. "Who are you?"

"Anna Beck. Gen-Y Security. I just met with King. Gave him a map. I imagine he's on his way." She smiled slightly, laughing at his scrutiny. "I'm on your side." She turned her weapon around, holding it by the barrel, and handed it to Knight. "You're going to need this."

Knight took the weapon and tucked it into his pants. "Why's that, exactly?"

"The facility is sealed down tight. There's no way out. Not until Ridley or Reinhart shuts down the system."

"In that case," he said. "Where can I get lost?"

Beck stepped into the elevator. "Science level. Lots of

nooks, crannies, and equipment to hide a little guy like you."

Knight looked at her wryly. She stood a good three inches taller than him and probably weighed more, too. At that moment, he realized he liked the size difference and decided to not take offense. He returned to the elevator and stood next to her. Looking over, and up, he saw she was closer to five inches taller than him. A lot of woman, Rook would say, was not necessarily a bad thing. Knight agreed. Still, her uniform bore a Gen-Y logo. He might fancy her, but he couldn't trust her. Not yet.

The elevator opened a moment later. An empty hallway yawed before them. "The science level. Go in deep, pick a room, and hold your position. I'll see if I can't put a wrench in things here."

Knight stepped off and turned around. "Thanks for helping."

The doors closed.

Fighting hard to not cover his ears against the earsplitting alarms, Knight ran into the science level, not worrying about tripping motion sensors or appearing on cameras. He needed to find a place to make a stand, and fast. He found what he was looking for at what he surmised was dead center of the level. The lab was large, perhaps fifty feet wide and three times as long. The room had only one set of double doors. Nowhere to retreat, but only one direction to shoot. Not knowing the layout of the facility, this would improve his odds of survival more than running pell-mell through the hallways.

He worked his way through the room, rounding computer terminals, refrigeration units, and large, granitetopped lab tables with built-in sinks. The place looked like a combo computer lab and college science lab. But there was a lot of equipment he didn't recognize. All that mattered to him was that it was made of metal and could take a bullet . . . or fifty, in his stead. At the center of the room was a long work table. It had metal sides and a granite top. He took up position behind it and leveled his Sig Sauer at the doors, ready to shoot anything or anyone foolish enough to enter.

As a long minute passed he noticed the large carrying case on the tabletop. It was gun metal gray and cold to the touch. Something important must be held inside. Something recently transported, possibly from Tristan da Cunha. Knight kept one hand aimed at the doors, while he unlatched the carrying case. He flipped open the lid. Steam rolled up and over the top. The object inside the case looked like some kind of statue head, snakelike and monstrous. The Hydra head.

Knight realized the head might be his ticket out of Manifold. If they still needed it intact, he could hold off an army for however long it took King and Bishop to track him down and raise holy hell. As he closed the lid, three rounds, fired in so rapid a succession they could barely be distinguished from one another, ripped through the air and smashed into the case. The case toppled, spilling the Hydra head onto the floor. It slid across the smooth tiles and slammed into a table leg, chipping chunks from its nose.

Some bargaining chip, Knight thought as he ducked down. He realized that Manifold would have never left the head unguarded and placed casually on a desktop if it wasn't completely irrelevant. In fact, they'd probably want it destroyed to keep anyone else from accessing its DNA.

He rolled to the side of the desk, poked his head around the side, and fired off two shots. The guard who'd fired at him dropped to the floor. Knight ducked behind the desk again and as he heard the doors open, popped up, and took aim. His eyes widened as six men poured into the room. He fired off two more shots, dropping another man, but the other five took up positions behind equipment and support beams. They returned fire with a devastating amount of raw power. With each pull of the trigger, each man fired three rounds without recoil. Holes punched through the

desk on either side of Knight as debris and shrapnel from
bullet impacts all around sprayed into the air.

What a pitiful last stand, Knight thought. He was a
sitting duck in a shooting gallery. Then he remembered
the Metal Storm weapon given to him by Beck. He drew
it, stayed low, and listened to the gun reports. Two men
on the right, three on the left.

The gunfire stopped for a moment as the guards stopped
and listened. They were, no doubt, trying to figure out if
they'd hit him. He rose from his hiding place, ready to fire.
But a barrage of bullets tore up the granite tabletop, spraying his face with shards of granite. He fell back down. His
face stung from where the stone had buried itself in his
skin. Quickly reaching into his pocket, he produced a small
eye dropper bottle. He sprayed both eyes, blinked rapidly to
clear the debris and discarded the bottle. A man rounded
the desk, weapon aimed.

Luckily for Knight, his knee-jerk reactions were faster
than the guard's planned actions. He squeezed the Metal
Storm weapon's trigger only once, but three rounds smashed
into the man. He cried out and spilled backward, flipping
over a computer terminal, taking the monitor with him.
Knight noticed the man's earpiece. He searched the back
half of the room and found four security cameras.

Four cameras. Too many to waste ammunition on, but
at least now he knew the guards were coordinating their
attack with whoever was watching. Knight fired a warning shot in the air, causing the guards to flinch, then dove
over a desk and worked his way around a second lab table. He then dove to the right, sliding behind a refrigeration unit, leaned out, and fired. The men, still catching
the audio description of his fast movements, were caught
off guard. Knight fired and dropped one of the remaining
three. The fridge exploded as a massive amount of rounds
struck. Bottles and beakers within burst as the rounds
ripped through. Liquid spilled from the unit like blood
from a wound.

Knight leaned out to fire again, but both men were hidden from sight. They'd learned that Knight didn't miss. Knight went into motion again, diving and rolling. Rounds filled the room as he popped up and ducked down again and again like a special ops whack-a-mole. He slid to a stop, found a clear shot along the floor and squeezed off a three-round burst. A man on the receiving end screamed as his ankle shattered. He hit the floor just as Knight fired again, silencing the screams. Knight went to stand, intending on dropping the last man with an Old West draw. But his foot slipped and squeaked across the floor. He fell back in a pool of multicolored liquid.

Fluids rushed around his body. He looked to the back of the room. More refrigeration units had been destroyed. This was bad. Not only was his footing ruined, but he had no idea if the liquids were poisons, chemicals, or somebody's rancid milk. At any moment he might succumb to a toxic gas created by mixing chemicals, or be blasted apart by an explosive reaction. But not knowing for sure meant the true danger still lurked at the other end of the room. Knight braced himself and prepared to stand and fire. When he came up his target was nowhere to be seen. A shadow moved. No, the man was hiding. But why? He must know about the liquid, about his unsure footing. Why not take aim and fire when he emerged? Knight knew a moment later when the doors burst open and ten more guards charged into the room: reinforcements.

Knight drew his handgun and along with the Metal Storm weapon, unleashed a barrage. Two men fell. The rest returned fire. Chaos reigned around Knight. Equipment exploded. Glass shattered. More liquid spilled. The Metal Storm weapon was empty. Having no ammo to reload and no idea how to do so if he came across some, he tossed the weapon to the side.

The pounded metal desk he hid behind relented to the bullets. A round struck his shoulder. He winced at the pain, but never slowed, angling his weapon up over the top and firing a spray of rounds across the room. As a man shouted out in pain, Knight launched toward the back of the room. Bullets ate up the floor behind him and obliterated the equipment around him. He dove behind the last lab table and slapped a fresh magazine into his gun.

He could hear the men sliding through the room. Whispering commands to each other, holding their fire as they closed in from both sides. Knight didn't stand a chance. He lay flat on his stomach. Placing his face half in the liquid rushing by his position, he looked under the two-inch space beneath the desk, hoping to see the locations of at least a few of the approaching men. He didn't see any boots, but what he did see stripped away what little hope of escape he had left. The Hydra head sat beneath a desk, deep in a puddle. Knight watched as the liquid was absorbed by the head. The fluids were pulled so quickly that they began flowing toward it. Turning fleshy and green, the head swelled near to bursting. But it didn't burst.

It grew.

FIFTY-FOUR

New Hampshire

David Lawson leaned in close, staring at the screen where he'd watched Knight dive behind a lab table. "Be advised. Target is partially obscured."

"Copy that," came Reinhart's voice. He stood by the doors in the lab overseeing the battle, but not taking part. He wanted to see how the men he trained fared without him. The grim expression on his face and the number of motionless bodies on the floor revealed things were not going as they should have.

But as three groups of three moved in on the target from different directions, Lawson knew the man would soon be a stain on the floor. At the same time he couldn't help but respect the Delta operator. He fought with spirit and his aim was uncanny. His partner, Simon Norfolk, with whom he'd been posted since the destruction of Manifold Gamma, failed to see why killing the man was a shame.

"They're going to get the prick now," Norfolk said. He rubbed a hand quickly over his crew cut head, then rubbed both hands together with nearly spastic excitement.

"Focus on your job," Lawson said.

Norfolk rolled his eyes, then noticed Knight laying on

the floor, looking beneath the lab table, handgun at the ready. "Middle team, watch your feet." The three-man team climbed onto chairs and desktops. All Knight would see was floor. As long as the cameras functioned, the team would coordinate based on every move their enemy made. The man was already outnumbered ten to one, bad odds to begin with, but with the cameras providing a kind of battlefield ESP, he didn't stand a chance, no matter how good his aim.

Motion behind the center team caught Lawson's eye. He looked at all four cameras. Not one of them provided a good angle. It could be nothing. Or it could be some kind of trap . . . but it didn't look that way. More like a fish flopping on the floor. A green fish. He tried to remember if the labs had any animal testing scheduled. He didn't think so, and they tended to use pigs and rats. Not lizards.

Lawson toggled the microphone, "Center team. Check your six. You've got—"

The jolt came fast, so fast that Lawson never shouted in pain or flailed. He simply stopped talking. Norfolk, now staring at the green writhing object on the lab floor, didn't notice his partner's silence until he turned around. "Dave, what the hell is that—gah!"

The electric shock baton caught him in the shoulder, sending eighteen amperes in ten microsecond pulses into his body. He seized and slumped into his chair. "Sorry guys," Anna Beck said as she stood above them, holding the shock baton by her side. "I was never keen on this peeping Tom stuff."

She could see the men on the four screens, nearly on top of Knight, holding their earpieces. Their intel had gone silent, throwing them into confusion. What had been a very organized approach fell apart as men began moving on their own. Reinhart was speaking into his headset, shouting actually. She couldn't hear him, but the four-letter expletives spilling from his mouth were easy to read. Heads would roll. Luckily neither Norfolk nor Lawson had seen her face. And after their screw-up letting Seth escape with classified information, these two would pulling duty in the arctic, or worse. Motion on the screen caught her eye. Knight had sensed the confusion and was attacking. The Gen-Y guards scattered, firing back as they did. But there was something else at the center of the room. Whatever Norfolk and Lawson were looking at was still there . . . and still moving. The thing writhed into view for just a moment before disappearing back beneath the desk. Beck gasped and stepped back. "Oh my God."

She had to warn Knight. If that thing kept growing no one would get out of that room alive.

Beck stepped past Lawson and jabbed the surveillance system with the shock baton. The system quickly overloaded, shutdown, and spewed smoke as the circuits fried. Gen-Y was officially blind.

She rushed out of the surveillance room, hurrying toward the barracks. She had to make a quick stop before she could help Knight.

Knight heard the sudden stop of feet sloshing through liquid and crunching on glass. Something had stopped the security force in their tracks, but it wasn't the thing growing behind them. They were too quiet for that. A voice by the door revealed the true nature of the problem. "Lawson. Lawson, get back on this com or so help me God I will make your life a misery!"

Knight sat up, using the lull and confusion to his advantage. He put several rounds in the closest man, then glanced toward the front of the room and dropped a second man without looking. He lay back down as return fire once again filled the room. He'd killed the two nearest attackers and got a glimpse of the man running the show—Reinhart. One of the Chess Team's Manifold most wanted. Knight risked sitting up again and squeezed off a round toward Reinhart, but a single shot was all he got before bullets began zinging past, and the shot was wide. He did manage to get Reinhart's attention. The man quickly gave up on reaching whoever had been directing the action.

Despite pain from the several shards of plastic, metal, and glass embedded in his face, and the sharp sting of the bullet wound in his shoulder, Knight couldn't help but smile. He lay on his back, looking beneath the desk. The thing on the floor had grown a body and legs were beginning to sprout. It looked about the size of a St. Bernard, but would provide a massive "holy shit" factor once spotted. These boys were about to experience their first true chaos, the kind that comes with urban warfare, and which Knight would cleave through like a katana blade through watermelon.

"Give yourself up," Reinhart shouted, still at the front of the room. The man was either a coward or smart. "Live to fight another day" was a motto that could win wars if abided by. "You won't be killed."

Knight remained silent. Confusion and stealth were his friends. Speaking gave away his position, physical condition, and mental state.

"You're outnumbered and the facility is locked down." Reinhart sighed. "You can't kill us all."

Knight knew Reinhart had experience. As head of Gen-Y he'd be their best-trained man. Ex-military. That he hadn't simply lobbed a grenade over the desk to flush him out meant he was either under orders not to do so or there was something in this room that made explosions a high risk. As a waft of something chemical hit his nose, Knight decided it was the latter. A chemical explosion at the heart of the facility could end up killing more people then just the men in this room. Motion on the floor caught his attention.

He lay back on the wet floor as the liquid continued rushing toward the growing creature. The Gen-Y boys would approach much more slowly now, if at all, so he was content to lay in wait. If someone was stupid enough to round the desk, he'd shoot them down. Otherwise he'd wait.

The screams would start soon enough.

FIFTY-FIVE

New Hampshire

It started with a startled "What the?" then descended into horrified screams of "Oh my God" and "What the hell is that!" The Gen-Y security team engaging Knight had seen the scaly green creature writhing at the center of the room. The loudest screams came from those, who, like Knight, were on the far side of the lab. Getting back meant getting past the creature. And as it reared up not one, but three heads, everyone realized how difficult that might be.

Each head held serpentine yellow eyes, split down the middle by black diamond-shaped pupils. Sheets of flesh, like thick insect wings, extended from slits on the sides of its heads, where the skull met the neck—like gills . . . or possibly ears. Rows of small horns rose up from its snout and tailed back across its face, splitting into two rows that rose up over the perpetually furrowed eyes. Its greenish brown body was covered in reflective scales except on the underside of its neck and belly, where large, hard plates overlapped all the way up and under its many chins. Muscles rippled on its legs as they hefted the now horse-sized body off the floor. A stubby tail grew down to the floor and twitched like an agitated cat's. Last but not least, its four feet held four toes, all connected by thick, webbed flesh and bearing sharply curved talons. Once caught in the creature's grip, nothing would escape.

Knight stood, knowing that everyone was too distracted to fire a round in his direction. They stood in awe of the mythological monster. Reinhart realized what it was just as Knight did. "The Hydra," he said.

The creature stood on four legs and stretched its still lengthening necks toward the ceiling. It gurgled—fleshy—as though its vocal cords were still forming. As the wet sound escaped all three sharp-toothed mouths, the sound came together, loud and clear. It was like a combination of an ocean-liner horn blast and a peacock's blare. Both high- and low-pitched, with each head producing a unique sound. The vocalization was accentuated by a sharp rattling sound that came from its winglike ears as they vibrated madly, slapping against the thick necks. The shriek made Knight's hair stand on end. It also sprung Reinhart into action.

The head of Gen-Y security drew his Metal Storm weapon, shouted "Kill it!," and began pulling the trigger. Knight ducked down, content to wait and watch while his enemies fought it out. If Gen-Y got the upper hand, he'd start dropping bodies. If the Hydra took control, he'd make a stealthy, and fast, exit.

Firing rapid, three-round bursts, the Gen-Y team riddled the Hydra with bullet holes. Chunks of flesh burst onto the walls, floors, and men's bodies. The water still rolling across the floor becoming red. The beast roared and twisted, flailing its tail. Computer terminals exploded from the impact. Desks shattered. Equipment flew across the room. One of the Gen-Y guards nearest Knight was caught in the face by a gene sequencer. The heavy metal unit compressed his skull upon impact. The man dropped his weapon. Knight snatched it up.

Bullets continued to pound the Hydra in a relentless assault. Then, one by one, the Gen-Y guards ran out of ammunition. Several hundred rounds had been fired, nearly all of them striking the large target. Silence filled the room as the men frantically reloaded.

Knight peered over the granite tabletop. The Hydra was bent inward, all its heads facing the floor. It shook. Blood oozed from hundreds of small holes and a few large ones. But despite the wounds, the body grew larger. Knight's eyes widened as the wounds began to heal. The small wounds disappeared within seconds. The large ones began to fill in from the inside out. But the Hydra didn't wait for its body to become hale again before lashing out. Two of its heads snapped out like striking snakes, snagging men on either side of the room, pulling them screaming toward the ceiling and then smashing them down to the wet floor. Their screams cut short as powerful jaws opened and closed, peeling away chunks of flesh, bone, and organ and swallowing them whole.

Gunfire began to ring out again as the Gen-Y team tried to make their way back toward the exit. But it appeared the Hydra had no intention of letting any of them escape. It launched itself across the room, smashing one man against the wall and bashing another into the air with its tail. Seeing an opening, Knight ran for the exit side of the room, but a burst of gunfire sent him to the floor. He caught sight of Reinhart standing by the exit, aiming his weapon at him while the two remaining Gen-Y guards continued to pepper the Hydra with Metal Storm rounds.

Knight looked up as the two men ran out of ammo and fled out the doors. The Hydra roared at them as they left and as it did, Reinhart pulled a grenade pin and tossed it into one of the creature's open maws. He ran from the room, closing the doors behind him. Knight ran for the doors again. Being the only human being left living in the room, he wasn't concerned about being shot. He leaped over desks, rounded columns, and did his best to move quickly without getting too close to the Hydra. But it had other plans. One of the Hydra heads shot out toward him, snapping shut a moment too early. It missed clamping down on his arm, but managed to knock him to the floor.

Knight hit the floor, rolled back to his feet, and unloaded the Metal Storm weapon. He got off four three-round bursts, pegging the central Hydra head square between the eyes. The head reared up with an awful shriek. But the sound was cut short as an explosion in the head on the right blasted it clean off, halfway down its neck. Reinhart's grenade.

The Hydra staggered back, shrieking while its ears vibrated. Knight made for the door and slammed into them, gun at the ready in case Reinhart had stayed behind. But the doors were locked solid and sent Knight sprawling back to the floor. He stood quickly and began kicking the door. They weren't budging. He turned to face the Hydra. What he saw made him forget all about escaping for a moment. The severed neck was not only regenerating, it was splitting, like a cell dividing. The flesh stretched, split, and continued to grow two separate necks. The myth was true. As the nubs of two new heads began to form at the end of each new neck, Knight focused on the door again. He kicked at it, then fired his weapon at the lock. That proved just as fruitless. As he slammed a new clip into his non-Metal Storm hand-gun, Knight turned again to face the Hydra, and just in time. He dove to the side, narrowly avoiding one of the new heads striking out at him. The impact sent the door flying into the outer hallway. As the head pulled up and a second prepared to strike, Knight dove for the door. When the second head lunged at Knight, he twisted in the air, aimed, and fired a single shot. The head snapped crazily to the side as Knight's round smashed into its eye. Knight landed on his back, sliding to a stop on the floor. He moved to stand but a third head struck out for his legs.

The teeth snapped just short of his feet as he was pulled away from the door. It shrieked at him as the other heads still inside the lab joined in the rattling roar. Yanked to his feet, Knight found himself standing next to a wide-eyed and petrified Anna Beck. "Which way!"

"Follow me," she said, dashing through the hallway. He ran behind her, looking over his shoulder as three Hydra heads spilled into the hallway writhing back and forth. The floor shook as the creature slammed its large body into the door frame, tying to break free of the lab. The slamming continued as they rounded a series of corners and approached an elevator.

"Where's Reinhart?" he asked.

"Saw him head in the other direction when I came down. We're safe."

"I'll need to find him when we get topside. Ridley, too."

Beck nodded.

The elevator chimed as the doors opened. Weapons raised. Fingers gripped triggers. But no one fired.

King lowered his weapon. Bishop, too.

Knight smiled. " 'Bout damn time."

A boom and roar echoed through the hallways.

King's brow furrowed. "What . . . was that?"

Knight and Beck entered the elevator. "You remember the artifact recovered from the Nazcan desert?"

King cocked his head to the side, eyes widening. The Hydra.

"Yea, well, it got wet . . . and now it's pissed."

A corner wall burst into chunks of plaster as the four-headed Hydra slammed into the hallway. Heads searched in every direction. When one saw them standing in the elevator, side by side like sardines ripe for the eating, all four heads snapped in their direction and roared. The sound hit them like an explosion. Then the beast launched forward, bearing down on them.

Beck was already pushing the floor button, then she hammered the close door button. The doors began to close as Hydra closed the distance. They slid shut and the elevator began ascending. Elevator music replaced the Hydra's roar for a moment before a massive force struck the doors below them. The elevator shook and screeched but continued to rise. A second, but less powerful blow shook them again. Then silence and the music returned.

King turned to Beck. "Are there any other ways up?"

"Four stairwells." Knowing where King's questioning was leading, she added, "All big enough for the creature. I doubt it will be contained."

Knight slouched against the wall, out of breath. "And it can't be killed. King, it can heal faster than any regen, and its heads . . . the legends are true. If you take one off, two grow back. If we try to fight this thing on the ground it's going to make a quick meal out of us."

Bishop knelt down in front of Knight and drew his knife. He cut a small slice into his thumb and held it up for Knight to see. A drop of blood slipped away and fell to the floor. By the time it struck the wound was healed.

Beck saw this and moved away from Bishop. Knight just stared at the healed thumb.

"Leave the fight to me," Bishop said. "You could die, but I won't."

Knight looked at King, who said, "We have an agreement. If he loses control—"

"Shoot me in the head," Bishop finished. "It won't grow back."

FIFTY-SIX

New Hampshire

Reinhart barreled through a set of double doors and sprinted down the following hallway. He was followed closely by six men, all armed with Metal Storm handguns and Metal Storm rifles, which were more accurate than the handguns and carried twice as many rounds. Each man also carried an assortment of fragmentation, stun, and incendiary grenades. Reinhart wanted them ready for any potential enemy, human or beast.

The occasional shake or distant scream of some scientist signified that the creature had escaped the lab level and was making its way up, toward them. Soon there wouldn't be any place left to run. And after what he saw, he didn't think all the bullets in their arsenal would do much more than piss the creature off. But he couldn't act without Ridley's say so, not to mention that Ridley's welfare was his number one priority. Not because he cared about the man. He just wanted to keep getting paid.

After having his men take up positions outside Ridley's office, he gained entry by swiping his key card, having his eye and thumb scanned, and then letting Ridley know it was him. Ridley alone had complete access to the office. The door unlocked and slid open.

Maddox sat in a love seat, sipping Ridley's damned mint tea. Whenever either man was stressed, they clipped some mint from the plants in Ridley's office, brewed a pot, and sat around like a couple of five-year-old girls at a tea party. Didn't even use sugar. Despite the tea, Maddox's leg bounced and his eyes shot to the door as Reinhart entered.

"What's happening?" he asked quickly. "Are we under attack again?"

Ridley was leaning against his huge, solid mahogany desk, gingerly sipping at his china teacup. Seeing such a large, commanding man sipping from a teacup always looked odd, but it wasn't until he spoke that the sight became surreal. "I'm assuming we have Delta issues again? King and his merry men?"

Reinhart nodded. "As best we can tell there are three intruders. Heavily armed and not taking prisoners. We have nearly twenty dead already."

Maddox sat up straight. "Scientists?"

"No . . . just my men." He looked at Maddox. "But seeing as how you're such a key player in all this, I'm sure you're on the hit list. As am I." He looked at Ridley. "I suggest we leave right—"

"I will not be abandoning another facility," Ridley said. "Not yet. Not when we're so close." He looked at Maddox. "How much time until the final batch is complete?"

Looking at his watch, Maddox said, "Two hours. Then we need to test it. Another two hours. But if they reach the lab . . ."

A smile stretched across Ridley's face and he clapped his hands together. "Four hours. I think you can handle these *three* men for four hours, Reinhart. Yes?"

"Actually, sir. There is a bigger problem, a *much* bigger problem."

His smile disappeared. "And that is?"

"The Hydra sample—"

"Is of no use. If the Delta team has it, destroy it with them."

"Sir, the sample got wet." Reinhart crossed his arms and waited for Ridley to put the pieces together.

As he raised the teacup to his mouth once more, Ridley stopped. His hand shook briefly. He placed the teacup down. "How . . . wet?"

"Very."

"It's alive?"

As though in answer, a distant boom shook the floor slightly.

"Very."

"What's alive?" Maddox asked.

"The Hydra."

Ridley paced back and forth in front of Maddox, who put down his tea and placed his sweaty hands on his bouncing knees. "Is it contained? Where is it?"

"No, and we don't know."

"How can you not know?" Ridley barked. "Every room in this facility is monitored by your men. How can—"

"The surveillance system was sabotaged."

"King."

"I . . . don't think so."

Ridley's bald head turned red with fury. "This is unacceptable, Reinhart."

Through the floor they could hear people screaming. Then, more distant, Hydra's inhuman, rattling roar.

Reinhart looked at the floor with a frown. The creature was moving through the facility faster than he would have guessed. Probably following a terrified sea of humanity. "I agree, but there is nothing I can do to remedy what has already happened. Right now I am concerned about your survival and the welfare of the project."

"Yes. Yes. Very good." Ridley turned to Maddox. "You have the most refined sample with you, yes?"

He nodded and lifted his briefcase off the floor. "Everything we need is in here."

"Give me one of the vials."

Maddox looked at him with suspicion. "This has yet to

be tested . . . don't do anything . . ." He didn't finish the statement, as doing so would insult Ridley. His point was made, though.

Ridley reached his hand out. "I want to make sure your legacy does not die with you . . . if something unfortunate should happen."

Maddox blanched, popped the briefcase, and handed Ridley a sealed test tube. He scribbled some notes on a sticky pad, tore it off, and handed it to Ridley. "These are the two genes currently being tested. One is regeneration. The other is unknown. If something should . . . happen to me, pick up the testing there."

After taking the note and pocketing it with the test tube, Ridley turned his attention back to Reinhart. "And you must destroy the creature at all costs. If our competition or, God forbid, the U.S. government were to get their hands on it, they may be able to duplicate our formula."

"It's worse than that," Maddox said. "They may find a way to undo it."

Ridley looked panic-stricken. The idea had never occurred to him. Immortal life achieved could be stripped away? "That's possible?"

"It'd be a simple matter of blocking the function of the new gene."

Ridley glared at Reinhart. "Reduce the creature to slurry. Then burn it to ash."

"Yes, sir."

"Now, how do you recommend we survive the next four hours?"

"Open the doors and run like hell," Reinhart said with a lopsided grin. "Being outside will allow us to use heavier weapons against the Hydra. It might be enough. But more than that, it will provide time for Maddox's computers to finish their tests. The results can be sent to you wirelessly, I hope."

"If I'm within range of the virtual private network, yes."

"And the Delta team?" Ridley asked.

"We'll have a mountainside buffet of science personnel in need of saving. And below that is the campground. Once outside, the Delta team will be preoccupied with saving themselves and the civilians. If they show, they'll get the same treatment as the Hydra. We'll prep the helicopter and have it ready to leave in four hours. In the meantime, we need to open the gates and get the race started. If the creature makes it to this level before we leave, well, we don't want that to happen." He looked Ridley in the eyes. "Once we're gone we'll level the site. The mountain, Delta team, and Hydra will all be destroyed."

FIFTY-SEVEN

New Hampshire

With Beck leading the way, Knight, King, and Bishop
made their way to the main level. As they entered the loading dock area Knight had used to enter the facility, they
saw a crowd of people rushing through the main tunnel,
toward the glow of daylight beyond. The exits had been
opened.

"Something isn't right," Beck said.

"What is it?" Knight asked.

"There's no security." She looked at King. "They're using these people to lure the Hydra outside. They're bait."

"Probably for us, too," King added, then sighed. He
looked at Knight, now armed with his MSG3, and Bishop,
who held his machine gun toward the ceiling. "Knight,
Bishop, take up position at the end of the tunnel. If the Hydra shows up, slow it down. Give these people a head start."
They nodded. He looked at Beck. She was one of them for
now, and received the call sign any temporary member of
the team had to live with. "Pawn, you stay with me.

Beck flashed a grin. While most people took the call
sign as an insult, she recognized it for what it was, a chess
piece. She was on their side, on the *right* side, for the first
time in a long while. It felt good.

"We'll cover your backs outside," King added, "and make sure Gen-Y isn't setting a trap for us. Go."

With that, all four descended the small staircase that led into the loading tunnel, merged with the moving mass of humanity, and continued to the end. Upon reaching the exit, Bishop and Knight split up and took positions on either side of the door, aiming their weapons back down the hallway. Knight knelt behind a fallen tree, steadying his aim. Bishop placed his machine gun on top of a boulder, letting its bipod hold the gun's weight while he took aim. They knew at that moment that the people fleeing the facility had seen the Hydra in person. Not one of them looked at the armed strangers with fear. One even said "good luck" as he passed.

Outside, the flow of people didn't continue down the road. People seemed to know that staying together was a bad idea. They split up, some in small groups, some on their own, fleeing into the woods in different directions. Rounding them all up, let alone eating them all, would prove a challenge.

King knelt to one knee, scanning the area for Gen-Y security. Beck stood behind him. "I disabled the security cameras and sensors. They won't be able to track us so they'll want to be more organized before launching an attack."

King lowered his weapon and took his PDA out of his pants pocket. "Cover me for a minute. Just in case."

After switching on the PDA, it connected to the satellite network, then sent a request signal to Deep Blue. Forty seconds later, the line picked up and Deep Blue's silhouette appeared. "Sorry for the delay, King."

"Check the satellite imagery. Infrared. You should be seeing something."

The screen went blue for a few moments as Deep Blue worked things on his end. A satellite image of the area emerged on the PDA, along with his voice. "It looks like the mountain is bleeding people, King. What happened?"

"You feeling open-minded?"

"Your friend looks like an alien and has a body bonded by heavy water. I'll believe whatever you tell me."

"The Hydra is alive. Back from the dead. Fully regenerated and hungry as hell."

Deep Blue's image appeared on-screen again. "Funny you should mention that. I've got Rook and Queen inbound. ETA one hour fifteen minutes. They say they have a potential cure for your friend. Something used by Hercules to stop Hydra's regeneration abilities long enough for him to sever its immortal head. Activate your GPS transponders. I'll get them to you ASAP."

"Copy that, but see if they can squeeze another mach or two out of the *Crescent*. I'm not sure if we'll be around in an hour."

Deep Blue's shadow nodded. "The satellite feed will stay open. Use it to coordinate your actions. Who's that behind you?"

King looked back. Beck was looking over his shoulder. "A friend. Pawn."

The designation of Pawn said all that needed to be said. They could talk details later. "Good enough. God speed, King." The screen returned to the infrared satellite imagery. Orange splotches wove through the forest in a wide swath, but eventually turned in a single direction. Downhill. Toward the campground.

Before King could curse their bad luck, a burst of gunfire turned him around. He ran to the exit with Beck, fighting against the flow of people and looked inside. At the far end, where the last few stragglers fled, the Hydra rampaged. Bodies flew through the air missing limbs, spewing blood, and splattering against walls. The four Hydra heads took bites from the bodies, but never slowed its motion as it seemed to prefer still-living flesh over the freshly killed. King wondered if the creature was intelligent enough to know it was a man that had imprisoned it for so long and was exacting a kind of revenge. Or maybe it had simply gone mad, like a regen?

Bishop unloaded with his machine gun, sending high-caliber bullets whizzing over the heads of the last few people running down the hallway. The Hydra fell over as the stream of bullets struck its front legs, spilling the creature to the ground. Knight fired his weapon, one accurate round at a time, focusing on the Hydra's eyes. Blinding it. Stumbling it up. But only slowing it down. Each burst eye and ruined leg quickly healed. As the last of the fleeing Manifold personnel ran past, Bishop's belt ran out of rounds. A moment later, Knight's magazine ran dry.

They watched in awe as the Hydra pounded down the hallway. It moved clumsily at first, as its legs and eyes finished healing, then picked up speed. When it roared with all four heads stretched out toward them, King shouted "Run!" and all three men leaped into the woods, bunny hopping fallen trees, plowing through brush, and, within thirty seconds, passing the slowest of the Manifold personnel. King wanted to stop and help, but with ammo needing to be switched out and the Hydra hot on their heels, they wouldn't stand a chance. Until they'd regrouped, the scattered mass of people were on their own. That is, unless their own security force stepped up.

King remembered Beck and looked for her. She was gone. *Damnit,* he thought. How could he have let her disappear like that? Better yet, why did she leave?

A roar rolled down the mountain from behind them and propelled them forward. As they slid down a steep incline they heard a voice call out to them, "Here! Over here!"

A woman wearing glasses and a lab coat waived to them from inside a small cave. King ran for the cave, followed by Bishop and Knight. "There's room for all of you." She ducked inside the cool, dry cave that descended slightly into the mountainside—a gift left from the passing of ancient glaciers. King motioned Knight and Bishop inside as a rustle of leaves told him someone else was approaching from above.

One of the stragglers, an overweight man, working for each breath, stumbled down the incline. King lunged for him and took him by the shirt. The man shouted in fright at King's sudden appearance, but silenced quickly upon realizing he wasn't being eaten. King shoved the man into the cave where he was caught and sat down by Bishop.

King ducked into the cave and was about to tell the man to stay quiet when the earth around them shook. The man fell silent.

King backed into the darkness with the others as a single Hydra head appeared from above. It tasted the air with its tongue, flapped its ears against its neck, and let out a shriek. A second head joined it, searching the fringe of the cave with its snout. As the head slid into the cave, King aimed his assault rifle at it. He knew he couldn't kill the creature, but he wouldn't go down without a fight. If he was lucky, it would back off enough for a few of them to make a run for it.

A distant scream—a man in pain—caught the Hydra's attention. The head pulled up out of the cave and rose up, out of sight with the other. Hydra's roar, just above them, shook the ceiling of the cave. The overweight man began to sob, but Bishop's large hand covered his mouth.

The Hydra jumped down from above, landing elegantly, like a cat, despite its size. And its size is what King noticed most. It had nearly doubled in size since he saw it in the Manifold facility. It looked to be the size of an elephant now, sporting four ten-foot necks and a long whip-like tail. The creature landed lightly and bounded off into the woods, heading toward the screaming man.

King looked back at the others in the cave. Bishop removed his hand from the fat man's face, allowing his jowls to shake as he said, "Whoever that is doesn't have a hope in the world."

Knight and Bishop reloaded their weapons and slipped past King, exiting the cave. King shot the man a serious glance before exiting and said, "He has us." Then they were gone, giving chase to the world's oldest living predator.

FIFTY-EIGHT

New Hampshire

As King rounded a tree and entered a blood-soaked clearing he realized the fat man in the cave had been right. Body parts were strewn about. Flesh dangled from broken tree limbs like jerky set out to dry. A severed leg had rolled over and flattened a stand of ferns. And the body, missing several large chunks, lay facedown, compressed in mud. The Hydra had killed the man savagely, eaten very little, and then stomped him flat.

Knight said what he was thinking. "This doesn't fit any feeding pattern I've ever heard of."

"I think it's pissed," King said.

Knight knelt down by the severed leg as Bishop swept the area with his machine gun. "Check this out." He peeled back the man's blood-soaked sock. A deep slice severed the man's Achilles tendon. "The cut is clean."

King inspected the deep gouge marks cutting across the man's back. They were wide and jagged. The cut through the man's ankle was made by something else entirely. "A knife."

Knight agreed. "Someone is stacking the odds in the Hydra's favor. This man didn't stand a chance because he couldn't walk."

A distant scream rang out. High-pitched. A woman. But the direction was impossible to gauge. King produced his PDA, and watched the dance of infrared figures on the screen. A few distant dots were still moving fast—the fittest and most agile of the Manifold employees. Others were huddled together. Probably hiding like the group they'd left in the cave. Some wandered aimlessly, and a few looked to be lying down, perhaps hiding. King zoomed in. Or perhaps struggling to run away with sliced Achilles tendons.

King watched as the human shape on the small screen reached up its hands. A scream rolled through the forest, matching the woman's movement. It was her. He was about to launch toward the woman, but the image on-screen kept him from moving. Her glowing orange body lifted from the ground, flew back and forth, then apart. As pieces of her rag doll form cooled and disappeared from the infrared, King realized what he'd seen.

"The Hydra is cold-blooded. We won't see it on the infrared."

"But we can see where it's going," Knight said, pointing at the right side of the screen. A second person, struggled to crawl away. Then a third. And a fourth. A human bread crumb trail. King scrolled farther to the right, following the trail. "That doesn't look friendly."

A crescent of orange dots, upwards of forty people, sat still and silent. An ambush. King recognized the cold, square shapes mixed in with the small army. The abandoned kid's camp.

"Let's go."

The three were up and running, led by King, straight toward the next victim. King glanced at the screen as a man's shriek filled the forest. On-screen, the next orange blob in line burst into pieces. The Hydra wasn't even slowing down now. A second man began screaming. Hydra's roar followed.

King picked up the pace. People were dying because he was too slow.

The man screamed again, closer this time. He was silenced as his body burst beneath the Hydra's pounding foot, sounding like an overfilled water balloon exploding.

They ran past the man's body, which had been crushed upon a rock. The Hydra hadn't even paused to bite him. The next bread crumb, now screaming, posed too much temptation. As another woman screamed out, King paused. The scream meant they were too late to save her, but it also meant Hydra had entered the campground.

Approaching low to the ground, King, Knight, and Bishop peeked up over a rock at the fringe of the campground. Hydra stood at the center, its four heads snatching chunks of flesh from the woman's body. King noted her uniform. Gen-Y had sacrificed one of their own to set the trap.

Knight saw the uniform, too, and raised his scope to his eyes. He saw the face and sighed with relief. It wasn't Beck.

"Fire!" The voice belonged to Reinhart, hidden somewhere out of sight. But the men obeying his order were not. They stood atop and inside the old cabins, rising as one and unleashing a barrage, at close range from their Metal Storm rifles and handguns. The number of rounds fired in the first thirty seconds was impossible to count, but the effect was clear. Hydra snapped at the air and twisted in pain as chunks of its body were blown away. Blood coated the pine needle–covered forest floor and clung to the sides of trees. The Hydra was being torn apart.

Some of the men focused on one of the necks. It severed and fell like a tree, crashing to the ground, where it writhed for a moment, then began to dry and flake. A leg burst and Hydra fell to its side, immobilized.

King wasn't sure who he should be cheering on. The Hydra was a monster to be sure. It would most likely go right on indiscriminately killing every human being it came across. And he wasn't sure they had the means on hand to kill it. Gen-Y clearly did, but if they survived, he,

Bishop, and Knight would be facing a three on forty fight that he doubted all of them would survive. Maybe none of them would.

"Spray it down!" Reinhart shouted. Five men with large containers on their backs emerged from the cabins. They sprayed gouts of foam that expanded and hardened, locking the Hydra in place. Bishop recognized it as the same foam used on him, only a lot more of it.

"They're pinning it for something," Bishop said.

"Okay, fall back!" Reinhart's voice rang out again. "Incoming!"

When the Gen-Y team hit the deck, King, Bishop, and Knight did as well. "Incoming" was a universal term for "duck or die." King couldn't help but watch, though. He peeked one eye around the rock. Hydra was attempting to stand as its leg regenerated, but the foam kept it stationary. The creature shook with exertion and the foam began to shatter away, but a cloud of high-caliber rounds hammered Hydra from above. Trees disintegrated. The hard foam turned to dust. The ground shook. Hydra shrieked as its body became like wet Swiss cheese. As the rounds continued to rain down from above, King realized this was the same Metal Storm weapon used to nearly sink the USS *Grant*. As Hydra continued to shriek he couldn't help but feel bad for it. What kind of creature could sustain a barrage like this and still have enough fight to whimper, let alone wail. It had to die, but it deserved respect.

For a full thirty seconds after Hydra's wails were silenced, the storm of metal falling from the sky continued. When it stopped, a cloud of dust hung in the clearing like a curtain. King could hear the voices of the Gen-Y soldiers checking in, but their words couldn't be discerned over the ringing in his ears. The dust settled in minutes and King got his first look at the Hydra. Its body was mangled, almost beyond recognition. More bloody pulp than living thing.

Gen-Y soldiers descended from their rooftop positions while others exited the cabins. They approached the Hydra, some reloading weapons, some already taking aim at the fleshy pile. They split as Reinhart, Ridley, and Maddox appeared from behind a row of cabins. "Is it dead?" Ridley asked.

"I'd say so," Reinhart replied.

"Burn it."

As Ridley turned to leave, King took aim. Ridley and Reinhart were their targets as much as, if not more than, Hydra. Then he paused. "Does something about the Hydra look different to either of you?"

Knight shook his head.

Bishop squinted. "I'm counting seven heads."

"How many did it have before?"

"Four," Knight answered.

King lowered his aim. Even while being pummeled by the Metal Storm rounds, the Hydra had continued regenerating heads, three of them. He watched as the wounds on the side of the immobile creature began to fill in. The Hydra still lived. "This is going to be messy."

FIFTY-NINE

New Hampshire

The first man snatched screamed like a wounded cat before he was flung through the roof of a nearby cabin. A few of the men standing closest took aim, but the other six heads snapped out like whips, squeezing the life from them as rib cages cracked and internal organs ruptured, then tossing them aside and striking out at other men.

Chaos ensued as the Hydra, still healing, stood again.

Some of the Gen-Y men turned and fled without a second thought. Others fired their weapons, but with their force already cut in half they could do nothing to slow the rapidly regenerating Hydra. Some men threw grenades, which had an impact, but more than a few went wide and one bounced back. The concussion sent three men flying. One legless.

Hydra threw itself into the remaining men. Their gunfire did little to slow the enraged beast. As one man became mush beneath its foot, another was eviscerated by its snapping tail. But the majority of damage came from the lightning-fast heads, snapping out like a twisted game of hungry, hungry hippos.

Five more Gen-Y men fled, all running in the fastest direction: downhill. Maddox was among them, clutching his briefcase.

Reinhart and Ridley, however, fled away from the others, heading back toward the Manifold facility.

Hydra spun in circles, looking for more attackers, but found only bloody, oozing corpses. It roared, louder than ever as the last of its wounds finished healing. Then all seven heads spread in different directions, tasting the air. Snapping branches caught their attention. All seven heads looked downhill, where the fleeing men were doing little to conceal their frantic flight. The Hydra roared again, then smashed through a cabin, reducing it to splinters, before barreling down the hill.

King cursed. He'd watched the whole gruesome event alongside Knight and Bishop. The Hydra was a killing machine. That a single man had managed to subdue the creature seemed impossible. If Deep Blue was right, and its regenerative ability could be stopped, it would be possible, but it had withstood a barrage powerful enough to destroy anything man-made and had come out stronger. And to make matters worse, it was heading for a campground full of families.

The Hydra had to be stopped.

But he also couldn't allow Reinhart or Ridley to escape. He turned to Knight and Bishop. "I'll go after Reinhart and Ridley. Do your best to slow it down. Make protecting the people in the campground your—"

Bishop was already up and moving. He passed through the decimated kids' camp and launched down the hill.

"—priority," King finished, then added, "Switch weapons. You'll need the heavier firepower." Knight took King's M4 and handed him the MSG3.

"You might need this, too," King said, handing him the PDA.

As Knight pocketed the PDA and jumped up to follow Bishop, King added, "Keep an eye on him."

Knight gave a thumbs-up and sprinted after Bishop. He was faster than Bishop and could normally catch up, but he was still human, and already breathing heavily from the past hour's action. Bishop, on the other hand, seemed right as rain; no doubt a benefit of his regenerative abilities. He couldn't get tired.

As Knight reached the drop-off behind the kids' camp he paused and looked downhill. In the distance he could see six small figures popping in and out of view as they moved between trees. Behind them ran the Hydra, its heads flailing, rattling, and roaring. Though it gained on the fleeing men, it did so slowly. It ignored trees and other obstacles, preferring to smash through them than run around. The result was a chaotic stumbling stride that left a cleared patch of forest in its wake. Knight stole a glance at the PDA map. They were just under a mile from the campground. They'd reach the quad in ten minutes. Maybe less.

Clutching his weapon, Knight dashed down the hill, leaping stones and running along fallen trees. His chest heaved from the exertion, but he was happy to see that he could still move faster than the average man, or regenerative man for that matter. He gained to within twenty feet of Bishop, just as Bishop caught up with the Hydra . . . and Hydra caught up with the fleeing men.

Knight had to duck as a man was snatched up and flung backward. The man soared over his head, screaming as blood seeped from a myriad of tooth punctures. A loud crack issued from behind him as the man struck a small but sturdy maple tree, folding his body around its trunk, backwards. He wiped the man's blood from this face as he leaped a fallen tree.

The Hydra struck a rock and careened head over heels, rolling over three more men, crushing them into the mountainside. Without missing a beat, the creature was back on its feet, nipping at the heels of the lone remaining Gen-Y guard and Maddox, whose scream undulated with every rapid footfall like Axel Rose squealing on a scratched Guns N' Roses CD.

The Gen-Y man tripped and screamed as his leg snapped. The Hydra snapped down at him as it passed, taking an arm and portion of the man's chest with it.

"Help me!" Maddox screamed, realizing he was next. "Somebody help me!"

Knight slowed some as he passed the armless, dying man. The fear stitched across his face turned to placidity as his life ebbed. He had never come across something as unforgiving and capable at killing as the Hydra, and for the first time in his life he felt his steady hands shaking.

Bishop, on the other hand, seemed undaunted by the Hydra's massive size and ability to quickly kill every human being it came into contact with. After discarding his weapon, he ran up a half fallen tree, coming alongside and above the massive creature. He drew his machetelike knife and dove onto the Hydra's back, plunging the blade deep into its flesh. Like a rodeo rider, he clung to the Hydra as it kicked its legs and arched its back, but never stopped its downward pursuit of Maddox.

Knight could see the trees thinning in the distance and the blue sky beyond. They were approaching the fringe of the camp. Bishop saw it, too, drew his handgun and fired several rounds in the back of the creature's flailing heads. Two turned to face him, but the bulk of the beast kept on running and the other heads had eyes only for Maddox.

Bishop fired as one of the heads came toward him. The bullets tore into its snout, turning it away as the stinging wounds regenerated. He ducked as a second head struck. It missed and quickly pulled back for a second strike.

But the strike didn't come. A gut-wrenching scream caught the head's attention. Maddox rose up, held in the jaws of two Hydra heads. He wailed as they pulled at his body. A leg came off, and a third head snatched on to the other. The tug of war began again. His hands shook. The briefcase fell and was trampled, destroyed. Just as the second leg was about to come loose, Bishop pulled the blade free and swung it at the head gripping Maddox's torso. The blade cleaved the creature's flesh. The neck and head fell cleanly away, taking Maddox with it.

Hydra roared in pain, but continued charging through the woods, heading toward the clearing ahead. Bishop stabbed into the Hydra's back again, and hung on as it ran forward. A head snapped back toward him, but a bullet from Knight smashed into its eye.

As Knight continued the chase he saw Maddox reaching out to him. Blood seeped from his leg and an arc of deep puncture wounds where he'd been bit. He was trying to talk. Knight slowed and listened. "They're going to clean the site. Get . . . people . . . away." Blood gurgled from his mouth. Dead.

Knight continued his pursuit, but was dogged by the man's statement. Clean the site. Clean . . . "Damnit," he muttered. The Manifold facility was a bust. Hydra was loose. Reinhart and Ridley were skipping town. He doubted a volcano hid beneath the mountain, but had no doubt Manifold had the means to destroy the whole facility. And the only people Knight could imagine Maddox worrying about were those in the campground. If they were in danger, too, then . . . too many possibilities for mass destruction existed. A nuke was the simplest thing, but that would probably attract too much attention. In the Amazon it was a fire, which could be chalked up to lightning. On Tristan da Cunha, a volcano. Both could be blamed on natural destructive forces. Here . . . he had no idea, but whatever it was had to be big if people at the campground, more than a mile away, were in danger, too.

With no way to reach King he had to trust he would catch Ridley and stop whatever madness he had in mind. Right now, he had to focus on not being killed by a mythological monster.

He looked up as Hydra pulled away. Knight was tiring. Slowing. He couldn't keep up much longer. But Bishop was . . . One of the Hydra heads swung around toward

Bishop again. He shot it twice in the snout, but a second had come around from the other side, this time targeting Bishop's arm—the source of its pain.

Knight stumbled and stopped in shock as he watched the Hydra bite down on Bishop's arm and tear it clean away. Bishop grunted in pain and fell away. As the Hydra pounded onward, charging for the campground, Knight dashed to where Bishop had fallen. He stopped short when he saw Bishop standing, holding his left arm . . . the missing arm . . . as it grew to its former bulk. As new fingers expanded from his hand, Bishop tensed and let out a roar of his own.

Knight took aim at Bishop's head.

Not now, Bish.

Bishop looked at him, fire in his eyes. His chest heaved. Drool fell from his gritted teeth.

Please not now.

Knight let out his held breath and lowered his weapon when Bishop spoke. His single question told him that Bishop had yet to become a mindless threat. At least not to people. "Which way . . . did it go?"

Knight pointed. Bishop charged, blade in hand. Hercules reborn.

SIXTY

New Hampshire

Following a trail of broken branches, disturbed brush, and muddy footprints, King had no trouble tracking Reinhart and Ridley as they fled back toward the Manifold bunker. They weren't concerned about being followed. That meant they were either very stupid, which he doubted, or that they were evacuating. He thought the latter was the most likely, so he didn't slow his approach in fear of an ambush.

He cleared the woods onto a trail that led diagonally up and around the mountain. Not fifty feet in front of him, Reinhart and Ridley ran for all they were worth. Ridley's quick pace surprised him. The man was towering tall and had a rounded waist, yet he had little trouble keeping up with Reinhart. But King was faster than both men, and could catch them easily on the clear path. Then again, a bullet would be even faster.

King raised his rifle, looked down the scope, and pulled the trigger once. The bullet whizzed past Ridley's ear, causing him to instinctively dive to the side and struck Reinhart in the left shoulder. Reinhart fell with a grunt, but spun before landing, drew his Metal Storm pistol, and pulled the trigger once. His aim seemed nearly as keen as Knight's, but his weapon, firing three rounds at once instead of one, packed more punch.

The first round nicked King's rib, just beneath his armpit. The second two struck his chest, just over his heart, and would have been fatal if not for his flak jacket. The impact knocked him off his feet. He fell back onto the wet path, dropping his weapon upon impact. He fought for breath, but wheezed like an asthmatic in a dust storm. Spots appeared in his vision as a lack of oxygen threatened unconsciousness. But as Reinhart stood above him, aiming the weapon down at his head, he fought to stay awake. He didn't want to die without looking his killer in the eye.

"Always wondered how hard it would be to kill a Delta," he said with a grin. "It's kind of disappointing, actually. I thought you'd be a challenge."

King sucked in a hard breath, forcing his lungs to expand. If he could clear his head and take control of his locked-up body . . .

"Hold it!"

Reinhart turned toward the voice, but didn't move his gun away from King.

"Put the gun down, boss."

King looked up enough to see Anna Beck sliding out of the woods. She had her own weapon trained on Reinhart, but didn't see Ridley approaching her from behind. He tried to warn her, but hadn't recovered his voice. He decided his voice wasn't what he needed. Ignoring the spots in his vision and the pain in his chest, he unclipped a small pouch on his belt and reached inside.

Reinhart laughed at Beck. "Stupid bitch. I always knew you were too soft. If you weren't such a—"

Ridley struck the distracted Beck from behind, wrapping his arms under hers, then up and around her head. Her weapon pointed uselessly toward the sky and the giant man picked her off the ground with ease. She cursed, kicked, and spat, but nothing loosened his grip.

"Like I said," Reinhart said, "stupid and soft."

"Not as stupid as you," King said, snapping Reinhart's attention back to him. He'd caught a breath, found his voice, and with a flick of his wrist sent three three-inch throwing spikes into Reinhart's left eye in less time and with more accuracy than a Metal Storm gun.

Reinhart screamed and staggered back, but didn't lose his desire to kill King. He had, however, lost depth perception. Reinhart squeezed the trigger three times, firing nine rounds, every single one of them missing the mark. But it wasn't just Reinhart's failing vision that kept the bullets from striking King—the agile Delta had caught his breath, rolled back onto his feet, and dove to the side.

Reinhart squeezed off another three-round burst. Mud splattered beneath King's feet as he dove again. Reinhart smiled despite the pain in his eye and shoulder. King moved in the same direction twice. His momentum would carry him forward. Reinhart adjusted his aim, leading King, adjusting for his lack of depth perception. But when he fired, King came up short, stopping instead of rolling again.

Reinhart adjusted his aim again, but as he brought his weapon around he saw the muzzle of King's rifle cough a single round. It was the last thing he saw. His body slumped to the forest floor like God had simply shut off the power switch.

King looked at the clean hole in Reinhart's head. It didn't heal. The man would stay dead. A groan caught his attention. Beck was on her hands and knees, picking herself off the ground. Sometime during the gunfight Ridley had clubbed her and made his escape. King took her hand and helped her up. "You coming?"

She stood. "Let's get him."

He started off in a sprint.

Beck ran after him. "King, this whole valley sits on a deposit of natural gas. It's why Ridley chose it. I went back in to see if the detonation sequence had been initiated, but it hasn't been."

"So?" King said, vaulting an old stone wall. "What can we do?"

"Ridley carries a PDA with him. He can remote detonate. If he does, this whole valley will implode—the campground, town, everything, will be blown to bits, then sucked inside a mile-deep crater. Whatever happens, that PDA needs to stay in one piece. It's the only way to access the system once it's engaged."

"Can we destroy it on site?"

"It's a mile underground."

A distant chop of rotor blades caught King's attention. With each chop the noise grew louder. Ridley hadn't left yet. "Can you cancel the detonation sequence?"

"No. Only Ridley can."

King stopped. The trail turned up at a sharp angle. As he began ascending the trail, the chop of the rotor blades grew loud and pine needles spun into the air like mini-sized missiles. He caught a quick glimpse of the chopper before it landed—a severely modified, sleek black Eurocopter. Both hatches were open, one to receive Ridley, the other containing a manned Gatling gun, already spinning and ready to fire.

King ducked down and looked back at Beck.

She slid up next to him. "What now?"

"I'll take care of the Gatling gun and pilot. You get the PDA from Ridley."

She nodded.

"Try not to kill him."

She nodded again.

They scrambled up the incline as the helicopter touched down on the landing pad. As they cleared the rise King saw two things simultaneously. The first was Ridley diving into the chopper. The second was the Gatling gun swiveling toward them.

SIXTY-ONE

New Hampshire

The thinning trees gave way to a dirt road. As he burst from the trees a glint of sun on metal caught Knight's eye. After a moment of looking he saw a pattern he recognized as camouflage. The shape of the SUV emerged next. *Yes!* Knight thought, running toward the vehicle.

Bishop continued chasing down the Hydra, whose violent charge was marked by a path of flattened birch trees.

Knight yanked the camouflage from the SUV, jumped inside, and started the engine. He peeled from the hiding spot, leaving a cloud of dust and shredded pine needles in his wake. Passing the abandoned mess hall, he drove down a stony hill, turned a sharp left, and slammed on the breaks as he nearly ran Bishop over.

Bishop climbed onto the hood of the vehicle and then onto the roof. He held on to the roof rack with one hand and slammed on the roof with the other, shouting a savage-sounding, "Go!"

Knight floored it through the cleared patch of forest left in the Hydra's wake. The Chevy Tahoe bounced over the small limbs as Knight did his best to steer around the larger felled timber. Bishop held on tight with both hands while his lower body was picked up and smashed against the SUV's roof over and over. He ignored the pain and had no worries about permanent injuries, not to his body anyway.

Then they were through it and onto a road. Knight's sense of direction was turned around by the endless sea of tall pines, but then he saw a street sign: Praise Street. A dog barked.

Thor.

Knight hit the gas and drew a fully automatic pistol capable of firing fifteen rounds in 1.9 seconds, one of the many weapons hidden within the vehicle. As the SUV raced down the street, Knight's view of the Honeymoon Cottage was blocked by a mass of green, scaled flesh. Thor stood on the small, red porch, barking up at the seven-headed behemoth as it reared up to strike. Knight leaned from the driver's side window and held the pistol's trigger down for a full two seconds, unleashing all fifteen rounds. Every one of them buried into the creature's side.

The bullets did no serious damage, but the sting got its attention. Seeing the approaching SUV, the Hydra roared and continued its mad flight through the campground. It pounded through a nearby cottage, completely flattening it, before charging toward the open quad.

Knight skidded to a stop in front of the cottage, looked at Thor and said, "Stay!" Then he peeled away again in pursuit of the Hydra.

Worst fears became realized as distant screams filled the air. Children. The SUV exploded from the forest, catching air as the road changed from dirt to tarmac, turning the Tahoe into a blunt missile. The vehicle slammed into the Hydra's side, toppling it over in a mass of twisting heads and limbs. Bishop was sent flying. He cleared the Hydra and landed on the grassy quad, sliding to a stop halfway between the road and the shuffleboard court where four children stood in shock.

Knight, unable to rapidly heal, having gone from sixty to zero upon impact with the Hydra, fared the worst.

Unconscious and pinned by an airbag, he slipped to the side, bumping his head against the door. He jolted awake when the Hydra roared. After kicking the door open and falling to the road he looked up and saw the Hydra, heads up and snapping at the only thing standing between it and the children: the machete-wielding Bishop.

SIXTY-TWO

New Hampshire

The man behind the Gatling gun had quick reflexes, but they were geared toward self-preservation. Even though he had the superior weapon and his sites lined up, when King fired his rifle from the hip, sending rounds pinging off the side of the chopper, the guard ducked down with his hands over his head. King suspected the man never thought he'd actually ever have to use the gun, and certainly not under attack. With the way clear, he ran for the open side of the helicopter as Ridley ran for the other.

Upon reaching the hatch, King dove straight through the chopper, striking the larger man like a linebacker, knocking him out of the chopper. But the impact knocked the wind out of him, too. When he regained his footing, Ridley was already throwing a haymaker. The first punch connected with King's injured side, sending a flare of pain to his toes. But King sidestepped the second swing, causing Ridley to hit the helicopter's metal side. The sound of his pain-filled shout was drowned out by the thunderous roar of the chopper, but was cut short entirely by King's heel connecting with his temple. The roundhouse kick sent Ridley to the ground.

Ridley stood as the helicopter pilot began to lift off.

He came at King again with enough force to take both of them off the helipad and into the woods below, but King saw the attack coming, took hold of the rising helicopter struts, and planted both of his feet square on Ridley's face. The man fell back like his feet had been pulled out from under him and cracked his head on the hard pavement. His eyes fluttered for a moment, then stilled. To King's surprise, the helicopter began to lower again.

As much as he would have liked to allow the six-ton helicopter to land on top of Ridley there was still the matter of stopping the implosion of Pinckney Valley. He dragged Ridley clear as the Eurocopter landed. Beck crouched inside, aiming King's rifle at the two terrified men there. She gave King a smile and a salute.

King searched Ridley's suit jacket and found the PDA. He pulled it out and unlocked it. The screen showed a small countdown ticking away in the lower-left-hand corner. "I think he's activated it!"

"I don't know how to stop it," she replied. "How much time is left?"

"Just under ten minutes."

"Get on board. We'll figure it out in the air!"

King dragged Ridley on board the chopper with the help of the timid Gatling gun operator. The man pleaded with King that he was just doing his job. Never wanted to hurt anyone. When King saw tears in the man's eyes he realized he was closer to being a kid. Probably still a teenager. Barely Gen-Y.

King ordered the kid and pilot to take them to the campground. Neither argued or had any intention of doing so. The gun in Beck's hand would have been enough motivation, but the phony CIA badge—one of many badges the team carried for similar situations—flashed by King was enough to make them fear disappearing off the face of the planet.

The group held their breath as the pilot flew the chopper out of the trees at a perfect angle. A shift to the right or left would send the blades into tree trunks. A little too much height would cut into the canopy, and a downward shift would plow them into the trees rising at a steady angle in front of them. Anyone watching from above would see the helicopter emerge, almost magically, from the forest.

As they cleared the trees and rose higher, King pulled out his cell phone and activated his direct line to the only person he thought could help.

"This is Aleman. What can I do you for?"

"Ale, it's King."

"What's up?"

"We've got . . ." He looked at the timer on Ridley's PDA. "Eight minutes and thirty-three seconds to stop an explosion triggered by a remote signal sent from Richard Ridley's PDA."

Aleman groaned. "What did they rig?"

"There's a massive natural gas deposit beneath the valley here. He's going to light it up, destroy the whole town and kill thousands of people."

"Okay. Call me back."

King was incredulous. "What!"

"Call me back from *Ridley's* PDA. Hurry."

King didn't argue. This was Aleman's forte. He had no choice but to trust the man. He dialed Aleman from Ridley's PDA. But when the phone on the other end picked up, a loud squealing sound came through, like a dial-up modem. A text message appeared on the screen.

Just need a few minutes.—Lew

A flash of movement tore his eyes away from the PDA message. As he turned, the moving object coalesced into a muddy wing-tip shoe. Ridley. King moved away from the kick, but only managed to soften the blow. Ridley's heel connected with his cheek, knocking him across the cabin where he spilled onto Beck.

When King spun, he expected Ridley to press the attack,

but was greeted by a gust of wind and the unhindered noise of the rotor blades cutting through air. Ridley stood at the open door, clutching the sides while his suit coat flapped violently around his waist. "I could have offered you the world."

"You would have destroyed it," King said as he righted himself.

Ridley backed out a little farther, glancing down. His face twisted with nausea from the height.

"Don't be stupid," King said.

"Death is a more becoming alternative to imprisonment. I was meant to be free." He looked at Beck. "Eternity awaits." He let go of the door frame and fell back as a smile stretched across his face.

King and Beck looked out the side, watching his body twist in the air. His face struck a horizontal pine branch tree that sent his body into a rapid head over heels flip. A second branch tore his arm away. He disappeared in a spray of blood as the pine canopy swallowed him up.

King slid away from the open door and closed it. He turned to Beck, who had already moved back inside. "I don't think that was quite the noble fall he had intended."

Beck glanced out the window as she began to reply. "Ridley was— Oh my God!"

Beck's cry drew King to the window. The campground quad spun beneath them as the pilot circled. The scene looked hopeless. Knight was on the ground, motionless next to the wrecked Chevy Tahoe. Bishop stood alone on the quad, backing slowly away from the Hydra, whose body and heads lowered to the ground like a cat about to pounce. In seconds Bishop would be a stain on the grass. And if he happened to survive the attack thanks to his regenerative abilities, his mind would most certainly be lost. His heart sank as he thought for sure he'd have to watch his friend die gruesomely.

Then he remembered the Gatling gun.

SIXTY-THREE

New Hampshire

Bishop swung high, bringing the blade straight down as the first Hydra head shot toward him. The razor-sharp machete cut cleanly through the snout of the Hydra's open maw. But as the injured head reared back, stitching back together, a second was already striking. A third followed seconds later.

Moving backward, Bishop swung the blade as fast as he could, hacking at the barrage of heads. The Hydra kept on healing and striking, but its low tolerance for pain kept an injured head from attacking until it was fully healed. Despite Bishop's efforts, each attack pushed him back and came closer to striking home. It was a losing fight.

As two heads struck at once from the front, Bishop swung horizontally, hoping to cut through both heads, but he failed to see a third head striking from the right. Instead of biting, it rammed his legs. Bishop fell to the side, causing the two striking heads to miss the mark, but the impact was enough to break his leg and jar the blade from his hand. The blade twisted through the air and fell into the grass, hard to see, impossible to reach.

An intense itch ate at Bishop's leg as the bone reset and mended. He could feel the sinews and veins as they stretched out to each other and bonded. He growled in annoyance and fought to stand, but the Hydra was upon him. Pain shot through his legs as jaws clamped tight around both his calves. The Hydra's hooked teeth easily pierced and clung to his flesh and bones. The head yanked him off the ground and tossed him into the air. When he landed, twenty feet away, already healing from the deep puncture wounds, the beast was upon him. This time it took him by the waist and threw him again, playing with him like a cat does a mouse.

Bishop landed hard on his side, breaking his arm. He screamed with rage as he stood again. The Hydra pounded toward him. But rather than run away or wait to be tossed again, Bishop charged with a battle cry. As he ran he took out a small throwing knife and clutched it in the hand of his freshly healed arm. It wouldn't do much damage, but it was something.

Knight pulled himself up using the Tahoe's rear door handle. He leaned against the SUV's side and watched with horror as Bishop was tossed into the air like a rag doll. As Bishop was released by the Hydra, a trail of blood followed his arc through the air, but disappeared before he landed, fully healed. He was being torn apart and put back together again, over and over, and he was taking it all without losing his mind or focus on his enemy.

Not yet, anyway.

Bracing himself against the SUV, Knight limped to the back of the vehicle and threw open the rear hatch. He lifted a plastic panel, revealing a keypad, and typed in a code. A lock clicked open. He pulled the panel up and looked at the assortment of weapons, from small arms to claymore mines to heavy-hitting assault rifles, which is what he was after. He took out a spare SOPMOD M4 with attached 40mm grenade launcher, already loaded, and hobbled back around the SUV.

When he faced the battle once more, a smell carried by

the breeze struck him. It was a mix of coppery blood tinged with something foul, like fish that had been left to rot and bloat in the sun. Knight watched as the Hydra, charging at Bishop once more, slipped in the grass. Red liquid splashed around its massive paws. The field was covered in blood, both Bishop's and the Hydra's. The copper smell was Bishop's blood. The rancid smell belonged to the Hydra.

Fighting his gag reflex, Knight took aim, but what he saw next kept his trigger finger from squeezing. Bishop was charging the beast head-on like he was Superman about to stop a runaway train. It was madness.

He watched as three of the heads launched forward, jaws open. They would have torn Bishop to pieces if he hadn't slid down onto the grass like a baseball player stealing second. The momentum carried him forward as the Hydra's charge carried it over him. He slid beneath its belly, jabbed the small knife up, and carved a three-foot incision into the creature's belly. As the blade cut through the thick flesh it made a sound like paper being torn. The knife snagged on a bone and was torn from Bishop's hand. But the damage had been done.

The Hydra toppled onto its side as its entrails spilled out and dragged through the grass behind it, unraveling like an anchor line. Its head swung up and around, biting at the exposed guts as the wound tried to seal. But with too much flesh in the way, the wound remained open, seeping more rank blood into the grass. The Hydra flailed madly, but soon focused on the source of its continuing pain. It quickly bit away chunks of its own organs, snapping through them and discarding the shriveling meat. It stopped when the wound was clear and free to heal over.

Knight took aim at the stationary Hydra, but Bishop stood in his line of fire. "Bishop!" he shouted. "Get down!"

Before the big man could move, one of the Hydra heads, attracted by the sound of Knight's voice, turned and found Bishop. It struck out, catching him by the waist. The head clamped down and twisted like a crocodile, tearing out a large chunk between his rib cage and hip bone. Bishop cried out and fell to the ground. A second head shot toward the prone man as the Hydra righted itself. But the strike never finished. A glowing burst of tracer bullets shot from the sky like a laser beam, striking the head and reducing it to the consistency of pulled pork. The headless neck flailed like a dying snake as the other six turned upward.

Knight followed the Hydra's gaze. A helicopter circled and unleashed a second round of Gatling-gun fire, striking Hydra's side. With a rattling roar, the Hydra quickly healed and stomped off in pursuit of the helicopter, which stayed just high enough not to be caught, but low enough to entice the beast.

As the chopper spun around the quad, laying down bursts of powerful Gatling rounds, Knight noticed a small black speck in the sky above. Its boomerang shape brought a smile to his face. The cavalry had arrived.

SIXTY-FOUR

New Hampshire

Wind tore through the rear compartment of the *Crescent* as the rear hatch opened. It was cold enough to blister skin and powerful enough to suck a man's breath away, but Rook and Queen didn't feel its effects from within their thermal jumpsuits, face masks, and helmets. As the rear hatch continued to open, Rook looked over at Queen.

"You sure that's going to work?"

Queen looked down at the weapon she and Rook had rigged during the flight from Gibraltar. They had raided supplies from the both the onboard armory and medical suite. With advice from experts quickly assembled by Deep Blue they were able to create a high-power dart gun capable of firing three rounds full of Alexander Diotrephes's serum, which they had yet to test. Any number of things could go wrong. The gun could jam. The injection mechanisms could fail. The serum might not work.

"Without a doubt," Queen replied.

The hatch finished opening and the pilot's voice came over the comm. "Target sighted. Jump on my mark. Three . . ."

Rook hefted a heavy AT-4 SMAW (shoulder-launched multipurpose assault weapon) over his shoulder and strapped it down tight. It was loaded with a single high-explosive antiarmor rocket capable of obliterating any tank or armored vehicle in service.

"Two . . ."

He nudged Queen. "Hey, if I don't see you at the bottom . . ."

"You'll see me in Hell."

"I would have said—"

"One. Go! Go! Go!"

Queen and Rook leaped from the back of the *Crescent* and quickly reached a terminal velocity of 124 miles per hour. The air pressure pushed against their top-heavy, weapon-laden bodies, threatening to make the fall an uncontrolled tumult, but both kept arms and legs spread wide, controlling the descent and staying on target.

The first minute of the two-and-a-half-minute drop passed in a blur of clouds that covered their face masks in mist. Once through the cloud cover, the mist evaporated, revealing the scene below.

The Hydra twisted and writhed under a constant barrage of Gatling-gun fire, shooting from the side of a small jet black helicopter. A pool of blood covered the field and reflected the sun. A small figure by a ruined SUV launched grenades, which blew gouts of blood and flesh away from the roaring creature. The sound of the roar was so powerful that it covered the distance to Rook and Queen, who heard it over the wind and through their helmets. But what caught Rook's attention as they closed in was the body laying in the grass, fifty yards from the Hydra. The man's size and dark skin made him wince. It was impossible to tell from this height, but his gut said the body was Bishop's. He lay twisted and still. A dark red pool covered the grass to his side.

He wanted to fall faster, but they had long since reached terminal velocity and would greet the ground in less than thirty seconds . . . far fewer if he forgot to pull his chute.

He took hold of the ripcord and waited for the last possible second to cheat death.

Knight held his fire as the two falling specs grew in size. Rook and Queen were taking the express route down. He watched as both chutes popped and unfurled, snapping the two soldiers violently, but only slowing their decent enough to avoid death. After a quick semicircle decent, Queen hit the ground with a roll and came upright in a crouch. She intended to take aim and fire upon landing, but Hydra lunged at her billowing parachute, took hold of it, and yanked hard. Queen was tossed low and fast. She landed in the blood-soaked grass, sliding to a wet stop. She fought past her revulsion of being covered in rank-smelling blood, wiped the grime from her helmet's face mask, and took aim from where she lay. Lining up the Hydra was easy and she pulled the trigger three times in rapid succession. Three small projectiles shot from the weapon's muzzle. The first ricocheted off at an odd angle. The next two pierced Hydra's back and stuck there, dangling limply from its hide.

Hydra turned toward the source of what was merely a pinprick and saw Queen's parachute billow once more. It shrieked and charged the large fluid intruder.

Queen discarded the makeshift weapon and tried to stand and run out of the path of the oncoming behemoth, which now had its eyes on her. But she had become entangled in her parachute lines. She drew her knife, intending to cut herself free, but it was easy to see she wouldn't get loose soon enough. She drew her pistol and fired at the beast as it stormed toward her.

Rook landed hard on the shingled roof of the Snack Shack, denting it. But his momentum didn't slow. He rolled down the roof's incline, toppling head over heels, and fell over the edge. But the ten-foot drop to the grass below was stopped short when the chute snagged on the roof's cupola. He hung, three feet above the ground.

A shriek brought his head up as he swung back and forth on the parachute lines. He looked up and found the Hydra, massive and horrific, bearing down on Queen, who was firing a pistol at it. He had no idea if Queen had managed to inject the Hydra with the serum, and if she had, how long before it took effect. But there was no way he was about to let this thing trample Queen.

Rook unclipped and raised a beige cylinder to his shoulder and did his best to aim while hanging from the parachute lines. Not only did he have to line up the Hydra, he had to lead the fast-moving creature. With only thirty feet between Hydra and Queen, he pulled the trigger. The SMAW boomed as a blast of flame burst from its back and a rocket shot from the front. The recoil, not normally enough to phase a crouched soldier, flung the hanging Rook back and up, smashing him against the roof's overhang, knocking the now spent antitank weapon from his hands.

Queen heard and recognized the noise. She dove down and curled into a tight ball, hoping the thick jumpsuit, flak jacket, and helmet would protect her from the blast.

The rocket blazed through the air, leaving a twisted coil of smoke in its wake. It covered the distance in seconds, striking the Hydra in the side before the beast could react. As the rocket penetrated the Hydra's side, it let out a wail—seven octaves of pain—before its body burst. Its bulk came apart in every direction, as its flesh was liquefied by the force wave and then charred by the flames. Fiery entrails rolled across the grass, leaving slick stains behind them. Necks and heads shot free, twisting in the air like loose ropes before landing. A wet crater was all that remained of the Hydra's body.

Rook shed his harness and helmet and ran to Queen. He helped her up out of the bloody soup, which covered her from head to toe. She wobbled for a moment, shook up by the explosion. With Rook's help, she removed the helmet, freeing her clean face and hair. "I'm okay," she said, looking up at him.

"Good," Rook said with a slight smile. Then he remembered the body he'd seen when descending. "Bishop!"

Together, they headed for Bishop. Knight approached from the SUV. The helicopter landed and idled as King and Beck exited. They all arrived by Bishop's body at the same time. No greetings were exchanged. No job well done. One of their own was down and they all wanted an answer to the same question. Was Bishop dead?

King knelt and checked Bishop's pulse.

His hand was angrily swatted away.

King jumped back as Bishop growled and stood. He took aim with his handgun.

"King . . ." Rook said.

"Two minutes ago he had a chunk the size of my head missing from his side. He's been torn apart, burned to a crisp, and doesn't have a scratch."

Queen shook her head. "He's a regen." She drew her side arm and took aim, as did Knight.

"Is that why he's been so pissy since Tristan?" Rook asked.

King nodded.

Bishop's face was twisted with rage as he stood. He grunted, stumbled, then straightened, glaring at them.

King placed his finger on the trigger.

"No way this is happening," Rook said, stepping forward, reaching a hand out.

What happened next was so quick, neither Queen nor King could get off a shot. Bishop stumbled forward, reached out, and fell into Rook's arms. He winced, grit his teeth, and clenched his eyes shut. When he opened them he looked at King. "You need to shoot me."

He tried to move away from Rook, but he held on tight, straining against the stronger man's struggle. Bishop let out a growl, yanked an arm free, and swung it at Rook. But he was tired and slow. Rook ducked, caught the arm, and pulled it behind Bishop's back. He kicked out his legs and put him facedown on the ground. Rook put his weigh on Bishop's back, pulling his arm back tight and pinning him.

"You're still you," Rook said. "You're still Delta. Choke it down. Beat it."

Bishop winced. His clenched fists shook as an internal rage like nothing he'd ever felt ate up his insides. "Shoot me!"

The two men struggled for a moment before Rook let him go. Bishop stood in a flash, face-to-face with Rook.

"If you go regen, I'll be the first to die," Rook said. "Now get a fucking grip."

Bishop stumbled, shaking, and was caught again by Rook. But he wasn't alone this time. King helped support Bishop's body, extending him help and trust, and like Rook, making himself vulnerable. Bishop fought harder, taking control of himself. He let go of them and stood on his own. His face calmed. He closed his eyes and took several deep breaths. Control returned. His muscles cooled and stopped shaking. His breathing slowed. When he opened his eyes again, he looked at Rook and said, "I'm sorry. I—"

"Ahh, save it for when your future wife sees your little pecker."

Bishop smiled as his rage subsided further, then noticed the pungent smell of explosives and burned flesh hanging in the air. "Is it dead?"

They looked over the blood- and flesh-covered quad. King counted six unmoving heads, but movement caught his eye. One of the heads was still moving, writhing in a pool of blood. He ran to the back of the SUV and reappeared with a grenade. He strode to the head. It moved, but showed no response to his approach and it wasn't regenerating. Whatever Queen had shot it up with had done the trick. He pulled the pin on the concussion grenade, forced the Hydra's mouth open with his boot, and dropped it inside. He jumped back, shouted, "Fire in the hole!" and

moved behind the SUV with the others. The grenade detonated with a muffled and very wet boom. The head burst
like a melon, further adding to the rancid mess on the quad.

The Hydra, immortal once, buried for thousands of
years and reborn in the present, was finally, and perma-
nently, dead.

Motion in the forest caught King's eye. He spun toward it, taking aim.

"What's wrong?" Queen asked.

"Saw something."

The others looked on, peering into the dark woods. Light
filtered through the forest canopy as the trees swayed in the
wind. Then a shadow moved against the wind. Unnatural. It
hung between two trees, thirty feet up, watching them.

"What the . . ." King placed his finger on the trigger.

Rook recognized the ghostly shape and knew that gray
flesh hid beneath the surface of its loose-fitting cloak. Another wraith. He put his hand on King's weapon and lowered it. "Let it go."

"What is it?" King asked.

"Let's just say they were on our side this time around."

"What's it doing?"

"Making sure we got the job done," Queen said. She
was sure of it. What bothered her about its appearance
was that Alexander either had a way to get the creature
halfway around the world as quickly as the *Crescent,* or
he had an army of the things lurking in every dark nook
of the planet.

The black wraith shoved off, landing on a pine deeper
in the forest. It seemed to glide the distance between the
trees, like a flying squirrel. It continued leaping from trunk
to trunk, until the darkness concealed it.

King looked at Rook. "What about next time? Will it
still be on our side?"

Rook shrugged. "Personally, I hope there isn't a next
time."

Queen nodded. "I second that."

King looked away from the trees and was struck by a terrifying thought. *The PDA!* Fearing that the valley would implode at any second, he pulled it out and looked at the screen. The timer showed fifteen seconds remaining and was still counting down. He was about to shout for the others to get to the helicopter when his phone rang. He answered it. "Lewis, it's still counting down!"

"What? Oh! No. You're all set. Ridley's PDA must not have registered the change. I stopped the countdown five minutes ago."

King let out his held breath. *Thank God.*

Aleman continued, "I was just calling to let you know I piggybacked into Manifold's VPN, stole their data, and dropped a worm to destroy their database. Ridley won't be able recover anything."

"Ridley is dead," King said. "Jumped out of a helicopter."

"Well, what comes around . . ."

"And then some. Got to go." King hung up the phone. The helicopter whined as its rotors spun up. King looked. Beck was there, in the back of the chopper, gun pointed at the pilot. She gave a wave.

He didn't try to stop her, nor did the team. They all knew she'd be arrested and imprisoned, possibly without trial, thanks to Manifold's affiliation with terrorist organizations. But she had been as instrumental in stopping Ridley, Reinhart, and Manifold as the rest of them. She'd earned her freedom.

Frightened campers began to stream out of hiding, gasping and talking loudly. Some pointed at King and Bishop saying, "It's them!," "They came back," and "They blew up the devil!" Kids whooped and cheered. King saw the boy who had flipped him off upon entering the campground. This time he offered a thumbs-up and a smile. King returned the thumbs-up and then turned to the others as the helicopter banked away and disappeared over the trees. "So we've got a forest full of scared scientists, more than a few rogue Gen-Y soldiers on the run, one hell of a mess to clean up, and more than a few wounds to dress." He looked at Bishop. "Well, some of us. What's the game plan?"

Queen reached into her vest and pulled out a vial of brown liquid. "I say we have Deep Blue call in the feds, have them handle cleanup, and get this to your friend."

King took the vial, swished it around, and looked at the liquid. "Sounds like a plan." He paused and then squinted at Queen. "By the way, where did you find this?"

EPILOGUE

Rock of Gibraltar

King slid through the darkness, viewing the cave in a haze of green, night vision light. He'd been told to watch out for a maze of strings and small flags marking the areas where Neanderthal artifacts lay, but the floor was not only clear of strings and flags; he didn't see anything to indicate that anything had ever been dug up. He moved forward, leading with his Sig Sauer, wary of the shadow's dark recesses. What Rook and Queen had described encountering in Pierce's office and in this cave didn't sound human, and he'd had just about enough of inhuman, fast-healing monsters. If a pair of reflective eyes opened at the back of the cave, he'd put a bullet between them.

But there were no eyes. No sounds other than the distant crashing waves of the Mediterranean high tide. He found the hidden cave entrance at the back of Gorham's Cave, exactly where it was supposed to be. He held his palm up and open, stopping the others. "Let me check it out."

He rounded the corner and descended a rugged slope . . . not stairs. A jagged entrance at the bottom of the slope opened where there should have been a door. King passed through and saw exactly what he expected: absolutely nothing. The place had been cleared out. All that remained was a stalactite-filled cavern. He backtracked up the slope and joined the others.

"Lights up," he said, removing the night vision goggles. A moment later several blazing bright flashlights clicked on and scoured the cave.

"This is horse shit," Rook said, looking around the cave. He and Queen had joined King on this little expedition, determined to return to the cave and uncover the mysteries they'd left behind. Knight had passed, preferring to visit Grandma Dae-jung. Something about the old folks he'd seen experimented on had struck a cord with him. Having seen their surreal youth, he knew that growing old, and eventually death, was the way things should be. Death was life. Without it the journey was meaningless.

Bishop, on the other hand, had stayed behind under orders. They tried using the serum to undo the regenerative curse given to Bishop by Ridley, but, being designed to interact with Hydra's genes, it had no effect on the early, pre-Hydra, genetic tinkering. He was being evaluated to make sure he was fit for active duty and not a danger to anyone. Scheduled meditation and a regimen of mood stabilizers had proven effective enough that he felt like his old, quiet self, but no one knew what would happen if he was injured again. A bullet wound might send him over the edge. Then again, so might a paper cut. Until they knew for sure, or until his services were in dire need, he was benched.

"I think it's safe to say that there were never any Neanderthal artifacts here," King said. "What's your take, George?"

George Pierce, healed and fully human, searched the cavern with his eyes. His reaction to the serum had been as quick as the Hydra's, and so far, the change had been permanent. Several of the nonhuman genes bonded to his body had been located and all appeared blocked. He had been declared fit and healthy two days after first being injected with the serum. "I think you're right. The whole dig must have been a front for the Herculean Society."

"It's only been a week," Rook protested. "How could they have cleared out that fast?"

Gallo, who had been found innocent in the University of Athens incident, stepped farther into the cave. George had insisted she join them, to reward her for her part in saving his life. King suspected there was more, but that was a ribbing he'd reserve for another day. "They've been around for thousands of years," she said. "They have a lot of experience staying off the radar."

"Then why help us?" Queen asked as she inspected the floor, finding no evidence of any kind that would suggest someone had even entered the cave before them. Not even a single footprint.

"You said the man, Alexander, knew about the Hydra being buried in Nazca?"

Queen nodded.

"Then he knew how dangerous it was."

"Or how dangerous the secret of regeneration . . . of eternal life . . . could be," King added. "In a way, he was protecting the human race."

Pierce walked to the back wall, running his hand across the surface. "So he's a good guy, then? They nearly killed me to get the *Argo* crew manifest."

"Some secrets are worth killing for," King said.

Pierce looked at him, trying to gauge whether or not his old friend was speaking from experience. He decided he didn't want to know and turned back to the wall. "That was the first time I saw the Herculean Society symbol. On the Manifest. When I saw it again, later, on the shipwreck, and then on the map, I knew what I had found."

"And when you saw the same symbol on the geoglyph in Nazca—"

"It blew my mind. I had to see it for myself despite the exciting discoveries I was making in Greece. Of course, when I saw the Hydra sample reanimate on the lab table,

I knew there was even more to the story of Hercules and Hydra than had been passed down through history. I should have told you sooner, though."

King stood next to Pierce and put his hand on his shoulder. "You told me just in time. Saved a lot of lives."

Pierce smiled. "Don't give me too much credit. I was just trying to save my green, scaly skin." His hand paused on the wall. "What's this?"

Rook and Queen shined their lights on the stone wall where Pierce's hand had been. The symbol for the Herculean Society was still etched in the stone.

"Maybe they missed it," Rook said.

Pierce shook his head. "It's not an oversight."

"It's a warning," King said.

"For who?" Queen asked.

Pierce turned to her. "For us. You've seen what they're capable of. They want to be left alone, but they want us to know you two didn't conjure the story."

"You think it's safe to let them stay in hiding?" Queen asked.

"I think I'm alive today because of it," Pierce said. "And I'll be glad to leave them alone from now on."

Queen mulled it over and shrugged. "Then my only remaining question is, who is Alexander Diotrephes?"

Pierce smiled. "You mean you haven't figured it out?"

The three of them waited for the answer.

"First, he knew about Hydra's resting place. That's a secret of the top order. You've seen the kind of danger that knowledge could bring to the world. I doubt anyone beyond the leader of the Herculean Society was privy to that bit of trivia. Then there is his choice of name. Diotrephes. It means, 'nourished by Jupiter.' Jupiter is the Roman name for Zeus." Pierce drew a small blade from his pocket and began scratching away at the Herculean Society symbol. When he stood back, the alteration drove home what he'd been insinuating. The Pillars of Hercules were now joined at the center by a horizontal line, turning the symbol into an encircled H.

Queen gasped and whispered the name. "Hercules."

King had seen enough over the past months to believe anything was true. The idea of the mythical Hercules still living among them would have been ridiculous two months previous. But so would the Hydra. He'd never experienced anything so primal. It really had been a force of nature. At times he felt remorse for destroying it. He wondered if that had been why Hercules, or Diotrephes, if they really were one and the same, had buried Hydra to begin with. He decided he would never know, and having had enough mythology for a lifetime, exited the cave while the others finished searching for clues of the Herculean Society's passage.

Standing at the edge of the azure sea, King thought about his sister. He hadn't had a chance to reflect since Pierce's abduction. The world had become a messy place since her death. A worse place. But that only made her passing that much more difficult to bear. She'd made the world, his world at least, a better place. Pierce's, too. Before the calm surroundings allowed him to slip deeper into thought, his cell phone rang. He checked the caller ID and answered it. "What's up?"

Deep Blue's voice came on the line. "We found McCabe."

King caught his breath. The last time anyone had seen the woman she was a psychotic regen on a killing spree. "Is she—"

"Alive," Deep Blue confirmed. "But barely. Severely dehydrated. Starving. Barely put up a fight."

Without meaning to, Deep Blue confirmed King's fear. She'd put up a fight. She was still a regen. "She'll be cared for?"

"We've got some brilliant people working on her. Bishop, too. We'll figure out how to reverse the effects. For now we're keeping her sedated."

King heard an unusual tension in Deep Blue's voice. "There's something else?"

"You know me too well, King."

"I don't know you at all."

"Better than most. Listen, they just finished sweeping the forest around the campground." They'd been finding scientists hiding in the woods and Gen-Y soldiers on the lam for the past week. King doubted Deep Blue had called him to tell him about them. There was something more important.

"You found Ridley."

"Pieces of him. An arm. Bits of organs. A lot of blood. The man fell through the trees, apparently tore himself open and hit the ground at terminal velocity."

"But no body?"

"They say there were a lot of coyote tracks. That the arm had been gnawed on."

"But no body."

King listened as Deep Blue let out an uncharacteristic sigh. He knew as well as King what the answer meant. "No. No body."

Richard Ridley was alive.

He always would be.

Instinct

The Annamite Mountains—Vietnam
1995

Three months had gone by since Dr. Anthony Weston had begun his search for the elusive creatures, and now that he'd found them, they were going to kill him.

A cascade of sweat followed a path of crisscrossing wrinkles down his forehead and dripped into his wide eyes. The salty, dirty sweat stung and brought forth a welling of tears, blurring his vision. He couldn't see the creatures clearly, nor the ground on which he ran, but he could hear them all around, calling out to each other.

The sheer volume of their booming hoots and hollers filled him with a kind of primeval dread that quickened his pace and made his heart pound painfully in his chest. He feared a heart attack for a moment, but the crunch of dry leaves all around signaled that his life was fleeting, heart problem or not.

Weston rounded a bend on the overgrown path that wound its way through the jungle and eventually up into the mountains. He picked up speed as the trail straightened out. If not for the assistance of the steep grade and gravity, the beasts would most assuredly have already overtaken him, but as it was, Weston found himself running much more quickly than on level ground. Even still, the task of outrunning the savage tribe was taking a grim toll on his body. With each labored breath, his ruddy-brown beard and mustache, which had grown long and ungainly during his months in the bush, was sucked in and pushed out of his mouth. His light blue eyes sparkled with wetness and his hands, which held off approaching tree limbs and bushes, shook violently, smearing the blood drawn from his fresh wounds.

Brush exploded to his right as one of the creatures toppled through it. They were tumbling and tripping as they barreled clumsily in pursuit, focused more on their quarry than their surroundings. They were single-minded hunters. He knew this from watching them take down yellow pigs and the antelope-like saola—even that fine creature's keen horns couldn't fight off the savages when they were hungry.

And they were hungry now.

Weston first knew something was wrong when, that morning, the creatures began sniffing vigorously at the air. He'd been watching them from a distance, higher up on the mountain for an entire week. He'd observed them hunting, grooming, sleeping, and playing. But it hadn't been enough. Seeing through binoculars and hearing only distant calls could not quench his thirst for discovery. So the previous night, he'd worked his way carefully, silently, down the mountainside until he was a mere fifty yards above with a clear view of the glade and mountain cave that served as their home. After carefully concealing himself with brush and debris, he'd waited eagerly for daybreak.

As the morning sun burned off the previous night's fog, the group emerged from their cave, stretching and yawning. Typically, grooming would come next, but a new smell had caught their nose—Weston. As a cool breeze tickled the back of his neck, he realized the winds were rolling down the mountainside from above, and being so close, the odor of his unbathed body was fresh in the air.

He'd only just begun debating what he should do next

when the group started jumping up and down, slapping the earth. A moment later, each and every one of them, forty-three in all, charged up the mountain. Their brown hair stood on end, bouncing madly as they ascended. For a moment, he sat still, stunned by the display, but as the creatures made eye contact with him and began their wild hoots, he too began to climb. Upon reaching the top, he wasted no time looking back to see how close they were. He knew them to be excellent climbers. They were no doubt already nipping at his heels.

And now, not two minutes after reaching the mountain's peak and beginning his frantic descent down the other side, they were on top of him.

Weston lost his footing for a moment and screamed. He was surprised by the volume and high pitch of his voice. It sounded as inhuman as the unclassified creatures pursuing him. As he sensed the front runners of the group closing in, he searched for any hope of escape. In the movies this was the point where the hero would trip and slide down a perfectly formed mud-covered waterslide and escape. But the forest was an unending assemblage of tall tree trunks, the occasional low level scrub, and a detritus-coated, downhill-sloped forest floor. There was nowhere to go but down.

And then where? The river was two days out on foot and from there it was a week, at least, to the nearest pocket of civilization. And what weapons did they own that could defeat such a group as this?

None.

Hopelessness settled in and his limbs grew weary. He thought of his wife and only regretted not having been able to tell her how angry he was that she'd left. In the end, she'd grown to hate him and taunted his profession; said that being a cryptozoologist was a job far better suited to children or imbeciles prone to flights of fancy. He'd thought she'd understood him, but he'd been wrong. And he would have never known if not for—

Shaking his head, Weston cleared his thoughts of his wife. She was not the image he wanted to see when he died.

With sure footing beneath him and the slope growing steeper, Weston felt himself moving faster. The pain in his lungs began to subside and the sweat on his forehead evaporated before it reached his eyes. He'd never before experienced a "second wind" but recognized it, and for a moment, felt some degree of hope.

That's when he saw the flickering shadow surrounding him, as though something above were blocking out the sun that filtered to the forest floor between breaks in the canopy. He glanced up into a pair of red-rimmed, deep yellow eyes. The beast shrieked at him and reached out. Its fingers found his field vest and gripped tightly. A moment later, Weston's feet left the earth and he found himself airborne, propelled through the air with stunning ease.

As the forest spun, he saw the entire group descending toward him, some charging, some taking to the trees and some rolling clumsily through the brush. What may have been a ten-foot flight took Weston much further as the ground continued to drop away. Twenty-five feet later he landed, but the same grade that made his fall further also minimized the force of his impact. He rolled and slid another fifty feet and came to rest at the foot of a tall, slender Aquilaria tree.

Having never lost consciousness, Weston knew he was lucky to be alive, but even luckier to not have sustained any broken bones. He struggled to his hands and knees, acutely aware that the wave of hair-covered flesh roaring down the mountain was almost upon him. He stood on wobbly legs and held the tree for support. It was shaking.

Weston looked up and found the same deep, red-rimmed eyes staring back at him. The creature, suspended upside down on the tree, reached out and backhanded Weston's head. He fell to the ground, stunned and despairing. They had him. Escape was impossible.

He began weeping as the creature climbed down the tree with an agility he'd witnessed all week. In many ways the creatures were more suited to a life in the trees than on the ground. Once on the ground, the beast stood erect, stretching its height to a mediocre five feet. If not for their physical strength, Weston might even be able to fight his way out. But he remembered how easily he'd been thrown, as though he were but a child.

As the beast stood above him, it hollered to the others, who quickly surrounded his prone body. They hooted and slapped the ground in a wild display, the likes of which he had not observed in the last week, even when they were hunting. A few stayed in the trees where they shook branches and shrieked. The one who caught him, Red Rim, stood above him and looked into his eyes. Red leaned in close and smelled him, moving slowed from his feet to his head, sniffing diligently.

Perhaps they're trying to decide if I'm edible, Weston thought. He tried to think of a way he could make himself less appealing, but that was impossible. Inside his pants, his legs were already coated in shit and his urine had leaked through the front. He smelled terrible, though he noted now, not as terrible as the creatures standing guard around him. Their scent was fecal and raw, like moldy egg salad. As Red sniffed his head and blew its breath onto his face, he could taste the decaying flesh of some previous meal that clung to its two-inch long canines. While Red sniffed his hair, Weston became aware of a gentle caress upon his chest. He glanced down, past his frazzled beard, and saw two large hair-covered breasts dangling down onto his body. Red . . . was a female.

Then she was up and hooting again. The cacophony reached an apex and the group descended on Weston like a starved pack of hyenas, yelping and reaching for him. As his clothes were torn and yanked away from his body by tooth and claw, he began to scream and fight. It did little good and only seemed to lather the group into more of a craze. Then one was on top of him, straddling his naked waist and pinning him to the ground. The creature's face leaned in close.

Red.

She howled and then bit into the meat of his shoulder.

Gulf of Aden—Somalia

A stark white motorboat bearing no national symbols, name, or markings of any kind rose up over a wave, catching air for a beat. The motor buzzed as it left the baby-blue water before being muffled once more as the boat descended and the blades bit into the sea. The fifteen-foot craft leapt from wave to wave, dancing over the ocean as fast as that old engine could push it and its five occupants.

Dressed in loose clothing and head wraps, only the eyes of the five passengers could be seen. Four sets of eyes were locked onto a single target—the *Volgaeft*, a Russian cargo ship. The only one of the five not looking at the cargo ship sat at the back, guiding the flat-hulled boat through the maze of five-foot swells. The seas were rough for such a small craft, but as they closed in on the cargo vessel, none on board thought about the threat of capsizing; their thoughts were on the violence that would soon begin.

The *Volgaeft* was at full speed in a bid to outrun the band of pirates, and had no doubt issued a call for help, but the pirates knew they could catch the sluggish, heavily laden vessel. And with some newly acquired technology, they would easily board it before help arrived. And help would arrive. After a short period of successful pirating which brought in an estimated 30 million dollars, the international community had cracked down. Warships from India, the European Union, the United States, and China patrolled the waters off Somalia, sometimes escorting ships from their various homelands, but always rushing to the aid of any ship in distress. And the *Volgaeft* wouldn't have waited to put out a call.

The pirates' sources put the nearest warship, a Chinese destroyer, roughly thirty minutes away. But with the *Volgaeft* now making a beeline for the destroyer and the destroyer for the *Volgaeft*, that half hour would be cut in half. And it had taken five minutes to pull up alongside the freighter.

Ten minutes left.

Typically, once a cargo vessel was boarded and the crew rounded up, there was nothing a destroyer could do. The ransom would be paid. And after returning to port with hostages, the ship and crew would be free to go. But this was no ordinary pirate raid. They were after something specific, and they needed to be gone by the time the Chinese arrived.

As the freighter crew watched the small pirate ship far below, preparing to cut grappling hook lines, they saw something they'd never seen a pirate do before. All five of the pirates raised what looked like hand guns, but tipped with solid black cylinders. Pirates typically fired warning shots at the crew, forcing them away from the rail while they scaled the side, but these devices weren't weapons at all. All five fired as one. The black cylinders arced up over the rail trailing thin black wires. They landed atop a large metal container and snapped up into standing positions as their magnetic bases engaged.

One of the men armed with a machete tried to cut through the thin black wires, which were already taut with weight, but his blade could do no more to the wire than a plastic knife. Before the crew could discuss what to do next, the pirates were pulled up and over the rail, landing on their feet and drawing pistols. The stunned crew stared for a moment. Then ran.

Ignoring the fleeing crew, the pirates entered the maze of metal containers covering the deck of the massive ship. They were looking for one container in particular. Its contents were worth more than the bounty received from all previous pirate attacks in the last year combined.

They wove their way through isles created by the looming towers of containers, scanning the variety of labels, serial numbers, and ID codes. They knew what they were looking for: ID-432 out of Vladivostok.

Three minutes later, they found it.

A pair of bolt cutters emerged from beneath one of the loose robes worn by the pirates. The lock fell to the deck a moment later and the large metal doors opened. Flashlights rose to meet the darkness within, illuminating a single metal carrying case.

"Over there," one of the large men said, his English perfect, though tinged with a New Hampshire accent.

"I'm on it," the shortest replied, her voice feminine. The cheap black ski mask she wore covered her face and the black face paint beneath concealed her skin color. The only aberration in her pirate disguise was her indigo eyes.

The man, Stanly Tremblay, call sign "Rook," stepped inside the container, flashlight up, followed by the woman, Zelda Baker, call sign "Queen."

Queen knelt down by silver case and inspected the area around it. "No traps. Looks clear, King."

Jack Sigler, call sign "King," stepped around Rook and unwrapped his facemask. His hard jaw was covered in stubble. His eyes glimmered with what his mother called mischief, but what the U.S. military called intensity.

Outside the container, the last two "pirates" kept watch. Erik Somers, call sign "Bishop," brimming with muscles, and the smaller man, Shin Dae-jung, call sign "Knight," kept their silenced pistols aimed down either end of the shipping container walled hallway.

King pulled the case free from the bungee cords that held it secure to the back wall of the container. A digital touch-screen and ten numbered buttons, zero through nine, were inlaid on the side of the case. Low-tech travel and storage, meet high-tech security. The case could not be opened without the correct code, and though there were no traps guarding the case itself, no one wanted to test a last recourse defense mechanism by opening the case without the right code. "Deep Blue, you there?"

"Right beside you." In fact, the Delta team's handler, Deep Blue, was half a world away, watching them via satellite. Named for the chess-playing super computer that trounced world champion Garry Kasparov in 1997, Deep Blue was the only member of the team whose identity was unknown. The man was an enigma, but he had access to U.S. military resources that were unparalleled, an impressive strategic thought process, and an understanding of military tactics that only someone who had previously seen combat could have. "I can see Bishop and Knight outside the container. Are you in?"

"Affirmative. I'm about to access the locking mechanism," King said as he used his K-BAR knife to pry off the touch-screen. He plucked the cable free from the back of the screen, removed a small touchscreen of his own, and attached it. Once connected, the screen lit up, a similar light blue to the ocean outside, and scrolled through a series of numbers. Unlike other mechanisms that tried a myriad of codes, looking for the right one, this device actually rewrote the software so that a new code could be added.

"Once you confirm the contents, you need to bug out," Deep Blue said. "The Chinese destroyer will be at your doorstep in five minutes and it looks like they're warming up a chopper."

King shook his head. It was never easy. "Armed or transport?"

"Gunship."

"Shit."

"Bishop, Knight, the crew is getting brave," Deep Blue added. "Looks like they're armed."

"Just let us know where to aim," Knight said.

Bishop, as usual, remained silent at his post. Watching and waiting. Unlike the others, he had nothing to fear from bullets, not physically anyway. Thanks to an unrefined serum created by Manifold Genetics, Bishop's body could regenerate from almost any physical injury short of decapitation. The downside was that every injury, from a paper cut to a bullet wound, pushed his mind closer to the brink. The test subjects before him had all become what the team called "regens"—mindless killing machines. It was only Bishop's history of anger management and a regimen of mood-enhancing drugs that kept him stable. It had been almost a year since their run-in with Manifold and the regenerated mythical Hydra, but this mission was Bishop's return to active duty. He'd been deemed fit for duty only a week ago.

The numbers on the display stopped, and a blank screen with ten empty spaces appeared.

"Ready for the code," King said.

"Hey, guys, Lew here." The new voice in their ear belonged to Lewis Aleman, their tech-wizard who was not only hardened on the digital battlefield, but also on the physical battlefield as a Delta operator. "The legendary CD Key for Office 97 is the code."

"Lew," King said, "this really isn't a time for—"

"All zeros," Rook said.

"And the winner is . . ."

King didn't hear the rest. He was already typing in the ten zeros. Upon finishing the code, the screen went black. "Uh, Lew . . ."

The locks clicked open. They were in.

"Knight, now would be a good time for a warning shot." Deep Blue's voice was cool, but the speed with which he spoke conveyed urgency. The crew of more than thirty men were closing in on what they believed were five Somali pirates.

Hoping the noise would intimidate, Knight removed his silencer from his .45 caliber Sig Sauer 220 handgun and fired off a round. It pinged off the deck where a crewman's shoe was poking out from behind a container. The man shouted and the sounds of shuffling feet could be heard moving away.

"That did it," Deep Blue said. "But they haven't given up. Chinese heli is in the air. ETA, two minutes. The destroyer will be right behind it."

King ignored the timeline. It would only make him nervous and slow him down. He opened the case. Steam hissed from inside, rolling over the edge and out across the floor of the roiling hot container. When the steam cleared, twenty small vials were exposed. King removed a small kit from his cargo pants, which were hidden beneath his robe, and opened it. Moving with extreme care, he then untwisted the cap of one of the vials, inserted a Q-tip, and soaked up a small amount of the clear liquid within. He rolled the Q-tip across the white surface of a small device that absorbed and analyzed the liquid. Normally, to identify a mystery liquid would require more processing power and equipment, but they were looking for one specific liquid, or rather, what was contained within the liquid medium. A small light on the device flashed green.

"Confirmed," King said. "We've got ourselves enough Russian-made smallpox to wipe out the populations of ten major cities."

"Great," Rook said. "All headed for our buddies in Iran."

Cases of smallpox could be traced back two thousand years in human history, emerging in China. It moved across the Asian continent to Africa, claiming the lives of thousands including Pharoh Ramses V. After arriving in Europe in 720 B.C., it crossed the Atlantic to the New World along with Hernando Cortez and an army of conquistadors. Contrary to popular belief, it was not the brutal tactics of the conquistadors that wiped out the Aztec civilization, it was smallpox. Nearly four million Aztecs died from the virus. The last case of smallpox was recorded, ironically, in Somalia circa 1977. Since then the world has been smallpox-free . . . and more susceptible than ever. There was no cure for the virus and though the mortality rate of the infected was ten to thirty percent, ten percent of the population of

New York City was eight hundred *thousand* people. In the wrong hands, these small vials could be weaponized and kill millions.

"So much for Putin's assurance that their smallpox cache was secure," Queen said.

"I believe that as much as I believe Putin saved a film crew from a Siberian tiger," Rook said. "If the guy had been born and raised in the U.S., he'd probably be on Broadway by now. What I don't get is why this is still kicking around."

"Human nature," Queen replied. "We've been dousing the world in chemical and bio-warfare for thousands of years before we even understood what the stuff was. And the U.S. is just as guilty as any other nation. Just because we don't use chemical and bio-warfare now doesn't mean we never did. It's only because we have better tech and bigger bombs that we no longer need to fight dirty."

"Amen to that." King nodded as he placed the Q-tip and small device on the floor. He took out a long cylinder that had been strapped to his leg, opened it and doused the Q-tip and device with Thermate-TH3, a ruddy-brown powder made from an iron oxide variant of thermite, barium nitrate, sulfur, and PBAN as a binder. The powder would burn at 2500°C, incinerating all traces of the smallpox and melting a hole in the container and a portion of the decks beneath. He closed the case as another shot rang out from outside the container.

"Another warning shot," Knight said. "No worries. Scratch that. Big worries, incoming."

The *whup*, *whup*, *whup* of an approaching helicopter rose in volume. The Chinese had arrived. King stood, and shook the remaining Thermate onto the open case. Though more than a few science boys in the U.S. would have liked to examine the old smallpox plague contained in the vials, Deep Blue's orders were clear: Destroy it. The world would be a better place without another smallpox strain floating around, even in U.S. hands.

As King wrapped his scarf over his face once more, he

headed for the exit with Queen and Rook. He popped a flare and tossed it into the container, then quickly closed and latched the metal doors. The Thermate would quickly suck the oxygen out of the small container space, but the flames would not be smothered. The powdered hell contained its own oxygen source and could burn just as easily at the bottom of the ocean or in the vacuum of space. Once lit, nothing could put it out.

Outside the container, Knight pointed to the sky. A black Zhi-11 gunship was approaching low over sea, headed straight for them. As bursts of yellow flashed from the helicopter's twin 12.7mm machine guns, King shouted, "Go! Go! Go!"

The Chess team darted down a side alley, hiding them from view as rounds chewed up the deck where they had stood only moments before. Hidden from the chopper, they ran without fear of being cut down from the sky, but they ran with weapons out in case the crew still lingered about. As they reached the port rail, it was clear that the crew had hid with the chopper's arrival. They knew enough not to get caught in the crossfire.

The gunship roared above and out to sea, turning in a tight circle. It would be back in seconds.

The team hitched themselves onto their cables, still tethered to the cargo container, holstered their guns, and slid over the side of the ship, rappelling with large leaps down to the small, white, and defenseless motor boat. Once aboard the small craft, they disengaged the magnets, which automatically reeled in. Without looking up, King gunned the engine, which looked old, but was actually top of the line U.S. military. The small boat shot forward just as a line of 12.7mm rounds traced across the waves and ripped into the side of the *Volgaeft*.

King steered the small boat out and away from the cargo ship as the helicopter swung around for another pass. But the helicopter didn't return. It just circled at a distance.

Too easy, King thought.

"King," Deep Blue's voice returned. "Cut hard to starboard."

King glanced to port. Closing in was an ominous Chinese destroyer, its cannons swinging toward them. "They can't be serious."

"The Chinese have been in the Gulf of Aden for a year without any major conflicts," Deep Blue said. "They're eager to test their mettle. I think they—"

BOOM!

The ocean in front of the small boat burst skyward as a 100mm cannon round struck the water. The small boat launched off the resulting wave and cut through the mist, landing on the other side. King cut to starboard, but with the *Volgaeft* moving away, they were exposed. If not for the boat's small size and speed, they would be an easy target.

"You're on target," Deep Blue said. "Keep your current course for thirty seconds."

"Easier said than done," King replied.

BOOM!

The second round struck just behind them, pitching the boat up and forward, bringing the engine out of the water. If not for the quick thinking of Rook and Bishop, the team's two giants who threw themselves to the stern deck, knocking the back end back down, the bow would have caught water and flipped them too soon.

"Wait for the next round," King shouted. "Then—"

BOOM!

The round struck just off the port side. The small boat became lost in a plume of sea water. When it cleared, the boat appeared—capsized and immobilized.

Rather than apprehend the pirates involved, the Chinese destroyer tested its aim on a still target.

BOOM!

The small boat shattered and burst as the massive round, powerful enough to sink the multi-hulled *Volgaeft*, struck home.

Thirty feet below the explosion, five bodies descended,

unmoving after the shockwave struck. Then a hand flashed up.

Hold position.

A dark shape loomed below. Waiting. Listening.

King gave the crewman monitoring the hydrophone inside the submarine a moment to recover from the impact and explosion above. Then he shouted, expelling the last of his air, "Open the damn door." The message was garbled by the bubbles escaping King's mouth, but the message was received. The side dry-dock of the still classified HMS *Wolverton* opened. All five swam inside. The doors closed as the small cabin pressurized and filled with air.

The Chinese searched for the remains of the pirates they'd wiped out, but found only debris of the small boat. Regardless, the front page of China's most popular newspaper, the *Southern Metropolis Daily*, heralded the encounter as a bold Chinese naval victory. And despite the pirates' best efforts, the only losses were minimal damage to the *Volgaeft* and the total destruction of one container destined for Iran, reported full of toys donated by a charitable Russian organization.